Man oh man, what a perfect day this was turning out to be!

Mattie Rowland had happened onto an employee who shared her love of art and woodcraft, and whose masculine, dynamic presence put a quick-charge on her feminine battery....

Mattie's thoughts skidded to an abrupt halt. Good heavens, what was she thinking? Joe Gray, as attractive and appealing to the eye as he was, was off-limits. She was his employer and she couldn't, wouldn't, jeopardize their working relationship.

No, the head honcho, who sat on his duff on his velvet throne at corporate headquarters, would undoubtedly frown on a personal relationship developing between his store manager and an employee.

"Strictly business, and you'd better not forget that," Mattie told herself. It didn't matter that she was mesmerized by Joe's whiskey-colored eyes and dark hair. It didn't matter that she was thirty years old, and her biological clock was ticking loudly. She was his boss and he was her hired assistant and never the twain shall meet, as the saying goes.

Who ever made up that dumb saying, anyway?

For more, turn to page 9

Great kisser or not, Rick Taylor wasn't a keeper.

Kim had had more than her share of infatuations and letdowns, and she really, sincerely wanted to find the one man right for her. Her quiet, serious sister had. Jane was soooo lucky to have Luke. They were perfect soul mates, and together they made beautiful babies. Kim couldn't imagine anything more wonderful.

A miracle like that couldn't happen with a man who disliked weddings. Rick might look like a love god—even kiss like one—but he wasn't the real thing. What kind of guy would try to stop his own brother's wedding? He was probably acting out of misguided concern, but Kim was determined not to put her heart in the hands of Rick Taylor, the scourge of romance.

She rolled over and hugged the pillow, trying to ignore the lingering tingle on her lips. And the voice inside that said it was already too late... She was a goner.

For more, turn to page 197

HARLEQUIN DUETS

ISBN 0-373-44111-8

A REGULAR JOE
Copyright © 2000 by Connie Feddersen

MR. RIGHT UNDER HER NOSE
Copyright © 2000 by Pamela Hanson and Barbara Andrews

This edition published by arrangement with Harlequin Books S.A.

® and TM are trademarks of the publisher. Trademarks indicated with
® are registered in the United States Patent and Trademark Office, the
Canadian Trade Marks Office and in other countries.

Visit us at www.eHarlequin.com

Printed in U.S.A.

A Regular Joe

Carol Finch

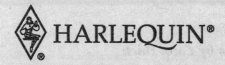

HARLEQUIN®

TORONTO • NEW YORK • LONDON
AMSTERDAM • PARIS • SYDNEY • HAMBURG
STOCKHOLM • ATHENS • TOKYO • MILAN • MADRID
PRAGUE • WARSAW • BUDAPEST • AUCKLAND

Dear Reader,

One of my favorite old movies, *Teacher's Pet,*
starring Clark Gable and Doris Day, inspired me to
create a hero who masquerades as someone he's
not. Combine that potentially explosive ingredient
with a lively, trusting heroine who takes truth,
honesty and honor very seriously and you have a
recipe for trouble. No matter what pretty name, or
justifiable reason, you attach to deception, it *is* what it
is and, inevitably, it returns to haunt you—usually in
the worst way, at the worst of all possible moments.

Just ask Daniel Grayson, the hero of *A Regular Joe.*
Too late, he realizes he's on a collision course with
self-imposed disaster and that he's head over heels in
love with Mattie Roland, the bubbly, unique female
he thoroughly deceived. If Mattie discovers the truth,
the fur will fly—most of it Daniel's, no doubt. Since
Daniel lied about his identity, how can he convince
Mattie that he speaks the truth when he says he loves
her? Like she'll believe *that,* coming from his lying
lips!

The moral of this story? *The lies you tell are gonna
get you if you don't watch out!* And so, dear readers,
the charade begins...

Enjoy!

Carol Finch

Books by Carol Finch

SILHOUETTE SPECIAL EDITION
1242—NOT JUST ANOTHER COWBOY
1320—SOUL MATES

This book is dedicated to my husband, Ed, and our children, Kurt, Jill, Christie, Jon and Jeff, with much love. And to our grandchildren, Blake, Kennedy and Brooklynn. Hugs and kisses!

A special thanks to my editor, Karen Kosztolnyik, and my agent, Laurie Feigenbaum.
It is a privilege to be working with you!

1

DANIEL JOSEPH GRAYSON, co-founder and CEO of Hobby Hut Enterprises, was running away from home. He wished he'd done it a year ago, because this hiatus was long overdue.

Daniel was desperate to regain his enthusiasm for the family-owned business. He needed to get back in touch with himself, because sitting in his plush executive office, surrounded by yes-men and -women, constantly staring at profit-loss spreadsheets, was distorting his perception of life. Hobby Hut's version of Stepford wives—those nauseatingly agreeable robots whose sole purpose was to protect their high-dollar salaries and prestigious positions—were driving him absolutely nuts!

No longer could Daniel bounce ideas off his junior executives or expect constructive and innovative input, because he couldn't trust their hidden motives. A year ago, when his grandfather officially retired, things rapidly deteriorated. J. D. Grayson was the only person Daniel could depend on to tell him the truth, and now the old man was spending his golden years in leisurely pursuits.

Therefore, Daniel decided to leave his executives holding the bag, *forcing* them to earn their exorbitant wages. He was hotfooting it out of Oklahoma City—without leaving a forwarding address. For one month

Daniel was going to become a regular Joe and hope like hell that the working stiffs in this world were nothing like corporate society with its patronized schmoozing—along with a little treacherous back-stabbing thrown in for good measure. Daniel craved a breath of fresh country air, longed to shed the cloak of executive privilege, and dodge the entourage of glossy females who saw him as a blue-chip bachelor.

Hell's jingling bells! He wasn't sure if he was liked for himself these days, or if his power, wealth and influence formed the world's perception of him. There was only one way to find out, Daniel mused. When he became your everyday average regular Joe Schmo he would discover how many true friends he could acquire.

Daniel steered the clunker truck that he'd borrowed from his grandfather off the interstate and cruised down the two-lane road toward Fox Hollow. The town was situated in a valley, surrounded by timbered hills and clear blue streams. The community was only a hop, skip and jump away from a scenic lake.

The quaint, off-the-beaten-path hamlet was just what the doctor ordered, he thought to himself. This area of the state catered to hunters, fishermen, lake-goers and retirees. This was the perfect getaway for a cynical, jaded executive—namely him—who needed to get back in touch with the simple pleasures in life.

Feeling his tension and frustration ebb, Daniel cruised his bucket-of-rust truck from one end of Main Street to the other. It took three minutes—less if he hadn't stopped for the white-haired old woman who jaywalked in front of him. There was one stoplight, dozens of parking spaces without meters, and several wooden barrels—belching riotous collections of flowers—sitting in front of each business establishment. A hardware store, with a sign that read If We Don't Have What You Need We Can Special Order It, sat on one corner. A floral shop, antique store, tractor-mechanic shop, mom-and-pop grocery, hole-in-the-wall café, tag agency and furniture store lined the street. There were no traffic jams in which road-raging motorists shouted at one another and saluted with their middle fingers. Daniel didn't hear the screech of brakes or blast of horns. What he heard was the sound of peace and quiet, the warble of birds and local citizens greeting one another as they passed friends and acquaintances on the sidewalk.

Ah, so this was what life was like in the real world. He'd almost forgotten. Daniel glanced down to check the time, then remembered he had stuffed his Rolex into the corporate safe. It was his intention to blend into the scenery and keep a low profile. He'd just as soon no one knew he could afford more than these casual clothes and clunker truck.

Looking west, Daniel spotted the local Hobby Hut. The doors should be opening soon, and he wanted to be first in line to apply for a job. He had selected this specific town for his hiatus for two reasons. Number one—it was only forty-five minutes from his office in the city. And two—this store manager's sales reports were impressive. Mattie Roland was doing more business in this little town than other Hobby Huts were doing in major cities in a five-state area.

Determined to acquire a job at his own store, Daniel hiked down the street, amazed that strangers nodded and greeted him as if he were a long-lost friend.

He felt welcome immediately, and he hadn't been here more than ten minutes.

Daniel pulled up short and stared in amazement at the window displays at Hobby Hut. They were divided into four sections—nautical, folk art, colonial and Americana. Original and print reproductions of landscape and still-life paintings, accentuated by Hobby Hut frames, were bookended by hand-painted curio and knickknack shelves that boasted figurines and collectibles. Small console tables, deacon's benches and storage chests had been painted to match the theme of each display. Daniel stood there for several minutes, absorbing the ambiance, admiring the artwork and cleverly arranged displays. No wonder Mattie Roland was one of the top managers in the company. Her displays practically reached out and grabbed you off the street and lured you into her store.

The words *inspiring* and *imaginative* came quickly to mind. These examples of decor made you want to give your home a makeover, to fill each cubbyhole, niche and wall with these intriguing combinations of art, woodcrafting and antiques that created a homey, welcoming appearance.

Finding the door unlocked, Daniel entered, hearing the tinkling sound of delicate chimes that announced his arrival.

"I'll be with you in a minute," came a sultry female voice from somewhere in the near distance. "Browse to your heart's content."

Daniel blinked, startled. Who was minding the store? A dozen expensive items could be shoplifted before the manager emerged from the back room. Maybe Mattie Roland wasn't Employee of the Year after all.

While Daniel surveyed the items on the aisles the white-haired woman who'd jaywalked in front of his rattletrap truck waddled inside. She nodded cordially to him, then stared toward the workroom in the back of the store.

"Mattie? How's my project coming along? You about finished, hon? My son and grandchildren are coming tomorrow, ya know. I want to have my shelves and family pictures hung before they arrive."

"Not to worry, Alice," said the disembodied voice. "I'm putting the finishing touches on your shelves right now. Come on back and have a look-see."

Daniel was surprised the hunch-shouldered senior citizen could move so fast. She scurried off in her orthopedic shoes, her cotton dress swishing around her as she went.

While Alice and Mattie did their thing in the workroom, Daniel circumnavigated the store, marveling at several other eye-catching displays of woodcrafts, ceramics and unusual antiques. Mattie Roland was obviously a whiz when it came to interior decorating. Daniel never would have thought to assemble these particular items and arrange them as she had, but the effect was extraordinary. The woman definitely had a gift!

Daniel's brain short-circuited when he glanced over his shoulder to see a petite but voluptuous female, dressed in paint-splattered jeans and T-shirt, walking toward him. There was a smudge of Lucky Shamrock Green on the tip of her nose and a streak of Longjohn Red on her elbow. Her raven-colored ponytail was slightly off center, but amethyst-colored eyes, rimmed with incredibly long lashes, dominated her pixielike face. Mattie Roland was five feet four inches, one hundred fifteen pounds—give or take—of arresting female who reminded him of an enchanting leprechaun.

Mesmerized, Daniel stood there like a tongue-tied doofus. This vivacious young woman was Mattie Roland? Employee of the Year?

"Hi," Mattie greeted cheerily. "Is there something I can help you find in Hobby Hut?"

The sizzling jolt of awareness caused his tongue to stick to the roof of his mouth. He, who spent the past several years with prima donnas latched to his arms like English ivy, had suddenly encountered the girl-next-door variety of female. Mattie wasn't what Daniel was accustomed to, but he definitely approved of the look of her.

Daniel was excessively pleased that he'd selected Fox Hollow for his hiatus. And speaking of *fox*, Mattie Roland was definitely that, in his opinion. She appealed to everything male in him. She had that wholesome, vital appearance that he much preferred over the bottled variety and surgically implanted artificial beauty women relied on to enhance their facial features and figures. The indifference he'd been experiencing with his shallow, glamorous companions of late took a flying leap when Mattie, with an energetic spring in her walk, strode up to him and blessed him with a two-hundred-watt smile.

"Sir?" she prompted when he continued to stand there, absorbing the refreshing sight of her. "Are you looking for a gift for your wife or girlfriend? Need supplies for a woodcrafting project?"

"No wife, no girlfriend," he said when his vocal apparatus began to function. "I'm looking for a job."

"Really?" She seemed startled. "Are you serious?"

"Yes, I just arrived in town, and I'm looking for work," he lied convincingly. Then he inwardly winced when he realized he was no better than his yes-executives who would lie through their smiles if it would get them onto a higher rung on the corporate ladder.

"I'm surprised you came in here," she said, as she absently reached over to rearrange a porcelain figurine that wasn't perfectly aligned on the shelf.

"Why?" He wanted to know.

"Most men in town consider this a sissified store where their wives and girlfriends shop. Most of my customers are women."

"Other men think woodcrafting is sissy stuff?" he asked, affronted. "That is beyond ridiculous. Table saws, miter saws, and nail guns are not for the faint of heart. You could lose a finger if you accidentally cut skin and bone rather than wood. I spent my teenage years in a workshop, creating shelving, tables and cabinets. Sissy stuff?" He snorted in objection. "No, I don't think so!"

Her bubbling laughter filled the space between them. Her violet eyes danced with amusement, and Daniel blushed, realizing this was the first time in a year that he'd expressed much sentiment on any subject. Mattie probably thought he was wacko because he had such strong feelings about woodcraft—the same kind of passion that he and his grandfather experienced while they labored on their craft projects in the old days.

"Obviously you have experience and a love for woodcrafting," she said, chuckling. "I share and appreciate your enthusiasm. And you probably won't believe this, but I just received a fax from the corporate office an hour ago, indicating that I should hire an assistant.''

Of course he believed it. Daniel had sent that fax from his office immediately before he headed south to Fox Hollow. He was here to fill the position he had created.

''As it happens,'' she was saying when he tuned back in, ''I've been swamped, and my only other employee is a high school art student who helps out after class and on Saturdays. I have so many special projects going that I can't keep up, even though I've been working double days.''

She pivoted on her heels, allowing Daniel an alluring view of her inverted heart-shaped derriere wrapped in faded denim. ''Come back to my office and fill out the application.''

He followed the enticing sway of her hips like a kitten on the trail of fresh cream. The past few years Daniel had begun to think his sex drive had withered away. However, one look at Mattie Roland's hourglass figure and infectious smile and his male body woke up and was ready to party on. It *had* been a long time since Daniel felt such a spontaneous attraction.

He really shouldn't have been surprised Mattie affected him instantaneously, he told himself as he followed his fantasy version of the Pied Piper. Mattie was *real* people. She was warm, outgoing, friendly and seemingly content with life. She was obviously doing what she loved and loved what she was doing. Daniel envied that about her.

Enthusiasm personified, he realized. That's what

she was. Mattie was exactly what he needed—someone who cared as deeply for his business as he once had. He could use an injection of her spirit and zest. He needed to bottle her up so he could take daily doses to counteract the mounting frustration he had been experiencing in his corporate office.

"Here you go," she said, handing him the application. "Park yourself at my desk and fill this out. This is just red tape sent down by Double H at Double H."

"Double H?" he questioned curiously.

"The head honcho at Hobby Hut," Mattie informed him. "Ask me, the man requires entirely too much paperwork, which prohibits a manager from going one-on-one with customers. But you know how those highbrow executives are. They don't trust us little guys and gals to manage business properly, especially way down here in the boondocks. Probably think that we small-town folks only operate with half a brain." She shrugged, and her dark ponytail rippled over her shoulder. "But the big boss in corporateland didn't ask my opinion, even if I'm the one out here in the trenches selling his products."

Daniel inwardly cringed when she confided her complaints about the head honcho. If Mattie knew she was talking to the CEO of Hobby Hut, she'd be thoroughly embarrassed.

"So, do you dislike all company executives on general principle or just this big boss in particular?" he asked as he plunked down in her chair at the desk.

"I had a personal run-in with a hotshot executive before I landed this job," she explained. "He seemed to think it was *my* company duty to offer *him* fringe benefits and that *he* was doing *me* a tremendous favor by suggesting that I join his corporate harem. He also thought *who* he was should impress me enormously, which it didn't. I quit and applied for this position.

"I strongly dislike the type of executive who uses his power and position to get what he wants. Although I don't know Double H personally, I suspect he possesses the same character flaws." Mattie relocated a stack of papers to give him the needed space on the desktop so he could fill out the application. "I bet I can peg Double H," she declared. "High-dollar Rolex on his wrist to match the expensive rings on his fingers. BMW sitting in his personal parking space that no one else is allowed to use under penalty of death. Glitzy cover-model types of females on his arm. A different glamour goddess for each day of the week, no doubt. Carries a state-of-the art cell phone, dresses in the best clothes his money can buy, and surrounds himself with every power and prestige symbol known to mankind to impress the rest of us peons."

Daniel inwardly grimaced. So far, Mattie had been right on target. He wasn't sure he wanted to hear the rest of her speculations.

"Double H's interest, I suspect, is the enterprise's bottom line of dollars and cents. He probably doesn't give a rip if customers are getting their money's worth, only that the profit margin pads his pocket. And his sales policy," she added with a snort. "His so-called big sales are his way of getting rid of stuff no one wants. I'd like to see a sale on expensive items that customers on fixed incomes can purchase, instead of stare at whimsically."

Head downcast, Daniel filled in the blanks on the

application, while listening to Mattie comment on company policy.

From behind him, Mattie glanced over his shoulder. "Joe Gray, is it? Nice to meet you. I'm Mattie Roland, your new employer."

He lifted his head. "You're pretty trusting. I haven't even filled in the blank about whether or not I have a criminal record."

"You don't," she said with great confidence. "You aren't the type."

"You know several criminals personally, do you?"

She laughed, and the sound whispered through him like a breath of spring air. God, she was good for him—all that vibrant spirit and enthusiasm. Not to mention the arousing effect she had on him when she was close enough for him to pick up her enticing scent.

"The small-time criminals I deal with in Hobby Hut are easy to spot. In your case, the way you dress, the way you speak, and your passion for working with your hands comes through loud and clear. I think you're just what this store needs. It's time some of the Neanderthal males in Fox Hollow realized that art, woodcraft and interior decor are not sissy stuff. Having you mind the shop will put them at ease—once they get used to the idea," she tacked on, then took another peek at his application.

"Thirty-five years old. Last permanent address in Oklahoma City. Hmm," she said thoughtfully. "Got tired of the hustle and bustle, did you? I presume you like to hunt, fish, and get in touch with nature. You'll like it here in Fox Hollow. I also expect the eligible females hereabout will be on your trail once they've spotted you."

Daniel—or rather, Joe Gray—glanced over his shoulder to see Mattie grinning impishly. "You think I'm a babe magnet? Me? In my faded polo shirt that's been through too many spin cycles in the washing machine, and these old jeans?"

She rolled her eyes at him. "Clothes don't make the man. It's what's inside, but yeah, I'd have to place you in the babe magnet category, Joe. You're tall, handsome, and those amber eyes of yours are gorgeous. They remind me of sunrise and sunset all rolled into one. But not to worry, you won't get the slightest pressure from me. I'm your employer, and we'll be friends who share mutual interests."

He was disappointed to hear that, he really was.

"If you need background information on prospective dates, I'll be happy to fill you in, since I've lived here most of my life."

They were going to be just pals? Damn, his suddenly rowdy male body didn't like the sound of that one little bit. After a long dormancy, his masculine engine was revving up, only to be shut down by this spunky, spirited little pixie who had captured his interest without trying. Maybe that was what he deserved for being lukewarm toward those cover-model types who fluttered around him because of his wealth and reasonably good looks.

Having completed his application—falsified though it was, and his conscience was nipping at him for that—Joe handed her the paper. He watched as she perched a shapely hip on the edge of her desk to scan the information.

"You left your current residence blank," she noted. "Where do you plan to live, Joe?"

He shrugged. "I noticed that Hush-a-Bye Inn on

the outskirts of town rents rooms by the week. I can store my stuff there while I'm looking for something else.''

"Or you could move into the furnished garage apartment where I used to live," she suggested. "Now that my grandfather has moved into Paradise Valley Convalescent Home I've taken over his house. At Pops's insistence, I might add. He wouldn't be in the nursing home if his arthritis and diabetes hadn't flared up on him.''

"Judging by the sound of your voice, I presume Pops isn't enthused about the assisted living center.''

"Hardly.'' Mattie bounded to her feet and paced the narrow confines of her office.

He noticed that standing or sitting in one place wasn't Mattie's thing. She had so much energy that she needed to be in constant motion.

"Pops is a lot like me, I'm afraid," she confided. "He has to be doing something constantly, and inactivity has never agreed with him. Lately, he's been giving me fits because he keeps escaping from the home at odd hours, putting the doctors and nurses into one tizzy after another, because his ability to escape reflects on their reputations. They don't like to keep *losing* him, and he delights in sneaking off.''

Joe chuckled in amusement. Pops reminded him of his own grandfather. One year ago, J. D. Grayson announced he was leaving the company to take life easy. Since then, J.D. had taken an Alaskan and Caribbean cruise, offered his supervisory services for two Habitat for Humanity projects, and volunteered as director of activities for the nearby senior citizen center.

"Mattie!''

Mattie gestured for Joe to follow her. "You might

as well take a tour of the work area while I wrap it up with Alice Dawson. Part of your job involves handling tools for special projects.''

Curious, Joe followed in Mattie's wake, his gaze still magnetically drawn to the hypnotic sway of shapely hips wrapped in denim that molded to her fanny like gloves. Damn, there was such an intriguing aura about this woman, he marveled. An hour ago, he'd felt tense and frustrated. Then, poof! It was as if he'd been transported into another dimension in time with this delightful pixie as his tour guide.

Joe skidded to a halt the instant he entered the workroom. His eyes popped as he panned the area that reminded him so much of the workshop where he and J.D. had designed crafts almost two decades earlier. It was where Joe had spent his spare time, working with his hands, dealing with the frustration of his parents' abandonment, then the loss of his grandmother. Together he and J.D. had poured their grief and disappointment into creative projects that somehow turned into an enormously lucrative business.

"Does all this equipment belong to you?" Joe croaked. It had to, because he knew perfectly well that the work space at Hobby Hut Enterprises did not come equipped with state-of-the-art power tools like these!

Mattie glanced up from her consultation with Alice Dawson, then nodded. "Most of the tools are mine. Some of them were donated by my grandfather. He used to help me until his arthritis hampered him."

Amazed, Joe surveyed the various and sundry of saws, drills, sanders and clamps that Mattie had at her disposal. A woman who shared his love of working with his hands? A woman who felt as at home in a workshop as he did? This woman was every wood-crafter's dream come true. Joe couldn't believe his luck. Working here would be the therapy he needed.

An amused smile pursed Mattie's lips as she watched him inspect one tool after another. "You look surprised, Joe. But then, it's not the first time I've gotten that reaction from men. Although I have a degree in art, my minor is woodcrafting and carpentry."

"I really do get to play with your tools?" he asked, delighted.

She nodded, causing her shiny raven ponytail to shimmer in the florescent light. "Although Hobby Hut sells generic wood furniture and crafts, I customize and personalize projects for customers. Like this project, for instance."

When Mattie motioned him forward, Joe strode over to study the framed original painting and shelves she had designed for Alice Dawson. His jaw dropped to his chest as he studied the artwork that featured what he presumed to be the old Dawson homestead, done in earth-tone colors. The shelves that were to be placed on either side of the painting—made of barn wood that probably came from the Dawson barn—boasted country antiques, small decorative frames, and portraits of Alice's children and grandchildren.

"Doesn't Mattie do fabulous work?" Alice said, smiling proudly at the display. "She came out to my place to gather up odds and ends so they could be included on the shelves. When I saw Josie Foreman's homestead painting and antique display last month at our home extension club meeting, I knew I had to have one of my own."

"Impressive," Joe complimented.

"Now that you're employed here, Joe, I can run over to Alice's place during my lunch hour to hang the painting and shelves without worrying about being back a minute too late." Mattie glanced at him hopefully. "You are willing to start work immediately, aren't you?"

He grinned. "No problem, boss."

Alice clapped her hands together in delight. "You can decorate my wall this afternoon? Wonderful!"

When Alice scuttled away, beaming like a fog light, Mattie chuckled. "I hope you're getting the impression that working at Hobby Hut isn't just a job for me. Making customers happy, rather than tallying dollars and cents, is the name of my game."

Yes, he could see that. Mattie Roland was the epitome of Joe's, and his grandfather's, vision for their company. She kept what had become commercialized on a personal level by making specialized projects for her customers.

A warm, fuzzy feeling spread through Joe's body. Oh yes, this hiatus in Fox Hollow was exactly what the doctor ordered. This was the cure for the affliction of frustration and indifference that had been tormenting Joe—or rather, Daniel Joseph Grayson, CEO. For that, and a few less than honorable masculine-oriented reasons, Joe wanted to hug the stuffing out of this little carpenter's elf. A month in Mattie's company and Joe was reasonably certain that he'd recapture his lost enthusiasm.

The chime above the front door heralded the arrival of another customer. Mattie smiled up at him, displaying the cute dimple in her left cheek. "You wanna handle that? I need to measure and mark another project this morning. If you want, you can make the cuts, since you look as if you're eager to get your mitts on my power tools.''

''My pleasure,'' he said, then wheeled around and strode toward the front of the store, a renewed spring in his steps.

Mattie watched her new employee depart, her gaze magnetically drawn to his six-foot-one-inch, power-fully built physique. Her artist's eye approved of the looks of her employee. Joe Gray was definitely the answer to a prayer, and she couldn't believe her good fortune. She had received the directive from corporate headquarters, indicating that she could hire a full-time staff member. And wham! Joe Gray showed up out of the blue.

It was almost as if fate had dealt her a winning hand. She needed someone responsible to mind the store so she could devote time to special projects re-quested by customers. She also needed someone to rent the efficiency apartment so she'd have extra money to pay her grandfather's expenses at the con-valescent home.

Man, oh man, what a perfect day this was turning out to be! Mattie had happened onto an employee who shared her love of art and woodcraft, someone eager to tackle the hands-on projects, someone who saw this business as more than a job that paid rent and put food on the table, someone whose appealing, dynamic presence put a quick charge on her own fem-inine battery…

Mattie's thoughts skidded to an abrupt halt. Good heavens, what was she thinking? Joe Gray, as attrac-tive and appealing to the eye as he was, was off-limits. She was his employer and she couldn't, wouldn't, jeopardize their working relationship. Although Joe was the first man to come along since her college years to inspire arousing feelings, she couldn't possibly allow herself to form an interest in him. That would be unethical. Probably even went against company policy, if she sat herself down to read the fine print in her managerial contract.

No, the head honcho, who sat on his duff on his velvet throne at corporate headquarters, would undoubtedly frown on a personal relationship developing between his store manager and an employee. Mr. Higher than the Almighty head honcho would *not* approve of her feminine admiration for Joe Gray.

"Strictly business, and you better not forget that," Mattie told herself as she grabbed the tape measure to mark the lumber. It didn't matter that she was mesmerized by Joe's whiskey-colored eyes and dark hair, that his good looks and masculine scent inspired basal reactions. She was his boss, and he was her hired assistant and never the twain shall meet, as the saying went. Who ever made up that saying, anyway? Well, she had to strive for a pleasant but ethical working situation, a mutual love for hobbies and crafts. Anything else was out of the question.

Too bad, really, she mused as she designed the new curio shelf. She was thirty years old, and her biological clock was ticking. She wanted a family, wanted children who would not be raised and abandoned the way she had been. If not for her beloved grandfather, there was no telling what would have become of Mattie. Bernard Roland had taken her in, shared what little worldly possessions he had with her, put a roof over her head, placed food on the table, and instilled his love for creating with his hands. True, he had inadvertently turned her into a hopeless tomboy who would rather wield saws, drills and create unique woodcrafts than power shop. Yet, she was content with her life. Well, except for the fact that managing the store, teaching a class in art during the winter at the local vo-tech, and working on special projects prevented her from having time to enjoy any kind of social life whatsoever.

"Stop whining, Roland," Mattie muttered as she laid out the one-by-six board for Joe to cut. "And don't get any ridiculous ideas where Joe is concerned. You can't be anything but friends."

2

WHAT A DAY HE'D HAD! Joe thought as he ambled down the street toward his rattletrap truck. He'd manned saws, routers and drills to his heart's content, then waited on customers and familiarized himself with the layout of the store. He had thoroughly enjoyed himself, and the hours had whizzed by at amazing speed.

Joe also gave Mattie Roland high marks for her rapport with customers. Everybody in Fox Hollow adored her. He'd heard her praises sung by every woman who entered the store.

Joe grinned, remembering how he'd been given the third degree by female customers he'd waited on. Everyone wanted to know where he was from, when he'd hired on and where he was staying. He was invited to a church supper and community bazaar by several customers. Typical small-town activities that he wouldn't mind attending if time allowed.

He had artfully dodged a few personal questions by offering half-truths so he wouldn't blow his cover. As far as anyone in town knew, he was just a regular Joe who liked the looks of this town, and the surrounding area, and decided to make a life for himself here.

Joe applied the brakes and slowed down so Mattie could pull out in front of him and lead the way to her house. He hadn't quite figured out what had happened between them after he exited the workroom to wait on his first customer this morning. Mattie, friendly and outgoing though she had been when he arrived, had become standoffish and reserved around him. What the hell had happened? They'd hit it off big time. Then suddenly, she was careful not to invade his personal space, nor he hers.

While she was giving directions for cutting and constructing the customized knickknack shelf, she had maintained a noticeable distance from him. He hadn't wanted distance. He'd wanted to work shoulder to shoulder with her during the lull in customer traffic at the store. Instead, Mattie gave him directions for the project, then ambled off to work on another customized design.

For a man who'd never had a problem attracting females, he was beginning to think his theory that money and corporate power lured the opposite sex to him was on the mark. Maybe he wasn't all that personable, he mused pensively.

Doubts clouded his thoughts as he followed Mattie through a residential section to a small acreage located in a grove of blackjack trees. His thoughts scattered when he turned into the driveway of a small but well-manicured gingerbread-style home. His gaze swung to the detached two-car garage that had been converted into an efficiency apartment. Joe, who had been living in a five-thousand-square-foot brick home in the city's suburbs, figured he was in for another culture shock.

Climbing from his truck, he ambled alongside Mattie, noting that she refused to encroach on the minimum requirement of three feet of personal space surrounding him. Damn, what was there about him that repelled her?

"I don't know what you're accustomed to, Joe, but this garage apartment is cramped quarters," she said as she pulled a set of keys from the purse that was slung over her shoulder. "The rent is reasonable and the utility bills minimal."

She opened the door, and Joe immediately fell in love with the place. The open area was paneled in glossy pine. Bay windows provided a spectacular view of trees that skirted the creek. A large mural on the west wall created an optical illusion that the inhabitant of this cracker-box apartment could wander through the tall pines and scale the mountains that lay in the background.

"Did you paint this mural?" he asked, incredulous.

Mattie nodded. "It was Pops who framed the art to give it the three-dimensional effect. It keeps the apartment from crowding in on you."

"You are an exceptionally talented artist, Mattie," he complimented as he strode across the carpet to closely examine the detailed artwork. "With the right backing and promotion you could go places in the art world."

"I'm not interested in national recognition," she informed him as she came to stand beside him, maintaining a respectable distance. "I paint for the love of it, not the money. I reside here in Fox Hollow because it's my hometown and because I feel a fierce loyalty to my grandfather who raised me."

"What happened to your parents?" he asked curiously.

Mattie's smile became reflective, rueful. "I'm sorry to report that I'm the biological product of parents who were too young to want a kid toddling along, cramping their lifestyle. My parents never married. My father wanted to shake the dust of this small town off his heels and see the world. My mother dumped me on my grandparents' doorstep when I was four and took off for parts unknown. I lost my grandmother three years later and the people in this community have become extended family to Pops and me.''

Joe nodded in understanding. ''Parents can be the pits sometimes, can't they? I was twelve when my dad took off to find himself. Hell, I never even realized he was lost! My mother is still looking for Mr. Right. At last count, none of her three ex-husbands fit the bill. It was my grandfather and grandmother who raised me, too. Gramps was determined that I didn't turn out to be the huge disappointment my dad was to him.''

''I can tell you one thing for certain, Joe. If I ever have a family, my kids are going to be top priority, and they won't be given a bunch of empty promises,'' she said with firm conviction.

''Same goes for me. I didn't enjoy feeling like unwanted baggage.''

''Ditto.''

''So, do you want to have kids together?'' Joe popped off.

Mattie stepped back a pace and gaped at him. ''I beg your pardon?''

When she shifted uncomfortably, Joe cursed under his breath. That was a dumb thing for him to say. They'd bonded on some level, and he'd blown it with his playful question. ''Sorry, I was only trying to lighten up our serious conversation. I really enjoy working for you, and with you, Mattie. I don't want to do anything to spoil our friendship. Which compels me to ask if I already did something to offend you this morning. I couldn't help but notice that your attitude toward me changed.''

Mattie inwardly winced. Had she been so obvious, so transparent after having that heart-to-heart talk with herself this morning? Apparently so. Well, she supposed now was the time to get things out in the open, explain the ground rules, just so there wouldn't be any misunderstandings between them. She was an open, forthright person, after all.

"The truth is that I like you, Joe," she admitted, keeping her gaze fixed on the gigantic mural.

"I hear a *but* coming," he murmured.

She nodded and managed the semblance of a smile. "The head honcho at corporate headquarters has a policy about relationships between managers and personnel. I know for a fact, because I dragged out my contract this afternoon and looked at the fine print. But even if Double H didn't frown on fraternizing with hired assistants, I have my own ethics. As much as we have in common, personally and professionally, we can have only a business relationship—"

"And nothing more, no matter what the potential," he finished for her. "I'm getting the picture, boss lady. Is there a significant other in your life as well?"

Mattie couldn't help herself; she burst out laughing.

Joe frowned, bemused. "That wasn't such an absurd question. One look in the mirror is all the assurance you need that you're attractive. And hell, isn't it every he-man's dream to happen onto a woman who shares his love for power tools?"

"Is it?" she asked. "I wouldn't know. I've never

tapped into the male psyche. But experience has taught me that some men don't like their male territory encroached upon by a woman. It's not feminine, or some silly nonsense. In addition, I've never had time for a social life, aside from community activities and projects. Up until two months ago I'd been caring for my grandfather and managing a store that brings in more business than I can keep up with. I put myself through college, commuting so Pops wouldn't have to be alone. Until God decides to add a few more hours to the day, I don't have time for more than professional and personal obligations.

"Which reminds me," she said, glancing at her watch, "I need to stop by the nursing home to check on Pops. He's a bit of a renegade. According to the staff, he's always stirring up trouble. Last month he and his gang of cantankerous senior citizens escaped before bed check. He sneaked over to our storage shed to confiscate fishing poles. To this day I don't know how those old rascals managed to get hold of the six-pack they were nursing while fishing at our creek."

Joe chuckled at the verbal picture she painted. Pops sounded like quite a character. J. D. Grayson would undoubtedly approve of Pops's shenanigans. J.D., after all, was a bit of a rascal himself.

"It wasn't funny," Mattie insisted, though she couldn't contain her grin. "The nursing staff was put out with Pops because booze doesn't mix with his medication. The staff warned him that he could have gotten dizzy, had a seizure and fallen into the water. His doctor threatened to put him in solitary confinement if he didn't behave himself."

Mattie pivoted, directing Joe's attention to the features of the small apartment. "Let me give you the quick tour before I go. The kitchen area is small but efficient," she said, gesturing toward the cabinets and appliances on the north wall. "The Hide-A-Bed sofa has a queen-size inner spring mattress for your sleeping comfort. The bathroom is on the back side of the closet. This place is yours if you're interested, Joe."

"I'll take it," he said without hesitation, even though the square footage of the apartment would fit easily into his living area in the city.

"The riding lawn mower is in my personal workshop behind the house. You're welcome to use it," she offered.

"I'll mow your lawn as part of our deal. That'll free up some of your time."

Mattie stopped short and gazed up at him. He fell into the depths of her violet eyes—and not for the first time, either. Damn, this woman had a fierce, intense effect on him. Too bad there were restrictions placed on their potential relationship. Also, too bad the head honcho had placed restrictions between managers and assistants. Joe would like to strangle himself for that.

"That is really nice of you," she murmured. "I accept your offer."

When she turned and walked away, his gaze followed her out the door. Joe glanced around his diminutive apartment, which Mattie had given such a homey, welcoming appearance. This apartment had her personality, her personal touch. It was going to be hell on him, feeling her presence, observing her rules. Damn, he wished the head honcho's policy didn't exist. Of course, he had himself to thank for those blasted rules. What irony, thought Joe.

Muttering at himself, and at the complexity of this situation he had created, he ambled outside to grab his suitcase from the truck.

Look, appreciate, but don't get close enough to touch, he mused sourly. Okay, he could deal with a limited relationship with Mattie, he tried to reassure himself. After all, he'd only be here a month, and the prospect of explaining that he wasn't exactly who he pretended to be would be horribly awkward.

Better that Mattie never knew her hireling was really her corporate boss. She claimed to like Joe dandy-fine now, but he predicted she would despise him if she knew he hadn't been totally honest with her.

No, he would simply play out the role he had designed to recapture his enthusiasm for this business, then he would put what he learned in Fox Hollow to good use. End of story.

Great idea, Joe, he thought to himself. So how do you plan to cool your heels when this pixie is so damn appealing to you, huh?

Joe decided he'd figure that out on his way to the grocery store to stock the empty fridge and kitchen cabinets.

MATTIE SIGHED AUDIBLY when she entered Paradise Valley to see one of the staff wagging an acrylic-tipped forefinger in her grandfather's scowling face. More problems, Mattie predicted. What kind of trouble had Pops gotten into now?

Mattie braced herself when Nurse Gamble pelted forward, wearing an annoyed frown.

"Now what?" Mattie asked warily.

Gertie Gamble knotted her fists on her ample hips

and harrumphed loudly. "Now that old rascal has incited a riot against the cafeteria staff. I swear he enjoys being labeled a troublemaker."

"Hi, Shortcake!" Pops called cheerfully. "Glad you could stop by. Don't pay any attention to Admiral Gamble. It's her job to keep this place shipshape."

Gertie flung Pops a withering glance, then focused on Mattie. "See what I mean? Now he's got most of the bedpan crowd referring to me as 'The Admiral.' Deal with him, Mattie. I've had enough of him for the week." She spun around, then turned back to Mattie. "By the way, I saw that original painting and decorative shelving you designed for Arthella Lambert. It's so gorgeous. Could you do something for me in greens and maroon that will enhance the colors in my living room furniture?"

"Sure, Gertie, stop by the store when you have time and we'll work out the details."

"Thanks." Gertie's smile faded as she hitched her thumb toward Pops. "It's time for your weekly talk about behavioral modification. Your grandpa's memory only lasts seven days—tops."

Mattie trailed after Pops, who had turned toward his room, propelled along with the aid of his three-pronged cane that lent additional support for his arthritic knees.

"The bad boy of Paradise Valley strikes again, so I hear," Mattie commented. "What prompted this most recent rebellion, Pops?"

Pops half turned, his dark eyes twinkling with mischief. "So now you know what I went through during your teenage years, Shortcake. How do you like reversing roles?"

It was impossible for Mattie to remain irritated with

her feisty grandfather. He was right, of course. She had given him a few gray hairs while she struggled through adolescence to reach adulthood.

"So this is payback time, is it?" she asked as she looped her arm around his waist, then gave him a fond peck on the cheek.

"Don't be doing that around here," Pops grumbled. "You'll give all these broads who have the hots for me ideas, don't ya know. Good thing I carry a cane so I can fight off the feminine attention I've been getting."

Mattie giggled. "I guess it's true that ladies, no matter what their age, love outlaws. You, being the rebellious ringleader that you are, draw all sorts of attention around here."

"Well, somebody has to buck the system," Pops commented as he veered toward his room. "You try eating that slop served on trays and on the plates at the cafeteria. Hell, you wanna know how many ways you can prepare and serve prunes? Have lunch with me tomorrow, Shortcake. I guaran-damn-tee you'll join the ranks of rioters who are craving a decent meal."

"Last I heard, a proper diet contributed to health and longevity," she countered as she watched Pops ease a hip onto his bed. "You know perfectly well that the main reasons you're here are to adjust your dosage of arthritic medication and balance your diet to prevent diabetic flare-ups. You can't move back in with me until your doctor gives you a clean bill of health."

Pops pulled his wire-rim glasses from the bridge of his nose and cleaned the lenses on the hem of his shirt. "So I have a real weakness for fried foods and red meats. So shoot me, Shortcake. What's the point of living if you can't enjoy yourself occasionally?''

It was hard to argue with a seventy-eight-year-old redneck who believed in taking each day as it came and making the most of it. ''Is the food here really that bad?'' she asked as she sprawled warily in the worn-out recliner Pops had insisted on bringing from home.

''Dog food has more taste,'' he declared as he shoved his glasses back in place. ''The oven-broiled steak they serve here is so tough my dentures come loose when I eat. The smothered chicken tastes like wet newspaper. The beans are cooked to death, and the fat-free desserts taste like wax. Shall I go on?''

''No, I get the picture.''

Pops glanced toward the open door to insure he wasn't overheard, then leaned toward Mattie. ''Here's my plan, Shortcake. You can slip food to me when you come to visit. You can bring it to my window before you come through the main entrance. No one will be the wiser. Fred, Ralph, Herman and Glen are willing to pay you if you'll do the same for them.''

Mattie nodded pensively. ''I see. You want me to become an accomplice for the Roland Gang.''

He grinned unrepentantly. ''You catch on quick, smart girl that you are.''

''Pops, I have a reputation to uphold in Fox Hollow,'' she reminded him. ''I manage a store for a corporation.''

''So? I have a reputation to maintain here, too,'' he assured her. ''These old folks—''

As if he wasn't one of them, she thought to herself.

''—depend on me to lead the way and fight their battles. I bring problems to attention and see that the necessary changes are made. Old folks want and need respect, ya know. We don't like being put out to pasture on crummy rations. Ask me, boredom and feelings of uselessness are the two leading causes of death around here." He hoisted himself off the bed, then grabbed his cane. "Let me show you something, Shortcake."

Mattie frowned curiously when Pops gestured toward the landscape painting and knickknack shelf she'd brought to give his room a homey appearance.

"See this stuff?"

"Yes, but—"

"Just keep it in mind, then come take a gander at this." Pops shuffled from the room, leading her next door.

"Hey, Fred, my granddaughter is here," he called out.

Mattie poked her head inside the generic room to see one of her grandfather's cohorts perched on a straight-back chair, staring through the slats of the miniblinds that covered the window. "Hi, Fred. How's it going?"

"Lousy, but thanks for asking, girl."

"Just popped in to say howdy," Pops said, reversing direction. "Poker at ten o'clock tonight? Your place, right?"

The bald-headed Fred perked up considerably, then winked at Pops. "Right. I almost forgot this was Friday night. One night's about the same as another around here."

When Pops returned to his room, he pulled a deck of cards from his pocket and displayed the ace of hearts for Mattie's viewing discomfort.

"Pops! For heaven's sake! Those cards have naked women on them," she grumbled, offended.

"Sure as hell do," he said, undaunted. "I asked Herman's grandson to pick them up for me during his last visit. I plan to give the gang a cheap thrill to-night…and don't give me that look, Shortcake. Ain't a man in the Roland Gang who hasn't seen a naked lady a few times in his life. We're all World War II veterans. Those island women we came across when we were stationed in the Pacific didn't wear blouses. And you know what else? A bunch of men in our unit pooled some money to buy them brassieres to pre-serve their modesty. You know what those women did with the contraptions we gave them?"

"No, what did they do, Pops?" she asked, smiling.

"They used them to haul coconuts two at a time," he informed her.

Mattie cackled. Her grandfather had always been a source of amusement to her.

Pops tucked the racy cards into the pocket of his trousers, then settled himself more comfortably on the bed. "The point of taking you to see Fred is that his room has only the barest of necessities. The place doesn't feel like home to him because it doesn't look like home. There's nothing on the walls, no memo-rabilia, no family pictures. Zilch, nada. I had to throw a tantrum to get permission to hang your artwork and the shelves in here. I shouldn't have had to do that. We're paying hard-earned money for room, board and medical care. Yet, this chicken coop looks like a half-way house for criminal offenders. This place needs your touch of interior decoration to provide some stimulation and aesthetic beauty. If every patient demanded the right to personalize their living quarters we could get some results. That's my next crusade."

Mattie cringed at the thought of another crusade for the Roland Gang. Rebel that Bernard Roland had become, he refused to give up until he'd paved the way for improvements. Yet, Mattie was inclined to agree with her grandfather. The convalescent home looked more like perdition—a dull way station to the hereafter. That definitely wasn't the effect she would be going for if she lived here.

"Next week I'm taking the petition to the director and demanding some rights," Pops informed her. "If I can push this project through, the patients want you to decorate their rooms like you decorated mine. And believe me, I've had compliments piled on top of compliments, Shortcake. The thing is that we're talking limited budgets at the old fogies' home. Can you handle interior decor on a skimpy budget?"

Mattie sat there, stunned. Pops was drumming up business for her, adding to her already hectic schedule? Yet, the intense, determined look on his wrinkled features indicated that the upcoming crusade was vitally important to him. He was fighting to improve the quality of life for the senior citizens who required assisted living. Could she spare the time for a project of this magnitude?

How could she not? Several of the patients here had practically helped raise her while her grandfather worked construction. These elderly folks had fed her, baby-sat her and offered her the love and concern her own parents refused to be bothered with.

Now that Joe Gray had hired on at the store, she could make time to fulfill Pops's request. True, she would meet herself coming and going, but what else was new?

"Okay, Pops, you've got a deal," she told him.

The old man leaned over to give her a high five. "Thanks, Shortcake. This means a lot to me."

"I can see that. Fortunately, I received a directive from corporate headquarters this morning, allowing me to hire an assistant. I filled the position immediately. Joe Gray is skilled in woodcrafting and—"

"Joe Gray? Never heard of him," Pops broke in.

"He's new in town. I rented the garage apartment to him," she reported.

Pops's dark eyes narrowed suspiciously. "Who is this character? Where's he from? What do you know about him?"

Mattie took a moment to gather her thoughts and realized that she really did know quite a lot about her new assistant, although they had only spent eight hours working together.

"He's thirty-five, single. He is respectful and has excellent rapport with the customers because he's knowledgeable about hobbies and crafts. He thoroughly enjoys working with his hands in the workroom, and he isn't the least bit allergic to hard work. I had to remind him to take a break this morning and this afternoon."

"Single?" Pops inquired interestedly.

Mattie rolled her eyes at him. "Don't even think about playing matchmaker. You have too much on your plate already. Besides, Joe and I are business associates, and that is as far as the relationship can possibly go."

"Baloney," Pops said, then snorted. "Unless Joe is a serial killer on the loose and hiding out in Fox

Hollow, he sounds like your type. Some guys around here feel threatened because you can handle a power tool with the best of them.''

"Thanks to you,'' Mattie put in, grinning.

"But if this Joe person shares your common interests and is a decent sort of fellow, I say go for it. Unless there's something offensive about him. Is there? Ugly as original sin maybe?''

Mattie chuckled. "Just the opposite. My female customers constantly ask for his assistance, just to get a close look at him.''

"He sounds perfect. A Mary Poppins of the male variety.''

"Except that he works for me,'' Mattie repeated. "I'd have to fire him if I became interested in him. Either that or I'd have to resign. I can't do that, not when you've just handed me a time-consuming project to perk up your senior citizen friends.''

"Oh yeah, there is that,'' Pops mumbled. "But there isn't a single patient here at the home who wouldn't tell you to go for it if this Joe character suits you, even if you spend your time with *him* and the rest of us have to stare at these bare walls an extra month before the interior decorations arrive.''

"Pops,'' she said warningly.

He flung up his hand. "Don't 'Pops' me, kiddo. You aren't getting any younger, and I want you to have a life like your grandmother and I had together. Now that's something you shouldn't pass up.''

Mattie squirmed uncomfortably. They'd had this little talk before—about a thousand times, thank you very much. Pops wanted her married and settled before he passed on. She understood that, but you just couldn't rush love. It either happened or it didn't. So far it hadn't. She'd been infatuated once or twice in her early twenties, but the relationships had fizzled out because Mattie kept long hours and took on the responsibility of caring for Pops. Most men didn't like to compete with Pops. He was such a lively, energetic character that he tended to steal the show when he was underfoot. Her boyfriends—what few she had— demanded that she choose between them and Pops. It was no contest. This man had taken her in, raised her, provided for her, taught her skills and encouraged her to pursue her artistic gift.

Mattie glanced at her watch when her stomach growled, reminding her that she had skipped lunch in order to decorate Alice Dawson's living room. "I better go, Pops. I haven't had supper yet."

"Yeah, well, if you'd eaten at this cafeteria you wouldn't feel as if you'd eaten, either," he muttered. "I'm serious about those snacks. Graham crackers, vanilla wafers, pudding cups. Doesn't matter to me. Just bring some junk food for me and my cronies."

Mattie sighed, resigned to becoming an accomplice. "Okay, get a list from your gang and call me at the store tomorrow. I'll bring the goodies Sunday evening when I come to visit."

"You're a doll, Shortcake. Did I ever tell you that?"

"Yes, Pops, immediately after you'd dragged me into another of your schemes."

"Hey, you know I love ya, kiddo. You were always my very best sidekick. Now I have to settle for these yahoos at the home, but that doesn't mean I don't love you best of all."

Mattie rose from the chair to give Pops an affectionate hug and kiss. "Love ya, Pops, even if you are the mastermind of the wildest bunch of codgers in Paradise Valley.''

''And you remember what I said about this Joe Gray person. If he's worth your interest, then bend a few rules. I'm an advocate of that. You go, girl.''

Shaking her head at Pops's adolescent jargon, Mattie exited. Pops was, without a doubt, the youngest seventy-eight-year-old in the country. He'd told her once that the only thing he regretted in life was not taking more risks—and he'd taken plenty of them, in her opinion. But when it came to her unwilling, unproductive attraction to Joe Gray, Mattie was hesitant.

No, she wasn't going to fire Joe because she was interested in him, or because she really wanted to get to know him better. She needed him at the store, now more than ever—thanks to Pops's latest mission. She'd put her feminine needs on hold years ago, after all. She could control her urges. She and Joe were going to be good buddies, best pals, she told herself sensibly. This was one time she was definitely not going to take Pops's advice.

And that was all there was to that.

3

JOE WAS AMAZED at the number of customers who poured in and out of Hobby Hut on Saturday. When he commented to Mattie, she informed him that Fox Hollow was the closest community to the lake, and that cabin and cottage owners delighted in redecorating their weekend retreats. In addition, the retirees who lived in the wooded hills enjoyed keeping up with the latest seasonal fads.

Joe had never seen the likes of women, young and old, buying fall arrangements, Halloween and Thanksgiving decorations. When he and J.D. came up with the idea of the craft store that had expanded across the Midwest, they'd never dreamed of being so successful. But now that Joe was here in the trenches, watching these women, with a few reluctant husbands traipsing around the store, he realized why the business boomed. People liked to rearrange their homes by adding personal touches they could appreciate, then replacing decorations several times throughout the year. It was the variety that kept life new and interesting.

Twice during the day, the husbands of female shoppers had looked Joe up and down, then muttered "twinkie" half under their breaths. Joe probably should have been offended that he'd been categorized as effeminate because he actually liked creating knickknacks in the workshop and didn't mind selling them. Once, however, he'd had to bite his tongue when a grumpy old man scowled and referred to the inventory at Hobby Hut as "sissy stuff no man would be caught dead selling, unless it was a last resort to keep the wolves from the door."

Joe's thoughts scattered like a flock of geese going airborne when Mattie scrunched in front of him at the cash register. "Here come the Zimmers for a refund," she murmured confidentially. "Better let me handle them this first time so you'll know how to deal with them. Lovable as they are, they get their kicks from trying to pull a fast one every now and then."

Joe stepped aside, frowning curiously at the harmless-looking elderly couple who hobbled down the center aisle, a quart of paint clamped in each gnarled hand.

"Changed our minds about the accent colors in the bedrooms and living room," Coreen Zimmer announced as she set the cans on the counter, then produced her receipt. "Just want our money back until we can agree on which colors to put where."

Sounded reasonable enough to Joe. He couldn't fathom why Mattie thought she needed to handle this simple transaction. But to his surprise, Mattie grabbed a flathead screwdriver from beneath the counter and opened the paint. To his horror, she dipped her finger into the can to taste the contents.

"Colored water," she said, smiling wryly at her customers. "Pretty sneaky of you two, but no dice. You really are going to have to get up a few hours earlier to outfox me."

Homer Zimmer shot Mattie a disgruntled glance, then flicked his attention to Joe. "Could've pulled it off if you would've let him wait on us, I'd bet. We heard there was a new assistant at the store, and we wanted to see how sharp he was."

Joe was stunned that these old shysters were trying to get a refund on paint they'd obviously used up, then refilled the cans with water. He didn't know whether to laugh or curse their ingenuity.

Mattie set the four paint cans on the floor beside the trash, then smiled brightly. "Anything else you want to try to fly past me today?"

"Well, now that you mention it." Coreen retrieved a plastic bag from her oversize purse. "I bought this figurine of an angel a couple of weeks ago and didn't notice that one wing was broken until I got home. I'd like to exchange it for a new one."

Joe crossed his arms, waiting to see how Mattie handled this transaction. As usual, she smiled cheerfully, then scooped up the angel with its broken wing. "You realize that I personally shelved these figurines, with all the loving care angels should receive. They are one of my favorites, you know." She stared at Coreen, then focused unblinkingly on Homer. "Who dropped this accidentally? And don't even think about lying to me because we are discussing *angels*. It'd be like telling a lie at church, right there, down on your knees at the altar."

Seconds ticked by. Joe appraised one wrinkled face, then the other.

Apparently Homer couldn't stand the silence a moment longer. He caved in.

"Oh, all right, girl, it was me, blast it. I knocked the angel off the shelf. You got any of that industrial-strength glue that'd work on a broken wing?"

"Of course, Homer," Mattie assured him. "I'll be happy to get it for you."

When Mattie strode off, the Zimmers zeroed in on Joe.

"You're darn lucky to be working for that girl, you know," Homer declared. "Sweetest disposition in town...argh." He grimaced when Coreen gouged him in the ribs with her elbow. "Next to my lovely bride of forty-seven years, of course. Mattie's a talented artist, too, if you didn't know. I'd buy some of her paintings, but I can't afford it on our fixed income."

"The point he's trying to make is that we don't want you pulling any fast ones on our sweet Mattie," Coreen lectured.

This from two shysters who'd tried to exchange water for paint? They were hypocrites, both of them. But it was obvious they were immensely fond of Mattie. Yet, who around this town wasn't? Joe had heard her praises sung all the livelong day.

"I wouldn't think of cheating Mattie," Joe assured the Zimmers. "I like my job, and I plan to keep it."

"Good for you, boy." Homer leaned closer. Joe could smell the cheap, sticky-sweet aftershave. "But be warned that some of the ranchers over at the café were poking fun at you during lunch today. They think you're a sissy for working here."

"What do you think?" Joe asked.

"I think you've got guts to be working in a place like this," Homer replied. "Just hope you can take the razzing that's sure to come your way when those cowboys get to feeling ornery and decide to torment you."

"Thanks for the warning."

Mattie returned, handing Joe the glue. "Please ring

them up while I finish my painting project in the workroom. I promised delivery after store hours this evening.''

Joe manned the register, swearing the mold count elevated when Homer pried open his wallet, complaining that it was highway robbery to pay such a high price for one teensy-weensy tube of glue.

When the couple exited Joe reminded himself that working with the public was no picnic. He'd obviously been sitting in his ivory corporate tower too long. His employees deserved an across-the-board raise for working in the combat zone.

DURING HIS AFTERNOON BREAK Joe heard the phone ringing in Mattie's office. Since she was helping one of her regular customers, Joe made a dash to answer the phone.

''Hobby Hut,'' he said politely.

''Where the hell's Mattie?'' came a loud, gravelly male voice.

''She's with a customer at the moment. Can I take a message?''

''Is this Joe?'' the caller demanded.

He blinked. ''Yes, sir, it is.''

''Figured as much. This is Mattie's grandpa. I have my list ready for her. Got a pencil handy, boy?''

''Yes, sir.'' Joe plucked up a notepad and pen.

''Don't give me any more of that *sir* crapola,'' Pops objected. ''The name is Pops.''

Joe grinned. ''Okay. Fire away, Pops.''

''Double-stuffed Oreo cookies, a jar of peanut butter, smooth not crunchy. Apples and crackers,'' he rattled off. ''Chocolate chip cookies—the gooier the better. Chocolate snack cakes with vanilla filling. And don't buy that off-brand stuff. Stick with the brand names. Make a note of that for Mattie.''

Joe scribbled as fast as he could. "Is there some sort of party going on at the convalescent home?"

"Hell no, Mattie has to sneak the junk food into me and my friends. They treat us like a bunch of preschoolers here. Afraid we'll OD on sugar and caffeine and be bouncing off the walls at bedtime.''

Joe swallowed an amused chuckle. He really was looking forward to meeting this character in person. He wished J.D. could, too. "Anything else, Pops?"

"Yeah, how do you feel about my granddaughter?" Pops asked flat out.

"Er…"

"Not attractive enough for you?" Pops grilled him.

"Plenty," Joe replied honestly.

"Thought so. I may be old, but I'm sure as hell not blind yet. That girl has a terrific body and a pretty face. I'm sure you must've noticed, being a man and all.''

"Er…"

"Do you feel threatened because she can handle a router and circular saw as good as any man?" Pops fired off the question at the speed of a launched rocket.

"Not the least bit threatened," Joe answered.

"Think she has the personality of a slug, do you?" Pops quizzed him.

"Hardly. Mattie is one of the nicest, most personable women I've ever met.''

"So, what's the problem here?"

"Problem? We have a problem?" Joe questioned, totally dumbfounded. He thought things were going great between them.

"Can't see why you should have a problem. She's single, and so are you. She says you're a decent, good-looking fellow, and you say she's attractive and personable. So when are you going to ask her out? Hell, you're practically living in each other's pockets so you ought to know each other pretty well after only a few days."

"I think Mattie sees that as a potential problem," Joe commented. "If things don't work out, if we have irreconcilable differences, then we are still stuck working together and living next door to each other."

"So you're too chicken to give it a whirl. Is that what you're telling me, Joe?"

"I'm saying nothing of the kind, Pops. As her employee, I'm simply respecting Mattie's wishes."

"Hogwash, Joe. Take my advice and ask her out... I gotta go. It's time for the guards to herd the prisoners to the cafeteria to eat slop. Don't delay in giving Mattie that list, hear me? She has to make the drop tomorrow night. If you squeal on her, you'll be damn sorry for pointing the finger and calling her our accomplice. Got that, Joe?"

It was all Joe could do to prevent busting a gut laughing at the threat from this old man. "Not to worry, Pops. I'll make the drop myself if Mattie can't do it. Consider your junk food signed, sealed and delivered tomorrow night."

"You're okay, Joe," Pops announced.

Joe hung up the phone, then pivoted to see Mattie approaching him.

"Who was that?" she asked curiously.

"Pops." Joe grinned when Mattie winced. He waved the junk food list in front of her face. "Does he turn you into his accomplice often?"

Mattie slouched in her chair, hunched and rolled her shoulders, then nodded. "Pops is on a crusade to improve conditions at Paradise Valley. His latest mission involves me and the interior decoration of the generic rooms for other patients. According to Pops, the place is screaming for that lived-in, homey atmosphere to perk up the morale of the elderly."

"Naturally, you couldn't turn Pops down, even if you have enough extra projects to keep you busy for…oh, say, the next two years."

When she focused those beguiling amethyst eyes, fanned with long, thick lashes, on him, Joe's knees wobbled. He propped against the doorjamb for support.

"Pops has a legitimate point, and he's petitioning the director for changes. If you would have seen his friend Fred sitting next door in his room, surrounded by blank walls, staring through the miniblinds, I bet you would have caved in, too."

Joe held up his hands like a victim of a robbery. "Hey, don't get defensive on me, boss lady. I'm not judging or objecting. If my grandpa was in a bland convalescent home and requested paraphernalia and memorabilia to make him feel more at home, I'd do the exact same thing. Furthermore, I'll be glad to help you design, construct and paint whatever you need for the projects. I assume we're working for elderly customers on a limited budget."

"You'll help?" Mattie smiled gratefully. "Thanks, Joe, I can't begin to tell you how much I appreciate it."

"But it'll cost you," he warned in mock seriousness. "You have to promise to fix Sunday dinner while I'm ripping lumber on the table saw and constructing curio shelves, keepsake chests and benches for the patients.''

"How do you know I can cook?"

"Boss lady, thus far I haven't seen anything you can't do exceptionally well," he complimented. "From handling power tools, creating art and interior design to dealing with devious customers, you can do it all."

She cocked her head and studied him from a different angle. "Are you buttering me up, hoping for a raise?"

"No, just stating the facts, ma'am." Yet, there was one fact Joe was reluctant to state. He had the wild, crazy impulse to walk right up to Mattie, snatch her from her chair and kiss the living daylights out of her.

It was the damnedest thing he'd ever experienced. He, who had escorted glamorous socialites and seen his name and picture linked with a half-dozen women in tabloids, was turned on by a carpenter's elf who had sawdust in her hair. Penny Candy Red, Frosty Glade Green, and Biscuit White were splattered on her fingers and on the hem of her T-shirt. None of that mattered. When she smiled at him it never failed to knock him for a loop and leave him wanting things he knew he couldn't have.

"And may I say that after two days of nonstop work, without a single complaint, I can give you nothing less than a rating of exceptional on your evaluation sheet, Mr. Gray. I suspect the head honcho, lounging on his throne in the city, will applaud your work ethics."

Joe inwardly flinched. Every time Mattie mentioned the all-powerful CEO, his conscience took a bite out of him. Maybe he should tell her the truth.

Or maybe not. Mattie lambasted the high king of woodcraft often enough that she would feel deceived and mortified. No, he was willing to bet that his Employee of the Year would take this the wrong way, wouldn't understand why he was here, incognito.

"So, how about if I treat you to a burger and fries before I hang Gladys Howser's painting and curio shelves this evening?" Mattie offered.

"Have you already locked up for the night?" he asked.

"Yes, right before I came back to the office. I'll count the till and we can be on our way."

"Fine, except I'm buying." When she tried to protest, Joe touched his forefinger to her lips to shush her. That simple, seemingly harmless touch sent a jolt of awareness sizzling through him. Joe swore he'd been electrocuted. Her lips felt like velvet beneath his fingertip, and he had to battle another insane urge to replace his fingertip with his lips and make a feast of her.

Damn it, if he'd had the slightest idea that he'd have such an incredible reaction to Mattie Roland he never would have hired on. Now it was too late. He felt involved in this particular store, involved in her life, and in the complications she faced with her rebellious grandfather.

Of course, if he followed Pops's advice, he'd just thumb his nose at his own rules and go for it. For sure and certain, his male body would applaud his decision.

"Buying dinner is my way of thanking you for this job, for the apartment and the chance to buck the establishment, on behalf of your grandpa, my grandpa, and everybody else's grandparents who want to improve the quality of life during their golden years…''

His voice trailed off when her gaze lifted and locked with his. Time screeched to a halt. The office shrank and silence descended around him. Joe had the unmistakable feeling that Mattie, despite the rules and regulations, was wondering the same thing he was. Did they dare to test this mutual attraction and risk what seemed to be the makings of a beautiful friendship?

Scratch that, Joe decided. Being the devious jerk that he was, there couldn't be a trusting friendship between them. He'd botched that up the instant he'd introduced himself as Joe Gray and allowed Mattie to confide that she thought the head honcho of Hobby Hut had lost touch with the purpose of his multimillion-dollar business.

In effect, Joe Gray was Daniel J. Grayson's corporate spy, an internal investigator who was staking out one of his store managers. He hadn't considered those ramifications when he came to Fox Hollow, hoping to rediscover his purpose and enthusiasm. But Mattie wouldn't view the situation the same way he did. He could sugarcoat his actions however he wished, rationalizing that his intentions were honorable and that he had tried to guard against being catered to so he wouldn't have to endure preferential treatment because of his title and position. However, he didn't think any of that garbage would fly with Mattie. She would misunderstand, he predicted.

Damn, he'd dug such a deep hole that he'd need an extension ladder to climb out.

Mattie stared into the entrancing amber eyes that were embedded in that all too handsome face and heard her grandfather's words echoing in her ears. According to Pops, every risk ignored was a chance never taken. Challenge the rules, he'd said, don't meekly accept them. Pops advocated grabbing for the gusto.

Should she or shouldn't she kiss Joe? This was really tricky, after all. She was the manager, and he was the hired assistant. If she up and kissed him, would he kiss her back because he thought his job might be in jeopardy or because he truly wanted to? If he kissed her—and he looked as if he, too, was pondering the prospect, for whatever reason—would he wonder if he was putting his job at risk, a job he claimed he was pleased to have.

Catch twenty-two, she thought. This was the proverbial two-edged sword, yadda, yadda.

After what seemed a century of standing on uncertain ground, wrestling with consequences, Joe traced the curve of her lips. Mattie's knees wobbled unsteadily beneath her.

"Mattie, I think we'll both feel a lot better if we just get this over with. You're the boss, so you need to call a time-out from the job. It is after hours. Despite my good intentions, I just don't think this good-buddy relationship between us is going to work. I'm too damn aware of you as a woman. Sorry, but that's just the way it is."

Mattie didn't pretend to misunderstand what he meant. Apparently, they were on the same wavelength here. He was wondering, as she was, if an experimental kiss would relieve the sexual tension that had been building since he set foot in the store.

Yes, Mattie *had* tried to ignore the frissons of desire that assailed her when he was in close proximity.

Which was like trying to ignore an emotional cyclone spinning around you all the livelong day. Impossible.

"*I'm* thinking that *you're* thinking that you don't want to step on a land mine of sexual harassment by kissing me," Joe murmured huskily. "*You're* probably thinking that *I'm* thinking I might risk losing my job—which you know I really like—if I kiss you first and you end up not liking it very much. So, what say, we meet in the middle like two consenting adults. All rules and regulations will be dispensed with for the moment. If things don't work out, we'll just slip back into our roles as boss and assistant, chalk this up to an experiment gone sour, and get on with our lives. Sound fair to you?"

"And if this experiment isn't sour?" she asked, afraid to breathe too deeply for fear the tantalizing scent of him would wrap itself so completely around her senses that her brain would fog up and she'd lose the common sense she'd spent thirty years cultivating.

"We'll cross that bridge when we come to it," he murmured, his voice rough and raspy. "The suspense is killing me, Mattie. On three. One, two—"

Repetitive, staccato raps on the glass door forced Joe and Mattie to leap apart.

"Yo, Mattie! Yoo-hoo, it's me, Gladys Howser. Are you still in there?"

Mattie didn't know whether to curse or bless her impatient customer. "Coming!" she hollered.

When Mattie sailed off like a flying carpet, Joe half collapsed against the desk. Damn, he probably should have kept his trap shut, but his unruly hormones had stormed his brain and executed a coup d'état. He'd wanted to kiss that cute little elf. Badly. Worse than badly, he amended. It was as if he were starving for the taste of her and wouldn't be satisfied until he'd sampled her petal-soft lips.

"You're nuts," Joe said to himself, then scowled. "Just goes to show how desperately you needed this vacation from the office. Of all the glamorous women you've dated, you go bonkers over a tomboy who smells like paint and sawdust rather than expensive perfume, a tomboy who dresses in faded jeans and T-shirts instead of sequined evening gowns. And to complicate matters *she* actually works for *you*, despite what she thinks. She also thinks Double H is a money-grubbing executive whose bottom line is profit. Have you left anything out?

"Oh yeah, you're a devious, lying impostor, and Mattie is too damn sweet and tenderhearted to deserve your deceit. If you had the sense God gave a gnat you would hand in your resignation and hightail it back to the city."

"Joe!" Mattie called on her way down the center aisle. "There's been a change of plans. Gladys wants her new painting and shelves hung now. Her bridge party has been changed to seven o'clock this evening to accommodate one of her friends. I need a rain check on supper."

Joe nodded agreeably. He figured this was for the best. Fate had intervened, or perhaps the powers that be in the universe decided that that kiss was a very bad idea. But you couldn't convince his rowdy male body of that, not without a bolt from the blue that fried him to the tiled floor.

"I'll count the till and lock up," he offered. "That is, if you trust me."

She smiled, stared him squarely in the eye, and said, "I trust you, Joe. If I didn't, you wouldn't be here, and we wouldn't have been on the threshold we were standing on five minutes ago, either.''

Now he really felt like a card-carrying jerk. He had lied to her, deceived her, misrepresented himself, and she trusted him. He suspected each and every one of her acquaintances felt the same way, when honored and graced by Mattie's trusting nature. Hurting someone like Mattie Roland ranked right up there with the seven deadly sins that could earn you a one-way express flight to hell.

Gee, maybe he should author a book on how many ways there were for a man to screw up without really trying, he thought to himself.

While Joe was counting the till, he heard someone pounding on the back entrance that opened into the alley. "Now what?" he muttered crabbily.

He yanked open the steel door to see five elderly men staring back at him. The Roland Gang, he presumed. He appraised the ringleader, who leaned on his three-pronged cane. Pops wore knit jeans that were snagged with twigs and a faded cotton shirt that emphasized his sunken chest. Pops had a full head of silver hair, wire-rimmed glasses and an attitude that shouted spirit.

J. D. Grayson would fit right in with this bunch, thought Joe.

Behind Pops stood four men—more or less bald—sporting spare-tire paunches, glasses and outdated clothes. Joe nodded a greeting to them.

"So you're Joe," Pops said, still appraising him astutely. "So, whaddya think, boys?"

Boys? thought Joe. That obviously implied these old codgers were enjoying their second childhood.

"Looks all right to me," said Fred. "What do you think, Herman?"

Herman raked Joe up and down—twice. "Decent stock, I'd say. What's your vote, Ralph?"

"Okay by me," said Ralph. "What about you, Glen?"

Glen's gaze narrowed solemnly behind his thick glasses. "You got a criminal record, son?"

"No, do I need one?" Joe asked straight-faced.

"A smart ass, I like that," Pops said. "Has Short-cake seen this side of you yet?"

"Shortcake? As in Mattie?" Joe guessed.

"Yup. So has she?"

"No."

"Well, don't hold back on her, son. Make sure she knows the real you, right off. Always better that way."

Joe inwardly grimaced. He couldn't follow Pops's good advice. Joe had already lied six ways to Sunday.

"I saw Mattie drive off a minute ago," Pops said. "Figured that clunker truck parked back here belonged to you. Are you about finished here?"

"Yes," Joe said carefully.

"Don't give me that look," Pops muttered. "We're not going to ask you to join in a bank heist or anything like that. We just need to hitch a ride is all. Don't want Mattie to know we broke loose until after the fact. We've had all we can stand at that funny farm this week. We're going fishing."

Pops raised his pointy chin, all but daring Joe to protest.

He didn't.

"The poles are in the shed at Mattie's house,"

Pops informed Joe. "We already walked a mile. Can you give us a lift?"

Joe finished counting the till, switched off the lights, then locked the door behind him. Although this wasn't as good as losing himself in a kiss with Mattie, aiding and abetting the Roland Gang was the next best thing.

"It'll be crowded in my pickup. It only has one seat," Joe commented as he lead the way.

"Sardines don't complain about cramped cans, so neither will I," Pops said, hobbling at his swiftest pace. "You ask her out yet?"

"No," Joe grumbled as he scrunched himself against the driver's side, giving the gang every inch of space the cab of the truck would allow.

"You have our stamp of approval, so what are you waiting for?" Glen demanded.

"Thanks, that means a lot coming from the nursing home escapees," Joe shot back wryly.

"Fine, pal, you keep pussyfooting around and you'll end up like us, all alone and on the prowl," Herman put in. "They don't come better than Mattie. I watched her grow up. Hell, I helped raise her when her grandpa was in a bind with a job that took him out of town for a week at a time."

"So did I," Ralph added proudly. "Me and Wilma, God rest her, were honorary aunt and uncle in the old days."

"Same went for me and Jean," said Fred. "Even attended her high school and college graduation as part of her family. You don't think Mattie is good enough for you, just because she's a tomboy at heart? Is that the problem here?"

"She's better than I deserve," Joe murmured.

"Speak up, son," Pops demanded. "The batteries on my hearing aids are fizzling out."

"I like Mattie just fine," Joe all but yelled.

"Sheesh, keep it down," Glen groused. "We're hard-of-hearing, not stone-deaf."

Joe pulled out from the alley and took the back streets to Mattie's house. Amused—in an exasperated sort of way—he listened to the old coots give sales pitches about why he needed to see Mattie socially. If she had the slightest idea that the fearsome five were trying to play matchmaker, she'd probably pitch a fit.

Joe, however, thought it was touching to observe their loyalty and devotion to Mattie. She might not have excessive material wealth to rank her among Fortune's 500, but she was well respected and loved here in Fox Hollow. Her customers heaped glowing accolades on her. Her grandfather and honorary uncles adored her. Mattie had a wealth of friendship, while Joe had numerous acquaintances and associates, but few valued and trusted friends.

Joe had come to Fox Hollow to regain his touch with reality, to wander among the real people in this world. In forty-eight hours he'd received a full dose of life. His own life had become an endless string of profit-loss spreadsheets, cabinets filled with files, corporate meetings and shallow social gatherings. But here in the timberland he felt himself coming alive, not merely existing.

"You boys had supper yet?" Joe inquired.

The question drew a round of scoffs, snorts, and a couple of colorful obscenities.

"I told you on the phone that we were herded to the cafeteria for the slop-of-the-day special, topped off with glazed prunes for dessert. If you call that eating, then yeah, we already ate,'' Pop grumbled. "You got any junk food at your apartment?"

Joe grinned. "You bet your asses, boys. You provide the fishing poles, and I'll bring along the junk food and dig a few worms for bait."

Pops beamed in approval, then leaned sideways to give Joe a high five. "You're my kind of people, son."

"So, what time do you have to report to the home tonight?" Joe asked as he turned into the driveway.

Glen grinned. "We already crammed our pillows and spare blankets under the bedspreads and switched off the lights to make it look as if we hit the sack early. We've got hours to burn before they call out the dogs and begin the search."

Joe chuckled while the old men squirmed restlessly in the cramped space of his truck. Ah yes, life here in Fox Hollow was interesting, to say the least.

Briefly Joe wondered how Mattie would react when, and if, she discovered he'd acted as chauffeur and accomplice for the Roland Gang this evening. Then he decided Mattie should thank him for keeping an eye on these old coots. After all, if one of the men tripped and fell in the river, he had enough brawn and muscle to handle the rescue. He was actually doing Mattie a favor, now that he thought about it.

4

MATTIE SQUATTED ON HER HAUNCHES, then assembled the miniature deacon's bench. Grabbing the nail gun, she secured the boards in place. While the *whack-thump* of the gun serenaded her, she reflected on the enjoyable hours she'd spent the previous Sunday, while she and Joe designed drop-leaf tables, storage chests, curio shelves and peg racks for the convalescent home. Using spare lumber from previous projects, leftover paint, and damaged merchandise from the store, she and Joe had created arts and crafts that depicted country life. They had worked side by side for hours on end, chatting about little or nothing, really. They'd just talked, discussed their projects, and got to know each other better.

Joe hadn't mentioned the Near-Kiss Incident and neither had she. She told herself it was for the best that they had been interrupted. But that incessant little voice kept repeating, *You go, girl.*

For a full week now, Mattie had worked alongside Joe, who proved to be a dream employee. She had heard the razzing he'd taken from the macho types who happened into town to gawk and taunt the "girlie-man" who had hired on at Hobby Hut.

For the most part Joe ignored the teasing, secure enough in his masculinity that he didn't feel intimidated by the cowboys and sportsmen who frequented Watering Hole Tavern on the outskirts of town.

Grimacing, Mattie rose from a crouch to work the kinks from her back and legs, then glanced at her watch. It was long past closing time at the store, and she had made good progress on the three projects for customers who purchased her landscape paintings and requested theme shelves to display their folk art and Americana knickknacks. Working with Emerald Pool Green, Footprint Cream and Longjohn Red, Mattie had added colorful, hand-painted designs to the shelves and benches.

She'd managed to fill another lonely Saturday night, she thought glumly.

Her social life stank.

Mattie had offered to buy Joe's supper after work, but he'd left the store at closing time, commenting that he'd already made plans for the evening. However, he promised he'd start bright and early Sunday on the projects for the nursing home. Mattie wondered if he'd grown tired of her company and lost interest in the kiss that never happened—and probably never would.

Story of her life, actually, she thought as she unplugged the power tools, tapped the lids onto the paint cans, then swept up sawdust. She'd always been one of the guys during her high school and college days. She was the misfit female in woodwork classes who took her projects seriously. No one had been interested in dating a girl who showed the guys up in class through her skills with a saw, drill and can of paint.

Same probably held true with Joe, she mused. Undoubtedly, he had decided to look elsewhere for a hot date. Women had been hovering around the store for a solid week, flirting outrageously, asking his opinions and making purchases, just so he would wait on them, spend a few extra moments with them.

So why was she complaining if Joe had a hot date on Saturday night? Hadn't she wanted to keep their relationship platonic? Hadn't she been wishing for a skilled assistant to mind the store while she created new window displays, which usually sold within a few hours of being set up? Hadn't she craved more spare time to pursue her private craft projects? She was getting what she wanted, and she wasn't as happy as she thought she'd be. And all because she had developed an infatuation for a man whom she'd labeled as off-limits.

You go, girl.

"Just shut up," Mattie muttered at that annoying little voice. She was going home to soak in a hot bath, stuff her face with snacks and sprawl in her recliner. Another exciting, fun-filled evening at the Roland homestead.

Feeling immensely sorry for herself, Mattie closed up the shop, piled into her old model car and drove home. An hour later, dressed in an oversize T-shirt that served as a nightgown, flip-flops, and not much else, Mattie stood at her kitchen window, staring at a distant campfire that cast swaying shadows on the trees that lined the creek behind her house.

"Well, damn," Mattie grumbled as she headed for the back door. She suspected Pops and his cohorts had sneaked away from the nursing home to fish in the creek. Either that or aliens had landed their flying saucer on the far side of the hill and were conducting scientific experiments.

Annoyed, Mattie picked her way down the dirt path

and peered around a tree. Sure enough, Pops was tossing his fishing line into the creek with one hand and holding an aluminum can in the other. Damnation, if he upset the chemical balance his doctor and nurses were trying to align, she'd murder him. This nonsense had to stop!

As far as the other old men were concerned, Mattie would threaten to tattle to their families if they didn't cease these moonlight capers...

Her murderous thoughts scattered like buckshot when she saw Joe Gray rise up from his lounging position near a tree. She knew it was him. His broad shoulders and narrow hips gave him away as he leaned over to retrieve a beer can from the ice chest.

That did it! Mattie was plenty mad. She stalked forward to put a stop to this latest shenanigan. She was royally PO'd, and she didn't care who knew it.

"All right, party's over," she snapped brusquely. "Blast it, Pops!"

Pops clutched his chest and staggered to support himself on the three-pronged cane beside him. "Damn it, Shortcake, what are you trying to do? Give us a collective heart attack?"

"Why not? It's bound to come sooner or later if you and your friends hang out in this damp night air, chugging beer and munching on high-cholesterol snacks." Her chest heaved with frustration. "Have the whole bunch of you lost your minds? When the director finds you missing he'll have a conniption, order you restrained or boot you out, depending on his mood. And you—" She rounded on Joe, gearing up to read him every paragraph of the riot act.

Pops waved his arms in expansive gestures to gain Mattie's attention before she laid into Joe. "Calm down, Shortcake. We just came down to the creek to try out the new rods and reels Joe bought for us. And this isn't booze," he informed her. "It's sugar-free, decaffeinated fruit juice. See?" He held the aluminum can in front of the lantern so she could read the label. "And besides, that uppity director at Paradise Valley didn't catch us when we sneaked off last Saturday. So what are the odds that he'll notice we're missing when the other patients agreed to cover for us?"

"Last Saturday?" Mattie's gaze targeted Joe like a heat-seeking missile. "You chauffeured them down here last Saturday, too?"

"Don't go blaming our pal Joe," Fred broke in. "We wrestled him to the ground and twisted his arms every which way until he agreed to help us make our getaway. He's totally innocent, isn't he, boys?"

Four heads bobbed in agreement.

"Yeah, right," Mattie said, then smirked. "Like I can see that happening. You boys tackling Joe and manhandling him? Uh-huh, sure. Now gather up your fishing paraphernalia. I'm taking you back to the home."

"It's only nine o'clock," Ralph complained. "We have an hour of freedom before we have to worry about curfew."

"Tough, you're AWOL, and we all know it. Pack it up and haul butt!" Mattie ordered succinctly.

Pouting like children, the senior citizens gathered their gear and cast her mutinous glares at irregular intervals. They were making her out to be the villain here, and she didn't appreciate it one damn bit. She wasn't backing down, no matter how many times their glares branded her a traitor.

"I'll get the car," she announced, whirling around.

"Mattie," Joe called softly.

"What?" She didn't do him the courtesy of looking at him.

"Maybe I better take the boys home. Although you look spectacular in that flimsy T-shirt, especially when the lantern light shines through it, I don't advise parading around town, dressed as you are, with these escapees in tow. People might get the wrong impression."

Mattie's face blazed Congo Red. "I apologize if I made you uncomfortable, Joe," she chirped.

"You did, all right," he confirmed, his voice raspy. "You realize, of course, that this is going to affect my perception of you on the job. You may have to fire me for daydreaming."

Covering herself as best she could, Mattie pivoted to meet Joe's ornery grin. He was teasing her, and loving every minute of it, she realized. "Jerk," she flung at him.

"Sex goddess," he tossed back.

That stopped her cold. Sex goddess? She'd never considered herself any such thing. Furthermore, no man had ever referred to her as such. Obviously Joe was teasing her again. "Very funny. Hardy-har-har. If you're finished having a laugh at my expense, then you can haul those elderly hoodlums to the home. Plus, I will reimburse you for the refreshments and fishing rods. Catering to my rascally grandfather and his cronies is not part of your job description."

He cocked a dark brow. "As my employer, do the sacred rules and regulations state that you can tell me how to spend my paycheck?"

"You haven't received your first paycheck," she reminded him.

"Yeah so, what's your point, Ms. Roland?" he smarted off.

Like Pops suggested, it was best that Mattie see his bad side, his good side, and all sides in between. The fact was that his rioting hormones were making him testy. He'd spent a miserable week following company rules, as well as the Regulations According to Mattie, and *not* touching her, *not* kissing the breath out of her had put excessive strain on his willpower and his temperament. He *wanted*. He *ached*. He tossed and turned half the night.

Now, seeing that glorious mane of raven hair cascading over her shoulders, staring at her shapely feminine physique, which was silhouetted against the lantern light and campfire, took his awareness of her to another dangerous level. Her arousing image was probably going to be plastered on the billboard in his brain for the next week—or ten.

"My point, Mr. Gray," she growled, "is that these rogue retirees are not your responsibility. They are my family, every blasted one of them. They raised me."

"So I've heard, but I've adopted them. They entertain me. They distract me."

She elevated a perfectly sculpted brow. "Distract you from what, may I ask?"

Joe strode past her to bring up the rear of the procession of senior citizens who were hobbling uphill toward his truck. "Trust me, you don't want to know."

"Don't I?" she called after him.

"Take my word for it, boss lady," he bit off as he disappeared into the shadows.

Exasperated, Mattie smothered the small campfire,

then tramped up the path that led to her house. She had no idea why Joe needed a distraction. Was he pining for a lost love? Grieving for a loved one? Getting over a broken marriage? Just because he claimed to be sans wife or girlfriend did not mean that he hadn't had one or the other in the recent past and that he wasn't trying to cope with the emptiness in his life.

The more she pondered that possibility, the more she was convinced that Joe had run away from an upsetting situation, or was on the run from himself and tormenting memories. It would explain why he'd shown up in Fox Hollow with little more than a few changes of clothing and no personal possessions.

Now what was she supposed to do? she asked herself as she mounted the back steps. Should she apologize for digging up unpleasant memories when she interrogated him? Should she pretend the conversation hadn't happened, just like she tried to pretend they hadn't almost shared a kiss?

Mattie grabbed a glass of water, then plunked into her recliner. The drone of the television provided very little distraction from her thoughts. Damn, there was that word again. Why did Joe need a distraction? Was he battling private demons? Should she offer to listen to his woes?

The roar of an engine and headlights glancing off the windows brought Mattie upright. She set aside her glass and padded to the front door.

What now? Had the Five Musketeers been overtaken before they could sneak in the same window they sneaked out? Had they been evicted from the home?

It only took a moment to recognize Joe's rattletrap

truck and note that he was alone. "Did you get them tucked into bed?" she asked as he strode purposefully toward her porch.

"May I come in?" He didn't await a reply, just shouldered past her, moved her aside, then closed the door.

He loomed over her, looking more intense and somber than she'd ever seen him. Mattie involuntarily stepped back and attempted to shield herself, because she was still wearing the revealing T-shirt he'd commented on down at the creek.

"First off, I like your grandfather and his cronies. A lot," Joe declared. "I grew up with my grandfather, and I miss having him around, like in the old days. He's healthy enough to enjoy an active retirement and he travels, so I don't see him as much as I used to. So, if I enjoy a substitute grandfather, times five, that's my business.

"For your information, I got permission to take the gang out for the evening. They don't know that, of course, because I don't want to spoil their fun thinking they've pulled a fast one on the director and the nursing staff. In fact, I also have permission to take the gang on outings, as long as the joy rides don't interfere with taking their medication on time. I realize that this leaves you playing the heavy, but that's the role they've come to expect of their honorary, concerned granddaughter."

Mattie was greatly relieved to hear Joe had gone through the proper channels for these evening outings. She could kick herself for not thinking to ask permission when the breakouts started.

"I'm sorry I came down on you like a semi load of bricks," she murmured.

"Don't be, because I'm not finished yet," he assured her. He took a step closer, his gaze bearing down on her, making her squirm self-consciously. "I've decided you need to know what is causing the problem that requires a distraction."

"If you don't want to discuss it, I understand," she bleated, her voice reacting to his overpowering nearness. "Really, Joe, if it's personal and you aren't comfortable confiding in me, it's okay. If you're recently divorced, or have ended a serious relationship, I know it must be difficult to discuss. Considering that you arrived here with little more than a suitcase of clothes and a clunker truck, I put two and two together. But believe me, I—"

At that point, he barked a laugh, confusing her.

"Is that what you thought?" He raked his fingers through his tousled dark hair. "I guess I did invite that impression, didn't I? The truth is that I ran away from home, from a job that was bringing me down. I had to get away because I wasn't sure who I was anymore. Or maybe I didn't like what I'd become. Whatever the case, leaving that other life behind seemed the only solution. I just needed to be...away."

That much he could confide in her. As for the rest of it, he couldn't bring himself to tell her that he was the high king of woodcraft, who left his tufted throne to regain touch with a company that had ballooned out of proportion. He couldn't tell her that tonight anyway. Not when he'd come here to straighten out her misconception. The fact of the matter was that he was going berserk because he'd vowed not to touch her—thanks to some stupid rule he'd made in his office, during a momentary lapse in judgment. And it was a dumb rule that he was going to rescind, soon as he returned to corporate headquarters.

Didn't it stand to reason that people who hired on at Hobby Hut shared mutual interests? Who was he to discourage what might turn out to be a mutually satisfying relationship between business associates? If, however, a relationship interfered with production or caused problems that affected the store, then that was something else entirely. As far as Mattie's rule of thumb went, then it was up to her to make the choice. Joe had made his decision during the return drive from Paradise Valley.

Joe sighed audibly, then glanced down to see Mattie staring up at him, waiting for him to continue. Damn, she looked so tempting in that ragged T-shirt, her glorious hair tumbling over her shoulders, those expressive violet eyes dominating her pixielike face.

Desire landed a blow below his belt buckle. Nothing new there. Joe had been in a permanent state of arousal for damn near a week. Mattie, however, seemed oblivious that he worked extra hard at maintaining self-control while she was underfoot. It was high time she knew the effect she had on him. If he had to deal with it, maybe she should have to, too.

"*You* are the problem that requires distraction," he blurted out.

Her eyes popped. Her jaw sagged on its hinges. She stared at him as if artificial ivy dangled from his ears. "Me?" she peeped. "What did I do?"

"You live, you breathe," he muttered, annoyed at her because she was so unaware of how attracted he was to her.

She stared quizzically at him, as if trying to decide if he was teasing her again.

"Hell yes, I'm serious," he answered her unspoken question. "You want me to quit before or after I kiss you? But I definitely plan to kiss you, unless you are totally repelled by the thought. If so, speak up, Mattie."

She didn't speak up, didn't say a word, just smiled at him. Then she looped her arms around the taut muscles on his neck and tilted her face to his.

His hands molded against the trim indentation of her waist and he pulled her against him. His body reacted instantaneously to the feel of her supple curves meshed to his masculine contours. "On three," he whispered, hypnotized by the sparkle in her eyes. "One, two, three..."

Joe felt her lips part invitingly beneath his. That's all it took to set him aflame. Need burgeoned, overriding thought. He responded mindlessly, devouring her, savoring her, plundering her mouth until he swore he was about to go into cardiac arrest. His heartbeat went off the charts when he heard her moan, and then she pulled his head down to devour him as thoroughly as he had devoured her.

His hands glided lower, mapping the swell of her hips, her bottom, then ventured up to cup her breasts. He teased the beaded nipples beneath her cotton T-shirt and felt her arch helplessly toward him. When she ground her hips against the hard length of his arousal, he restrained himself from throwing back his head and howling in torment.

"Oh, Mattie," Joe croaked, pretty sure his voice sounded as if he'd been sucking helium.

He opened his eyes, then stared down at her kiss-swollen lips. All the while, the heat of unappeased passion swamped and buffeted him, egged him on.

He slanted his lips over hers and clutched her tightly to him, delivering and receiving a kiss that packed enough wallop to send his senses reeling.

Mattie felt her mind whirling like a pinwheel. Her body sizzled with sensations she couldn't begin to describe. She'd known she was attracted to Joe. That was a given. But my gracious! She hadn't expected to feel so completely out of control the moment his lips first touched down on hers, the moment his hands glided over her quivering body, setting fires that burned deep in her very core.

Even now, when he raised his head and came up for breath, she still felt as if her bones were melting into puddles and her skin was turning into steam. She'd never known anything like this, certainly not that one time in college when she allowed sexual curiosity to sweep her away momentarily. She'd realized her mistake immediately afterward. The encounter had left her feeling foolish and ashamed, and she had never allowed another relationship to go beyond casual dating.

This, she decided, was what desire and passion was supposed to feel like—this spontaneous, ungovernable, delicious and wildly disconcerting wave of sensations that left no part of her untouched. Mattie had always regarded herself as an in-control kind of person. But when Joe kissed her, caressed her, she felt helplessly *out* of control—and didn't mind that she was.

The fascinating discovery made her bolder, giddy. She draped her arms around his shoulders, marveling at the feel of his body's reaction to her, feeling empowered by the intimate knowledge that she aroused him.

"Pretty impressive kisses, Mr. Gray," she said playfully. "What do you say to the best two out of three? We'll suspend my rules and the king of wood-craft's regulations for a few minutes. You know, that whole space-out-of-time scenario you mentioned and see how this goes."

A rakish grin quirked his lips. He was intrigued by her playful sense of humor and aroused because she was asking for more. He trailed his thumb and palms from the underside of her breasts, over the flat plane of her belly to rest possessively on her hips. He felt her shivering reaction, and a ripple of satisfaction streamed through him.

"You nearly gave me a coronary with those first two kisses, Mattie. I'm not sure I can survive another one. If I do survive, I can't guarantee that I'll be able to stop with a kiss and caress. You turn me on, Mattie, in case you don't know it, and I can't imagine how you could miss the way my body reacts to you. Are you willing to risk what comes next? We're talking serious, intimate stuff here, Mattie. Are you ready for that?"

Her smile wavered when sanity crowded past the tantalizing sensations. She admired and respected Joe for giving her a choice, not overwhelming her. And she had no doubt that he could, because he was a devastatingly sensual man who obviously had oodles of experience with intimate relationships. In comparison, she was practically a novice. She was talking years since she'd allowed herself to get caught up in the heat of the moment. But it hadn't been so long that she hadn't forgotten that it had turned out badly.

Her arms slowly retreated from his shoulders. Her fingertips lingered to encircle the buttons on his chambray shirt. "You're probably right...no, you're exactly right, Joe," she amended. "We've only known each other ten days. And though we've spent an enormous amount of time together, it is a little too soon. I don't do affairs, rarely even have time to date because of my job and obligations to Pops."

Which was exactly why Joe had called a halt— though his body was screeching at him to go with the flow. He knew Mattie well enough to know she wasn't into one-nighters. She didn't feed her sexual desires the way she regularly fed her appetite.

She was not a woman who gave sexual favors heedlessly, or without forethought. In short, she was absolutely, positively nothing like the women in his previous social circle. Joe had too much respect and affection for Mattie to screw up their business and personal relations, just to scratch this itch—maddening though it most certainly was.

Gently he reached over to limn the velvety texture of her lips, the curve of her jaw, the rise of her cheeks. "You're one of a kind, Mattie," he murmured huskily.

She forced a smile. "Yeah, I know, that's a polite way of saying I'm the tomboy next door who gets a bigger kick from power tools than power shopping."

He didn't like to hear her put herself down that way, especially when he admired her unique qualities and talents. Joe shook his head in contradiction. "You're way wrong, sweetheart. You possess amazing gifts and creative skills. Power tools may be the tools of your trade, but it's what you create, the love and intensity you put into your art and crafts that make you special. You *fix* things and make them right, whether it's repairing broken knickknacks or solving problems in your grandfather's and his friends' lives. You are caring and generous of heart, and your neighbors and customers come to you for ideas, help and advice. And furthermore, glamour is superficial and short-lived. It rubs off with soap and water and it hangs in a closet. You have inner beauty that runs soul deep.''

Mattie stared at him, amazed that he perceived her as something special when she considered herself unremarkable and had never put forth the effort to make much of her physical assets. But what really hit her where she lived was that Joe didn't care that she didn't gussy herself up in attempt to gain attention and impress others. He seemed to appreciate her for who and what she was. She wanted to hug him for that, but, considering their explosive physical reaction to each other, she predicted they'd wind up naked on the living room floor—and things would get totally out of hand, or *in* hand, in this case.

''There's something else you should know, Mattie,'' he whispered as he wrapped his arms around her and drew her full length against him, nuzzling his chin against the top of her head. ''I like who I am when I'm with you. I had to get away from the life I was living because I wasn't sure if I was liked *for myself* anymore. You helped me find the person who got lost somewhere along the way. I enjoy being a part of your life. If the intimacy is too much for you to handle, then I'll suffer the raging hormones. I'll leave it totally up to you to let me know if, and when, you're ready to take the intimate step.''

Willfully, Joe set her away from him, though he preferred to hold her, to absorb her into him. He glanced over her head to notice several large paintings, surrounded and accentuated by curio shelves, a plant stand, deacon's bench, and Shaker-style reading table. Studying the interior decor of her home was the distraction he needed to keep himself from doing something crazy—like tossing good sense to the four winds and succumbing to the unruly urges of his body.

"Damn, woman, do you know how talented and gifted you are?" he said as he strode up to the painting that had reached across the room to draw him closer. "You put so much life, detail and color into your artwork that it grabs hold and won't let go."

Joe forced himself to move to the next landscape painting that depicted the old wooden bridge south of town that he'd noticed while cruising with the Roland Gang. Mattie's artwork transported him to the scenic location, filled him with a sense of peace. It dawned on him while he appraised the third painting that Mattie's artwork depicted all those safe, serene havens where a person might go to achieve a sense of inner tranquillity. When she added memorabilia and collectibles to the surrounding shelves and tables, the entire wall became a peaceful sanctuary of sorts.

Lord, what a creative, artistic knack she had. She always managed to come up with just the right combinations of arts and crafts. Oh, how he'd love to have her in the creative design department of Hobby Hut Enterprises. She was a font of unique ideas.

"Joe, would you like a cup of hot chocolate? I get the feeling you'll be wanting the whole tour of my arts and crafts, considering how fascinated you seem to be with the living room walls." Mattie was enormously pleased and proud that Joe appreciated and admired her art—and said so.

"Cocoa would be great, thanks," he said without glancing at her, so intent was he on the seaside painting that hung above boat-shaped shelves filled with hand-painted knickknacks. "When did you find time to do these detailed paintings?"

"It's been several months since I've worked on time-consuming paintings like these. The store monopolizes my time, and customized jobs for clients fill up my evenings. Running back and forth to check on Pops takes up the remainder of my spare time. I keep thinking the custom projects will slow down, but word of mouth appears to be promoting my work, and clients keep showing up with requests."

While Mattie ambled into the kitchen to mix and heat the hot chocolate, Joe went from one wall to the next, mesmerized, fascinated. Mattie's home was a veritable showcase of art and crafts that gave the place a personality all its own. Subtle, understated themes were carried out in each display. But it was the painting hanging above her bed, bookended by curio shelves, that sucker-punched him.

Children, laughter etched in careful detail on their faces, played in the shade of a sprawling oak tree. In the background was the depiction of an old clapboard homestead, barn and outbuildings. A young couple was cozied up on the porch swing, watching contentedly while their children played on the lawn.

Joe stood there, motionless, feeling himself drawn into the circle of the loving, close-knit family he'd never had—and probably never would if he remained on this same course in his corporate world. He felt as if he was falling into the artist's unspoken dream of a simple life, surrounded by a caring family.

Suddenly Joe wanted to be there, sitting on the

swing, watching his children, cuddling up with his wife. He wanted it all—the good life—not the executive suite, surrounded by yes-men and -woman who kept telling him what they thought he wanted to hear. He wanted honesty, true friendships, the opportunity to create with his hands as Mattie did. Love. He wanted that most of all. To love and be loved. To matter, to be wanted and needed. To make a difference...

Feelings, deep and intense and sentimental, bombarded him with the force of tornadic winds. He staggered, realizing how empty and materialistic his life had become. Mattie's life was full, and complex, because of her dedication to customers, friends and to Pops. Yet, he realized that on some level this painting depicted what Mattie needed to complete her life. She filled her time with substitutes for love, but this painting was her elusive dream.

"Joe, the hot chocolate is ready."

He pivoted to see her smiling at him, and he just couldn't bear to be alone with her until he pulled himself together, got these spinning emotions under control. If he didn't leave now, the feelings squeezing at his heart, and this abrupt sense of desperation, were going to overpower him. He might do something stupid—like appease the sense of vulnerability that had overcome him by seducing Mattie, right here, right this minute. He just couldn't do that to her, not after he promised he would give her time to make her choice.

"I gotta go," he said as he whizzed past her, refusing to glance at her.

"Joe? What's wrong?" she called as he made fast

tracks toward the front door. "Are you feeling okay?"

"No, definitely not." He was feeling too much, too fast, too intensely…and it scared the hell out of him. He had to sit himself down and think. He would go to his apartment, park himself in front of that gigantic mural of towering pines and sky-scraping mountains, and stare at them until he pulled himself together.

"Joe?"

Mattie's shoulders slumped when the door closed on his heels. Damn, he'd been in a strange mood. Curious, Mattie retraced her steps to the bedroom and stood where he'd stood, peering at the painting of an old homestead and family. Is that what had shaken him up?

"Why on earth…?" Mattie's voice evaporated when she remembered what had compelled her to paint this picture. This was the family she decided she was never going to have, after she gave up on meeting the man of her dreams, a man who shared her need and desire for a loving family, shared her appreciation for art and crafts.

Had this painting reminded Joe of what he didn't have?

Mattie couldn't answer that question, because Joe had only confided bits and pieces of his past to her. Oh yes, he told her that his parents had taken off, much as hers had. Told her that his grandparents had raised him. But she didn't know where he'd worked during the years in between. Didn't know who had come and gone and influenced his life. Obviously something was bothering him, something he hadn't confided in her.

"Give it up, Mattie. Dr. Freud you're not," she

told herself as she ambled to the living room to sip the two cups of hot chocolate. "This is your life, and you liked it well enough until Joe showed up. Just be thankful for what you have and don't dwell on what you don't have."

Having given herself that sound advice, Mattie flicked on the TV news broadcast and lounged in her chair.

There was no sense wasting time trying to figure out Joe, when she couldn't even diagnose what caused this restless, edgy feeling that was thrumming through her. Must be the caffeine in two cups of cocoa, she tried to convince herself. But deep down, Mattie had the unshakable feeling that the affliction ailing her went by the name of Joe Gray. She was becoming emotionally involved with him, whether that was a good idea or not. She sensed that he was only going to be a temporary resident in Fox Hollow, considering what he'd told her tonight. If she let herself fall in love with the man she would get her naive heart broken.

Take a few risks, Shortcake. You'll always regret the opportunities missed.

Mattie vaulted to her feet, shut off the TV, the lights, then went to bed. The last thing she needed right now was Pops's devil-may-care philosophies spinning in her head. What she *needed* most of all was a good night's sleep.

5

SITTING IN THE DILAPIDATED recliner, Joe stared at the large mural of pines, a crystal-clear lake and towering mountains. A sense of peace stole over him—as long as he concentrated on the lifelike scenery. He still wasn't sure why the painting hanging over Mattie's bed had shaken him so badly. He hadn't spent much time dwelling on what lay in his future, or regretting his past, just worked to build the company until it exploded into a multimillion-dollar business. But that painting represented a circle of family he'd never had as a kid and probably wouldn't have as an adult. He'd programmed himself to be satisfied with the life he led—until he just couldn't take it anymore.

"God, listen to you," Joe muttered at himself. "There are people all over the planet who would like to be in your shoes."

On impulse, Joe bounded up to retrieve his cell phone, then punched in his grandfather's number. The phone rang three times before J. D. Grayson picked up.

"Hello?"

"Gramps, it's me."

"D.J., where the hell are you? I've tried to reach your cell phone, but all I get is voice mail," J.D. said. "Your junior executives have been calling and leaving messages all week, wondering where to reach you so you can tell them what to do.''

"That's why I skipped town," Joe replied. "It was time to force the whole lot of them to earn their salaries and stop depending on me to make every decision.''

J.D. obviously noted the undertone of bitterness and frustration in Joe's voice, because he chuckled. "Told you that you'd spoon-fed them too long. They definitely need weaning, but it's not like you to just take off to parts unknown without leaving a forwarding address. So where the devil are you, D.J.?''

"First you have to promise you won't disclose my whereabouts," Joe requested.

"Me? Shoot, no. I won't tell those candy-ass executives where you are if you don't want me to.''

"I'm in Fox Hollow, working incognito as hired assistant at the local Hobby Hut.''

"What the blazes are you doing that for?" Gramps crowed.

How to explain without sounding like the irresponsible, self-serving father who had bailed out to follow his own rainbows. It was a touchy subject with Gramps. "Because I needed to get back in touch with the reason you and I started designing and constructing crafts and knickknacks in our garage workshop," he said finally.

Dead silence.

"Gramps?" Joe prompted.

"Tell me you're not turning into your father or your social butterfly of a mother," J.D. said, then scowled.

Joe was afraid Gramps would get the wrong impression. Sure enough. "No, I'm not my father,

Gramps. I just needed to take the off-ramp from the fast lane of life and wander the backroads to recapture the enthusiasm the business held for me when it was just the two of us pitching our woodcraft creations to other companies.''

"So you lost sight of our original purpose," J. D. paraphrased.

"Yes, and I'm giving myself another three weeks of R and R. Mattie has so many projects going that she needs my help."

"Who's Mattie to you?"

Joe noted how J.D. phrased the question. Leave it to Gramps to hit the proverbial nail on its head. "She manages the local Hobby Hut, and she loves arts and crafts as much as we used to," he said, tap-dancing around the direct question. "She's also a very gifted and talented artist. As we speak, I'm sitting in front of her eight-by-eight mural of the Rocky Mountains, and I feel as if I've been transported to one of the rugged peaks."

J.D. chuckled. "That's not what I asked you, boy. Is she one of those glamour-pusses I've seen on your arm in the city?"

"Just the opposite."

"Wealthy?"

Joe smiled for the first time in an hour. "Immensely. She is rich with dozens of true and honest friends, and she cares nothing about national recognition for herself and her paintings. All she wants is to bring artistic beauty to her friends and acquaintances in her corner of the world."

"Hmm," J.D. said. "And does she know who you are?"

Joe squirmed uneasily. "No, she knows me as Joe

Gray, her hired help who showed up at the store immediately after she received a fax from the corporate office, telling her to hire an assistant.''

J.D. snickered in amusement. "Clever move, Deeje. I think I understand why you did it, though.''

"It seemed the perfect solution at the time," he mumbled.

"And now?" J.D. prodded.

"I'm afraid it's going to get complicated.''

"Ah..."

Joe was pretty sure Gramps was reading his grandson loud and clear. "Yeah, ah..." he murmured.

"Well, well, isn't that something. 'Bout damn time, if you ask me. I never was too keen on those porcelain dolls who followed you around social gatherings. So this Mattie person is *real people?*"

Joe explained Mattie's dedication to managing the store, her after-hour projects for clients, her situation with Pops and the Roland Gang. By the time he finished relating Pops's escapades, J.D. had had several good laughs.

"Fox Hollow sounds like my kind of place," J.D. said. "I'd like to meet Mattie and her grandfather."

"Thought you would, but that might complicate the situation more than it already is."

There was a long pause, then J.D. said, "Are you happy, Deeje? Are you enjoying yourself down there in Fox Hollow?"

"Yeah, Gramps, I'm happier than I've been since you announced your retirement and left me to handle our brownnosing executives."

"Then you have yourself one whale of a time in Fox Hollow," J.D. ordered. "I'll field the calls up here and tell those knothead executives to take charge during your absence because you won't be back until the end of the month.''

"Thanks, Gramps. Any plans for another trip or cruise?"

"Naw, the last tour to the East Coast wore me out. I'm not going anywhere that requires more than an hour's drive from the house. Be happy, Deeje.''

When Joe disconnected he felt more settled. The old man was the only contact Joe needed from his other life. The fact that Gramps didn't condemn Joe's decision, wanted to see him happy, was a load off his mind.

Joe sprawled out in bed. Although he wished he could be in someone else's bed, he vowed not to push Mattie. He might be ready and willing, but he had placed the decision of where they were headed in her hands.

Damn, he thought when his body reacted to the enticing vision that materialized above him. Being honorable where Mattie was concerned was taking its toll on him.

MATTIE GLANCED OUT the kitchen window to see Joe working industriously outside her workshop Sunday morning. Rather than operating the nail gun and saws and disturbing Mattie's sleep, Joe had painted several curio shelves, coat racks and storage chests. His consideration made her smile, gave her a warm, fuzzy feeling.

After grabbing orange juice and toast, Mattie donned her work clothes and walked down to her workshop to assist him. "Morning," she murmured as she studied his arresting profile.

"Hey, Mattie. Thought I'd get an early start so we

could take our collection of crafts to the convalescent home in the middle of the week—''

Without preamble Mattie walked up to him, looped her arms around his neck and kissed him full on the mouth. When she stepped back, Joe stared incredulously at her.

"What did I do to deserve that?" he asked.

"For helping me with these projects, for being you, and just because I felt like kissing you."

He grabbed her to him and planted a steamier version of her kiss to her lips. Need blazed through her, reminding her of her reactions the previous night. No doubt about it, the man sent her up in flames. Despite whatever unsettling thoughts had sent him dashing from her house last night, he seemed to be his old self again. Mattie was relieved to know that. She'd grown accustomed to having Joe around, wanted to be with him. Which was why she kissed him. She was trying to alert him to the fact that she had thought it over and she knew that she wanted more than a working relationship even if the high king of woodcraft frowned on fraternizing with the help. Mattie had spent the night tossing, turning, listening to the echo of Pops's advice about living life to its fullest, taking chances.

Joe raised his head, his amber eyes glowing with the passion they ignited in each other. "That's an interesting way to start the day, boss lady. Are you trying to tell me something?"

Mattie nodded. Her off-center ponytail glistened like a raven's wing in the sunlight. "I'm thumbing my nose at Double H of Double H," she announced.

He grinned wryly. "So kissing is allowed?"

"As long as it doesn't interfere with work or with this project Pops talked me into," she stipulated.

"Fair enough, Mattie." Joe shifted awkwardly, then looked away. "About last night and the abrupt way I took off—"

She held up her hand to forestall him. "It's okay, really. No need to explain, because we're starting all over today. Deal?"

Joe reached out to trail the pad of his thumb over her velvety lips. "Deal." His head dipped to graze her mouth with his. "I agree with you about the head honcho's stupid rules. Who is he to stick his nose into other peoples' relationships?"

Mattie backed up a pace, before she lost all interest in crafting tables, benches and barn-wood frames for the paintings she was donating to Paradise Valley. "We better get to work," she tweeted, her voice indicating the devastating effect he had on her.

"You're right." He gestured toward the workshop. "I suggest you go measure and cut the lumber for the shelves before I forget why we're here. You seem to have difficulty realizing what a distraction you are to me, lady."

"Last night you said I was the problem that required a distraction," she reminded him saucily.

Gosh, it felt good to be at ease around a man for the first time in ages. Joe was good for her feminine ego.

"You're the cause and the cure, Mattie." He swatted her playfully on the fanny. "Now get to work, woman."

She arched a quizzical brow. "You certainly are a take-charge kind of guy, aren't you?"

"Can be," he hedged, then quickly changed the

subject. "I'll treat you to lunch at the café if you'll let me finish a few of these projects without more distractions."

Smiling, Mattie sauntered off to grab the tape measure and man the saws. Taking the next step with Joe seemed so easy, so natural. She'd decided to let it happen and it had. There was a man in her life now, a man who shared her likes and dislikes, who didn't resent her devotion to Pops, a man who made her feel feminine, made her feel desired.

The heady feeling remained with her while she worked. The projects fell easily into place, and Mattie worked by Joe's side all morning with the perfect precision of two efficient carpenters. He handed her tools she needed before she asked for them, and vice versa. By lunchtime they had constructed yet another four sets of curio shelves and cut lumber for a deacon's bench, small console table, rustic hat rack, and plant stand.

Satisfied with their progress, Mattie piled into Joe's truck, eager to feed her growling stomach. Her light, carefree mood lasted until they ambled down the sidewalk toward the café. Four cowboys, who looked as if they were sporting hangovers, compliments of Watering Hole Tavern, blocked their path.

"Well, lookie here, boys, it's the tomboy and the sissy," Buck Reynolds said, then smirked disrespectfully.

"Hey, girlie-man, still arranging flowers at the Hobby Hut?" Harlan Barker taunted.

Mattie had little use for her former high school classmates, who had razzed her for showing them up in woodwork classes. It incensed her that men who had done nothing positive with their lives felt the need to stroke their egos by badgering Joe, who had done absolutely nothing to them.

"Back off, bozos," Mattie commanded. "I realize you're out of sorts because Watering Hole Tavern doesn't open on Sundays, but you need time off to recover from your hangovers."

"Damn, Mattie, you're as sassy as you were in high school," Leo Sampson said, then gave Joe a condescending glance. "*This* is the best you can do? A *sissy?*"

That did it! Mattie refused to allow these mental midgets to insult Joe. "I'll have you know that Joe is more man that the four of you put together. And for your information, we are having a steamy, satisfying affair. If any one of you had Joe's impressive skills in that department, you wouldn't have to hang out at Watering Hole Tavern every night, fabricating tales about your nonexistent love lives!"

Joe nearly choked when Mattie rushed to his defense and announced they were intimately involved— when they weren't…yet. The fact that she risked her own reputation to save his left an odd lump in his throat. No one had ever stood up for him like that before. Not that he needed anyone to run interference, because he'd been fighting his own battles for years. That she cared enough to spare him ridicule and boasted his sexual prowess amazed him.

For a moment, Joe was too flabbergasted to string words together. The four bozos, however, didn't have that problem because they didn't engage their brains before opening their mouths.

"You're getting your kicks from a twinkie?" Harlan smirked.

"Joe is not a twinkie," Mattie snapped. "Now get out of the way. Go loiter on another street corner."

When Buck reached out to grab Mattie's arm, Joe reacted instinctively. He put a hatchet-chop to Buck's wrist, which prompted the other three hooligans to pounce. Two rapid elbow punches to Harlan's midsection sent the man to his knees, gasping for air. A forearm to the nose sent Leo staggering backward. Joe's uplifted knee caused bozo number four to double over and howl in pain.

It was Sunday, for heaven's sake, and here he was, involved in a street fight with a bunch of local yokels whose opinion of him didn't matter in the least. Yet, he felt inclined to prove to these clowns, and to Mattie, that he was as tough and macho as the next guy. He did admit, though, that it inflated his pride when Mattie stared at him as if he were some action hero who had taken out an entire squadron of military terrorists, using martial art techniques.

"Wow," she said. "That was something."

"High school football," he said by way of explanation. "I butted heads with the best of them." He took her arm to usher her to the café, pausing beside the cowboys, who struggled to get their wobbly legs beneath them. "If you'll excuse us, boys, I promised to buy Mattie's lunch. Nice to meet you, by the way. Maybe we can share a beer at the Watering Hole and get better acquainted."

"Why'd you say that when you know perfectly well that they aren't your type?" Mattie questioned as they entered the café.

"Why'd you tell those imbeciles we're doing the horizontal macarena?" he questioned her question.

He stopped dead in his tracks when she said, "Wishful thinking, maybe?"

Joe stood there, immobilized, when she ambled toward the empty booth in the corner, greeting friends and acquaintances as she went. He noticed he drew stares and speculative glances when he joined her in the booth. Mattie had linked her name to his by accepting the lunch invitation on Sunday, suggesting they shared more than a business relationship.

Joe wasn't sure how he felt about Mattie placing herself in a compromising position, hadn't thought about it until the relationship between them altered. Oh yes, his body was in favor of taking their friendship to the next level. But then, his hormones didn't really care how an affair would affect her life in this small town where she lived, where she'd grown up—and never planned to leave.

What did he have to offer a woman like Mattie? A few weeks of sexual fun and games and labor for her community projects?

That same question had hounded him the previous night while he stared at the painting over her bed. He found himself wondering if he could be the man in that painting—if he wanted to be, if Mattie might want him to be. And all the while he knew that, because he had misrepresented himself, there wasn't a chance in hell that he would ever find out for sure.

Nagging guilt descended on Joe. He should tell Mattie who he was, explain why he'd come here, before he became more involved with her than he already was. "Mattie, there's something we need to get straight."

She reached across the table to link her fingers in his. Her smile, the expression in her violet eyes, rendered him speechless. "Don't, Joe," she murmured. "I made up my mind this morning to dispense with the rules where you're concerned. Let's just take things as they come, okay?"

He regarded her for a pensive moment. Maybe she had the right idea. Maybe they should discover the possibilities of this relationship before he botched it up with his confession. She might be ready to see him go a few weeks from now, and he might be ready to leave.

Joe also pondered what Gramps had said during their conversation. Enjoy yourself. Be happy. Joe was, and he didn't want to lose these contented feelings so soon.

And so, Joe listened to his grandfather's advice. He simply sat back in the booth, enjoyed Mattie's company, lost himself in that mystifying sparkle in her eyes and let whatever would be, would be. For the next few weeks he was going to be the regular Joe she thought he was, and he wasn't going to stare too far into the future.

Couldn't. Because, at present, Joe couldn't see past that enchanting, pixielike face across the table from him.

MATTIE STARED AT HER REFLECTION in the mirror, then added eyeliner and mascara that emphasized the shape of her eyes and length of her lashes. She had gone to extra effort applying makeup and donning the most feminine dress she owned. It was nothing spectacular, because she never dressed to attract male attention and usually downplayed her femininity. But tonight she had a statement to make to Joe Gray. And since she didn't own any of those lacy, provocative undergarments, she went *without.*

The thought put a wickedly playful smile on her lips as she stared at her reflection. Imagine her planning to seduce her hired assistant who lived in her efficiency apartment. Talk about breaking all the rules!

"First time for everything," Mattie told herself as she sprayed on perfume. "Tonight or never. You go, girl."

Mattie was reasonably confident she wouldn't be rejected when she showed up at Joe's front door. The past few days Joe had sent her several smoldering glances at work and expressed mutual desire when he kissed her good-night, after they logged in extra hours at her home workshop, putting the finishing touches on the arts and crafts for the nursing home.

He had told her that when, and if, she wanted more than a kiss from him, it was up to her to let him know. She was pretty sure that going commando beneath this formfitting cotton knit dress was statement enough.

Mattie exited her house to make the short jaunt to Joe's apartment. Her nerve wavered momentarily, but she knocked on the door, then inhaled a steadying breath. The tomboy of Fox Hollow had an interest in a man, and she was going to let him know it.

When the door opened Mattie watched Joe's eyes bug out, watched his gaze roam over the lavender dress. The look of appreciation gave her the confidence needed to sashay into his apartment.

"Good gad, woman," Joe croaked. "Are you trying to give me another seizure? Worse than I suffered down by the creek?" He raked her up and down once again. "You don't have anything under that dress, do you?"

"I've got *me*," she assured him, smiling elfishly.

He stepped back, as if he didn't want to be within five feet of her. That was not the reaction she'd hoped for when she mentally planned this tryst. Feeling awkward, Mattie's gaze dropped to her open-toed sandals.

"What are you doing here, Mattie?" he asked, his voice thick and husky.

She didn't look at him, couldn't. "I decided to have the flaming affair I announced I was having. I don't like being a liar."

Neither did Joe. He knew Mattie valued honesty, but telling her the truth about himself now seemed very inappropriate. Plus, when he looked at her, every sensible thought launched into orbit around a galaxy far, far away. Desire was hammering at him repeatedly. Mattie had yet to touch him, nor he her, and he was already aching in places he'd like to forget he had.

The television droned, but Joe couldn't hear much else besides his drumming pulse. His hormones were cheering like a pep squad. He wanted this night to be spectacular, especially since Mattie had gone to the effort of dressing seductively for his benefit. Of course, it didn't matter because he found her appealing and sexy, no matter what she wore. But he did appreciate and take note of the effort.

"Joe?"

His gaze lifted to her face, after a slow, all-consuming sweep of her curvaceous assets that were displayed by the clingy lavender dress. "Yeah?" Was that his voice? He sounded like a cockatoo.

"I've never tried to seduce a man before," she said nervously. "I could use a little help here, if you're so inclined, that is."

So inclined? He wanted to be *reclined* with Mattie, and he was afraid the hungry needs prowling through him would frighten her off if he took a step closer.

"You look absolutely gorgeous," he complimented, forcing his hands into fists at his sides, battling the urge to grab her, toss her over his shoulder and carry her to the sofa to ravish her.

She sighed audibly. "This isn't going as I'd planned," she murmured, eyes downcast.

"What had you hoped for?" Far be it from him to destroy whatever fantasy had brought her to his door. "Tell me, Mattie. I really need to know."

She peeked up at him from beneath long, thick lashes. That look nearly drove him to his knees and left him howling at the moon.

"I was kind of hoping you'd be so overcome with desire that you'd just kiss me and the rest of the evening would take care of itself."

A slow, wickedly seductive grin spread across his lips as he reached down to unbutton his shirt, then carelessly tossed it aside. "Sweetheart, that sounds like a good plan to me."

When he reached for her, she came into his arms without the slightest hesitation. Joe forgot about feeling guilty, forgot about everything except this ravenous need that had been gnawing at him for days on end. The moment he kissed her, and she kissed him back, his brain shut down and sensation after sensation exploded to life.

His hands glided over the supple terrain of her body, memorizing each luscious curve and swell. Her soft moans, the instinctive way her body arched toward him, drove him wild. The feel of her fingertips skimming his chest to trail along the band of his jeans caused his body to clench with barely restrained need.

Damn, he knew Mattie worked on him like a fast-acting poison. But he thought he had enough self-control to proceed at an unhurried pace. They had all night, if that's what they wanted. Yet, he kept forgetting that. He wanted her hot and naked in his arms, beneath him, surrounding him, welcoming him.

With a lack of patience and finesse that appalled him, he tugged the dress over her head and sent it the same way as his discarded shirt. She was everything his imagination anticipated—and more. The tomboy of Fox Hollow was one-hundred-percent woman, and the sight of her silky skin, bared to his devouring gaze and his bold caresses, left him panting, as if he'd run a hundred-yard dash.

"Absolutely gorgeous," he wheezed.

"You already said that," she whispered unsteadily, her face pink.

"I can't emphasize that fact enough."

Joe picked her up and carried her to the lumpy sofa. He kicked off his boots, peeled off his jeans, then stretched out beside her. He told himself to slow down—for all the good that did! He feasted on her like a starving man, suckling her breasts, drawing the sweetest sounds from her. He curled his hand around her inner thigh, caressed her, then delved his fingertip into the soft nest between her legs. He felt the liquid fire of her desire burning him alive, and he groaned when she melted in his hand. He stroked her, again and again, until she cried out his name and arched helplessly toward him. He felt her quivering in sudden release, and he wanted to be buried deeply within her—now, this very instant.

He moved above her, teasing the nub of her passion, then drove himself into her the instant before she came undone in his arms. Her undoing was his, as well. Joe couldn't remember feeling so out of control, so overwhelmed. His body pumped into hers, harder, faster, deeper...

And then he was spiraling through space in a mindless blur, clinging to Mattie as he cartwheeled through a universe teeming with incredible sensations that splintered into a zillion pieces, then regenerated, intensified and bombarded him again.

Gasping for breath that was slow in inflating his collapsed lungs, Joe sagged heavily upon Mattie. The moment he regained his senses, he cursed himself but good. Damn it to hell! This was not the way he envisioned making love to Mattie. He had behaved like a randy teenager in the back seat of the family car!

Hesitantly he lifted his head and watched her watch him. "Sorry about that. I guess I blew your perfect fantasy right out of the water."

To his vast relief, she smiled. "I'll admit I had visions of slow and languid, with me doing my share of the touching. But I got a little carried away myself."

Indeed she had. She'd been with Joe every step of the way, responded to his kisses, his caresses, the feel of his muscular body gliding perfectly over hers. Every moment had been so wildly exciting, so breathlessly sensual that Mattie could do nothing but respond to the unprecedented sensations.

It didn't take a genius to figure out why, either, Mattie acknowledged. Everything Joe did aroused her because she was already in love with him. Yes, that was utterly foolish, because they had known each other less than two weeks. Yet, she had become emotionally involved with him before they became physically involved.

She liked the fact they were both out of control when they made love, that they were hungry for each other and nothing seemed to matter except communicating and appeasing their ungovernable needs.

Her thoughts trailed off when Joe cupped her breast in his hand and flicked her nipple with his tongue. He eased down beside her, his hands moving at a slow, less hurried pace. Mattie felt herself sinking into another world of erotic sensations when Joe aroused her degree by tantalizing degree, kissed her with unexpected tenderness.

"Slow and languid this time," he promised as his lips skimmed her belly, then ascended to devote more attention to the budded peaks of her breasts. "Just the way you want it."

"Mmm, a man of many talents," she murmured raggedly. "But the next one's on me."

He raised his tousled head and smiled at the implication that she was determined to get her hands on him before the night was over. "I'll be all yours, sweetheart. Any way you want me, but right now, you're all mine."

When she placed herself in his skillful hands he taught her the meaning of that exquisite little death. She swore she was about to die of pleasure several times before he came to her, filling her, appeasing the ache he summoned from her, time and again.

Never in her wildest imagination had Mattie expected lovemaking to be like this. Joe made her feel cherished, as if her pleasure was even more important than his own. He taught her things about her feminine body that she'd never known. And later, he taught her how to make a man beg—and love every minute of it.

Sometime after midnight, her body spent, her mind blank, Mattie drifted off to sleep, oblivious to the fact that she and Joe were snuggled up on the lumpy sofa and barely had room to move.

6

JOE AWOKE TO THE SOUND of birds chirping and squawking in the overhanging trees outside his apartment. His left arm was asleep. His legs were tangled up with Mattie's. They'd slept without pillows or quilts. Wearing nothing but each other.

He glanced at the clock above the TV and speculated on whether he had time to love Mattie awake before reporting for work. Then he decided he'd already overdone it the previous night. He'd known immediately that she was barely above novice status, had suspected as much after all those "tomboy" references he'd heard. He rather liked the fact that he was the one who had taught Mattie about a dozen ways to make love—on the narrow confines of the sofa.

Joe grinned, wondering how many inventive ideas he could come up with for the kitchen counter, the table and the shower.

Tamping down his vivid imagination, Joe eased away. He barely had time to shower, dress and grab a bite to eat before opening the store. He glanced down at Mattie's shapely form huddled against the sofa cushions. Her raven hair cascaded over one shoulder, and she looked so alluring that he had to battle against rejoining her on the couch.

He wished he had her artistic ability so he could

paint the tantalizing pose that exposed the line of her back, the gentle curve of her hips. Now here was a painting he'd like to have hanging in his bedroom!

Quietly Joe ambled off to shower. When he returned, Mattie was still sleeping. He decided to let her catch up on her rest. No telling how long she'd been putting in double days.

Joe slipped outside a few minutes later, then strode toward his truck. It dawned on him a mile later that he hadn't given a moment's thought to protection. Hadn't even checked his wallet to see if he had brought a few foil packets with him from the city. Fact was, he hadn't planned on needing protection during this hiatus. Boy, had he been wrong about that!

And what if—after last night—buying the needed items was a waste of time and money?

Another wave of guilt crested on Joe. Not only had he *not* been honest with Mattie, but now he had behaved irresponsibly. Hell, and here he thought it was impossible to complicate the situation worse than he already had. Boy, he had been wrong about that, too! He was taking the risk of bringing a child into the world the same way he'd arrived—unexpectedly.

No way did he believe Mattie would purposely entrap him. That wasn't her style. No, whatever happened, she would accept responsibility, just as she accepted the responsibility of her grandfather and his friends.

Joe drove to work, stopped for junk food to tide him over until lunch, then unlocked the shop. He waited on four young female customers who batted their eyelashes at him and hinted at their availability.

Not one of the women who sidled up next to him in their tight-fitting shorts and scoop-neck knit tops appealed to him. He was pretty sure he was losing his heart to a raven-haired pixie with violet eyes and a heart-stopping smile.

That was the good news—and the bad news. It was going to make it impossible for Joe to walk away— and impossible for him to stay, because Mattie didn't have a clue who he really was.

The moment Mattie walked in the back door and made eye contact with him, he saw a blush stain her cheeks. He wanted to chuckle, but he kept a straight face so he wouldn't embarrass her more than she already was.

"Good morning, boss," he greeted cheerfully.

Mattie noted the four women who were hovering around Joe like humming bees after nectar. She caught his intimate-looking glance, and she turned a deeper shade of pink. Knowing they shared private knowledge of each other, that he'd seen her lying naked on his couch and had left her sleeping while he opened the store was unsettling. Not to mention the things they'd done to each other half the night!

When her face turned Congo Red, his brow quirked and he made an attempt to hide a grin. Spinning around, Mattie retreated to the workroom in the back of the store.

"Morning, Joe," she said over her shoulder. "If you have things under control out front, I'll work on a few projects in the back."

This was definitely going to be awkward, Mattie decided as she rat-tat-tatted with her hammer, securing boards for a customized project. She couldn't look at Joe without remembering the passion they'd shared, knowing he was the only man on the planet who'd seen her totally naked and slept in her arms.

She'd just have to get used to the idea, she told herself sensibly. Because, more important than this work-related relationship, Mattie wanted this personal involvement that had escalated to incredible proportions. She'd simply have to get better at hiding her emotions and control the arousing effect Joe had on her in these business surroundings, was all. She could do it if she really tried.

She glanced up to see Joe leaning casually against the doorjamb, smiling roguishly at her. "Yep, you do look good in red," he murmured. "Are you going to blush every morning?"

Mattie felt the color spread up her neck to heat her cheeks. "You should have awakened me this morning," she muttered as she measured and marked a pine board.

"Disturb the living portrait on my couch? Not a chance," he said, then snickered when she turned Penny Candy Red.

"I don't know if I can do this," she grumbled, busying herself with her woodcraft project. "I don't have experience at it. Maybe Double H was right about that fraternizing business. It's awkward."

His smile vanished. "About Double H of Double H—"

"Don't bring him up," she cut in without glancing in his direction. "I'm having enough trouble adjusting to *us,* without bringing *him* into this. And don't forget we promised to load up our arts and crafts and haul them to the convalescent home this evening. According to Pops, we're expected."

"I haven't forgotten." Joe turned away to man the store. There were a lot of things he hadn't forgotten—and wished he could. Like, for instance, who he was and how Mattie would react if she discovered she had been face-to-face, body to body, steamy passion to steamy passion with the head honcho of Hobby Hut himself.

BY THE TIME MATTIE AND JOE had carted all the woodcrafts, print reproductions and knickknacks inside the lobby of Paradise Valley Convalescent Home every resident who could ambulate under his or her own power, or with the aid of walkers, canes and wheelchairs, had congregated to browse through the crafts.

Joe got a funny feeling in his chest as he surveyed the delighted expressions on the patients' faces. It was like bringing Christmas gifts to Paradise Valley. The older generation, with the help of their nurses and staff, were selecting and gathering hand-painted figurines, curio shelves, keepsake chests, benches, and plant stands that he and Mattie had labored over on Sundays and after hours at the store.

The lump in Joe's throat expanded when Mattie, smiling in satisfaction, walked over to stand beside him, then slipped her hand in his.

"This is what it's all about," she murmured, tears clouding her eyes. "Can you feel it, Joe? You and I have created gifts that bring people joy and regenerate their spirit. This is why I paint, why I spend my spare time working so that others might enjoy. It's not for the money, it's for the personal satisfaction."

Joe understood completely. The feeling that tugged at his heart and fueled him with immense gratification was what he had been searching for when he came to Fox Hollow. He'd also come here to figure out why the manager of this store was doing such a thriving business. The answer was obvious. Mattie gave of herself so that others might enjoy her artistic talent and her labors of love. She wasn't in business for profit; she was in the business of dispensing happiness like a year-round Santa Claus.

Blinking rapidly to fight back tears, Mattie raised her arm and waved it in expansive gestures to gain the crowd's attention. Ripples of conversation ceased, and all eyes swung to Mattie and Joe.

"Despite what Pops originally told you about these crafts, you'll notice there are no price tags on the items," Mattie pointed out. "The reason is that Joe and I decided to make these gifts for you."

Murmurs spread rapidly through the crowd. Mattie waved her arm again, requesting silence. "Joe and I used spare lumber and paint from other projects to construct these items. Most of the craft items were actually damaged merchandise from Hobby Hut that we repaired rather than discarded. We want you to take whatever you like from the collection. If there is anything you want specifically, in addition to what we have here today, we'll make a list and construct more crafts to bring here next month."

A round of applause went through the crowd. Beaming faces focused on Mattie and Joe, and thank-yous were heard around the lobby.

"That was mighty generous of you," Joe murmured, giving Mattie's hand a squeeze. "Especially since I know that not all that lumber was spare wood and that you had to dig into your own pocket to pay for supplies."

She grinned impishly at him. "I'd like to keep that little secret confidential, if you don't mind. I've been satisfactorily repaid for my labor and expense. In addition, I'll pay you for your time—''

He held up his free hand to silence her. "Oh no, you won't," he objected. "You don't get to have all the fun here."

She stared pensively at him. "You really don't mind donating so much time for nothing?"

"Nothing? You call this nothing?" He indicated the delighted patients who were making their selections. "You can't put a price on the feelings that hit you right where you live when you make so many people happy."

"So you do understand," she murmured.

"You taught me to understand, Mattie," Joe told her.

He wanted to haul her into his arms and squeeze the stuffing out of her for putting him back in touch with the truly important things in life—those things that were priceless, those feelings of pride, satisfaction and generosity. Joe was pretty sure that he had received more from this after-hours project than the patients who excitedly made their selections.

"Told you this was a grand idea," Pops said, grinning. "You don't see smiles like these around this place every day, ya know."

Pops gestured toward his friends. "Just look at 'em over there, picking out all those colorful crafts to decorate their rooms. Hope you brought along hammers and nails to hang up the shelves." He chuckled wryly. "Bet the director will have a conniption when you start pounding and poking holes in these bland walls."

"Actually, I called the director this afternoon to ask permission," Joe spoke up. "He didn't object."

Pop's gray brows jackknifed. "He didn't? You mean he has a heart after all?"

"Apparently," Joe confirmed.

Pops harrumphed. "You probably just twisted his arm a half-dozen different ways to convince him to go along with the idea before I started a riot."

Joe didn't comment. He had done some serious talking to get the director to agree to personalizing the rooms at the home. However, one glance at the director indicated the man was also stirred by the scene before him. It was hard not to be touched by the pleasure and joy radiating around the lobby.

Joe grabbed Mattie's hand and towed her alongside him. "C'mon, little elf, let's get started hanging these shelves and racks so we won't interfere with lights out around here. You take the east wing and I'll take the west."

"Pops, get one of the staff members to start a list of other items desired, will you?" Mattie called as Joe hustled her away.

"Sure thing, Shortcake…hey, Joe, same time this week?" Pops questioned enthusiastically.

Joe glanced back and winked at Pops. "You bet. Tell the gang to be ready."

Mattie gazed quizzically at Joe. "What was that all about?"

"Another adventurous expedition. The Roland Gang thinks we're sneaking away without permission again. Not to worry. I cleared it with the director."

"Thanks, Joe. I hope you realize how much I appreciate your effort with this project and your willingness to entertain Pops and friends."

He grinned wickedly. "You can repay me later." When she blushed profusely, he chuckled. The thought of *how* and *where* he'd be spending the night was the inspiration needed to get to work hanging the shelves and woodcrafts that Mattie had generously donated to the patients at Paradise Valley.

JOE NEARLY SWALLOWED his tongue when, two days later, his grandfather, dressed in casual clothes and a baseball cap, hobbled into the shop. Joe was standing at the counter with his jaw scraping his chest when Mattie strode forward to ask J.D. if he needed help locating the items he wanted.

What the hell was J.D. doing here? Criminey! Joe recalled that he had specifically requested that Gramps didn't get involved in this situation.

"You are the manager?" J.D. asked Mattie.

She smiled and nodded.

"Pretty little thing, isn't she?" J.D.'s eyes twinkled as his gaze darted to Joe. "Well, young lady, I could indeed use some help, if you don't mind. I'm looking for an artificial flower arrangement to perk up my living room. And some knickknacks, too. Do you have any suggestions?"

Mattie led the way down the aisles, wondering why this senior citizen looked familiar. She swore she'd never seen him in the shop before, but there was something about him that reminded her of someone, though she couldn't figure out who.

"Do you live around here? Have family around here?" she asked as she gestured toward the rows of flower arrangements.

"No, I'm just passing through the area," J.D. informed her. "Nice community you have here. I noticed the signs indicating there's a lake nearby. Thought I might do a little sight-seeing. Hmm...this arrangement is bright and colorful,'' he said, quickly changing the subject.

When the phone rang in the office, Mattie glanced toward the counter to see Joe stride off to take the call. When he motioned her to the phone, she excused herself and passed Joe as he was coming down the aisle.

''It's a customer requesting your advice on interior decoration,'' he reported on his way by. ''I'll handle this customer.''

When Mattie walked off, Joe rounded on his grandfather. ''What are you doing here?'' he demanded.

Grinning, J.D. plucked up the flower arrangement. ''I'm shopping.''

''No, you aren't,'' Joe grumbled. ''You came to see me working as a hired assistant, so don't deny it. Couldn't resist, could you, Gramps?''

J.D. grinned, undaunted. ''Nope, I couldn't. You got something going with Mattie?'' he asked in the same breath.

''I believe we already covered that subject to my satisfaction on the phone,'' Joe said, striving to keep his temper under control.

''Not to *my* satisfaction, however,'' J.D. countered. ''I'd also like to meet Pops. Are you, by chance, picking him and his friends up tonight?''

Joe sighed in resignation. ''Yes, as a matter of fact. I'm taking the Roland Gang to the lake after we grab a bite to eat at the café. The gang pooled their money to rent a pontoon boat, and I was elected to drive.''

''Good, then I can come along,'' J.D. invited himself.

''And how do you propose that I explain you?''

J.D. stared him squarely in the eye for a long moment. "The truth would be best. It wouldn't hurt for Mattie and her grandfather to know who I am."

No, Joe supposed not. Things with Mattie were going splendidly. She had overcome her initial embarrassment of sleeping with the hired help. They spent their nights in her bed, or on his hideaway sofa, and he had purchased the necessary protection that he'd neglected that first night. Joe reckoned he could explain his grandfather's appearance without arousing too much suspicion.

"All right, Gramps, come to the counter and I'll introduce you to Mattie."

Happily, J.D. followed in Joe's wake, then set his purchase beside the cash register.

When Mattie emerged from her office, Joe motioned her to the counter. "Mattie, this character who showed up unexpectedly is actually my grandfather. Mattie, this is J.D....Gray," he added belatedly.

She extended her hand and smiled. "That explains it. I thought there was something familiar about you. It is a pleasure to meet you, J.D. Your grandson has had wonderful things to say about you. Will you be staying a few days?"

J.D. glanced at his grandson. "I'd hoped to, when I planned to come here and surprise him. Joe tells me that he's taking your grandfather and friends to the lake this evening. I was hoping to tag along. Will you be coming, too?"

Mattie shook her head. "I promised to bring a few items from the store to one of my regular customer's home after hours. She's having difficulty getting the decorative look she wants in her living area."

"Mattie is the guru of interior decor in these parts," Joe inserted. "If you noticed the displays in the windows, you were looking at her original paintings and her amazing gift of combining a variety of crafts to brighten up a wall.''

"I did notice," J.D. affirmed. "Very impressive, Mattie. That painting in your nautical display, the one with the lighthouse beaming through the fog, really caught my eye. I'd like to have the entire display."

Joe winced.

Mattie blinked, startled.

"I can afford it," J.D. rushed to assure her.

Joe wanted to kick the old goat in the shins for implying that money wasn't an issue for him—which, of course, it wasn't. "Gramps has a nest egg set aside," Joe felt compelled to add.

Realizing his blunder, J.D. said hurriedly, "Joe has told me many a time to enjoy my money, not stash it away for his inheritance. So I'm taking his advice and splurging when the mood strikes."

Mattie checked her watch. "I'll wrap up the artwork and crafts before I give my consultation this evening. Joe, if you want to take the rest of the afternoon off to show your grandfather around town go right ahead. The part-time assistant will be here in an hour to help me with the rush we usually get just before closing time."

"Thanks, Mattie, you're a sweetheart," J.D. said, then smiled wryly. "Joe is lucky to be working for someone like you."

Exasperated, Joe ushered Gramps from the store, then drove to the cracker-box apartment so the old man could take a load off his feet before the boating expedition with the Roland Gang. Joe also cautioned Gramps to watch what he said in front of Pops and friends.

Having Gramps underfoot put Joe on edge. One misstep and this situation could blow up in Joe's face. Damn, he needed to tell Mattie the truth, he told himself grimly.

Tonight, he decided. After he got all the senior citizens tucked in bed, he would trot over to Mattie's house, set her down and explain why he was here and who he was. He had several hours to rehearse what he intended to say. He would assure her that none of his reasons for coming to Fox Hollow had anything whatsoever to do with their relationship, that he truly cared about her.

Yeah, he told himself. Honesty was the best policy. Better late than never, he supposed.

Having delivered those consulting platitudes to himself, Joe loaded up Gramps and headed to the nursing home to wait for Pops and the gang to sneak away from their rooms. He still hadn't told Pops that all that secrecy was unnecessary because the director was happy to have the old scoundrels out of the home for a few hours. Of course, Joe wouldn't think of spoiling Pops's fun of sneaking out the window and scurrying around the shrubs to prevent getting caught.

MATTIE ANSWERED THE KNOCK at the door and greeted Joe with an eager kiss. She had his shirt unbuttoned and cast aside before he closed the door behind him.

"Eager, are we?" he asked playfully.

"Yes, indeed." She ran her hands across the solid, muscular wall of his chest, loving the feel of him beneath her questing hands. "How was your adventure with the senior citizens?"

"They had a grand time on the lake. Gramps had

the time of his life, too, but I came over here this evening to—''

Mattie had had enough conversation to last her for the night. The hours she'd spent alone made her realize how vital Joe's presence was to her happiness. There was a time when her extra projects occupied her. No longer. Joe had taken up permanent residence in her mind. She was in love with the man, despite her previous policy and the head honcho's regulations.

Joe forgot what he intended to say, couldn't remember one word he'd rehearsed, when Mattie's soft lips whispered over his chest. He felt her hands gliding over the band of his jeans, heard the metal rasp of the zipper easing downward to admit her prowling fingers. His breath hitched when she stroked him, and the desire he forced himself to hold in check during the workday broke loose from the dam of restraint.

Urgency claimed him and he took her down to the carpeted floor, knowing he didn't have the patience to make it all the way to the bedroom before he possessed her and became her willing possession.

It was always like this with Mattie, he realized as he peeled away her clothes, his hands sweeping over her silky skin. The first time they made love, each evening, was a wild rush to completion, as if they couldn't get enough of each other, fast enough. Need was such an intense, overpowering instinct that it knew no master save itself. Their hunger for each other was an all-consuming kind of passion that, like a wildfire, fed upon itself and devoured all within its path.

Only the second time around could Mattie and Joe savor all the inexpressible sensations they summoned from each other. It was the damnedest thing Joe had ever experienced, and he knew he was getting in over his head with Mattie. She mattered so much to him that he couldn't remember when she wasn't a part of his days, his nights, his life.

He came to her in a whirlwind of unrestrained passion, burning alive in the wildfire that constantly blazed between them. His days never seemed complete until he was one with her, until he was buried so deeply inside her, and she was clinging so tightly to him, that he couldn't tell where her passion ended and his began.

Much later, when Joe recovered enough energy to raise his head and marshaled the nerve to broach the subject that played havoc with his conscience, Mattie left him speechless when she whispered, "I love you."

Before his mind stopped reeling from her quiet confession, she set about to express her feelings by savoring every inch of his ultrasensitive body with intimate kisses and caresses that blew his mind and stole the breath from his lungs. And when she came to him, settling exactly over him, he was so desperate with need that he couldn't even remember his own name—the real one or the fictitious one.

Of course, he couldn't tell her the truth about himself so soon after she whispered—twice—that she loved him. And he couldn't return her words because he felt like a devious jerk and guilt was eating him alive.

Heaven and hell at once, Joe realized when he finally found the willpower and the strength to ease from Mattie's bed and return to his apartment.

She loved him. This honest, kindhearted little elf

loved him, and he was caught up in a lie of his own making—no matter how innocent, harmless and necessary it had seemed in the beginning.

Frustrated with the situation, Joe tiptoed into his apartment, then sank down on the pallet he'd made for himself so Gramps could sleep on the Hide-A-Bed.

He had just stretched out when J.D.'s voice erupted from the darkness.

"Did you tell her the truth?"

"Er...no."

"You're sleeping with her," J.D. guessed correctly. "Mattie doesn't strike me as the kind of woman who goes in for affairs. Not if Pops and his friends are to be believed, which I'm sure they are. Don't hurt that girl, *Joe*. She deserves better."

"I know," Joe murmured.

"The longer you wait the less she will understand," J.D. told him.

"I figured that out all by myself."

"Then why delay?" J.D. wanted to know.

"Because she's pure of heart, and she's the best thing that ever happened to me, Gramps. She brings out the best in me, makes me like who I am when I'm with her. When I tell her the truth, I'll break her trust in me. She gives it unconditionally. She accepts me as I am unquestioningly. I'm afraid she'll take it the wrong way when she learns the truth. I'm afraid things will never be the same between us again. I'll lose the happiness I've found here, and I'm not ready to face that yet, Gramps," Joe said miserably. "It's hard to make yourself confide the truth when you know the repercussions will tear your world apart."

Thankfully, J.D. piped down. But then, Joe figured

Gramps didn't have a fail-safe solution for the problem, either. Joe *wanted* to be who he was when he was with Mattie, *wanted* to forget that Daniel Joseph Grayson existed because, for sure and certain, that head honcho at Hobby Hut would ruin the best thing that had come along in Joe's life.

"So, SHORTCAKE, when are you gonna marry Joe and make a respectable man out of him?"

Mattie hadn't even had a chance to sit down in Pops's room before he sprang the question on her. Furthermore, she had her doubts that Joe was as serious about her as she was about him. Although they had been inseparable the past two weeks, during and after work, he'd never once said that he loved her, though she continued to whisper the words to him each night while they nestled in each other's arms.

She was pretty certain Joe cared about her, enjoyed her company. But then, she reminded herself that she had such limited experience with romantic relationships that she probably couldn't recognize the signs and signals that other women's internal radar picked up on. Or maybe Joe was the kind of man who had difficulty with verbal expression of his affection. Maybe he was trying to show her, rather than tell her, how he felt about her.

"Well?" Pops prompted impatiently.

"Gee, Pops, I've only been seeing Joe for a month, give or take a few days. We haven't discussed future plans."

Pops rolled his eyes. "Kids these days. They do things back-ass-ward, if you ask me."

Mattie battled down a blush. She suspected Pops guessed that she was no longer sleeping alone. "The thing is, marriage is a giant step. I want to be sure that I make a mature decision about something that is going to affect the rest of my life.''

"Mature decision?" Pops snorted at that. "I've got a news flash for you, Shortcake. Nobody can make a mature decision until he or she approaches the age of fifty. And from where I'm standing, even that seems a little young. Folks just don't have enough life experience to pull it off. You're in love with the man and it shows when you're with him, the way you look at him, the way he looks at you."

"The way he looks at me? It shows?" she asked.

"Sure it does. Joe cares about you. He cares about me, too. Not like some of those yahoos you dated occasionally. They saw me as an inconvenience and burden they had to bear in order to go out with you. Far as I'm concerned, Joe is as good as they come, and so is J.D. That old coot is worth a few good laughs himself. Wouldn't mind having them both in our family."

"Well, if Joe mentions marriage I'll be sure to tell him that he has your stamp of approval," Mattie replied.

Pops leaned forward on the edge of his bed. "I've got one more crusade to conquer around here, before the doctor gets my medication properly adjusted and dismisses me."

Mattie held her tongue. She had conferred with Pops's doctor the previous week and the physician wasn't too keen on dismissing Pops for at least two months. Not unless Pops agreed to regular visits from home health-care nurses who could monitor his vital stats and diabetic condition. Mattie decided to withhold that information until Pops needed to know.

"So what's your new crusade, Pops?" she questioned.

"I have this idea about energizing the senior citizens by inviting some preschoolers or kindergartners to the home once a week. There's nothing like children to raise flagging spirits."

"That's a wonderful idea, Pops," Mattie enthused.

"Told you," Pops replied, smiling. "But you'll have to make the arrangements for me."

"I'll contact the day-care center and see what we can arrange," Mattie promised.

She wasn't sure when she could find time to do that, but she would handle it, nonetheless. After the showing of hobbies and crafts at the home, more orders had come pouring in to consume her spare time.

Mattie decided to take Pops's idea one step further and contact the florist to see if she would donate flowers for the children to bring to the convalescent home occasionally. The children would have a special gift, in addition to their youthful presence, to rejuvenate the elderly.

"Ask Joe to clear it with the director," Pops requested. "He pulled off the hanging of shelves and racks in the rooms, so we'll let him be the one to fly the idea past the director."

"I'll let Joe know what you're planning," Mattie promised as she rose from her chair, then pressed a kiss to his wrinkled forehead. "You better get some rest. With all the activities you have going I don't want you to wear yourself out."

"I'll rest when I'm dead," Pops said. "I gotta make my rounds to visit my friends. Herman and Glen's family haven't been around to see them much lately. Somebody has to keep their minds occupied.

Hell, they are living from one of Joe's grand adventures to the next. They aren't fortunate to have an angel like you showing up at regular intervals to visit."

Mattie hugged him impulsively. "I love you, Pops."

"Me, too, Shortcake." He patted her arm, then steered her toward the door. "Now, don't forget to tell Joe to swing the arrangements for the preschoolers with the director," he repeated, as if her memory was as short as his.

"Done," Mattie confirmed, then walked away.

Recalling what Pops said about families neglecting the elderly, she detoured down the hall to spend a few minutes with each of Pops's oldest and dearest friends.

7

MATTIE HURRIEDLY STRIPPED off her clothes and hopped into the shower. Joe had announced that he was taking her out dancing at Watering Hole Tavern where the live country-and-western band was scheduled to play on Saturday night. Mattie wasn't sure that was such a hot idea because of Joe's confrontation with the cowboys who had harassed him outside the café. Mattie expected Buck Reynolds and company would be in attendance. After all, they were regular fixtures at the tavern. But Joe assured her that he could handle any situation that might arise. Nevertheless, Mattie was apprehensive. A barroom brawl wasn't her idea of fun.

Now that gossip linked Joe and her as an official item in town, she fully expected to be harangued by Buck Reynolds and his sidekicks. But, as Joe said, this was their first official date and it was long overdue. For almost a month, they had worked side by side every day and on weekends to complete the craft projects for the nursing home. Yet, they hadn't actually been out on a date. Joe had promised dinner at the café and dancing. This date seemed important to him for reasons Mattie couldn't understand, but she agreed to go, despite her reservations about mixing with the rowdy crowd at the dance hall.

Mattie had splurged on a new dress from Lindsay's

Boutique, and she had styled her hair to lie in frothy curls around her face and shoulders. She didn't look half-bad, if she did say so herself. The black dress she'd purchased during her lunch hour was sleek and provocative and probably a bit too dressy for the country-and-western atmosphere, but she wanted to look elegant and feminine so Joe would be proud to have her at his side. Maybe that would perk him up a bit—or at least distract him from whatever was disturbing him.

Joe had been meditative and preoccupied the past couple of days. It was as if there was something he wanted to tell her and just couldn't quite bring himself to say. Was he considering making their relationship permanent? she wondered. Was he wrestling with the possibility of giving her an engagement ring?

The prospect of a proposal delighted her. Truth was, despite how she'd two-stepped around the question Pops had tossed at her, she did want a long-term commitment with Joe. Mattie had never felt this way about any man. Although Joe still hadn't professed his feelings for her, he gave the impression that he cared, that he enjoyed their time together—whether it was at work or play.

Mattie kept waiting for Joe to confide where he had been working before he came to Fox Hollow, and she refused to push him into disclosing information he apparently didn't want to discuss. But why was he secretive? It was as if there was something he didn't want her to know, something in his past he was ashamed of, embarrassed about.

Didn't he understand that she trusted him explicitly, that she cared so much for him that she was willing to listen if he had problems in his past that he wanted to get off his chest?

The rap at the front door sent Mattie scrambling to retrieve her shoes from the closet. "Come in," she called.

Mattie scurried down the hall, shoes in hand, then skidded to a halt. She gaped at Joe's expensive shirt, slacks and western boots. "Wow, you do clean up nicely," she complimented. *Nice* didn't begin to describe how devastatingly handsome Joe looked. The man was most definitely a babe magnet when he got all spruced up in expensive duds.

Joe stood and stared in astonishment. His petite elf, who usually wore faded jeans and T-shirts, was decked out in a knock-'em-dead black silk dress that should have had a warning sign posted on it. Damn! Mattie looked positively stunning.

Too stunning for his comfort. Possessive feelings bombarded him when his gaze dipped to the satiny swells of her breasts, which were displayed to their best advantage by the diving neckline. Ah jeez, he thought as his gaze tumbled to the trim indentation of her waist, lingered on the curvaceous swell of her hips, then drifted down her shapely legs.

For a few seconds he suffered flashbacks of dates with glamour queens who had dressed to entice him. But none of them appealed to him the way Mattie did, because he knew damned good and well that it wasn't the sensational dress that made this woman so alluring to him. *She* accentuated the dress, not the other way around. When Mattie did decide to call attention to her feminine beauty, rather than downplay it, she was an absolute knockout!

For the life of him Joe couldn't find his tongue,

must've swallowed it. Worse, his body grew more aroused with each passing second that he appraised her, then reappraised her. His silence obviously made her self-conscious, because she fidgeted, then glanced away.

"Don't like it much, huh? I don't claim to have the knack for buying appropriate clothes, only gathering interesting crafts for displays. This is probably too dressy for the countrified dance, but—"

"Not like it?" he bleated, his gaze roaming over her again. "Are you kidding?"

She met his gaze. "So, you do like it then?" she asked earnestly.

"I like it way too much," he finally managed to get out without his voice sounding like shattering glass. "And so will every other man in town. Sheesh, Mattie, you really don't have the slightest idea how beautiful you are, do you?"

Mattie smiled at his compliment, then spun around so he could view the dress from every angle. "Think so?"

"Know so." His body hardened and clenched painfully.

"Yeah?"

"Yeah, yeah, oh yeah," he confirmed as he moved deliberately toward her. "Nobody cuts in on me at the dance tonight. Got it? Hell, I'll be ready to murder any man who looks at you for more than a split second, because I know exactly what he's thinking. I won't appreciate other men having X-rated fantasies about you."

"Won't matter," she murmured as she pushed up on tiptoe to kiss away his frown. "All I care about is you."

Joe couldn't resist. He clutched her to him and kissed her with the sense of desperate frustration that had been gnawing away at him these past few days. His time was running out and he'd all but given up on finding the right time, the right way, to tell Mattie that he hadn't been honest with her. Neither was he certain the love she claimed to feel for him would weather the storm of the brutal truth.

He had misrepresented himself from the very beginning. He'd gotten involved with Mattie when he knew that complications would arise. But Mattie had trustingly, generously made him a part of her life, a part of her extended family. He had been welcomed and quickly accepted in Fox Hollow because of his association with Mattie. That old cliché about any friend of yours is a friend of mine held true, because of Mattie's rapport with people in her hometown. She was the reason Joe had rediscovered the meaning and enjoyment of life, the reason doors opened and welcome mats were placed at his feet. In short, she had paved the way for his acceptance.

Now he had to give it all up and return to his world. The prospect of leaving Mattie behind was killing him, bit by agonizing bit.

In order to spare Mattie's feelings, to prevent hurting her deeply, he would call regularly, visit her on weekends, and continue searching for the right way to extricate himself from impending disaster.

It had taken a good deal of forethought, but Joe had finally devised a plan to keep himself in Mattie's good graces—until he felt comfortable coming clean. First off, he needed to change those stupid rules he'd made from his executive office at corporate headquarters. Then he'd put Mattie's suggestions and ideas to good use in the company. She would realize that he cared what she thought and approved of her ideas. Surely that would soften the blow of his deceit when he worked up the gumption to tell her the truth, the whole truth and nothing but.

Furthermore, Joe planned to make some generous donations to Paradise Valley to improve the quality of life and provide entertainment for the patients. He wanted all those senior citizens he'd come to know and love to enjoy a few luxuries that might brighten their days.

"Joe?" Mattie murmured softly. "Are you okay?"

No, he wasn't okay, because he was scrambling to find a way to hold on to the best thing that had ever happened to him. He couldn't shake the cloud of doom that had been hovering over him the past few days. One minute he was reassuring himself that he could successfully find a way to hold on to Mattie. The next minute he was overwhelmed by the unshakable feeling this situation was going to blow up in his face. Talk about manic-depressant!

"I'm fine," he lied through a smile. "We better get out of here before the tantalizing vision of you in that dress, and the erotic fantasy of getting you *out* of it, makes me forget I promised you a night on the town, an official date."

He took her arm and shepherded her toward the door. Mattie frowned at his tense grip on her arm, the odd note in his voice and his peculiar mood. She was perplexed by the urgency in his kiss and his intense need to show her a good time. What the devil was bothering him anyway? Was he stressing out about mentioning a wedding engagement, for fear she would turn him down?

Yeah, right. Like that would ever happen. She would marry this marvelous man in a New York minute and take her Texas time proving to him how much she adored him.

Well, there was no sense anticipating something that might not happen, Mattie told herself sensibly. *She* might have engagement on the brain, but there might be something else entirely on Joe's mind besides wedding bells, babies and happily ever after. She would do herself a tremendous favor if she didn't let herself get carried away. After all, the man hadn't come right out and told her that he loved her, now had he? This affair could be mostly physical on his part. It wasn't as if Mattie was well-versed in the nuances of relationships or anything. She didn't have a clue what Joe saw in his future. All she knew was how she felt and how she *hoped* Joe felt in return. Assumptions could lead to crushing disappointment, she reminded herself.

No matter what, though, Mattie vowed to make the most of the evening—their first official date. She felt happy and alive, and she refused to let anything spoil the evening. Clinging to positive thoughts, Mattie sailed out the front door on Joe's arm.

JOE DECIDED THE LOUD MUSIC and noisy crowd at Watering Hole Tavern was just what he needed to distract him from his glum thoughts. This was the beginning of the end, but he didn't want to dwell on that tonight, just wanted to show Mattie a grand time. Thus far, she seemed to be enjoying herself. She had stuffed herself on the Saturday-night special of catfish and didn't seem to notice the masculine glances that came her way—repeatedly, continuously. Joe certainly had noticed. The male customers at the café had gawked when Mattie strolled in, looking as if she had walked off the pages of *Vogue*.

Things got progressively worse when Mattie stepped into the tavern. Men's heads turned in synchronized rhythm, eyes popped, then roamed over her alluring figure and smiling face. Hell's jingling bells, she had visual fingerprints all over her!

Possessive feelings grabbed Joe by the throat and wouldn't let go. Joe knew Mattie was going to attract considerable male attention, but this was even worse than he imagined! Damn, he would have to remain on guard duty the whole livelong night.

When the band struck up a slow ballad, Joe pulled Mattie into his arms. This way, he wouldn't have to endure other men staring at her bosom, which was so enticingly showcased by her clingy dress. He could relax and enjoy the feel of her soft, luscious body molded full length against him. Of course, that presented another kind of problem, but since Joe had pretty much been in a constant state of arousal since he'd gotten close enough to stare into her beguiling amethyst eyes, to touch her, to kiss her, that was nothing new.

"Mmm, this is nice," Mattie murmured against his shoulder. "I haven't danced since my college days. I didn't have much time for it then, either, because I was usually too busy working to pay my way through school."

"Me, too," Joe said, then glowered meat cleavers at the cowboy who was visually measuring Mattie's hips while she swayed to the music.

When the song ended, Joe clasped Mattie's hand

and shouldered his way through the crowd to reach the bar. "I could use a beer. How about you?"

"Just a cola for me...hey!" she squawked abruptly.

Joe stumbled sideways, then glanced over his shoulder to see that Buck Reynolds had taken hold of Mattie's free hand and was trying to drag her back to the dance floor. Well, damn, it looked as if Joe was going to have to kick some ass before the night was out.

"Let her go," Joe demanded sharply. "The lady is with me."

Buck ignored Joe. "Aw, c'mon, Mattie," he slurred. "It's just a dance. Figured you'd appreciate holding on to a real man instead of that wuss you're with."

Before Mattie could object further—and she looked as if she wanted to—Buck tugged her onto the dance floor to two-step. Joe silently seethed when Buck's cohorts appeared to restrain him from going after Mattie.

"Settle down, twink," Harlan growled in Joe's ear. "Buck just wants to dance with her. He's had the hots for Mattie since high school, but she would never give any of us the time of day, so we had to razz her unmercifully to make up for that. But damn, if she didn't turn into a knockout. Like to have a piece of that myself."

Joe debated about initiating a barroom brawl—if that's what it took to wrest free from these three drunken cowboys and rescue Mattie from Buck's octopus arms. But before he could act, he saw Mattie discreetly knee Buck in the crotch while he tried to clutch her to him in full body contact. The cowboy's knees buckled, and he dropped to the floor like a feed sack. Joe silently applauded Mattie's acting ability when she pretended concern for the hooligan, who couldn't catch his breath after she had gouged him accidentally-on-purpose.

"Your good buddy looks as if he isn't feeling so hot," Joe pointed out. "Too much booze, do you think? Maybe you better go help him to his feet before somebody dances on him. That'd be such a shame."

When the threesome swaggered off, Joe circled around the crowd to take Mattie by the arm before some other doofus beat him to it. His tension eased, and he grinned when the cowboys hauled Buck to a nearby chair and dropped him in it.

"Nice move," Joe complimented Mattie as he steered her toward the bar.

"Pops always told me that when in doubt, punt," Mattie explained. "Besides, I was afraid if I didn't handle that bozo myself, you'd feel obligated to be chivalrous and take out those other three clowns like you did outside the café a few weeks back. You were considering it, weren't you?"

Joe looped a possessive arm around her waist as he leaned against the bar to order drinks. "Yes, I considered it. A guy can only take being called a wuss a couple of times, can only stand to see some lame-brained bozo manhandle his best girl *once* before he gets PO'd. It ticked me off to watch Buck try to give you a physical examination, right there on the dance floor. I definitely wanted to hit something—beginning and ending with good old Buck."

Her violet eyes sparkled at him and his heart

banged against his ribs—and stuck there. "Jealous?" she asked.

"Insanely, murderously," he assured her.

"Good, then you can imagine how I feel when all those women at the store undress you with their eyes. You've captured plenty of feminine attention here tonight, too. You look good enough to eat, Joe."

He glanced around, surprised to note that he was drawing feminine stares and come-hither smiles. He'd been so busy being protective of Mattie that he hadn't noticed the attention he was receiving.

Mattie giggled at his surprised expression, then frowned when one of the store customers, who had been panting after Joe for the past couple of weeks, sashayed toward him, dressed in skintight jeans and a formfitting knit top.

"Trouble at three o'clock," Mattie warned. "Prepare for your own physical examination. Candice Green has quite a reputation around Fox Hollow. Her favorite sport is men chasing."

"Yeah?" Joe asked, glancing in Candice's direction.

"Yeah, and I'd guess she wants you to be her new flavor of the month."

Joe slapped a couple of bills on the bar to pay for the drinks that had yet to be delivered, then steered Mattie toward the door. "I'm ready for a drive around the lake. I've had about as much fun here as I can stand for one night."

"You and me both," Mattie agreed as she dodged bodies to keep up with the swift pace Joe set to reach the exit.

Once outside, Joe expelled an audible sigh. "Next

time I suggest a night at the tavern, remind me what a dumb idea it is,'' he requested.

"You've got it. Although I admit I'm a people person, I don't enjoy the crush of crowds. Give me wide-open space any ol' day.''

Joe opened the passenger door to his clunker truck, then derailed from his train of thought when Mattie eased onto the seat, revealing a generous amount of nylon-clad leg. "Mattie, about that moonlight drive,'' he murmured huskily.

"What about it?''

He smiled, then waggled his eyebrows suggestively. "I'd rather go to your place.''

"Just the two us? All alone in the dark?'' she asked.

"Yeah, like that.''

She leaned out to give him a wispy kiss. "I can't think of anything I'd like better myself, Joe.''

Joe practically sprinted to his side of the truck, then climbed beneath the steering wheel. He made tracks to Mattie's house and wasted no time getting her behind closed doors. He honestly wondered if this ravenous need that had been such a constant thing for nearly a month would taper off if he had years, rather than days, to spend with her. He really doubted it, though, because Mattie affected him intensely, got to him on so many different levels. She oozed sexuality, character and personality. He never could get enough of her.

Incredible really, all these indefinable sensations she called from him. And what terrified him was that he could destroy this magic between them with one careless misstep. If the sequence of his plan to reveal who and what he was didn't follow the proper progression, he didn't even want to think about the consequences he'd face. Timing was so damn crucial!

Later he would wrap his mind around initiating phase one, he told himself before he picked her up and carried her to the bedroom. But definitely not now. When he had Mattie on the brain there wasn't room in his head for anything else.

Joe was certain he had died and gone straight to heaven when Mattie's caresses meandered over the padded muscles of his chest, teasing one nipple and then the other. His body felt so sensitive, so responsive to her touch that he swore fires burned in the wake of her arousing caresses.

When her hand descended along the dark furring of hair on his belly, Joe hissed a breath through his teeth—then forgot to breathe at all, couldn't remember why he needed to. She traced the throbbing length of his arousal, enfolded him, stroked him until he groaned in sweet torment. Then she flicked her tongue against his rigid flesh and Joe felt desire roiling out of control, felt his body tremble in helpless response.

"No more," he gasped when another lightning bolt of pleasure sizzled through him, very nearly stripping away his restraint. "Mattie—"

When she suckled him, held him in the palm of her hand, Joe knew he wouldn't last another minute if she didn't stop what she was doing to him—and so expertly, so tenderly. Before Mattie realized how it happened, Joe flipped her onto her back and braced himself on his elbows.

"My turn," he rasped, then dipped his head to make an erotic feast of her nipples and the satiny swells of her breasts.

Mattie arched into his lips, into his roaming hands,

reveling in the magical pleasure that Joe spun around her. She quivered and burned beneath each heated kiss, each splendorous caress. When his hands and lips drifted lower, exciting, arousing her, she moaned aloud.

He traced her heated softness with his fingertips, held her suspended in wondrous torture. He shifted, nudging her legs apart, granting him access to the sensitive flesh of her inner thighs. Mattie came unraveled when she felt his hot mouth searing her, his tongue flicking at her. Bone-melting sensations consumed her, inflamed her, boiling up like lava from the very center of her body.

"Come here," she gasped when the first wave of ecstasy crashed and rolled over her. "Joe...please!"

Joe drew her legs around his hips, lifted her to him, sank into her and felt her shimmering exquisitely around him. He thrust into her, then withdrew, setting a slow, gentle cadence that gradually accelerated to match the pounding rhythm of desire that spurred him like a merciless rider. He made love to Mattie—savoring and memorizing each ineffable sensation—as if there were no tomorrows, because there weren't too many tomorrows left for him.

When her voice shattered on a cry that was his name, immense satisfaction consumed him, took him with her into a wild, spiraling free fall of passion. Joe shuddered once, twice, three times. He uncurled above her, clutched her tightly to him, burying his head in the tangled strands of raven hair that lay against the curve of her neck. His pulse pounded like hailstones and he suspected his highly accelerated heartbeat would bruise a few ribs. He struggled to catch his breath, but the alluring scent of her surrounded him, leaving him dizzy, light-headed and totally spent.

Making love to Mattie demanded all he had, all he was. Even minutes later, he was still engulfed with pleasure too immense and profound to put into words.

"I love you," she whispered to him.

His heart twisted in his chest, just as it always did when she confided her feelings for him so sincerely, so simply yet eloquently.

Joe lay there for several minutes, with Mattie nestled possessively against him. He was tormented to no end that he had made such a mess of this situation. Damn, this riptide of emotion was tearing him apart.

Finally he said, "Mattie, we need to talk."

"Do we? What about?" She waited with bated breath, hoping he was going to spring the big question on her, knowing what her answer would be. It didn't matter that she had only known him a month. She knew she loved him with all her heart and soul. That was all that mattered. They could make a life for themselves here in Fox Hollow. There was no question that Joe could be happy here. He seemed to like the community as much as she did.

"Mattie, I have to give notice that I'm quitting my job," he told her.

Her breath stalled in her chest, and she felt a sinking sensation in the pit of her stomach. Of all the things she expected him to say, that wasn't even on the list!

She angled her head on his shoulder so she could stare into his shadowed face. "What? Why? I thought you liked it here. I thought——"

"I do," he cut in quickly, determined to get through this carefully rehearsed explanation. "Unfortunately, liking it here, being with you, doesn't automatically relieve me of the obligations I left behind." He nuzzled against Mattie's cheek, feeling her tension, her disappointment and confusion. "When I came here I told you that I needed to get away from the unpleasant situation I'd left behind. I had lost my enthusiasm and direction. Because of you, Mattie, I have recaptured my lost spirit."

The thought that she had been a tool to help him recover from whatever emotional pothole he had tripped over left Mattie with mixed feelings. She felt he had offered her a compliment and insult in the same breath. Her heart shattered, knowing her love for Joe wasn't going to be enough to hold him here. Naive fool that she was, she had believed that loving Joe was all that mattered.

Just showed what she knew, didn't it?

"I know you don't understand, and I can't fully explain where I have to go and what I need to do when I get there," Joe went on, stroking her arm in a soothing gesture.

Mattie, however, didn't feel the slightest bit soothed. She felt hurt and raw and rejected, and she couldn't imagine that anything Joe could add would make her feel better.

"My last day will be Wednesday. And I'll spend my spare time completing as many craft projects for Paradise Valley as I can before I leave. But I'll be back late Friday night to stay the weekend. I plan to return every weekend until I have my life and my obligations in order. I don't want to lose you, Mattie," he whispered.

Mattie couldn't be sure, because she was a novice at affairs, but she suspected Joe was handing her a line, making all the right noises, in an attempt to tell her what he thought she wanted to hear so he could continue to string her along. He claimed he didn't have a wife or girlfriend that he had left behind when he arrived in Fox Hollow with nothing but a suitcase and a rattletrap truck.

Unfortunately, however, comments about dealing with situations in his previous life and making weekend visits sounded highly suspicious to Mattie. When he said, "I care about you, Mattie, and I don't want to lose you," she thought he sounded about as clichéd as you could get!

Come to think of it, she had wondered why Joe's grandpa had shown up out of the blue, intent on surprising Joe. Had J.D. come to encourage Joe to return to the mysterious life he had left behind? Undoubtedly!

Damn him! Damn her for reading more into their affair than was actually there!

Mattie tried to recoil into her own private space, but Joe refused to let her. "Don't withdraw from me, Mattie," he murmured. "I was afraid this would happen, which is why I've had a devil of a time trying to find the right time to bring this up. But in fairness to you, I wanted you to know I was leaving before I left. I also want you to know that I'll be back."

Yeah, sure, thought Mattie. He was only letting her down easily. But he was still giving her the brush-off. She could imagine what he was thinking but was too tactful to say. *So long, sugar, the sex was fun and your grandfather amuses me. And I do enjoy woodcrafting a lot, but this was just a temporary fling between us.*

"I'll call you every night," he promised.

Mattie inwardly smirked. Sure he would, and she was the Queen of Sheba.

"I'll be here every weekend, rain, shine or blizzard."

Uh-huh, here comes another snow job, she mused. The flakes were already piling up, knee deep.

"Mattie?" he prompted.

She didn't reply. It was all she could do to keep from bawling her fool head off and blubbering in self-pity.

"I know how this sounds, and I can just imagine what you're thinking."

"Can you?" she managed to say without her voice cracking.

"Yes, I can," Joe confirmed. "You think this is the beginning of goodbye, but you're wrong. This isn't goodbye, Mattie, I swear it."

Sure, next he'd be swearing on a stack of Bibles. Lord, the things men said and did to string women along!

"I swear it on a stack of Bibles."

Her heart fractured. His attempt to convince her had the reverse effect. The trust she had offered him, unconditionally, shattered. Her belief in him wavered and tumbled. Or maybe it was her uncertain belief in herself, her long-held feelings that she wasn't quite woman enough to capture and hold a man's attention that was the root of the problem.

The more she thought about it the more she wondered if she hadn't been convenient for Joe. Naive, lacking in experience, too trusting, too eager to find a man to love. Yup, that was good old tomboy Mattie for you. Princess of the power tools could only hold on to the things she could nail down. To Joe, she had been accessible to appease his sexual cravings. Gawd, what an idiot she had been. She hadn't seen this coming because Joe was a master at concealing his purposes and using her until he was ready to cast her aside like a piece of scrap lumber.

When he tried to kiss her—as if *that* would convince her of anything ever again!—Mattie twisted from his arms. She felt used, ashamed, discarded and disillusioned. Without a doubt, she had just received the verbal version of a Dear John letter.

"Mattie, please don't—"

"I'd like for you to leave, Joe," she interrupted, blinking rapidly to ward off the tears welling up in her eyes. "I need time to think about what you've said—and haven't said."

Joe eased from bed and grabbed his discarded clothes. He'd known this wasn't going to be easy, so he had rehearsed it a half-dozen times, a half-dozen different ways. Not that it helped, because some things never came out right.

This was definitely one of those things.

Well, he just needed to give her time to adjust to the idea, he tried to reassure himself. Hopefully, the shock of his announcement would wear off, and he could make a few more attempts to smooth things over, to convince her that he would call, that he would be back each weekend.

Surely when he showed up Friday night she would realize that he was sincere...wouldn't she? And he would keep coming back every weekend until she realized that she could depend on him to be there. Then, he would tell her the truth, the whole truth—every last, damning word of it.

God, he dreaded that more than the explanation of

phase one of the plan to acknowledge that *he* was *her* corporate boss and that it had no bearing whatsoever on how he truly felt about her.

With only a quiet good-night that received no response, Joe made his way toward home, then changed direction at the last minute. Although it was late, he made a beeline for his truck and headed out to Paradise Valley. He needed an ally—Pops. He had to make Pops understand that he wasn't brushing off Mattie, no matter what she told Pops to the contrary.

Joe cruised into the parking lot at Paradise Valley, then skulked along the west wing to tap on Pops's window. He waited a few seconds, then tapped again.

"Fred? That you? What the hell are you doing out there? Our great escape to the bowling alley isn't scheduled until tomorrow night. I swear your memory isn't what it used to be!"

Troubled though he was, Joe smiled and poked his head in the window Pops had opened. "It's Joe, Pops. Can I crawl in and talk to you for a minute?"

"Joe?" Pops whispered. "Tarnation, boy. I thought it was one of the Roland Gang who was prowling around in the dark. Haul your butt in here, but be quiet about it."

Joe slung a leg over the windowsill, then climbed inside. Miserable though he felt, he smiled when he noticed Pops had the latest issue of *Playboy* laying on the bed beside him.

Pops was definitely *not* reading the articles, Joe decided. No, the old coot was gawking at the pictures.

8

Pops TUCKED his racy magazine under his pillow, then settled comfortably on his bed. "What brought you out here in the middle of the night?"

Joe plunked into the wobbly old recliner, then, with a scowl, he realized that he'd left Mattie's house in such a flaming rush that he had buttoned his wrinkled shirt haphazardly. He probably looked as wrung out as he felt. He only hoped the old man's eyesight wasn't acute enough to notice.

"I need your help," Joe burst out.

Pops, dressed in his baggy blue pajamas, linked his gnarled fingers together to pillow his head. "Sure thing, Joe. What can I do for you?"

Joe leaned forward in the chair, forearms braced on his knees, gaze focused intently on Pops. "I have to leave town to attend to unfinished business. I don't think Mattie believes I'll be back, though I have tried to assure her that I will. I was hoping I could count on you to insure that she doesn't start thinking negative thoughts."

Pops's brows shot up. "Leaving Fox Hollow? Why would anybody in his right mind leave a paradise like this?" His gaze narrowed suspiciously. "You got some filly waiting in the wings that I don't know about, boy?"

"No, absolutely not," Joe assured him adamantly.

"What I do have is a business that needs my attention after a month's absence. I tried to explain to Mattie, but I think she thinks I'm hightailing it out of town, never to be seen or heard from again."

"Will you be?" Pops grilled him, his gaze probing and intense.

"Hell yes! But only on weekends, until I can get things squared away in the city."

"Are you toying with my girl, Joe?" Pops raised up on one bony elbow, then shook an arthritic fist threateningly. "Better not be, boy. I may be old, but I haven't forgotten how to throw a punch if one needs to be thrown. I'll not have my girl hurt, not by anybody."

The prospect of Pops decking him would have been amusing if Joe hadn't been roiling with turmoil. "No, I'm trying to play for keeps here, but things are pretty damned complicated. Bad as I hate to, I have to proceed in the proper sequence of events before I can return to ask Mattie if she'll marry me."

"You tell her that? That marriage part?" Pops asked.

Joe shook his head. "She stopped listening, stopped believing, about the time I got to the part about calling her every night and returning on weekends," he grumbled sourly.

Pops reached for the pitcher beside the bed, then poured himself a drink of ice water. "You've got to remember that Mattie was left behind as a kid. She heard the same kind of promises from her parents about calling regularly and returning for visits. Only it never happened. She got stuck with me and her grandmother. I did my best to raise Mattie, but she kept waiting for calls and visits that never came. Then she grew up enough to realize some promises were never meant to be kept, to realize the empty promises are the ones that hurt the most. My guess is that you must have hit a raw nerve with her. It'll take time and effort to convince her that you aren't abandoning her, that you aren't offering the same empty promises her parents made to her.''

Joe groaned, remembering that comment Mattie had made about empty promises the first day they met. He hadn't realized what a touchy subject that had been. He had been standing on top of a land mine and hadn't realized it.

''Damn, I wish I'd known all that beforehand. I might have tried a different approach with her. In my case, no promises were offered before my parents dumped me off at my grandparents' house, then hightailed it off, separately, to find their own happiness.''

''Well, I'll try to help Mattie keep the faith in you, Joe, but if you make a liar out of me, you'll have to deal with the Roland Gang. You have to know that my friends are as fond of Mattie as I am. She's about the only one who cares enough to stop in for a visit with Fred, Herman, Ralph and Glen. So that sort of makes her like family to all of them, see?''

''I understand. So, if I screw up I've lost every friend I've made here, because of everybody's affection for Mattie,'' Joe paraphrased.

''That's it in a nutshell, boy,'' Pops confirmed. ''That granddaughter of mine has touched too many lives here in Fox Hollow.''

That wasn't news to Joe. He had figured that out the first week of his stay.

Joe rose from the chair to shake Pops's hand. ''I

appreciate all the support you can give while I get this mess straightened out.''

"But you won't say what the mess is. Sounds a little fishy to me, Joe."

"Complicated," Joe clarified.

"Fishy," Pops repeated emphatically. "So, when are you leaving town?"

"Wednesday."

"So...the trip to the bowling alley is still on for tomorrow?" Pops asked.

"Yes, it will be our last fling before I return to the city. I'll only be able to drop by for short excursions on weekends for the next month or so."

"I'll hold you to that," Pops said, staring surreptitiously at Joe.

Joe slipped out the window he'd come in and walked silently through the darkness to reach his truck. Loneliness crowded in on him as he drove off into the night. He decided he better get used to the feeling of loneliness, because he would be sleeping alone until he left town in the middle of the week—and every night thereafter. He could feel the distance expanding between him and Mattie, knowing she had lost faith in him.

But hell! How was he supposed to handle this convoluted situation? He couldn't wait until closing time on Wednesday to spring the news on her. She already thought that he'd taken her out on the town this evening as a prelude to the big kiss-off. Damn it, that was what he had been trying to *prevent* her from thinking!

Grimly Joe strode into his apartment. He considered calling Gramps, just to hear a sympathetic voice. Or maybe not. Gramps had advised getting at the truth sooner rather than later. No, Gramps probably wouldn't be very commiserating, now that Joe thought about it.

Joe thought he'd come up with a good plan to untangle this situation, but it would take time to execute the various phases. He was going to ease gradually into revealing his identity, to assure Mattie that his intentions toward her were honorable and sincere.

Damn, how was he to know that he'd offered her the same kind of promises she had heard from her parents before they hotfooted it out of her life and never bothered coming back?

Joe plopped down on the Hide-A-Bed and willed himself to sleep. That didn't work any better than willing Mattie to believe him when he offered her verbal guarantees she couldn't accept as truth.

It was several restless hours later before Joe dozed off into a fitful sleep.

IRRITABLE FROM LACK OF SLEEP, from the nagging sense of hurt and disappointment, Mattie got up and dressed for work. She wasn't sure how she was going to endure a second day of having Joe underfoot at the store. Yesterday she had pretended he didn't exist, took a wide berth around him and spent most of her time in the workroom, putting her frustration to good use on customized projects.

Joe had approached her several times, but she refused to let him within ten feet of her. He had been excessively polite and courteous to her, giving her no reason to snap his head off. Which was a damn shame, because that was exactly what she wanted to do.

He'd hurt her, damn it, and she couldn't imagine

feeling worse. He claimed he would return for the weekend but Mattie didn't believe him. From childhood experience, Mattie had learned how easily lies were spoken and how quickly promises were broken.

Practically numb from experiencing too much troubling emotion in a short amount of time, Mattie moved mechanically around the workroom. In an effort to get Joe out from underfoot, she had sent him over to Candice Green's home to hang the curio shelf and deliver the special-order nautical chest Mattie had decorated. Mattie suspected Candice would be thrilled to get Joe all to herself, since the woman had been making passes at him every chance she got.

When the chimes sounded at the front door, Mattie set aside her nail gun and ambled off to wait on the customer. She frowned curiously when an executive-type male, carrying an expensive black leather briefcase, and looking as if he had walked straight out of corporate America, glanced around, then spotted her. He pelted down the center aisle in his high-dollar suit, not a hair out of place despite the stiff morning breeze. Mattie had never had the slightest use for men who clung to power symbols like babies clung to security blankets.

"May I help you?" she asked.

"I certainly hope so," Eric Shaffer said as he turned up his nose at Mattie's casual attire of jeans and T-shirt. "Is the manager here?"

Obviously the suit thought she was a peon. She took extreme pleasure in saying, "You're talking to the manager."

The suit didn't bother concealing his smirk. "Oh. I came here looking for Daniel Grayson."

Daniel Grayson? The name rang a distant bell.

Mattie racked her brain for a moment. Grayson. Oh yes, that would be the head honcho of Hobby Hut Enterprises. Mattie had referred to the CEO as Double H for so long that she had almost forgotten his name. Now why in the world would the suit expect Daniel Grayson, the high king of woodcraft, to be down here in Fox Hollow, of all places?

"Daniel Grayson isn't here," Mattie assured Eric. "We are speaking of the CEO of Hobby Hut, aren't we?"

"None other," Eric said in a haughty voice that made Mattie gnash her teeth. "But I was told that I could find him here. I have to deliver an important message. It's imperative that I contact him. J.D. has been asking for his grandson."

J.D.? Mattie felt as if she had been gut-punched. She staggered unsteadily on her feet, then braced a hand against the cashier's counter. Oh, God, no! It couldn't be! Joe Gray couldn't possibly be Daniel *Grayson*...could he?

Mattie was still gripping the counter for support, her mind spinning like a windmill, when the chimes clattered again. Dazed, she glanced over her shoulder to see Joe wedging his way through the door, carrying two empty boxes in his hands. Obviously Candice had approved all the crafts and figurines Mattie selected for her wall hangings.

"Eric, what are you doing here?" The moment the careless question was out of Joe's mouth he wanted to yank it back, wanted to pretend he didn't know this upstart executive.

Joe's gaze shot to Mattie, who looked as if she were staring at a monster that was about to gobble her alive. Apparently, she had already been doing the math, calculating that Joe wasn't who she thought he was. The haunted, disbelieving look in Mattie's wide violet eyes was like a lance through Joe's heart.

Joe was dead meat. Roadkill. No doubt about it, there would be hell to pay here today.

His heart dropped to his feet when Mattie, tears swimming in her eyes, stared at him as if he were Judas and Benedict Arnold rolled into one traitorous, devious, despicable, two-headed monster. Joe wasn't sure what a panic attack felt like, but he predicted he was having one. He couldn't breathe properly, and his heart was pattering like a bongo drum.

"D.J., thank goodness I've found you," Eric said, moving swiftly down the center aisle.

"D.J.?" Mattie crowed, glaring chain saws at Joe. "As in Daniel *Jo*seph *Gray*son. The reverse of J.D.? Joseph Daniel?"

She jerked herself upright, fists knotted at her sides, her body rigid as a flagpole. "How could you? Why did you? Lord, when I think of all the laughs you had at my expense..."

Her voice evaporated when all the comments and complaints she'd made to Joe about the great Double H of Double H came back to haunt her. She had mocked his rules, his corporate decrees, and she had spouted off a dozen times how she would run the enterprise if *she* were in command.

Oh, God! Joe Gray was D.J. Grayson's alter ego. He was a deceitful, sneaky corporate spy who had come here to evaluate his store manager and had decided to get his kicks from bedding her since she was so hopelessly naive, so inexperienced in worldly matters, so hopelessly infatuated with him. She had been nothing but fun and games to him, and he had been the real deal to her. Only he wasn't the real deal at all, she thought wildly. The man she had fallen in love with didn't even exist!

The pain of betrayal and humiliation axed through her. Mattie careened sideways. Her knees banged together like cymbals. Oh, God, oh God! She loved Joe, gave her heart to him, and he had manipulated her, lied to her, used her!

She had stupidly thought that nothing could possibly be worse than the brush-off he had given her a couple of days ago. Well, she was wrong. This was a hundred-thousand times worse—and still counting!

"Mattie, let me—"

Mattie wheeled around and dashed to the workroom. She refused to listen to more lies. There was nothing Joe could say to compensate for her mortification and outrage. Mattie was so embarrassed that she seriously considered taking a saw, cutting a hole in the floor and dropping out of sight!

"Mattie!" Joe called as she sprinted into the workroom without looking back.

"D.J., I need to speak with you," Eric insisted. He grabbed Joe's arm when he tried to chase down Mattie. "This is about J.D. He asked me to contact you."

Joe stopped trying to break Eric's hold on his arm. He lurched around, his gaze filleting his junior executive. "J.D. couldn't have sent you here. He promised to give me a month away from the office without you and the other executives hassling me."

Eric looked affronted for a moment, then managed to gather his composure. "D.J....er...Mr. Grayson, sir, J.D. wanted me to call you, but I decided to come here in person."

"Well, I sure as hell wish you had called," Joe

muttered, his gaze locked on the door of the workroom. "What the hell do you and my grandfather want?"

Eric turned the color of his starched white shirt. "I'm sorry, but you need to know that J.D. had a heart attack last night. He managed to dial 911 and get help. But his condition is serious enough that he wanted you there with him."

Joe felt as if he was being pulled in two directions at once. Joe would move heaven and earth to be there with Gramps. However, if not for the bungling Eric Shaffer, and his attempt to put himself on Joe's good side, a quick call to the store would have had Joe racing off immediately to reach the hospital. In fact, Joe would have been in the city, sitting at J.D.'s bedside long before now if Eric would have simply picked up the damn phone and placed the call.

Furthermore, Mattie wouldn't have accidentally discovered what Joe had planned to work up to in gradual phases to prevent her from going ballistic, which she just had, thanks to Eric, damn his hide!

"I brought my car," Eric said quickly. "I thought we might be able to go over a few business matters during the drive to the hospital."

Joe bared his teeth and clenched his fists, telling himself that he shouldn't bust Eric in the chops, though Joe couldn't think of anything that would satisfy him more. "Business matters?" he growled menacingly.

Eric shifted uneasily when Joe's glittering gaze bore down on him like a laser beam. "Well, yes, sir. Company matters, you know."

"Far as I'm concerned the company can go hang, and you can go hang with it!" Joe boomed furiously.

Eric was forever kissing up to him, brownnosing him. Hell's jingling bells! Joe wanted to beat this upstart executive blue and black—then do it all over again—for making this situation so much worse than it already was.

"Wait for me in the car," Joe said through clenched teeth. "And don't you dare bring up business when I get there. Got it?"

"Yes, sir...I mean...no, sir," Eric peeped like a sick chicken.

After Eric took off, his expensive Italian loafers slapping the tiled floor, Joe inhaled several deep, fortifying breaths. He was in a fine temper, but temper would only make this situation more explosive when he confronted Mattie. He figured *her* flaming temper would be volatile enough for them both.

Like a man headed to the guillotine, Joe approached the workroom. Mattie, it seemed, was determined to vent her angry frustration by working on her most recent project. Her back was to him, her spine fused with tension, her taut legs braced, her attention focused on the pieces of lumber she was assembling for a heart-shaped plant stand.

Joe strived for the softest, calmest, noncombative tone he could muster. "Mattie, I know this looks bad, and I'm dreadfully sorry. But this isn't—"

She wheeled around, nail gun in hand, murder in her eyes. Joe winced, fully aware of Mattie's skill with power tools. Judging by the expression on her animated features, he expected to be nailed to the wall—literally.

"Don't you ever speak to me again, Daniel Joseph Grayson," she spat furiously. "You *lied* to me, you *deceived* me, you *spied* on me, and you—" Her breath hitched and tears bled down her flushed cheeks. "And you *used* me. Like the absolute idiot, the naive fool that I am, I fell in love with you. I'm sure you hadn't expected that, in addition to the free sex you got during your spy mission. But not to worry, D.J.," she said in an irate hiss. "As much as I thought I loved you before, I couldn't despise you more than I do now, and will continue till the day I die. Or till the day you die, whichever comes first!"

Chest heaving, eyes snapping, despite the streaming tears, she raised the nail gun threateningly. "Now get the hell out of my store. And it still is *my* store, until you find a manager to replace me. Oh, and by the way, don't bother firing me, because I quit!" she blared at him.

Her booming voice blasted his eardrums. Her glare fried him to a crisp. Yet Joe refused to leave until he said what he had come to say, what he felt compelled to say. "I love you, Mattie."

His timing couldn't have been worse. If he'd had half a brain—which he obviously didn't—he would have known she wouldn't believe him when his heartfelt confession came so closely on the heels of what she considered the queen mother of betrayal.

"Oh, that's rich, rich man." She scoffed sarcastically and waved the nail gun wildly. "Do you tell all of your little managerial playthings whom you spy on that you love them, after you have finished using them? What is that supposed to be? Some kind of sick-minded compensation?"

"No…I mean…I don't spy on everybody," he said hurriedly.

"Just me? Well, rooty-toot-toot, aren't I the lucky one?" As if she just recalled she still had a potential weapon in her hand, she swung it toward him, aiming directly at his crotch. "Get out of here before I turn you into the twinkie that Buck Reynolds and his buddies think you are."

"I'll leave," he assured her. "But I wanted you to know that my grandfather had a heart attack. If not for that, I would stay to work this out."

Sympathy and concern filled her watery eyes momentarily, then she thrust out her chin and glared at him—again. "I'm sorry about J.D. I'm fond of him. I'm sure it makes his condition worse, knowing that he has a low-down, dirty, rotten, devious spy for a grandson. Did your well-dressed, well-heeled junior executive drive down here to tell you what happened to J.D.?"

"Yes, and I wish like hell that Eric would have picked up the phone and called," Joe muttered in a resentful tone.

Mattie smirked caustically. "Of course you do, for several reasons, I suspect. What a shame that I discovered who you really are and what a fool I've made of myself. Now get out!"

"Mattie, I don't want you to quit. You have been named Employee of the Year," he told her.

She barked a hysterical laugh. "Oh, gee, what a wonderful consolation prize. That makes me feel *sooo* much better." Her eyes narrowed into angry slits when a suspicious thought leaped to mind. "Or did you come here to investigate and spy on your Employee of the Year because you thought I was tampering with the sales reports to gain recognition?"

"Of course not." Damn, she was so mistrusting of him now that she was trying to make something devious of everything he said and did.

Mattie smirked at him. "I don't believe you. Now...get...out!"

"I'm not leaving until you agree to discuss this situation after I've checked on Gramps," he insisted.

She skewered him with a glower. "Then you better put on your waiting shoes, Mr. Grayson, because there will be glaciers in hell before I agree to listen to anything you have to say!"

Joe's shoulders slumped. He knew a lost cause when he was staring it in the face. Mattie was lost to him. The evidence against him was damning. Hell, if he were defending himself in a court of law, he wouldn't have given a plugged nickel for his chances of redemption.

"Goodbye, Mattie," he murmured.

"Good riddance, Double H," she flung hatefully.

Joe turned and walked away, feeling as if he had left the best part of himself—the only part of himself that really mattered—behind. Joe Gray was dead and gone, buried beneath the hatred in Mattie's tear-filled eyes. His hopes, his dreams, his best-laid plans scattered around him like the debris left in the wake of a tornado.

DANIEL STARED DOWN at his grandfather, who was sprawled in the hospital bed. The beep and hiss of machines were the only sounds to break the silence. According to the attending physician, J.D. had suffered a mild heart attack that would keep him immobilized for a few weeks. The thought of losing Gramps had hounded Daniel during the tormenting forty-five-minute drive to the city.

Eric hadn't dared to open his trap during the trip, not while Daniel sat there brooding on the passenger side of the car. But like the bootlicking, corporate puppy he was, Eric trailed after Daniel when he rode the elevator up to the room to check on Gramps. Still Eric was lingering in the corner, expecting to acquire a few brownie points for remaining dutifully by his boss's side during the time of crisis.

Daniel eased into the chair beside the bed, then wrapped his hand around J.D.'s wrist. "Gramps, I'm here," he whispered.

J.D.'s eyes fluttered open and he smiled weakly. "Knew you would be, boy, soon as you could. Sorry for the inconvenience. Promised you a thirty-day hiatus, but I blew it. How's Mattie? Pops and the gang?"

"Fine." Well, most of them anyway. Mattie he wasn't sure about. He had only to close his eyes, and he could see the tormented, humiliated look on her pixielike features. He had broken her trust and that was something a woman like Mattie couldn't forgive. He had witnessed the full spectrum of emotional upheaval in her fit of temper. In her eyes he had betrayed, manipulated, deceived and used her. He didn't know if she would ever recover enough to listen when he tried to explain.

Sure she would, came that snide little voice inside him. Give her about a million years or so, and she'll come around. Like she said, when glaciers are icing down hell.

"Did you tell her the truth?" J.D. whispered hoarsely.

Daniel shook his head. "Didn't have the chance. Blabbermouth Shaffer over there in the corner blurted it out before I had all my plans carefully in place so

I could explain in a manner that I hoped she would be receptive to.''

Daniel shot Eric a glare hot enough to melt steel. "You're fired, by the way, Shaffer. Clear out of your office by Monday.'' When Eric stood there, his briefcase clutched in his fist, his face white as salt, Daniel gestured toward the door, as if Eric was too dense to figure out where it was. "Out!''

Eric skulked away, much to Daniel's bitter satisfaction.

"A little hard on junior, weren't you, Deeje?'' Gramps asked.

"No,'' Daniel growled. "He's lucky I didn't strangle him. The imbecile used your condition as an opportunity to butter me up. Instead of calling the store and saving me time, he drove down to Fox Hollow to bring me the news, carrying his briefcase so we could discuss business on the way back. As if I thought he'd actually done the slightest bit of work during my absence. Hell's fire, that upstart hasn't done squat since I hired him eighteen months ago, except hover around the coffeepot and rearrange papers on his desk like some big shot. Instead of firing him, I probably should have sent him up to one of our stores in Nebraska where it gets cold enough to freeze that smarmy smile on his lips.''

J.D. grinned. "He's pretty full of himself. Never did have much use for the man, either, if you want the truth. Waste of a good salary.''

Daniel slouched in his chair. He was emotionally spent, physically exhausted because of the tension prowling through him. He felt a dozen years older and a hundred years wiser. The confrontation with Mattie had taught him things he didn't want to know.

Things like: Twisted truths and half lies formed the strands of rope that were exactly the right length for you to hang yourself.

"Just close your eyes and rest, Gramps," Daniel whispered. "I'll be here, kicking myself into next week and back for royally fouling up things with Mattie. If you need anything, just let me know."

J.D. nodded, then closed his eyes. "Only a damn fool would give up on a good woman like Mattie, no matter what a man has to do to win her back," he murmured before he drifted off to sleep.

Win her back? Now there was a laugh, thought Daniel. You couldn't win back a woman who couldn't be bought, who refused to listen. Besides, there wasn't enough money in the federal treasury to purchase the trust Daniel had destroyed. The way Daniel figured it, his chances were slim and none—and slim was entirely too optimistic.

Maybe Daniel couldn't return to Mattie's good graces, but he could compensate in every way imaginable. He was still going to follow through with the plan, put phase two into immediate motion. Mattie might go on hating him as long as he lived, but he was still going to do his good deeds.

Resolved to compensating as much as possible, Daniel picked up the phone to make several calls. Then he sat by J.D.'s side throughout the day and the night, offering Gramps moral support, encouraging the old man to rest so he could get back on his feet eventually.

9

MATTIE CURSED COLORFULLY when the delivery boy carted in another flower arrangement, courtesy of Daniel Joseph Grayson—the jerk. Every day for the past two weeks, flowers had arrived at the store. The message enclosed was always the same. "I'm sorry. I want you back. Daniel J. Grayson."

Some secretary had obviously ordered the flowers at Mr. Hotshot CEO's request. Double H was probably too busy to bother with the task himself, even though he wanted her to remain manager. That's what he meant when he said that he wanted her back.

Mattie had seen the sales figures lots of times, and she knew her store did a thriving business. Apparently, Daniel J. had come to spy on his Employee of the Year to find out *why*, to find out *if* she was breaking any of his precious rules, then uncover her secret to success. Well, she hoped it dawned on him that her love of arts and crafts, her attentiveness to customers' special needs made all the difference. If that sneaky, underhanded CEO figured out nothing else, she sure as hell hoped he figured that out.

"Just put the flowers over there." Mattie indicated an empty space beside the cash register.

The previous week Mattie had hauled the bouquets and arrangements to the local parcel post office and begged a favor from a friend who worked there. The young man had agreed to deliver the flowers to J.D. Grayson, in care of Hobby Hut Enterprises. She enclosed a note indicating that she wished J.D. a speedy recovery and that Daniel J. should spend his money on someone who meant a great deal to him. And that someone certainly wasn't her!

Mattie rolled her eyes in frustration when Candice Green pranced into the store, wearing another of her painted-on knit top and short-shorts ensembles.

"Is Joe here?" Candice asked, craning her neck to locate Joe.

"No, he doesn't work here anymore." Silently she added, *In fact, the man simply disappeared. Pfft!* It was as if he never really existed, which he hadn't. Daily, Mattie reminded herself that the man she had fallen in love with was a figment of her imagination, sort of like a fictitious character in a book.

"Joe quit?" Candice chirped. "Well, darn. I was hoping he could come by and help me rearrange my interior decorations. He has a wonderful knack for such things."

Didn't he though? He should have, being the all-powerful king of woodcraft that he was.

"Well, it sure is a shame about Joe leaving, it surely is," Candice went on—and on. "Just the sweetest man, you know? But I guess you already knew that." She sent Mattie a pitying glance. "I guess things got complicated around here when he tired of you. Suppose he had no choice but to move on. Dating the hired help never works out, does it?"

Mattie smiled past her irritation. "No. Is there something I can do for you, Candice?"

"No." She twirled around and sashayed down the

aisle. "I'll be back when I feel the urge to redecorate."

Relieved to have Candice gone, Mattie watched the woman's drumroll walk take her through the door. Now that there was a lull in the store Mattie could focus her concentration on hating Daniel J. Grayson and the fact that he had single-handedly ruined her life. Not only that, but he would force her to make a move she didn't want to make. When he finally got it through his thick skull that she refused to work for him, he would send a replacement. Then Mattie would leave the town where she had grown up. Relocating and finding a similar job would be difficult, but packing up Pops? The prospect didn't bear thinking about!

Mattie blinked in surprise when she saw her grandfather, with his friends on his heels, hobble into the shop. "What are you doing here?" she questioned, bewildered.

"We caught a ride into town in the new van," Pops reported. "Fanciest thing you ever did see, Shortcake."

"New van?" Mattie parroted.

"Joe donated it to Paradise Valley so we can get out and kick up our heels when we feel like it," Glen said delightedly.

"And that's not all," Herman spoke up as he tipped his head back so he could stare through his bifocals at the figurines on the shelf. "Joe started construction on a pond that he plans to build so we can stock it with fish. We won't have to hike off the grounds to the river when we're in the mood for a couple of hours of fishing."

Mattie's mouth dropped open. "You're kidding."

"Nope," Pops confirmed. "He called to tell me himself."

Mattie's eyes narrowed. She smelled a bribe. Butter up the Roland Gang so they would convince her to stay on as manager of the local Hobby Hut. That money-wheeling cad was appealing to Pops and company so they would side with him. Well, she suspected no less from that sneaky creep.

"Pops, may I have a private word with you?"

"Sure thing, Shortcake." Pops hobbled down the aisle so they would be out of earshot. "What's up?"

"Have you forgotten that I explained to you that there is no Joe Gray?"

"My memory works fine," Pops assured her.

"Then you remember that I told you that he is the owner of the company, and he came down here to spy on me," Mattie muttered resentfully. "You are letting the man buy your loyalty to him."

Pops waved off her protests. "First off, I'm too old to learn new names, so Joe is still Joe to me. Secondly, he told me in confidence that he had complications to work out but that he would be back. But since poor ol' J.D. got laid up in the hospital when his ticker tried to quit on him, it's understandable that Joe hasn't made it back to Fox Hollow." He stared steadily at her. "Would you leave my bedside if I was laid up in the hospital with all those contraptions plugged into me, Shortcake?"

"No, of course not."

"Well then, there you go. So Joe's doing the next best thing since he can't be here in person. He calls me every night because he says you won't respond to the messages he's left on your answering machine, and he's doing things to make life more pleasant for us at the convalescent home.''

It was still bribery, in Mattie's book, and she wasn't going to be taken in by Daniel J. ever again. The man had faxed her, flowered her, and called her dozens of times, but she refused to speak to him. If Pops got all sorts of gadgets, vans and fishing ponds from that jerk, fine and dandy. But Mattie was not going to play his games, and she was not giving him the opportunity to ply her with more lies.

She could not be bought or persuaded! The hotshot CEO would figure that out sooner or later.

"And get this, Mattie girl," Pops added. "Next week, Joe is having a big-screen TV delivered to the lobby, along with a VCR so we can watch shows and movies without squinting at the piddling little screen we have now. Never had a big screen before. I bet it's really going to be something. Not only that, but he's ordered a bunch of those fancy-schmancy electrical recliners that stand you right up when you're done sitting down.''

Mattie swore under her breath. Pops and his gang were like children with new playground equipment to entertain them. Daniel J. certainly was a master at buying loyalty and devotion and influencing people. He threw his money around, and she didn't doubt for a minute that he expected favors in return.

"So, when are you going to get over being mad and return Joe's calls?" Pops demanded to know.

"When hell looks like Antarctica. That should be soon enough," Mattie said, then scowled.

"Aw, c'mon, Shortcake. I keep telling you Joe is one of the good guys. Would I lie to you? Give the man a second chance.''

"Yeah, I'm sure this was all a big misunderstanding," Glen said as he poked his head around the corner, from where he and the rest of the old men had been eavesdropping.

"Joe wouldn't go to all this effort and expense if he didn't care about the whole bunch of us," Ralph put in.

Mattie wasn't buying any of this nonsense. If anything, Joe was soothing his conscience, which was probably on life support, provided it still lived and breathed at all. He was spending money freely for the intent and purpose of convincing Mattie to stay on as store manger. He had finagled and bought favors so the Roland Gang would hound her and put pressure on her to forgive Daniel J.

Sooner or later, Mattie knew she was going to have to contact Daniel J. in a written resignation to inform him that she was not staying in Fox Hollow, no matter how many schemes he devised to convince her otherwise. She would find a job and commute so she could visit Pops until he was dismissed from the home. Of course, now that Paradise Valley was becoming one of the most elite convalescent homes in the state, thanks to all the money Daniel J. was pouring into it, Pops probably wouldn't want to leave at all.

Damn the man for using her grandfather and his friends against her, she fumed. Mattie was definitely going to let Daniel J. have it with both barrels for that!

DANIEL PLOPPED into the chair in J.D.'s hospital room, scowling at the most recent delivery of returned flowers that he had sent to Mattie. The card she included said the same thing as last time. "Give the flowers to J.D. You obviously care about him, not me."

For three weeks Daniel had kept his promise to call every day, though he hadn't returned on weekends because he wanted to remain by his ailing grandfather's side. Truly, Daniel was at his wit's end. Mattie refused to return his calls and ignored the faxes. The only progress Daniel had made was with the Roland Gang, who kept telling him not to give up on Mattie. But damnation, nothing he did persuaded Mattie to speak to him.

"Still no luck?" J.D. asked when he awoke from his nap.

"No," Daniel said grimly. "I may as well beat my head against a brick wall. It would do as much good as trying to get Mattie on the phone so I can apologize and explain."

"Well, boy, I guess you're going to have to resort to the same tactic I was forced to use on your grandmother fifty years ago," J.D. decided.

Daniel glanced up, startled. "You had to convince Gram to marry you by using drastic measures?"

J.D. smiled. "Sure did. Ester thought I cared more about making money than about her. She turned me down twice, and I got desperate because I realized that I needed her more than I needed to become successful in the furniture business."

Daniel leaned forward, on the edge of his seat. "So what did you do to convince her that she mattered to you, Gramps?"

J.D. pushed the remote control to elevate the head of the bed so he could prop himself up. "I kidnapped her."

Daniel blinked in disbelief. "You did what?"

"You heard me, boy. I spirited her off into the woods and even had to tie her up to make her stay and listen to what I had to say," J.D. reported. "All you have to do is rent one of those cabins down by the lake and hold Mattie hostage until you've assured her that you are sincere and that you mean business."

"Right." Daniel smirked. "That tactic may have worked fifty years ago, but I would probably get hauled to jail for abducting Mattie. Then I would be in a worse mess that I am now, not to mention leaving myself wide-open for news reporters who feast on gossip and scandal."

J.D. grinned. His eyes had finally regained their usual sparkle, much to Daniel's relief. "You can pull this off if you make prior arrangements."

"The Roland Gang," Daniel said thoughtfully.

"Exactly. You'll also need to make arrangements for someone to man Hobby Hut during Mattie's captivity. Cover all your bases so you'll have Mattie alone long enough to say everything that needs to be said. You realize, of course, that a certain amount of groveling will be required to pull this off."

For the first time in three weeks Daniel felt a glimmer of hope rising from the ashes of despair. True, J.D.'s scheme was drastic, but Daniel was about as desperate as a man could get. Knowing Mattie despised him was equivalent to having his heart yanked out by the tap root and expected to go on living this empty existence.

"I'll do it," he said decisively.

J.D. beamed in delight. "That's my boy. The doctor said he would release me in the morning. I have decided to do my recuperating at Paradise Valley. Can you arrange for me to get a room there?''

Daniel gaped at his grandfather. "You're sure you're up to the trip?"

"Hell yes, it would take us forty minutes to drive home through rush-hour traffic. It doesn't take but a few minutes longer to drive to Fox Hollow. Since you've made all those generous donations to the convalescent home, I'd like to see what the place looks like now. Plus, I've got a hankering to rejoin the Roland Gang."

Daniel stared somberly at his grandfather. "You're sure this is what you want to do? You're health comes first, Gramps. I don't want my problems to influence your decision."

J.D. stared just as somberly at his grandson. "Are you certain that getting Mattie back is exactly what *you* want? You aren't trying to make amends, just because your conscience is bothering you, are you?"

Daniel didn't need time to think that over. Three weeks without his daily recommended requirement of Mattie's enthusiasm and infectious spirit were three weeks of pure, tormenting hell, and he had been suffering all the torments of the damned. Daniel knew what he wanted, needed—desperately. "Very sure, Gramps. She is the one and only."

J.D. grinned in satisfaction. "Then what the blazes are you doing, moping around in here? You've got arrangements to make. Get at them!"

Daniel sprang from his chair, spurred by his grandfather's words. He might get shot down again, but, by damned, Daniel wasn't going down without one hell of a fight!

MATTIE FLIP-FLOPPED IN BED, counting flocks of sheep, then cursed the insomnia that kept her awake night after tormenting night. She was suffering separation anxiety from a man who wasn't worth the wasted emotion. Her theory that time would heal her heartache and disillusionment wasn't working worth a damn. Furthermore, sleep deprivation was making her cross and cranky. Twice, she had even snapped at customers who had become wishy-washy about what they wanted for their personalized woodcraft projects. Mattie never did that—until Daniel J. Grayson's torturous memory played havoc with her temperament.

Curse that man's devious hide! He had turned her world upside down, then sent it caroming sideways. Mattie couldn't eat, couldn't sleep, couldn't function in her customary, cheerful manner.

A sound thump at the door brought Mattie straight up in bed. She glanced at the digital clock on the nightstand. It was two-fifteen in the morning. Her first thought was that Pops's diabetic condition had flared up again and that a staff member had arrived to bring her bad news.

Frantic, Mattie bounded from bed. Wearing her threadbare, oversize T-shirt that served as her nightgown, she raced, barefoot, down the hall. When she whipped open the front door, she didn't see anyone waiting on the porch.

Before she could close the door, a blanket—held by she didn't know whom—dropped over her head. She shrieked and cursed and fought like a wildcat, for all the good it did her. She found herself bound up like a mummy, restrained by duct tape that held her arms to her sides and clamped her knees together.

Mattie screamed bloody murder.

"Calm down, Mattie, I have no intention of hurting you."

Mattie froze up like a block of ice. "Joe? I mean...Daniel J? What the hell do you think you're doing!" she yelled through the quilt.

"Kidnapping you," he said pleasantly.

Mattie squawked when she was abruptly tossed over his shoulder and carried down the steps. Blood rushed to her head when she was toted, wrong side up, across the lawn. To her excessive frustration she heard the murmur of other voices nearby—and she had a pretty good idea who those voices belonged to. The traitorous gang of turncoats!

"Pops? Is that you and your friends?" Mattie called through the blanket.

"Sure is, Shortcake," Pops replied.

"Well, for crying out loud, call the police!" Mattie demanded.

"Can't," Pops said. "I'm an accomplice to this crime."

Mattie silently fumed. The Roland Gang had definitely been bought out by the high-and-mighty CEO of Hobby Hut. Daniel's outreach to the elderly program had produced the self-seeking results he wanted.

Mattie swore inventively when Daniel J. shifted her into his arms then plunked her down on what she assumed to be the leather seat of a car. The vehicle smelled new, though she had never owned anything except a used car and couldn't say for certain what a new model smelled like.

"Pops, if you don't do something to stop whatever it is that's going on, I refuse to speak to you for the rest of your life!" Mattie shouted.

Pops grinned, then glanced at Daniel. "Told you she'd be PO'd, didn't I?"

"I mean it, Pops. If the Roland Gang is along for this ride, I'm never going to speak to them again, either!"

"Now, girl, you know we wouldn't do anything to hurt you," Glen assured her as he eased down on the back seat beside her. "This is just another grand adventure. No harm done here."

Mattie sputtered a few more obscenities under her breath when the Roland Gang piled into the getaway car and slammed the doors. "You can tell Daniel J. that I fully intend to press charges against him, first chance I get."

"Tell who?" Pops questioned as the car sped away.

"Joe," Mattie muttered.

"Oh, yeah, I keep forgetting his real name." He turned to Daniel, who was steering his BMW down the highway. "Joe, Mattie says she intends to press charges against you. I gather she is refusing to speak directly to you."

"Tell her that I'm taking my chances with the law," Daniel replied.

Pops twisted around to glance into the back seat. "Joe said—"

"I heard what he said," Mattie snapped angrily. "Where are we going?"

"You'll find out when we get there," Daniel told her.

Mattie gnashed her teeth until she nearly ground off the enamel. "Tell Daniel J. that he better hope and pray that I don't get loose, because I plan to claw out his eyes."

"Vicious little thing, isn't she?" Pops snickered. "Hope you're wearing body armor, Joe. I think you might need it."

For fifteen minutes Mattie issued one threat after another and received nothing in response except snickers and wisecracks from the old coots who Daniel J. had undoubtedly bribed with expensive gadgets to improve their living conditions at the nursing home.

Finally the car came to a stop and the old men piled out.

"Okay, Pops, you know the plan," Daniel said. "You drive my car to the convalescent home and sneak back to your rooms. I'll contact you later."

"Is it okay if Ralph drives this fancy cars of yours?" Pops asked. "I've been bothered by night blindness for years. Ralph sees better in the dark than I do."

"Yeah, but we all know that Ralph gets disoriented easily," Herman put in. "He's liable to get turned around and we'll end up in Dallas. No way do I want Ralph behind the wheel in that kind of traffic!"

"Well fine, we'll let Fred drive," Pops suggested.

"I don't know the way home," Fred spoke up. "I was riding in the back seat on the way out here, and I wasn't paying close attention."

"I know the way," Glen announced. "Want me to drive?"

"No!" shouted the rest of the Roland Gang in unison.

"Never mind," Daniel said. "I'll drop off Mattie, then I'll take you back to the home. You might need help crawling up the stepladder and easing into Pops's window anyway. If we leave the stepladder in plain sight, the director might get suspicious.''

"Good thinking, Joe," Pops replied. "Don't want him to catch on that we've being flying the coop on a regular basis.''

Mattie silently smoldered when Daniel dragged her across the seat, then hoisted her into his arms. A moment later she heard the rattle of a key in the lock, then the whine and creak of a door. The scent of flowers filtered through the quilt that prevented her from seeing where she was. Nevertheless, she suspected she was being stashed on a cot in one of the rented cabins near the lake.

"I'll be back in a jiffy, Mattie," Daniel assured her.

"Don't rush on my account, because I am definitely not speaking to you!"

"You just did," he reminded her, chuckling.

"Go to hell!"

"Where do you think I've been for the past month?" he asked before he closed the door and left her alone.

10

MATTIE MUTTERED a few more obscenities when she heard the car drive away. Why would Daniel claim to have been hellishly miserable the past month when *she* was the one suffering heartbreak and humiliation? Probably just another of his deceptive comments, she decided.

Determined not to be here when he returned, Mattie wiggled and squirmed to the edge of the bed. Swinging her legs to the floor, she leaned forward, then stood up. That accomplished, she hopped like a jackrabbit—until she banged into the wall. Turning her back, she hopped sideways, using the wall as her guide to locate the door.

No matter what, she was going to gain her freedom. Becoming lost in the woods was preferable to being alone with Daniel J. Grayson.

Several minutes later, Mattie bumped against the doorknob, then realized it was going to take some doing to twist the knob when her arms were strapped against her hips. Difficult though it was, Mattie grabbed the knob through the fabric of the quilt, contorted her body and gave a twist.

After several attempts the door creaked open, granting her precious freedom. Daniel J. Grayson, high king of woodcraft didn't think she would press charges, just because he had money and influence and had bribed her own grandfather and friends to help him? Boy, did that jerk have another think coming!

Mattie hopped onto the wooden porch, unsure how she would manage the steps—wherever they were. She sank down on her bottom, then stretched out her legs to locate the edge of the porch.

Smiling victoriously, she scooted sideways until she could feel grass beneath her bare feet. She had taken ten leaps forward when she heard the growl of an engine and saw the glare of headlights filtering through the blanket.

Damn it! Five more minutes and she would have been home free.

The engine died, the lights flicked off, and the door slammed shut.

"Good grief, woman, I go to extremes to get you alone so I can talk to you, and you risk breaking your neck to avoid me," Daniel grumbled as he approached.

"Let me go," Mattie snarled. "I have nothing to say to you—ever! Put me down, damn it!"

Despite her barked command, Daniel carried her back to the cabin, then deposited her on the cot. Mattie had hoped Daniel J. would cut the tape, thereby giving her another opportunity to make a run for it. Instead, he used scissors to cut a hole in the blanket so she could poke her head out.

Mattie blinked in stunned disbelief when she panned the cedar-paneled cabin. The place was decorated with the four new displays she had created for the windows at the store. Damn, the man had been busy stealing from his own shop, hadn't he?

Her gaze darted this way and that, noting the colorful flower arrangements that sat beside the sofa, easy chair, and on the dinette table. Even the counter of the small kitchenette was lined with flowers.

"The answer is still no," Mattie muttered as her gaze settled helplessly on Daniel's tall, masculine physique, which was wrapped in blue jeans and a chambray shirt. Damn, she wished she didn't find him so appealing. Willfully, she looked the other way. "You can torture me if that makes you happy, but I refuse to manage your store. Considering the amount of time you spent spying on me, I should think you would have picked up on why I was named Employee of the Year."

Daniel frowned, puzzled. "What has that got to do with anything?"

Mattie, forgetting she hadn't planned to speak to him for the rest of her life, snapped, "What do you mean what has that got to do with anything? Your notes that arrived with the flowers always read the same. 'I'm sorry. I want you back.'"

He stared at her for a long moment. "You really don't get it, do you?"

"Of course, I get it," she spat at him. "You came sneaking down here to see why I made so many sales. You probably suspected that I was doing something illegal in the process, too, and you wanted to catch me at it. But you know perfectly well that I did special orders for customers after hours, on my own time, and that I paid your company a consignment fee for every one of my paintings that I sold in connection with items from the shop. There was absolutely nothing illegal going on."

"I know that," Daniel assured her as he came to stand in front of her. "But wanting you back has nothing whatsoever to do with the store. If you want to resign, then that's your business, though you will be difficult to replace because you're so good at what you do.''

She blinked, confused. ''Then why all the flowers and cards that asked me not to resign?''

''The cards said that I wanted *you* back, Mattie,'' he said emphatically. ''Not as store manager. Just *you.*''

Now she got it. Didn't believe it, of course, but she got it. He was trying to make her feel better about herself so she wouldn't quit her job. ''Right.''

''I want what we had before everything blew up in my face,'' Daniel told her.

''Tough. I don't date devious, manipulative corporate executives,'' she reminded him harshly.

Daniel sighed in exasperation, then dragged a footstool over to the cot so he could sit down and confront her face-to-face. ''Let's begin at the beginning so you'll understand how this whole mess got started.''

''Fine, talk until you're blue in the face, if that makes you happy, but don't expect me to change my mind about you, Grayson,'' she warned uncompromisingly.

Daniel took a moment to organize his thoughts, then said, ''I came to Fox Hollow because I had practically burned out on the company Gramps and I started in the garage of his home. He and I poured our grief of losing my grandmother into creating the kind of woodcrafts she always loved. We sold our arts and crafts and the demands increased so rapidly that we opened a store and hired more help to keep up with orders. The business became so popular that we continued to expand until we had stores in five surrounding states.''

Mattie stopped glowering at him and began to listen. So far so good, Daniel thought to himself.

"I was reasonably satisfied running the corporation until last year when Gramps decided to retire. Before that, he and I could bounce ideas off each other and create new designs. But when Gramps left, I was stuck with people like Eric Shaffer, who care more about climbing the corporate ladder and brownnosing the boss than focusing brain power on creating unique crafts."

"Where did you find that clown anyway?" Mattie asked.

"He was fresh out of college, and he could talk a good story," Daniel explained. "But he and the other junior executives got into the annoying habit of agreeing with all my ideas, never offering suggestions or constructive criticism."

"The proverbial yes-men of corporate America," Mattie presumed.

"Precisely. I had to get away from that pandering atmosphere before I went nuts. I had to rediscover my enthusiasm for the company, so I decided that the Employee of the Year might be able to put me back in touch with the real reason Gramps and I went into business. So I sent a fax from my office, telling you to hire an assistant."

Mattie gaped at him. "*You* sent the fax, then arrived to fill the job you created?"

"Well yes, I didn't want someone else to beat me to it," he said.

Mattie shook her head in disgust. "Playing God must be tough work if you can get it."

Daniel winced. "I needed that job, Mattie. I needed to get back to the grass roots of this business. I didn't tell you who I was because I didn't want you to cater to me the way my executives do. That's the last thing I wanted after a steady diet at the office.'' He stared solemnly at her. ''In all honesty, can you tell me that you would have treated me like a regular Joe Schmo if you knew who I was?''

Mattie scowled. ''Probably not, but that doesn't excuse the fact that you spied on me, that I was being evaluated and investigated without prior knowledge.''

''You didn't need to be evaluated,'' he told her crisply. ''Hell, you are the Employee of the Year! And I was *not* investigating you, either, damn it!''

''Fine. Okay, I yield that point to you,'' she shot back. ''You were looking for an injection of enthusiasm. I presume I somehow gave you what you needed. But that doesn't mean I intend to forgive you for what you did to me personally.''

Daniel studied her bitter expression, then said softly, ''What did I do to you, Mattie?''

Her chin elevated a notch, and she blistered him with a glare. ''You made me fall in love with you. But it wasn't really you. It was a regular Joe who shared my love of woodcraft and art, a man who *appeared* to be content with the simple life in a laid-back community. Joe Gray never really existed. You misled me, you misrepresented yourself to me, you used my feelings for you for sexual gratification before you decided to take your newfound enthusiasm and hightail it back to your corporate world. You promised phone calls and visits that I didn't expect to come. You *hurt* me, damn it, and I can't forget that!''

Daniel nodded grimly. ''I would never have made those promises if I had known you had been plied with empty promises in your childhood.''

"I suppose I have Pops to thank for passing along that little tidbit of information," she said resentfully.

"Yes, I went directly to Pops after I told you that I was quitting the job and returning to the city," Daniel informed her. "If it's any consolation, guilt ate me alive each time you made a comment about Double H of Double H. I tried to tell you the truth several times, but like a coward, I was afraid I'd lose what we had together."

"The sex, you mean," she clarified. "I can't imagine why you were worried about losing one plaything when Candice Green would leap at the chance of volunteering for the assignment."

"I didn't want Candice," Daniel grumbled. "I wanted you, Mattie! Can't you get it through that wooden head of yours that it's you I want?"

"Why? Because I came with the store and I have a lively, lovable grandfather who amuses and entertains you during your off hours? You didn't want to lose the whole package, huh?"

Daniel vaulted to his feet to loom over her. Mattie noted that he was exceptionally good at it.

"Pay attention to me, Mattie," he snapped in irritation. "Everything I have done, whether or not it backfired in my face, I did because I wanted you back in my life. Not as store manager, though the position is still yours if you want it, but as the woman I want and need to make my life complete."

He bent at the waist to get right in her face. "Do you hear me? Do you understand me? *You*, Mattie. I love you, but I couldn't say those words while I was trapped in a lie of my own making, because that would have been another form of deceit you wouldn't be willing to forgive. I wanted you to love *me*. Joe and Daniel, because both of them are who I am.''

Mattie stared at him, stupefied. No one but Pops had ever claimed to love her. No one had ever yelled it at her, either, which was exactly what Daniel had done.

He loved her? *Her?* The tomboy of Fox Hollow?

''Don't give me that incredulous look, damn it,'' Daniel growled. ''It never ceases to amaze me that you, who are surrounded by devoted friends and acquaintances, can't understand that you are worthy of love, that you are a beautiful, alluring woman, even if you prefer power tools to power shopping.

''Just because your parents lit out and left you behind doesn't mean there's a damn thing wrong with you. Hell, my parents bailed out on me, too. True, they didn't offer empty promises to write, to call, or to visit occasionally. I knew right off the bat that my accidental birth was an inconvenience my parents weren't willing to accept when they went their separate ways. If you're not assured of your self-worth, then you are still allowing your irresponsible parents to influence your perception of yourself. They don't deserve that privilege!''

Mattie thought that over for a minute, or three. He was probably right. She probably did have a tendency to put herself in situations that made her feel needed, to compensate for the rejection she had experienced when her parents abandoned her. When the promised calls and visits that she lived for, hoped for, never came, she figured there was something very forgettable about her. Something about her that was difficult to love.

Daniel dropped to his knees in front of her, then

framed her face with his hands, forcing her to meet his gaze head-on. "I love you, Mattie Roland. I love the way you put so much of yourself into your paintings, your crafts. I love the way you treat your job like a compelling passion. I love the way you have taken the responsibility for your grandfather, just as he took responsibility for you.

"I share those exact same feelings for my grandfather. I understand that kind of loyalty, which is why I hightailed it to the city when I learned about Gramps's heart attack. That doesn't mean that I didn't want to stay and fight for what we had together, to explain why I did what I did. I was pulled two directions at once."

"How is J.D.?" she asked.

"Doing quite well, thank you for asking. He is convalescing at Paradise Valley. He's been there for a couple of days, but I wouldn't let him join the Roland Gang this evening, much to his dismay. I wasn't sure he was up to that just yet."

"Daniel, are you ever going to untie me?" she wanted to know.

"Eventually. When I get the answer I want from you."

"What's the question?"

"Am I forgiven for handling the situation badly, for delaying in telling you the truth because I was afraid you would react exactly the way you did?"

"You're forgiven. Now untie me," she demanded impatiently.

He shook his head. "That's not good enough."

"Gee, you CEO types are pretty particular, aren't you?" she sassed him.

He traced her lips with his forefinger. "So, you are

telling me that you couldn't spend the rest of your life as a CEO's wife, the mother of his future children, ones who are never going to get dumped off and left thinking they are contaminated with some unforgivable personality quirk that makes them impossible to love?''

"That's a rotten trick, Grayson, playing on my deep-seated sentiments like that," she said, frowning darkly. "No child of mine is going to doubt his or her worth, you can bet on that. Of course, I'll have to guard against smothering my kids with too much love, because I'll probably try to compensate for what I missed out on as a kid."

"Yeah, I'll probably have to deal with the same problem myself," Daniel agreed. "Probably spoil my kids rotten, which is fine by me, as long as I can teach them not to *behave* as if they're spoiled rotten."

Daniel tried out one of his most charming smiles on Mattie. "So, what are the chances of a woman like you settling down with a man like me and raising a few kids whom our grandfathers will likely spoil rotten before we get to do it ourselves?"

"Not good," Mattie told him.

His face fell like a rock slide. His heart cracked wide-open. "God, Mattie, did I kill all the love you once felt for me? Or was it all about sex for you?"

"Apologize for that crack, right this minute, Grayson," she ordered, staring him down. "Maybe it's true that you're the only man I have ever loved and that I don't have a frame of reference, but the great sex—"

"Great?" He brightened considerably.

"Fabulous sex, actually," she amended, then went on, "was only part of what I felt for you. You shared my passion for arts and crafts. You cared about Pops and did all within your power to see that he and his friends were happy. You made me laugh, and you made me feel good about myself, made me like who I became when I was with you.''

''Past tense?'' he murmured, his smile fading once again.

''No, I still love you,'' she assured him. ''You don't get over something like that in a month, you know. You've been sticking to my heart worse than super glue.''

''Yeah? So what's the problem here?''

''It's that whole high king of woodcraft, ruler of the corporate roost extravaganza that I can't handle,'' she told him.

''So, you're saying that if I sell the company you'll marry me?''

''No.''

Daniel threw up his hands in exasperation, then bounded to his feet to circumnavigate the one-room cabin. ''You're tormenting me to repay me for hurting you, aren't you? Fine, I know I deserve it. Hell, I knew I was asking for trouble when we became intimately involved, because I was pretty sure what you'd think when I finally worked up the nerve to tell you who I was.''

He wheeled like a soldier on parade, then paced the opposite direction. ''So, what are your demands, Mattie? Put them on the bargaining table.''

''Gad, you sound like a CEO,'' she said distastefully.

He stopped in his tracks and rounded on her. ''I *am* a CEO. I *own* the company. I *run* the friggin' company! What in the hell do I have to do to win back your love? Tell me and I'll do it!"

"Untie me."

Daniel blinked like a mole emerging from his subterranean tunnel. "Untie you?" he echoed.

"That's what I said."

Daniel frowned, bemused. "You will love me if I untie you?"

She nodded. Raven curls cascaded over her shoulders, shimmering in the dim light of the cabin. "Yes, but I have a couple of stipulations. However, I'm not getting into that until the numbness leaves my arms and legs."

Daniel strode forward, retrieved the scissors from his pocket, then snipped the tape. Mattie tossed aside the quilt to massage her arms and legs.

"So, what are these stipulations?" Daniel asked impatiently.

"Got any more of that duct tape handy?" she questioned.

He reached into his pocket and then handed the tape to her.

"Now lie down," she ordered.

He quirked a brow. He suddenly wondered if he had gone through this entire fiasco for nothing. Wondered if Mattie was still so full of bitterness that she only claimed to love him in order to gain her freedom so she could have her revenge. He'd broken her trust and lied to her, after all. Why should he expect anything less than her?

Well, he didn't know what else to do but offer his trust and hope she wasn't planning to tape him up so he wouldn't resist while she skinned him alive.

Deciding to go for broke, Daniel stretched out on the cot, belly up.

Without cracking a smile, looking quite serious, Mattie taped his wrists and ankles to the metal frame of the cot.

"In case this has any bearing on your fiendish plans for me, I really had no intention of leaving you tied up overnight if you didn't agree to marry me," he felt compelled to inform her.

"Guess you're a better sport than I am, Grayson," she said while she secured his left ankle.

His hopes sank like the *Titanic.* "Mattie—"

"Clam up, hotshot CEO," she commanded as she stood over him. "Now, here's the deal. I will agree to marry you under two conditions. Number one— you will never, not in all our years together, refer to me as the high queen of woodcraft. That is an absolute no-no."

Daniel grinned. "That title will never pass these lips."

"Number two—you will not try to persuade me to attend all those stuffy social gatherings that you undoubtedly feel obliged to plan for your executives during the holidays."

"Fine. You're off the guest list," he said generously.

"Company picnics, however, I will attend," she allowed. "Number three—"

"I thought you said there were only two stipulations," he reminded her.

"Well, I just thought of another one," she told him. "You will not force me, now or later, to leave Fox Hollow, because I refuse to be separated from Pops and his friends."

"Wouldn't even consider such a thing," Daniel assured her. "In fact, I plan to build our home near Fox Hollow, because Gramps decided he wants to remain here permanently, even when he is dismissed from the convalescent center."

Smiling, Mattie leaned over to unfasten the buttons of his chambray shirt, then raked her fingers through the matting of hair on his muscled chest.

Daniel groaned. "I think agreeing to let myself get tied up was a very bad idea. You're going to torture me, aren't you?"

Her hands glided down to the band of his jeans, then she made short shrift of baring his body to her appreciative gaze. "Mmm, you look exactly like someone I used to know, Mr. Grayson."

Daniel wasn't quite sure how to take that. "Who?"

"A regular Joe," she whispered as she eased down beside him, spreading butterfly kisses over his chest, his belly, his thighs.

Daniel sucked in his breath when her moist lips skimmed his arousal. When she took him into her mouth and gently nipped him, need exploded like nitroglycerin. He was hot and shaky and writhing for freedom, aching to touch her as intimately as she was touching him.

"Mattie, let me go," he moaned when she added more splendorous caresses to her arsenal of erotic weapons to destroy him.

"Not in this life," she promised as she worked her seductive magic on him. "I love you too much to ever let you go."

"Woman, I was afraid I'd never hear you say that again. Without you I'm—"

"I know, you're a stuffy ol' CEO who lacks enthusiasm.'' She smiled against his aching flesh, then kissed and caressed him until he groaned and begged for mercy. Then she straddled him, sank down upon him and gave herself up to the wild crescendo of passion they created together.

These wondrous feelings that Mattie had thought were lost and gone forever, when Daniel broke her heart, returned with the force of a thermonuclear blast. She reveled in his urgent need for her, her desperate, all-consuming need for him. She shivered in helpless spasms when white-hot desire exploded inside her, sending her careening into ecstasy.

Mattie collapsed upon him, feeling that ineffable closeness that joined her soul to his.

''I love you, Mattie,'' Daniel whispered hoarsely.

This time she heard, and she believed. He had gone to tremendous effort and expense to convince her that she mattered more than anything. Smiling, she fished the scissors from his pocket and cut him loose. His arms came around her like steel bands, hugging her tightly, holding her close to his heart, nuzzling his cheek to her cheek.

''You really are here to stay, aren't you?'' she murmured against his chest.

''Absolutely, positively, without a doubt. I may have to make the occasional trip to the office, but Fox Hollow is about to become my personal headquarters for Hobby Hut Enterprises.''

''Okay, I can live with short business trips, as long as you're in my bed every night,'' she purred contentedly.

''Can't think of any place I'd rather be. Beside you, loving you all the days of my life.''

''Mmm...I love the sound of that,'' Mattie murmured, then drifted into blissful sleep.

POPS AND GRAMPS, surrounded by the rest of the Roland Gang, stood outside the church, waving farewells to the bride and groom. As the married couple drove away, strings of aluminum cans clattered against the pavement and neon-colored streamers flapped in the breeze, compliments of the Roland Gang.

"'Bout time they tied the knot," Gramps said. "None of us are getting any younger."

Pops watched the car disappear from sight. "Still can't believe those two younguns are only going as far as that cabin by the lake for their honeymoon."

"Ask me, they'll be lucky to make it that far before all the hugging and kissing starts," Glen predicted.

"No kidding," Herman put in. "They could barely keep their hands off each other during the ceremony and the reception."

Ralph grinned delightedly. "They are definitely crazy over each other, aren't they?"

"Absolutely nuts," Fred confirmed.

"They haven't been able to take their eyes off each other the past few months," Pops remarked. "I was afraid they were going to saw off a few fingers while they were building their new house."

Gramps snickered. "I thought it was kind of touching the way they insisted on building that house by themselves. Not surprising since they do everything together these days. Couldn't pry those two apart, even with a crowbar."

Pops hobbled around on his cane and headed toward the parking lot. "Let's get back to Paradise Valley. There's a fish with my name on it waiting at the new pond."

"Think I'll kick back on that soft recliner and watch the big-screen TV," Ralph said as he followed in Pops's wake.

"Suit yourself," Herman said. "I'm hankering for a swim in that new pool to cool down from all the excitement of the wedding."

"Sounds like a plan to me," Fred and Glen chorused.

Pops glanced at Gramps. "What about you? Are you coming with me or am I fishing alone?"

"I'm fishing," Gramps confirmed.

"Prepare to get your butt whipped, old man," Pops taunted.

"Won't happen, you old rascal. You haven't beaten me in a fishing contest yet."

Pops snorted at that. "Haven't had an official contest yet."

Gramps chuckled. "Like I said…"

While the Roland Gang was piling into the van to return to the home, Daniel and Mattie were cuddled up in the back seat of the car, which was parked in a copse of trees. Daniel had pulled onto a gravel road to locate a remote spot a few hundred yards from the highway.

As the Roland Gang prophesied, Daniel and Mattie didn't have the patience to wait until they reached the cabin in the woods before they got their hands on each other. Which they proceeded to do without delay.

"I'll love you forever, Mattie," Daniel whispered sincerely. "And you should know by now that I'm not a man who takes promises lightly."

Mattie smiled up at him, love sparkling in her violet eyes. "I know."

When he returned her smile, she saw all the promises of their future unfurling before her like a wave rippling across an endless sea.

Mr. Right Under Her Nose
Jennifer Drew

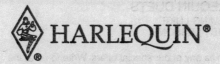

HARLEQUIN®

TORONTO • NEW YORK • LONDON
AMSTERDAM • PARIS • SYDNEY • HAMBURG
STOCKHOLM • ATHENS • TOKYO • MILAN • MADRID
PRAGUE • WARSAW • BUDAPEST • AUCKLAND

Dear Reader,

What's a romance novelist to do when writer's block hits and even massive amounts of chocolate chip cookie dough don't help?

We (Jennifer Drew is the pseudonym of mother and daughter Barbara Andrews and Pam Hanson) thank our lucky stars Debra Robertson is our editor. When she suggested giving the accident-prone sister of the heroine in our first Harlequin Duets, *Taming Luke,* her own story (and her very own special man!), we raced to the keyboard!

Sending Kim Grant on a cross-country trek with sexy traveling companion Rick Taylor was almost as much fun as going ourselves.

Enjoy the trip!

Jennifer Drew

Books by Jennifer Drew

HARLEQUIN DUETS
7—TAMING LUKE
18—BABY LESSONS

Happy birthday and happy traveling
to Maxine Fuller, with thanks for all the lives
she enriched in her classroom.
Everyone should have such a good friend!

Sharon, Jane's husband, was in Africa, checking on

1

SHE WAS A walking baggage cart.

Kim Grant pulled her overstuffed wardrobe-on-wheels with one hand and carried a hard-sided old garage-sale-bargain suitcase in the other. Every few steps her duffel straps slipped off her shoulder, and the purse she'd so cleverly hung around her neck to keep her plane ticket safe was flopping against her chest.

A friendly neighbor, Ben, had driven through blowing snow to the airport and dropped her outside the ticketing area at Detroit Metro at 6:00 a.m. Kim smiled, remembering his really sweet goodbye kiss. It had almost made her wish she wasn't leaving, though leaving was seeming less and less of an option. Ben was long gone when she'd learned her plane couldn't take off. The frigid wind had piled snow-drifts on the runway, and all flights were canceled.

Now that she was on her way to Phoenix, the city she called home, the delay was annoying. Her Detroit apartment was empty, her thrift-shop furnishings sold or given away, and the key was back with the land-lord. She'd checked out of the Motor City, and there was nothing to do but try to get to Arizona.

She had to get to her sister's as quickly as possible. For the first time ever, Jane really needed her. Luke Stanton, Jane's husband, was in Africa, checking on the construction of a new branch of the sporting goods firm he ran for his grandfather. He'd gone reluctantly because Jane was well into her second pregnancy, this time expecting twin girls. Kim was certain that if Luke knew Jane was having difficulty carrying the new babies to term, he would come home in a flash. But Jane was too stubborn to ruin his trip by telling him.

Fortunately, she did tell Kim when the doctor ordered lots of rest. Her sister had a housekeeper, but keeping up with four-year-old Peter was a labor of love. Kim adored her nephew, but he was practically a clone of the wild man his father had been before love tamed him. The pint-size daredevil climbed trees as easily as steps and took the word "no" as a personal challenge.

Kim had no regrets about giving up her job teaching computer courses to auto execs. She missed Phoenix with its golden hot sun and dry deserts, but especially she longed to be closer to the only family she had. It was sheer joy to know that, for once in her life, she could do something for her sister. Jane had raised her after their parents' untimely deaths, seeing her through one teenage crisis after another and helping her to get a college degree.

Kim fairly ached to see Peter again. No matter that he'd put sand in her suitcase and drawn pictures on the bathroom mirror with her lipstick the last time she'd visited. This time she'd be ready for his stunts. With her help, Jane would get the rest she needed, and Kim would have the time of her life trying to tame Luke's son.

First she had to get there. She had one possibility

of catching a plane to Phoenix that day: another airport.

The escalator loomed ahead, blessedly empty at the moment so she had time to load her cases on the descending stairs. She plunked the wheeled wardrobe onto a moving riser, quickly piled the old suitcase on top of it, clutched the duffel against her side, and hopped on a second too late to land on the step directly above her luggage. She didn't plant both high-heeled black suede boots squarely on one moving step, and her long skirt twisted around her ankles. She felt herself toppling forward and instinctively grabbed at the moving black handrail with the hand that was balancing the hardsider.

"Oh, no!"

She saved herself but lost the old suitcase. It toppled off its precarious perch, springing open on the second bounce and spilling the contents. She watched her silky lingerie fall out in a rainbow trail on the steps.

Blocked by her big case, she couldn't do a darn thing. Her intimate apparel followed the wretched case to the bottom, piling up where the steps flattened and disappeared.

At the bottom she stumbled in her eagerness to retrieve her underwear but managed to stay on her feet. Kicking aside her wardrobe-on-wheels, she dropped to her knees, so intent on rescuing her belongings that she nearly broadsided a pair of long legs clad in khaki chinos.

"Let me help you," said the voice that went with them.

She stuffed a pair of lacy peach panties into her jacket pocket, too embarrassed to look up at the deep-voiced man who'd made the offer. A silvery bra was practically under the toe of his boot. She snatched it away.

"Thank you, but I can manage." She kept her face averted, wondering what had possessed her to buy zebra-striped briefs.

"It's no trouble. Be too bad if all your things got trampled."

She followed his gaze to the top of the escalator where a group of people were poised to get on. Her would-be rescuer retrieved the battered old case and started tossing her most intimate garments into it. To his credit, he didn't eyeball them too closely except when he tried to fold her black lace chemise.

"It's for sleeping," she said, cheeks hot under his scrutiny.

People were midway down the escalator now. She snatched frantically at the remaining garments and moved aside just before a trio of noisy jocks in matching red-and-black jackets rode the last step onto solid flooring. She turned her back, ignored a suggestive whistle, and found herself looking up at sexy electric blue eyes. Her friend-in-need was a hunk indeed!

He was dangling a fire-engine red thong from one finger, but he dropped it like a hot coal, missing the suitcase, when she looked directly at him. She grabbed the garment off the floor and wadded it, intending to stuff it into her pocket with her peach panties. Instead she changed her mind and tossed it into the case along with the last fistful of silky underwear. To her relief, the old-fashioned clasp still clicked shut after she slammed down the lid.

"I can't thank you enough," she said, trying to

play it cool even though he was making her feel impossibly awkward.

"No problem. Can I give you a hand with your luggage?"

He pushed a strand of dark blond hair away from his forehead, giving her a chance to eyeball his strong-jawed, extremely okay face.

Men were always offering to help her. Her sister said it was because she looked vulnerable, but Kim knew she wasn't helpless. She just had an unfortunate tendency to stumble, spill and scatter. She was working on it, but sometimes things went wrong. Like today.

"Thanks a lot, but I never travel with more luggage than I can handle myself."

Some assistance would be nice, but how could she hand her suitcase over to a man who'd just had his hands on her undies? She was too busy noticing how gorgeous his long, spiky lashes were to be bothered by the skeptical look he gave her.

"Okay, but you may not want those stockings trailing behind you." He pointed at her navy panty hose sticking out of the suitcase.

He walked away, leaving her to reopen the case and stuff the tights into the jumbled mess inside so they wouldn't get caught in the crack again. She didn't have enough nerve to look at the horde of travelers moving in all directions and wonder how many had witnessed her gaudy display of underwear.

Slapped and thumped by her luggage, she hurried toward the car rental desks. If she left now—and if the roads were still passable—she could drive to Chicago and catch a late flight to Phoenix from O'Hare.

There was no line at the counter of the first rental

agency, so she rushed up, only to read a small printed sign: We Regret That No Vehicles Are Available At This Time.

At the second counter her broad-shouldered rescuer was only two places ahead of her in a long line. With a strong possibility of icy roads and more snow, she wanted the best car she could get.

Fortunately she heard the person at the front being turned away. No cars were available here except by reservation. She sprinted toward the last rental counter.

Halfway there she glanced over her shoulder and spotted the tall hunk race-walking toward Econo-Cars. If he hadn't stopped to help her, he might have gotten a car and been on his way. Her conscience told her she should let him get ahead of her, but renting one of the budget clunkers was her last chance. She had to get to Phoenix. Her big sister needed her.

Dang, he was fast! She ran full speed ahead, her big leather purse slapping her stomach as the strap cut into the back of her neck, the wardrobe trailing behind her on wobbly wheels.

She skirted around a giant of a man in a silver-and-blue Lions jacket and narrowly missed a head-on collision with a luggage cart being pushed by a pint-size traveler whose significant elder was struggling with a baby howling in a car seat. The little luggage-handler had pale blond hair like Peter, and she fairly ached to see her nephew again.

Distracted by the little guy, she'd let the competition narrow the gap between them. Forgetting he was her personal Good Samaritan, she sprinted and flung herself at the purple-and-white Econo-Cars counter in a photo finish.

"I was here first," she gasped, untangling the purse strap from her hair and slapping the heavy bag on the counter. "I have my credit card right here."

She was digging for it when the handsome hunk-turned-enemy interrupted.

"I was here ahead of you," he said, "but if you're in that big of a hurry, you can jump me."

"Sir, I'm afraid we only have one vehicle left," the rental agent said.

The woman behind the counter had streaked blond hair teased into a frizzy halo and bright red lipstick outlining a toothy smile. It was definitely a bad sign that she was focusing her attention on the hunk. She moistened her lips with her tongue and ignored Kim.

"I'll take it," the big guy said with a lopsided grin no doubt calculated to charm the fawning agent into turning over the keys.

"Wait!" Kim shoved her purse directly in front of him. "I really did get here first. I touched goal while he was still a full step behind."

"I'm really sorry," the blonde said with the sincerity of a telemarketer selling snail-ranch stock. "This gentleman has already spoken for our last car."

"Call your supervisor, please," Kim said, unwilling to debate with a woman who was staring at her male customer with pinwheel eyes.

"That really won't change anything." Miss Sweety-sweet sounded as if she'd just bitten into a lemon.

"Maybe you'd better do it to speed things up," her rival said. "I have to make a connection in Chicago. I need to get out of here before the storm closes the interstate."

"Chicago! That's where I'm going. Maybe we can

share,'' Kim suggested impulsively without considering that he could be a serial killer or a con man or a lousy driver.

He looked directly at her.

"I don't think so."

"I'll pay half—no, I'll pay the whole rental. Please, I'm desperate to get to Phoenix. My sister is expecting twins and—"

"Don't tell me she's expecting you to deliver them?" he asked in a disbelieving voice, presenting his credit card and slapping his wallet shut.

He wanted to play hardball. Kim lowered her lashes and gave him her never-fail, wounded-dove look. She wasn't proud of herself for playing dirty, but she was desperate.

He ignored her best effort at looking pathetic and turned his shoulder, subtly but effectively shutting her out of his transaction with the rental-car agent.

"Miss, I insist you call your supervisor," Kim said. She'd offered to share. What more could she do?

A pudgy man with wire frames and extra chins came through a private door carrying a Closed sign for the counter.

"Sir," Kim said, hailing him, "I'm afraid there's a misunderstanding. I hate to make trouble, but I really did get here first. I should get the last car."

She faltered, trying to think of a convincing argument. They probably had tied in the race to the counter, but she needed a vehicle urgently.

"Are you sure you saw who was first, Ms. Wheeler?" the supervisor asked.

His chins jiggled, obscuring the knot of his saffron-and-purple company tie as his eyes traveled the length of Kim's five foot nine inch frame. His gaze lingered for the usual extra seconds on her fairly spectacular bustline, visible under the open black squall jacket. He blinked three times—about par for the course—and she had to remind herself this was for Jane. She hadn't felt this rotten since she'd spoiled a rock climbing party by falling off a cliff.

"I'm desperate to get to Chicago and connect with a flight to Phoenix. My sister is pregnant, and she's supposed to get lots of bed rest so she can carry her twins to term. Her husband is out of the country, and I have to take care of her little boy and make sure she doesn't take any risks."

She told her story in a rush of words and really needed the deep breath that pulled her blush-pink cashmere sweater tight across her chest.

"This gentleman got here first," Ms. Wheeler insisted, making her silver-lined eyelids flutter.

"Our policy is first come, first served." Chins quivered regretfully.

"It was pretty much a dead heat, I guess," the hunk said. He pushed aside Kim's purse and put his credit card into the eager scarlet-tipped fingers waiting for it. "You can ride with me."

"Oh, wonderful! Thank you! I'll be glad to put the rental on my card." She started digging into her purse again.

"Never mind. You can buy breakfast after we drive out of the storm. We have to hurry. The way the snow is piling up, they might close I-94."

Kim heaved a sigh of relief. She was going to get to her sister as promised.

THE PAPERWORK seemed to take forever, but Rick knew patience wasn't a Taylor family trait. He urgently needed to get to Phoenix, but falling snow and tumbling underwear had conspired to hold him back. Now he'd rented a wreck that might or might not make it to Chicago. Worse, he'd taken on a walking disaster as a passenger.

He smiled automatically at the rental agent and resisted the urge to snatch away the form and fill in the blanks himself. Maybe he was overreacting, but his brother had already had one catastrophic marriage. Now Brian was rushing headlong into a second, as if he hadn't learned a thing from a costly divorce and the two messy affairs that followed it.

Rick seethed with impatience, automatically producing his driver's license and ignoring the agent's none-too-subtle come-ons. When would his kid brother learn there weren't any happily-ever-after scenarios? Their parents were a textbook case on the folly of marriage, ten tries between them and counting.

He shuffled from one foot to the other, bursting with impatience but trying to keep his cool. Whatever happened to sending wedding invitations early? Maybe Brian had deliberately held his back so there wouldn't be time for big brother to dash the cold water of common sense on the impending nuptials. Storm or no storm, he was going to get to Phoenix before the ceremony and try to talk Brian out of getting married. If his brother wouldn't cancel the wedding, at least Rick would see that his sibling had a good prenuptial agreement before he said, "I do." Rick had already contacted a family attorney to draw up the papers.

First, he absolutely had to get to Phoenix before the wedding.

As soon as the paperwork was done, Rick slipped the strap of his flight bag over his shoulder and picked up his passenger's duffel to speed things along. Reluctantly he grabbed the case that had done a header down the escalator.

"Is this thing going to fall open on me?" He eyed it suspiciously, remembering all too well the spill of soft, sexy lingerie.

"No, the clasp isn't broken, but I can carry my own—"

"I'm in a hurry, Ms.—what is your name?"

"Kim Grant."

"I'm Rick Taylor."

"Yes, I know. From the rental form. I can read upside down."

He hurried toward the parking area, too rushed to comment on her dubious talent. Hopefully the clunker he'd just rented would hold up the three hundred or so miles to Chicago's O'Hare Airport.

He didn't have any trouble spotting the vehicle. It stood alone in Econo-Cars' parking area.

His unwanted passenger laughed at the lavender dinosaur.

He didn't.

He had to save his addle-brained brother from marital disaster in a gas-guzzling relic that belonged in a demolition derby.

"It's a heavy car. Should be good on the highway," she said, her cheerful proclamation sounding forced.

"Yeah, it was a good used car when my father bought one like it for his second wife. He's on wife number five now."

He opened the trunk, relieved to stow the case of

lacy panties and silky bras out of sight—and hopefully out of mind. He'd darn near gotten aroused in
the middle of the airport when he helped her scoop
them up.

"Wow, five wives! Which one was your mom?"

Tact wasn't her strong suit, he thought sourly. How
many hours would he have to spend with her? The
way his day was going, she'd probably get the seat
next to his on the plane.

"Everyone needs a hobby." It was his pat answer
to comments about his father's marital escapades.
"My mother was number one. Aren't you worried
about riding with a stranger?"

He slammed the trunk and took a long, hard look
at the gorgeous but annoying woman who'd maneuvered him into giving her a ride. Were her eyes really
green? Probably just a trick of the light, but he
couldn't find fault with her bouncy sable hair and pert
nose. In fact, she had the look that attracted him when
he had time for women. Unfortunately, she probably
expected to marry Mr. Right and live in wedded bliss
forever and ever. He avoided that type like the plague.

"Are you an ax murderer?" she asked, waiting for
him to unlock the door on the passenger side.

"Possibly."

"Well, I took martial arts lessons, and these are
lethal weapons." She made a defensive gesture with
small hands neatly gloved in black leather.

He'd been awake, stewing over Brian most of the
night. He'd gotten up at 4:00 a.m. for a flight that was
canceled. He'd played Galahad for a woman who
scattered underwear on an escalator, then tried to steal
the last rental car from him. Enough was enough. In
one quick lunge he grabbed her around the thighs and

boosted her over his shoulder, rewarded by her little shriek of protest.

"Tell me when you get dangerous," he mocked, hoping she'd back out of going with him.

"Put me down!"

"What's the magic word?"

"Please!"

He lowered her slowly, liking the close encounter too much for his peace of mind.

"It's a very bad idea to accept rides with strange men," he warned. "Want me to unload your bags?"

"No. And I'll drive first."

"Thanks, but no."

"All right, you get us on the highway. But we will take turns."

"I'll do the driving. Get in. We've wasted enough time."

He closed the passenger door after she scrambled onto the purple leather seat. Taking a deep breath, he got behind the wheel.

"You expect me to trust your driving, but you don't trust mine?"

She sounded huffy. That was good. If she got the sulks, he wouldn't be as inclined to fantasize about how she'd look in those hot-pink bikini panties or the black lacy thing.

In the short time it took to merge onto the interstate, he realized she was the least of his problems. This was one serious storm, and he wasn't used to northern winters. A semi barreled past him, the driver impervious to the slick surface and the snow whipping across the road. The rental vibrated but held the road, making him glad he wasn't driving a light-weight compact.

"Where's your car?" she asked.

"My car?" He wanted to pass a slow-moving van in front of him, but another semi was coming up fast in the left lane.

"Didn't you drive to the airport?" she pressed, making him wonder whether he was saddled with a chatterbox.

"No, I used the motel shuttle."

"Oh, you don't live here."

He didn't like the way the truck swept past, making the car sway.

"Brilliant conclusion." Okay, he was cranky, but he had to concentrate on driving.

"It's not my business." She sounded hurt.

"Sorry. This isn't my kind of weather. I live in Phoenix."

"I grew up there. I've only lived here two years, but I'm moving back. My sister is there, and I'll miss so much if I don't see her children grow up. Her husband is a gem. I thought he was too wild for her when they met—wild, but exciting. I guess you might say she tamed him."

"I doubt that." He gnawed on his lower lip, finally switching lanes to pass the overly timid driver ahead of him. He didn't want to be rear-ended by a faster vehicle. The pavement was slick with drifts piling up in low areas, but it hadn't discouraged the heavy urban traffic.

"You don't think she tamed him?"

"No, but the poor guy has my sympathy if it's true. I don't believe in the domestication of the male of the species."

A truck was right on his tail, and he made it back to the right lane with relief.

"You don't believe in marriage."

"No."

"It can be a wonderful life. My sister and her husband couldn't be happier."

"Are you looking for a husband?"

"No...not exactly looking. I don't think people should marry too young. I'm twenty-six and still single, but my sister is living proof. Marriage can be a wonderful partnership. Two people working together, raising a family—"

"Cheating on each other, divorcing, remarrying, shuttling kids around like pieces on a chessboard."

"If you're an ax murderer, you're certainly a crabby one. Aren't you supposed to be charming? Lull me into a false sense of security?"

"Aren't you worried about this storm?" Her nonchalance was making him edgy. He didn't want the responsibility for her safety, and he didn't want her to be so trusting.

"I offered to drive. I've had two winters of Michigan weather. This is pretty bad, though. I'm glad I'm not driving all the way to Arizona. I sold my car. It was too old to make the trip. My neighbor brought me to the airport. I hope he got to work okay."

She was chattering, probably nervous about the blizzard. He couldn't blame her. If the snow got much heavier, he'd be driving blind.

"Your neighbor will be fine. The city plows are probably out in force." He surprised himself by wanting to reassure her.

"I hope so. He was awfully nice to me."

Imagine, a man willing to put himself out for this woman. Odds were, she never pumped her own gas or paid for a plumber to fix her sink. Back at the airport, she'd had him scooping up her undies when he should have been running to the rental car counters.

"This is going to be a long trip, isn't it?" she asked, peering through her side of the windshield.

"Yes. A very long trip."

2

"I CAN'T BELIEVE we made it." Kim thankfully patted the dash of the aging boat-on-wheels and realized she was talking to herself.

The wedding grouch was dialing his cell phone again, at the same time nonchalantly negotiating the access road to O'Hare with one hand on the wheel.

"I'm on standby, but... No, I'm at the airport now. As soon as I park this clunker... Brian, a day won't make that much difference."

"I would be one unhappy bride if my wedding were postponed," Kim muttered.

"They're getting married tomorrow on his patio—family only. The reception isn't until next weekend," Rick said in an undertone for her benefit.

"I was talking to the woman who's riding with me," he said into the phone. "No, she won't be coming to the wedding. I told you, we shared the last available car. I won't be in until late tonight.... Sunday would be much better."

Kim yawned, looking forward to sleeping on the flight to Denver and then to Phoenix. She'd had more relaxing rides on a roller coaster than she did racing across Michigan in a snowstorm with a man she didn't know.

"At least talk to Carlisle," her car mate urged. "Everyone gets a prenuptial these days. No reason for her feelings to be hurt...I understand, no promises. But see if you can pull off a one-day postponement."

"Do you know where to go?" she asked as soon as he clicked off the phone. She'd only been at O'Hare once before, but in her book the airport had all the charm of a Marines' obstacle course.

"I'm heading straight to the gate as soon as I park this antique. If you want to tag along, you'll have to move fast."

Tag along!

"I'm in a hurry myself. I'm on standby," she told him.

He gave her an evil look. "If there's one seat, it's mine. My brother promised he'd try to delay the ceremony until Sunday, but when he's in love, he'll do backward somersaults for the woman."

"Unlike his brother? No bride wants her wedding delayed. Don't you have any romantic ideas?"

"I've thought of creating a computer program to determine marital compatibility," he said.

He'd told her a few things about himself on the trip. He was a software engineer, had his own firm and traveled frequently on consulting jobs. She'd observed more than he'd shared. He was overly protective of his younger brother and the family assets. Behind the wheel he was cool and competent, stoic about the weather but impatient with drivers who took unnecessary risks. After maybe a dozen calls on his cell phone, it was pretty clear he was used to being in charge. When he couldn't control a situation, he bit his lower lip. He also had a deep, warm laugh, but she hadn't heard much of it.

He definitely didn't think she was funny, not even

when she described how Peter had packed every stitch of clothing from his dresser in a black garbage bag so he could go to Africa with his dad.

When Rick found Econo-Cars' drop-off spot, she was almost sorry to abandon the lavender relic. The heater was erratic, giving them a choice between the tropics or the Arctic, and a young couple had pointed and snickered at their mode of transport when they'd stopped for a quick lunch. But it had lumbered along with aging dignity, bringing her closer to Jane and Peter.

Rick was true to his word. He grabbed her duffel and suitcase and started race-walking toward the terminal, forcing her to run with the wobbling wardrobe-on-wheels toppling from side to side. The going was slow. The city of Chicago had emptied into the airport, judging by the congestion on all sides.

"Trouble." He stopped so abruptly she bumped into his back and let the wardrobe whack her legs.

"Look at the delays." He pointed at a bank of overhead monitors. "St. Louis, Omaha, Denver, L.A. Nothing's coming in from the West."

"But it's not snowing here!"

As she studied the monitor, two more arrivals moved into the column of delays.

"What's going on?"

"Nothing good. Let's check."

He shifted her hardsider to his other side, clutching it under his arm as though he expected an explosion of unmentionables at any moment.

They bypassed the ticketing area where long lines of surly travelers forced even a determined sprinter like Rick to slow down. At the security gate she caught him checking the latch on her suitcase after it went through X-ray. The man couldn't seem to forget her little mishap on the escalator.

He led the way to their gate. All the seats in the waiting area were occupied, and the aisles between them were serving as picnic area and playground. Kim saw a curly-haired rascal boosting his smaller sibling up the side of a drinking fountain, doing his best to push the younger boy's face into the jet of water. His mischief made her all the more eager to get to Phoenix. If Jane tried to lift her squirming four-year-old...

Rick left her standing with stacked luggage and went to the line at the counter. When he came back, he was frowning in irritation.

"No problem getting a flight—if we want to go by way of Mexico City."

"Funny," she said without much hope he was kidding.

"A second front is hitting the West. Denver is socked in. Nothing west of Des Moines is taking off. That's why so many arrivals are late."

"Where does that leave us?"

"Us?"

"Us, as in people who want to go to Phoenix," she said, embarrassed because she had started to think of him as a fellow traveler.

"It leaves us up a creek."

"Are you suggesting we go by boat?" She could be as flip as he was.

"Not unless you've always wanted to see the Panama Canal."

"How about a train? I went home on one last Christmas."

"A train?" He didn't sound enthusiastic, but he gave her a grudging, "Possible."

"Sure, it takes more than a little snow to stop the Desert Chief."

"Let's go for it."

He saddled himself with the straps of his overnight bag and her duffel, hoisted the hardsider under his arm, and grabbed her hand.

They hustled, running on the moving walkways and diving down escalators in a breathless charge to the nearest exit where they could get a taxi.

Half a million stymied travelers had the same idea. Kim and Rick burst out of the building and stopped abruptly. They had to jostle for standing room on the crowded pavement while buses, motel shuttles and taxis were caught up in a turtle derby in front of them. A block-long white limo was hemmed in at an angle beside the curb, assailed by the honking from cabs that couldn't get around it to pick up fares from the twenty-deep lines.

"No way," Rick grumbled.

"No choice!"

She cozied up close to use him for concealment, stuffed her dangling purse under the waistband of her skirt, buttoned the top three buttons of her squall jacket, and threw her shoulders back and thrust her hips forward.

"What are you—oh."

"Nine months and counting. Now snag one of those taxis."

"You'll never get away with it."

"I want to ride in a cab, not steal one." She moaned loudly enough to get a couple of sympathetic glances.

He grabbed the handle of her wardrobe and plunged into the traffic jam, leaving her to waddle after him doing her best to imitate a hugely pregnant female in distress. By the time she caught up, she had the moan down pat.

Rick was arguing with a burly driver whose nose had been broken so badly or so frequently he could sniff his left cheek. Kim could see her breath in the frigid air, but he was snug in his cab with massive hairy arms bare under the sleeves of a black T-shirt. He also had the best chance of squeezing into the outer lane and getting past the traffic snarl.

"I gotta take my turn. You want me to lose my license?" he snarled.

"You're the only cab with a chance of getting out of this mess," Rick argued patiently.

"Don't matter. I gotta—"

"Ever delivered a baby in your taxi?" Kim asked, yanking open the rear door and throwing herself inside with a few heartrending groans and a shriek for good measure.

"Okay, okay." He reluctantly popped the trunk and let Rick throw their luggage into it.

After taking time to yell a lurid description of his passenger's condition to the lead taxi still sandwiched behind the limo, the driver did a rhumba of starts and stops until he finally broke free of the traffic nightmare.

"Where to?"

"Union Station. Please hurry." She buckled over and groaned pathetically.

"Hey, what is this? You should go to a hospital."

She panted, squealed and poked Rick with her elbow. Let him field that one. She was in the throes of birth.

"My wi... Eh, we're meeting the doctor there."

He couldn't even say the word wife in a dire emergency.

"She's really a midwife, and she'll take us to her laying-in clinic," Kim elaborated, wishing she'd had more experience telling tall tales. She was always sure her guilt would come through when she fibbed, but her urgency wasn't fake. Jane needed her, and that meant getting to Phoenix as fast as possible.

The driver shrugged his beefy shoulders. "Just don't have it in my cab," he warned.

Rick patted her bulging purse with mock solicitation and shifted it just enough to poke a hard corner of the billfold into her navel. She groaned for real.

"This your first?" the cabbie asked. "First one takes a long time," he added hopefully.

"Fifth," she gasped.

"Fourth," Rick said at the same time. "That's counting the twins as one delivery."

"If you'd been the one in labor, you'd count them as two." She was beginning to enjoy being with child.

"At least you didn't have them on a bus that time." He did have a sense of humor.

Kim was too busy trying not to giggle to enjoy scenic Chicago, not that they were following a landmark route. Their driver nosed the cab from lane to lane wherever there was a six-inch opening and used his horn as a battle trumpet. With the imminent threat of motherhood looming large in his back seat, there was no worry he'd pad the meter by taking the long way.

The aging midtown station looked gloomy under a gray sky, and Kim felt homesick for the muted desert shades and clean lines of the buildings in Phoenix. The cabbie threw open the back door, and she ponderously crawled out into the biting winter wind.

"Pay the man, darling," she purred, reminding him she couldn't get her money without giving birth.

She watched Rick hand over a hefty tip to compensate for their charade. He had a conscience. That was good, although why she should care was a total mystery. They were oil and water. He barely tolerated her, and she thought he was bossy and overbearing. Maybe it was noble to be worried about his brother, but he'd stepped over the line between caring and meddling. She sympathized with his travel frustrations—she wanted to get to Phoenix as badly as he did—but he wanted to stop a wedding, not attend one.

Kim played pregnant until they were inside the cavernous depot, then delivered her bulky purse from the confines of her shirt. Walking with her stomach stuck out had made her back ache, and she had new sympathy for the woes of her sister's pregnancy. Even more urgently, she wanted to get home to help her.

Rick honed in on the row of ticket sellers, and she followed in his wake, oddly reminded of the windows at a horse racing track. She was no gambler, but the day's setbacks made her ready to bet they'd be thwarted here, too.

A line snaked in front of them and on either side. She was crowded behind Rick and had to nudge her stack of luggage forward with her knee and foot. Impatience making her fidget, she had nothing to do but admire his very fine back view. He'd taken his jacket off and stuffed it into his bag—not an option for her since every piece of her luggage was filled to capacity. He was wearing a burgundy soccer shirt with a pale fawn collar nearly the color of his chinos. His shirt was tucked in—showing off his muscular flat stomach—and a narrow mahogany belt circled his trim waist.

She admired his shoulders, broad without the exaggerated muscles of weightlifting fanatics. His hair was windblown with dark blond tendrils making his neck look boyishly vulnerable. She even liked the way his ears were close to his head with just a little curl in the lobes.

He turned and caught her checking out his backside, so she had to cover by bending over and fiddling with her wardrobe zipper.

"That one won't come open, will it?" he asked suspiciously.

"No, of course not. The other one came open because it fell down the whole length of an escalator, as you may remember."

He looked skeptical, but the line edged forward and he turned his attention straight ahead again.

He had a mighty fine rear end, she decided, rounded and firm. She'd like to see him in a bathing suit—all right, she'd like to see him *without* one. She hoped he wouldn't turn around to see her blushing! She was also a great admirer of long, strongly built legs. In fact, the biggest turnoff for her was a man with legs shorter than hers. It made her feel as if she were walking on stilts. Too bad that inside such an appealing package Rick was dedicated to ruining a wedding and breaking up a romance.

Finally it was their turn at the ticket counter. She crowded up to the window beside him, wanting to be darn sure he didn't grab the last seat and leave her behind.

"The Desert Chief left for Flagstaff two hours ago," the oily voiced ticket agent said with obvious satisfaction.

"What else do you have going west today?" Rick asked.

"The Prairie Wind, Superliner Number Five, leaves for Denver from platform five at 5:05 p.m."

"Five, five, five o'five," Kim repeated, hoping number five was their lucky number.

"How long does it take?" Rick asked.

"It'll roll into the Mile-High City in seventeen hours." The agent smoothed a handlebar mustache with chewed ends, seemingly in no hurry to sell tickets.

"We'll take two coach tickets," Kim said to speed things along. She'd slept well enough sitting up on her last train trip.

"Coach is sold out."

"What do you have?" Rick had his credit card out, ready to slap it on the counter, and she started digging for hers.

"We've got the deluxe first class for two, includes your meals, and the family bedroom for two adults and two children. Course, they're sold out. So's the accessible bedroom, but you have to have a mobility problem to book one of them anyway."

"What *is* available?" Rick spoke slowly, enunciating every syllable.

Kim was ready to reach under the glass safety shield and strangle the ticket seller with his own green pinstripe tie.

"That would be the standard compartment with sleeping accommodations for two."

"We'll take two." Rick was nothing if not decisive.

"Two beds. Yes, sir."

"No, two compartments."

"That I don't have. I've got the one because of a cancellation. Standard compartment for two on the upper level."

Rick looked at her. "Want to flip a coin?"

"No, I want to go."

He stared at her, crease lines furrowing his brow as he seemed to be waging some internal argument.

"I have to get to Phoenix. We'll take it," he said to the ticket seller.

"This isn't like sharing a car," she protested.

"No, it sure isn't. We want it." He handed his card under the glass partition.

"Put half on my card." She was going to regret this, but she gamely started to push her card under the window with his.

"Too complicated. We'll settle up later," he insisted, giving the card back to her. "Don't worry. You'll pay your share."

When Rick had their tickets in hand, they rushed toward a series of doors opening directly onto the platform. The daily commute to the suburbs was beginning, weary working people streaming to the gates on homeward treks. Again he had her lingerie case tucked under his arm as though he were guarding classified secrets.

She needed time to think. Should she share a sleeping nook with him? Part of her thought it was a very bad idea. Maybe they could leave the seats up, pretend they were traveling coach, but she doubted whether he'd go for that. He was too tall to sleep sitting scrunched up on a seat. Of course, they'd be in bunks, one above the other. They wouldn't even see each other once the lights were out.

Who was she trying to kid? She certainly would know he was there, snuggled in, all cute and sexy.

Wait, she wasn't even sure she liked the man! So what if his skin did have the sun-bronzed glow of a Phoenix native? So what if the shadowy bristles on his face were just long enough to give her goose bumps if he rubbed them against her cheek? She'd still be sleeping with—make that *near*—a complete stranger.

"Hurry up," he said brusquely.

Maybe she'd just murder him! She'd always enjoyed a good train mystery. There was something devilishly clever about doing the deed, then mingling with other passengers.

She didn't want to think about seventeen hours in Rick's company. Men liked her, and generally she liked them back, but she had to admit she didn't have her sister's luck finding the right man. Kim had been hoping to find Mr. Right for years, and Jane hadn't even been looking when she found Luke showering nearly naked in the company fountain where she worked. Kim was going to be stuck in a crowded compartment with a sexy killjoy who thought a computer program could pick a mate.

When she refocused on the killjoy in question, he was five steps ahead and not slowing on her account. It would serve him right if she stuck him with tickets for two and went back to the airport to wait for a flight. She would, if she weren't so darn tired and Jane didn't need her for the first time ever.

A porter stood inside the passenger car they entered to stow their luggage on a rack and direct them to their compartment on the upper level. By the time the train lurched forward promptly at 5:05 p.m., they were seated across from each other in their cozy little cubbyhole, ready for the train to speed them forward to their destinies.

No, make that destinations, she thought with a trace of panic, absolutely sure they'd go their separate ways as soon as the trip was over.

3

DINNER WAS FANCY by his fast-food standards. Kim had angel-hair pasta with clam sauce and a baked parmesan tomato. He had a stuffed pork chop with parsley-buttered potatoes and spinach salad. They shared a table with a retired couple who kept finishing each other's sentences—scary to be married so long their brains worked in sync. Rick was too tired to follow their lengthy account of a trip to British Columbia, but Kim nodded politely at all the right times and asked enough questions to keep them going.

Without the chatty couple, he would have had to talk to Kim. He wasn't at all sure he had anything to say to his traveling companion. He felt oddly grateful to the talkative pair and tried hard not to doze off.

The dining car gradually emptied, and their table-mates left. The staff hustled to clear away the last evening seating and set up for breakfast. Kim was clutching a cup of herbal tea, only pretending to sip what had to be cold dregs.

"Guess we'd better get out of their way," he said.

"Yes."

She looked longingly at the white linen tablecloth as though she'd like to lay her head down and go to sleep there.

He knew exactly how she felt—or thought he did. It was one thing to share a rental car or a cab with a stranger, but he wasn't sure how this compartment thing would work out.

Even though he was preoccupied with Brian's latest goof, he wasn't indifferent to the woman tagging along with him. Whenever he let down his guard, he found himself wondering how she'd look in a pair of her sexy panties or a lacy see-through bra. He wished he hadn't stopped to help her. The last thing he needed was a yen for a woman who exuded *eau de picket fence*. His brother was the marrying man; all Rick wanted from a woman was an occasional good time with no strings. His one try at cohabitation had turned into a fiasco when his roommate started window-shopping in jewelry stores and studying china pattern pamphlets.

He followed Kim back to their seats, trying not to admire the graceful way she walked to the sway of the train, moving seductively even when they went through the vibrating passageways between cars. He wasn't the only one watching her pass through the train. Men's eyes followed her like marbles rolling on a slanted board. If she had this effect wearing a long black nun's skirt and a schoolgirl pink sweater—albeit well filled—she'd cause a riot in a really hot outfit.

Most of the men on the train would sit up and beg like flea-bitten hounds for a chance to share a compartment with her, so why was he dreading it?

"Maybe I'll go to the lounge. See what movie is showing," he said. Better to nap there than lie awake wondering how she looked when she was sleeping.

"Okay."

She didn't offer to come with him, much to his relief. If she did, he might make the mistake of taking her hand, maybe stroking her wrist with his fingertips. He got a little shivery at the thought of feeling her pulse.

He walked her to their compartment, a fancy word for two seats facing each other in a tiny closet with enough legroom for a pair of pygmies.

"I thought maybe we could leave the seats up. It's not so bad, sleeping sitting up," she suggested.

He'd like to take off his boots and put his *feet* up, but where would he put them? He could tuck one on either side of her hips or squeeze both feet beside her on the seat, but not without imagining how it would feel to slide his toes up her legs, under her skirt, between her soft, sexy thighs.

Would it be worse to use the bunks? He'd be aware of every move, every little sound she made in her sleep. She'd give him nightmares about church aisles and bobbing bridesmaids.

At least if they used the beds, he'd have the thickness of a mattress between them.

"I'd like to stretch out," he said, feeling like a jerk for nixing her idea to sleep sitting up.

"Well, you bought the tickets—but we'll total up the charges in the morning. I'll give you a check for my share."

"No hurry."

He'd gladly cover the whole cost of the trip for an hour in the same bunk with her, but oddly enough, he was starting to like her a little too much to take advantage. He retreated to the lounge car, not feeling particularly good about himself. But he was determined to avoid entanglements with marriage-minded females.

Darn that Brian! He wished they were still kids so

he could take him behind the garage and lay down the law to him. Instead of learning from their parents' marital disasters, his brother seemed determined to repeat them.

Rick picked one of several empty seats in the lounge and stared out at snowy fields swept into surreal configurations by a frigid February wind. He didn't bother to watch the grainy screen of a television set at the end of the car. He had too much on his mind to care about a movie: Brian's impulsive wedding plans; his disdain of a prenuptial; the necessity of calling him again and asking for another postponement. If he waited until the train got to Denver, he could make arrangements for the last leg of the trip. Then he could say for sure when he'd get to Phoenix.

He tried to concentrate on Brian's foolishness, but Kim kept popping into his mind. He liked her hazel-green eyes and curly sable hair, even though he'd long ago become immune to her brand of dimpled cuteness. Wholesome girls always came with a steep price: matrimony. It was his misfortune to be thrown together with the tall, sexy brunette.

He was drooping with fatigue, but he didn't doze in the chair. The soft buzz of voices in the lounge was a distraction, and he found himself eavesdropping on a young couple.

"This is supposed to be our honeymoon!" the girl wailed plaintively. "What a joke! Your parents and your brother never leave us alone."

"Honey, we'll make up for it later."

"Why did your sister plan her wedding so close to ours? I can't believe we're taking our honeymoon trip on a train with your parents."

"It's only until tomorrow, and you did agree to it."

"I can't sleep in that bunk. It's like a casket."

Rick felt mildly ashamed of himself for listening to their private conversation. Other people's intimacy had that effect on him. But from what he'd heard, he would give the lovebirds three years. By then the little bride would get tired of her simpering husband and decide she wanted a real life, whatever that was. They'd have a kid by then, and junior would be lucky if he didn't end up with three dads and a few uncles with overnight privileges.

He might as well go to bed. He could hardly stand himself when he felt this cynical. He got his shaving kit from the luggage rack, made a quick stop to brush his teeth, and went to their compartment.

The porter had done his job while Rick was gone. Their seats were folded down into a bottom bunk, and the upper had been pulled from above. The crisp white bed linens looked inviting enough, but his bunkmate was gone. Her duffel was jammed between the sliding glass door and the bottom berth, a space barely allowing foot room to climb to the top on a small ladder.

He'd hoped to find her sound asleep in a buttoned-to-the-neck flannel nightgown. Instead he had to wait for her while his feverish imagination conjured visions of her in skimpy sleepwear. How he wished he'd never seen the contents of her suitcase!

He left the curtained glass door open, but flopped down on the lower bunk. He didn't own a pair of pajamas, so the best he could do was slip off his chinos after she was tucked into her bed.

He was dozing when she startled him to full wakefulness.

"I want the lower bunk."

She sounded petulant. Her squall jacket was buttoned to her neck, and pajamas covered her legs. Her fuzzy slippers made her feet look bigger than his, and he was grateful for a moment because she looked more silly than sexy.

Carefully closing and locking the door, she wiggled out of the coat and folded it on top of her duffel.

His impulse to laugh at her died. Her pajamas were an old-fashioned, man-tailored style, oversize and designed for comfort, but the creamy silk clung like plastic wrap and made her look so darn cute and sexy he wanted to tumble her onto his lap.

"I'll flip a coin," he offered reluctantly, pretty sure the upper would fit him about as comfortably as a baby crib.

"No."

He could see she'd left her underwear on. The pink of her bra was hard to make out, but only a hint of her nipples showed under the clingy silk shirt.

"You're a lot smaller than I am." He squeezed out of the lower bunk and wondered what kind of toothpaste she used. No woman should smell so sweet at bedtime—no untouchable woman, anyway.

"I may be claustrophobic," she argued.

"May be? Don't you know?"

"I've never tried to sleep in a bed where I can't turn over without bumping my bottom on the roof," she explained with the patient tone of a harassed kindergarten teacher.

He wanted to pack her out of sight in one bunk or the other. It was getting harder and harder to resist starting something. She was exactly the type of woman he tried to avoid: the happily-ever-after kind.

If he let their chemistry kick in, it would be impossible to make her believe he wasn't a marrying man.

"Take the lower," he said with resignation.

"No, I'm being selfish. You need it more than I do. Just let me get settled before you turn the light off."

The lounge car was looking better, even with the honeymooners' bickering.

She flattened herself against the curtained door to allow room for him to squeeze past.

"Wish me luck," she said in a breathy voice.

"I'll help you." That came out too eagerly. He'd love to give her sleek, silk-clad bottom a boost, but it was a really stupid idea.

"Here I go." She stepped out of the big fuzzies—they actually had ears and eyes—revealing slender feet with cute red-polished toes.

It was easy to see the panty line under her pajama trousers. The silk pulled taut across her shapely backside as she climbed the ladder. The hard part was keeping his hands by his sides, especially when she got to the top rung, leaned over the bunk, and froze.

"What's wrong?"

He was the one in trouble if she didn't plunk her gorgeous bottom under the covers soon.

"Ah...nothing."

"Get in, then tell me when you want the light off."

"Just give me a minute."

"To do what?" He had a very clear idea of what he wanted to do.

"I have to get used to having so little space."

Did she have to do it with her rear hanging over the edge and her thighs outlined by clingy pajamas? Did she know the effect she was having on him?

"You'll be more comfortable lying down," he suggested, conscious of the rhythmic motion of the train under his feet and the rising temperature in the cubicle.

She peeled back the blanket and top sheet and cautiously slid one leg onto the mattress. From his point of view, it made her even more provocative.

"That's the way. Now the other leg. Slide in there," he coaxed.

He was hot and aroused, tempted to give her a shove and pull the covers up for her.

"I can't." She sounded pathetic, and she made him feel guilty for his lusty inclinations, even though they were involuntary and contrary to his best interests and hers.

"Close your eyes and roll," he suggested.

"Easy for you to say."

Easy wasn't the word he'd use.

"Either get in bed or come down here," he ordered sternly.

"I can do this. I've been rock climbing—but not since I broke my ankle doing it. This is much easier—*should be* much easier."

"Then do it," he growled.

Her top had slid up, showing several inches of soft, eminently touchable skin on her back. She put her other leg up and buried her face in the pillow. He wanted to throw the cover over her himself, but he was afraid he might touch her accidentally—or on purpose.

"Are you okay?" Was that husky rasp his voice?

"I will be." She wiggled under the blanket and curled up in a fetal position facing him. Her eyes were shut so tightly he wanted to relax her lids by kissing them.

"I'll leave the light on," he offered.

"No! I don't want to see. My pet hamster had a bigger pen than this."

"Come on down." He knew when he was defeated. "I'll take the upper."

"You won't fit."

"You're imagining it's smaller than it is."

"No, it's shrinking even as I lie here. The roof is going to come down and crush me."

"Kim, get down here. This is silly. You must be claustrophobic."

"You think?"

Did he detect a note of satisfaction in her voice?

"Get out, or I'll roll you out."

"I'll hit my head."

"Slide your legs out, and I'll lift you down."

He didn't have to. She shimmied down the ladder and made a beeline for the lower bunk, bumping against his hip and leg, igniting a flash fire in his groin.

"Can I still leave the light on?" she asked meekly from where she huddled under the covers.

"Sure."

"Aren't you going to take your pants off?"

"I plan to."

"You'll never be able to do it up there."

"Probably not."

"You can do it here. I'll close my eyes and not peek."

"Big of you," he said dryly.

She was right, though. Sardines in a can had more room.

"Are you doing it?"

She was lying on her stomach, propped up on her elbows with the fingers of one hand across her eyes. Even fully covered, she made enticing bumps under the blanket.

He unbuckled his belt and let his trousers slide down his legs, bumping his hip painfully on the door as he tried to keep his throbbing arousal out of her range of vision.

Of course she peeked.

He would, if *she* were stripping.

He climbed to the upper bunk and hoped he would remember not to sit up in the night. Headroom was nonexistent. She was right about the space. It seemed a lot smaller now that he was actually in it.

He closed his eyes, determined to sleep, but the light bothered him. Not being able to turn freely made him uncomfortable, and every little sound she made seemed magnified. He could hear her soft breathing, the rustle of covers and the small sigh as she settled down. He even imagined hearing one delicate toenail click against another.

He was going back to the lounge as soon as she was asleep, but she turned and twisted with no indication that that would be happening anytime soon.

"Are you asleep?" she whispered in a sultry undertone, or at least his overactive imagination heard it that way.

"No." He felt as grouchy as he sounded.

"I can't sleep either."

"Try." He tried to sound firm and fatherly, not that his male parent had ever been around at bedtime.

"I feel too guilty."

"For what?" He wanted to shut her up almost as much as he wanted to crawl in with her.

"You're much too big to sleep up there. I'm being selfish. Let's change places."

"You're claustrophobic."

"Maybe I exaggerated."

"You mean you were faking?"

"Well, sort of. I mean—"

"I don't want to know what you mean."

He scrambled down the ladder, not caring how much his navy briefs were still bulging.

She chose that exact moment to wiggle out of the lower bunk, colliding with him as his feet hit the floor.

"Oh!" they said in unison.

"Sorry," she mumbled with a little giggle.

"Sure you are."

He didn't plan it, but their lips collided as the train jiggled underfoot. It was more smack than kiss as she tumbled against his chest and caught herself by grabbing him.

The damage was done. He parted his lips and tasted the sweetness of her mouth.

"Ohhh!"

He knew a kiss-me-again moan when he heard one. He kissed her again.

"I'm...I'm sorry," she whispered breathlessly.

"Isn't that my line?" He was trying hard to remember why he shouldn't pull her into the lower bunk.

"No, I think it was my fault."

"Is that what was keeping you awake? You needed a good-night kiss?"

"Certainly not!"

He was glad the light was on. Her cheeks flushed pink, and he could tell she was a lousy liar.

"Maybe you should put your pants on."

"You peeked, didn't you?" He tried for mock indignation but blew it by laughing and circling her waist with his arms, pulling her closer with no resistance on her part.

"Do you think this compartment is soundproof?" she whispered.

He didn't know whether she was shy or naive or just plain reckless, but now was his last chance to ignore the invitation he thought was in her voice.

"Get to bed," he said huskily.

"Yes, I'd better. There's no way I can like a grouch who wants to ruin his brother's wedding."

He couldn't tell whether she was relieved or miffed.

She squeezed past him with difficulty, no doubt confirming that at least one part of him was reluctant to have her retreat to the upper bunk.

"Do you want the light out now?" he asked.

"I couldn't care less."

Was that a sniff he heard?

He left the light on.

4

SLEEPING ON A closet shelf wasn't easy, especially since Rick was so close she couldn't help thinking about him.

Kim curled on her side, cradled her cheek on the pillow, and thought about the surprise kiss. She hadn't expected it, but she had been wondering how his lips would feel on hers. He had the cutest little Cupid's bow—a perfect licking spot for the tip of her tongue, not that it had been that kind of kiss. He was a wonderful kisser, but the delicious sample only made her want more.

She wiggled, trying to get more comfortable, then worried he could hear her restlessness. No way did she want him to think he was the cause of her fidgeting. Great kisser or not, he wasn't a keeper. She'd had more than her share of infatuations and letdowns, and she really, sincerely wanted to find the one man right for her. Jane had. Her quiet, serious sister was soooo lucky to have Luke. They were perfect soul mates, and together they made beautiful babies. Kim couldn't imagine anything more wonderful.

A miracle like that couldn't happen with a man who hated weddings. Rick might look like a love god—even kiss like one—but he wasn't the real thing. His way of dealing with his brother's happiness was to oppose the marriage. He was probably acting out of misguided concern, but Kim was determined not to put her heart in the hands of Rick Taylor, the scourge of romance.

The rhythm of the rails was mildly hypnotic, unlike the soft drone of her cellmate's breathing. He was sound asleep. Their little good-night peck hadn't kept him awake.

She wiggled and hugged the pillow, trying to ignore the lingering tingle on her lips.

Sleep, when it came, shattered so abruptly she sat up and hit her head on the ceiling. For a panicky instant she was in limbo, forgetting where she was as the train lurched to a stop. Reacting on instinct alone, she scrambled over the edge of the bunk. Her toes missed the first rung of the ladder, and she plummeted backward.

"Eeeeee…"

"Gotcha!"

Her bottom collided with Rick's chest as he broke her fall.

"Put me down!"

"No thanks?"

"Thank you—put me down!"

"Next time use the ladder."

He took a deep breath and lowered her to the floor. Her bare feet slid down his long, delightfully hairy legs and connected with the tops of his feet. She squirmed aside a tad bit reluctantly.

"What was that bump?" Her brain felt fuzzier than the bunny slippers she located with her toes.

"The train stopped."

"Are we somewhere?"

"I don't think this is a scheduled stop. It's not even 5:00 a.m."

Noises from the corridor outside reached the door. She edged aside the curtain covering the glass door and peeked out.

"There are people out there." Brilliant observation! she scolded herself.

"I'll see what I can find out."

He put on his pants, quickly yanking up the zipper but not before her unchecked curiosity kicked in. She was wide awake now.

The corridor was noisy and crowded, and Rick left the door open enough for her to hear excited comments.

A hush fell over the crowd, and Kim stuck her head out as far as she could, holding her jacket in front of her for modesty's sake.

"Folks, no need to worry," a tall, lanky man in a railway uniform shouted the length of the car, quieting the crowd. "A semi crashed into the overpass just ahead. It's temporarily closed."

"For how long?" Rick spoke for everyone.

"Until we're sure it's safe. If there's structural damage to the supports…"

"How long until you know that?" a portly man in blue flannel pajamas interrupted.

"There's an inspector coming from Omaha. He should be here in a couple of hours. He can't see much anyway until daylight. We apologize for the delay, folks, but don't worry. Go back to sleep, and the staff will have a nice breakfast ready in a couple of hours. Meals are free until we get going again, and there's plenty of food."

"Where are we?" Rick made himself heard over the babble of voices.

"Fort Powell, Nebraska, about thirteen miles south

of Kearney. Nothing wrong with the train, folks. Just an unfortunate delay.''

"What if the train can't use the overpass?" flannel pajamas asked.

The rail spokesman was trying to make his way toward the next car. "No decision has been made, but we'll get you where you're going.''

"Probably have to go back to Omaha to be rerouted,'' another passenger grumbled as the crowd dispersed.

Back in the compartment Rick flipped the seats into position and pushed the upper bunk against the wall to give them headroom. Kim peered out the window and saw lights ahead where the tracks curved.

"I can't believe this trip,'' she said.

"I'm going to take a look.'' He started putting on his boots.

"You mean, go down there?''

"The slope's not too steep here.''

"Can you do that, just walk off the train?''

He laughed dryly. "We're not prisoners,'' he said before bundling up and heading for the outdoors.

She felt terribly alone when he left. Below the window several other passengers were going down the slope with Rick. Men! What were they trying to prove by plowing through knee-deep snow in the dark? They couldn't move the train over the overpass by gawking at the accident.

She curled up on the seat, used her jacket as a blanket, and proved to her own satisfaction that the seat was comfortable for sleeping.

RICK PLUNGED down the hill, slipping and sliding on the rough snow-covered ground. He was so frustrated by yet another delay, he was ready to push the train across the overpass himself.

The accident site wasn't more than a half-mile ahead once he reached the highway. He stomped and brushed away the dry powdery snow on his pant legs, then jogged toward the cluster of lights. What he saw was anything but encouraging. A northbound semi had gone out of control under the train bridge. Rick speculated that the driver had been going too fast in the predawn hours and had hit black ice on the pavement. Or he could have fallen sleep.

There were enough lights from police cars and highway department vehicles to make the crash site as bright as day. Rick saw an eighteen-wheeler jack-knifed like a toy in a kid's sandbox and a concrete support crumbled from the impact. He approached a highway worker in an orange vest.

"Any chance of the train going over it?" he asked.

"Sure—in a couple of years when the paper pushers get around to rebuilding. I wouldn't ride my motorcycle on that overpass."

The man only confirmed Rick's own estimate of the damage. His trip home was playing out like a diabolical board game: advance four spaces, sit out a penalty, then throw snake eyes. At the rate he was going, his brother's new bride would be filing for divorce and asking for a hefty settlement before he got there.

He walked back along the road and stared across bleak empty fields more desolate than the deserts of the Southwest. When he was hurrying to get to the scene of the accident, he'd concentrated on the lights by the underpass. Now he saw a tall sign in a halo of mist: Truck Stop. Distances were hard to gauge in the predawn darkness, but it seemed about a mile south of the train.

A truck stop meant transport, and he was willing to ride in anything going west. No way would he sit on a train while Brian said "I do" to disaster.

The hill seemed steeper as he climbed back to the train, but the tough part would be leaving without Kim. She had made the long trip less tedious. Of course, nothing could come of it. He'd passed a major test: spending a night with her in a compartment the size of a coat closet. Except for one little kiss, no, two—and some harmless fantasies, a few pretty hot—he'd kept her at arm's length where she belonged.

Hell, she didn't even like him. Why should she? She got starry-eyed at the mention of a wedding, and he didn't owe her an explanation about Brian. If this were his brother's first big romance, Rick could live with it. He hadn't yet met the new woman, but he couldn't stand seeing his only sibling act like an idiot over who had to be another materialistic bimbo. The money part wasn't the point. He didn't give a hoot about the family fortune, even though their grandparents had left them more than comfortable. Brian did well as a civil engineer, and Rick had no complaints himself. He just resented women using his brother and hated seeing him get hurt.

When he reached the train, he climbed into the car where the luggage racks were and was tempted to grab his overnight bag and leave. All he had in the compartment was a shaving kit, but he couldn't be sure what Kim would do if he disappeared. He knew she'd worry. She was that kind of person.

She was sleeping under her coat, long, spectacular, silk-clad legs stretched across the aisle between the seats. He wasn't going to forget those pajamas for a while. He could almost envy the guy who coughed up a ring for her and staked a permanent claim.

Maybe he could leave a note. No need to wake her. He reached toward the small recess between the seat and the wall, intending to use one of the advertising postcards stuck beside a route map. He cautiously reached for it.

"Ohmigosh! I didn't hear you come back." She was so startled her bottom bounced on the seat and the coat fell to her lap.

The pajama top was a lot more clingy than it had been. A day or two stranded in a compartment with her wouldn't be all bad. He wavered but knew it was best for both of them if they parted company.

"I came for my shaving kit," he said, reluctant to break the news that he was leaving.

"Don't shave on my account," she said, all trace of sleepiness gone.

"Actually, I'm not going to."

"Did you learn anything?" She was yanking and smoothing her pajamas as though she could look anything but sexy in her silks.

"Nothing good for us. Fortunately the driver survived, but the semi took out one support."

"You're sure?"

"Ninety-nine percent."

"How long until we get going again? I'm worried about my sister."

"The train will be rerouted." He didn't mention the long delay. "You'll get there in good time."

"*I'll* get there?"

She was sharp. There was nothing to do but say goodbye and get going.

"There's a truck stop about a mile down the road. I'm going to hike down there and hitch a ride. The wedding will be over before I get there if I'm stuck here all day."

"You won't get there in time by truck."

"No, but maybe I can find an airport somewhere south of here that's open. I'll go nuts if I sit on this train much longer."

"I'll go with you."

"Not a good idea."

"Why not?"

"You can't hitch a ride with a trucker."

"If I'm with you, why can't I?" She scrambled to the edge of the seat and tried to reach around him to get her duffel.

"You're not coming with me. You're much better off waiting on the train."

"I'm going. If you don't want me with you, I'll go alone."

"That's crazy."

"Maybe, but I'll give you three-to-one odds I get a ride before you do."

"I thought you didn't gamble."

"Only on sure things."

She was trying to get her duffel by pulling it between his legs. He wanted to dig his fingers into those bobbing curls of hers and pull her upright.

"Be reasonable, Kim." He couldn't remember saying her name aloud before this moment.

"I'll be dressed and ready to go in two minutes. Wait or not, it's up to you."

"You're making a terrible mistake."

"And you're not? I guess that means you're leav-

ing without me. Bye-bye.'' She had the bag and was
using it as a battering ram to get past him.

''I'll wait two minutes. If you're not back in exactly one hundred and twenty seconds, I go and you
stay on the train. If you are, you can come with me.''

''You have a deal, mister! Synchronize watches.''

She held up a delicate wrist and checked the face
on her watch where tiny hands marked the time.

''You're five—no, seven seconds slow,'' she said.

''Why are you so sure you're not fast?''

This was ludicrous, bickering over a few seconds'
difference. He'd never known a woman to get dressed
in less than twenty minutes.

''On your mark, get set, begin timing.''

Coat over her shoulders, she sprinted into the corridor in her fuzzy slippers, holding her duffel and
boots like a shield and sword.

He wanted to cheat and leave immediately, but no
doubt she'd follow on her own. He wasn't usually an
alarmist, but he could easily think of thirty or forty
ways she could get into trouble on her own. And she
might catch up with him anyway if he didn't get a
ride right away.

He liked the precision of his Swiss watch, the lu-
minous dial showing the day, hour, minute and second with silent efficiency, but he'd never realized just
how long two minutes were. What could he do in one
hundred and twenty seconds? Shave, scan the front
page of the morning paper, open a document on his
computer and begin work? He was satisfied with the
routine of his life, no big highs or depressing lows.
Why did he have the feeling things were racing out
of control?

Thirty seconds left. She couldn't possibly make it.

To his surprise, he found himself rooting for her. Then his saner self took over, and he foresaw nothing but trouble if she tagged along with him.

"Three seconds to spare!" She ran up to their compartment with flushed cheeks and the smugness of a winner.

"What about your luggage? You don't exactly travel light."

"That's because I'm moving back to Phoenix, not just visiting. Before leaving Detroit, I shipped tons of stuff, but it's not cheap, you know. Anyway, I never travel with more than I can manage myself."

"Sure you do." He didn't think his comment was unwarranted, considering he'd been the one to help scoop up her undies.

He had to stop thinking about her rainbow of sexy lingerie!

"You're making a big mistake," he warned without much hope of dissuading her.

"A bet's a bet. I won, so I go."

He looked her over from the buttoned front of her jacket to the tops of her boots brushed by the long black skirt.

"The hill is steep."

"You said it wasn't bad."

"That was before I climbed it."

As if Brian wasn't giving him enough grief. Now he had to worry about Kim. She was a walking magnet for the wrong kind of attention, and he didn't like feeling protective.

"Let's go." He didn't care if he sounded surly.

The first problem was her luggage, and he led the way to the baggage car. He wasn't being noble when he offered to carry the big wardrobe. No way could she wheel it down the snowy slope.

"I'll take that."

"I'll just slide it down the hill."

"And rip it open on a boulder? No thanks. I've seen enough of your clothes. And this case has to go." He pulled the old suitcase off the rack. "You can divide the contents between your duffel and the big case."

"I can't. They're too full. Anyway, I want it." She tugged the old hardsider away from him.

"It has a resale value of what? Fifty cents? I'll buy you a new one, but I won't hitch a ride with that."

"There's no room to—"

He opened the lingerie case and duffel, afraid she might be right about the lack of space. He did manage to stuff in the black number and a handful of panties, but that was it. She cooperated by trying to put more in the wardrobe, but it was already bulging beyond the intended capacity.

"Stuff your pockets," he suggested.

"No, I look too bulky already with pajamas under my clothes."

"You're still wearing them? I call that cheating on the bet."

"No way. I won fair and square."

He knew what he had to do. His overnighter was packed for a short trip. There was plenty of room in the numerous slots and pockets.

"I'll put the rest in mine. We can re-sort later."

She pouted and didn't help. Fortunately she didn't often push her lower lip out like that. The temptation to nibble it was almost too much for his hands-off resolution.

He tried not to look at her intimate garments as he stuffed them by the handful into his own case, but touch alone was enough to make him hot and bothered. He hurried as fast as possible and let her check to make sure the old case was empty.

"Let's go."

His overnight felt fifty pounds heavier even though her things weighed practically nothing.

"I have to get the luggage tag." She removed it and put it in her purse. "I don't want some well-meaning porter sending it to me. And you don't have to buy me another piece of luggage."

He'd lightened the load by ditching one case, but he still felt weighed down by the responsibility of keeping her out of trouble.

The snow outside was trampled, making the slope a little easier to see but no easier to descend.

"Take my hand," he said.

"No, I'm fine." She plunged ahead of him, lost her footing, and slid the next ten yards until she stopped herself by rolling.

"Are you all right?" He climbed down anxiously, hoping she hadn't injured any crucial parts.

"My pajama bottoms are all snowy."

"Maybe you'd better go back to the train and take them off."

"Will you wait?"

"This isn't a good idea. You should wait and go by train."

"I can't. You have my lingerie."

"I'll mail it to you."

"I'm going. I just have to take off my pajama bottoms."

"You can just as soon as we get to the truck stop." He grabbed her hand and pulled her to her feet.

"Are you kidding? I have snow up my legs. The silk is freezing cold. Just turn around, and I'll slide them off."

He glanced up at the train. Most but not all of the windows were dark. How many lecherous old men—or young ones—were watching her strip them off? He couldn't leave her alone to hitch a ride.

"Okay, they're off." She waved the silk trousers like a battle flag, sending a sprinkling of powdery snow into his face.

"Sorry." She tried to help him brush the flakes off his shoulders and hair.

"Never mind. The trucks will start rolling at dawn." He didn't have a clue about truckers' driving habits, but the quicker they got moving, the sooner he could part company with this walking disaster. If he believed in that sort of thing, he'd say he had a premonition about this leg of the trip.

He wadded the pajama bottoms into his jacket pocket, feeling like a traveling lingerie salesman.

The trek was longer than it looked, he thought, moments later. The cold, gray, first light of morning was streaking the sky when he switched her wardrobe to his other hand and flexed his aching arm.

"I can pull it," she said.

"Just watch out for ice so you don't fall again." And stay out of my mind!

He walked a step or two ahead, but it didn't stop him from thinking about her. He thought of how cold her legs must be after plunging into snow. He would gladly massage warmth into her shapely calves and thighs. An icy Nebraska wind buffeted them, and he longed to warm her chilled body against his.

He tried to tell himself it was only because he'd had a long dry spell. He'd been too busy and too indifferent lately to go through the ritual required to have sex with the kind of woman who appealed to him. He was overdue. Any tall, shapely, beautiful woman would have the same effect on him.

Kim—he had to think a minute to come up with her last name—Kim Grant was naive, ditzy and accident-prone. He was only imagining how special she was. More to the point, she thought a man who didn't wax enthusiastic over weddings—and he'd never met one who did—was a grouch.

If she didn't have a head full of happily-ever-after fantasies, she might end up in his bed. He could guarantee a good time, but he couldn't promise heart and soul to any woman.

"I'm pooped." She came up beside him, her breath steamy in the frigid air.

"It's not much farther, and I think we've lucked out."

"How?" She did sound weary.

"Look. It's more than just a service station. I think this is a loading area where trucks pick up freight from trains for distribution. See the platforms."

"That's good?"

"More chance of getting a ride. The road under the overpass is only a minor highway. The main one is over there." He pointed to moving lights beyond the truck center.

"Good. I could sleep for a week."

She dragged behind, and he adjusted his pace to walk beside her. He relieved her of the duffel, and she gamely tried to keep up, but every few paces she fell behind again.

When they finally got close, he was reassured by the well-lit warehouses, loading docks and fuel pumps. The rest area was large with a restaurant, trucker facilities and even a bus station.

His feet and hands were numb and his legs smarted from the cold, but he was more concerned about Kim. The long skirt flip-flopping around her boot tops looked too breezy for comfort, and the frigid wind had reddened her cheeks.

She'd wanted to come, but he still felt vaguely guilty for bringing her with him. Like it or not, they were together for the long haul: He had her underwear.

KIM TRIED not to stumble, but her toes felt like marbles crowded into her boots. She was wearing the hood of her jacket for the first time ever, but the icy wind bombarded her face and made her forehead ache to the center of her brain.

"We're nearly there," Rick said.

"Good." Talking was an effort.

She should have stayed on the train. Warm, cozy lights were beckoning to her from where it still stood on the track.

Her nephew would be getting up soon. He thought sleep was an inconvenience to be avoided as much as possible. The rascal hadn't taken a nap since he was two. If any other member of the household dared linger in bed, he'd "scare" them awake with a flying leap or a stuffed lion in the face.

"I can smell the hot coffee from here," Rick said.

Drinking it wouldn't be enough to get warm. Kim needed to soak in a bathtub full of it.

They approached the truck stop from the rear, cutting through a snow-covered field with drifts higher than the tops of her boots. A little metal-sided building separate from the main facility served as a bus station, and Rick headed toward it.

"If I can rent a locker there, it would be worth it

not to haul all this luggage into the restaurant,'' he said.

"Very practical.'' She had to sound the words in her mind to make her tongue articulate them.

They walked into a drab little room with a few scoop-seat plastic chairs, a row of metal lockers and an unmanned ticket counter at the rear. A large notice board with moveable block letters showed the schedule for the day.

Rick dug into his pocket for change to rent a locker while she studied the list of departures. It cheered her to see it was possible to get to Denver from wherever they were. Anyone who had the price of a ticket and was willing to wait—she counted on her fingers—five and a half hours could board a bus and get to Denver where the weather was probably too awful at the spacious new airport for planes to take off. She felt trapped in a video game where every door was the wrong choice.

She should call Jane, but how could she give her sister a progress report when they were stranded who-knew-where hoping to get a ride from who-knew-who? Her sister would worry, and that wouldn't be good for her pregnancy.

Rick had to use two lockers for her belongings. He slammed the metal doors shut in quick succession, setting off rockets of pain across her forehead.

"Let's get some breakfast and see about a ride,'' he said.

She went with him to the restaurant, shuffling whenever she forgot to lift her feet. What was wrong with her? She felt drained. Two years in the midwest should have made her winter-proof, but Detroit seemed like a temperate paradise compared to this.

"Thanks," she said when he held the door for her, surprised that talking made her throat hurt.

They walked into the world of early-morning people. Kim felt overwhelmed by the pungent aroma of frying bacon and the din of male voices.

"Is that booth okay?" Rick asked, his voice sounding dreamy and distant.

"Sure."

She slid onto a red plastic seat and hugged herself to absorb the heat of the place. Her cheeks burned, and her fingers had all the mobility of popsicle sticks.

"What are you having?" Rick handed her one of two laminated menus stuck behind a holder with salt, pepper and sugar packets.

"Tea." She took off her leather gloves and massaged her fingers. "Hot tea."

"Number two looks good—juice, two eggs, bacon or sausage, hash browns, toast and a stack of pancakes."

Just hearing him read the breakfast special made her nauseous.

"Can you eat all that?"

"I wouldn't usually, but who knows when we'll have another meal."

"We're going to Denver, not the Antarctic."

"You're testy this morning. You didn't have to come—"

"Don't tell me I should have stayed on the train."

His face was swimming in front of her, and she wanted to put her head on the table and pass out.

"Are you all right?" He leaned closer and peered at her.

"I'll be fine, thank you for asking."

"This isn't a good idea...."

"Don't say it!" The upper bunk was beginning to seem like a heavenly loft.

The waitress hurried over to their booth, cheery but obviously rushed.

"You folks decided?"

"Number two with bacon, orange juice and black coffee," Rick said.

"Tea. Hot tea," Kim said. She'd like a pail full to warm her feet.

"She'll have number six—one scrambled egg with whole wheat toast," Rick ordered for her.

"No—just tea," she mumbled at the waitress's retreating back. "You didn't need to order for me," she said to him.

"Someone had to. Are you sure you're up to this—hitchhiking to Denver?"

The little worry line creasing his forehead was sweet. Another nice place to kiss. Not that Rick was her type. She had to remember that.

She intended to reassure him, but it was hard to talk when her teeth were chattering. She clenched her jaw and wished she were home, wherever that was. She couldn't stay at Jane's forever. The whole process of relocating loomed ahead like a concrete wall with no opening: interview for a job, search for an apartment, change her driver's license....

"Kim. Kim!"

"Sorry. I wasn't paying attention."

"You're not yourself."

"Who am I?" She gave the question serious consideration.

He reached across the table and gently touched her forehead. His fingers were warm and soothing.

"I wouldn't be surprised if you have a fever." He sounded worried.

"I never get fevers. I'll be fine." She tried to sound chipper, but her thick, fuzzy tongue muffled her words.

"I'm going to ask around for a ride. I'll be right back."

When he left, she slumped, resting her head on the padded back of the seat. Maybe she wasn't quite herself, but she still enjoyed watching him walk. All his parts fit together so perfectly. Too bad she'd never get a valentine from him. Her favorite day was coming up soon: lacy hearts, tiny chocolates in boxes with big red ribbons, red roses from someone special. A skeptic like Rick probably gave magazine subscriptions if he paid any attention at all to the most romantic day of the year.

What day was it? She vaguely remembered leaving Detroit on Friday. Her watch was no help. The little hands were dancing on the face. Funny, she'd never seen them do that before.

Breakfast came before Rick got back. She burnt her tongue on the scalding tea and wrapped the toast in a napkin, putting it in her purse for later. She got rid of the scrambled egg by adding it to the pile on Rick's plate.

"You've eaten already?" He sounded surprised. "You must have been starved. I've lined up a ride, but we'll have to hustle. You'd better use the ladies' room while I eat."

Not even her big sister told her when to go, but she couldn't sit there and watch him plow through the mound of greasy food.

He was waiting for her at the door when she got back.

"I didn't pay for my breakfast." The warm water she'd splashed on her cheeks made them feel burning hot—or maybe she did have a fever.

"I took care of it."

"I owe you a fortune."

"I have your lingerie as collateral."

Would he hold her panties hostage? The black-and-white checkerboard floor tiles made her dizzy. She tried to walk without stepping on a white square.

"It's the semi with the red-and-white logo on the side," Rick said, pointing. "I'll walk you over there, then get our luggage."

"What is it hauling?" She had no idea why this seemed important.

"I didn't ask, but nothing four-footed."

The truck motor was idling. The stench of diesel fuel filled her nostrils and made her want to gag. Who was she kidding? She was sick. Her teeth were clicking together like a set of wind-up false ones, and she didn't have enough energy to climb into the cab.

She hesitated, not quite sure what to do.

"Can you get in?"

He put his arm under her elbow to help, and she wanted to lean on his broad, inviting chest.

"Not a good idea," she muttered to herself.

"Climb in and keep warm. I have to get the luggage."

"I can't do it," she whispered in a husky voice.

"Can't what?" To his credit, he sounded concerned.

"I've changed my mind."

"I don't think you should walk all the way back to the train. You don't look too good."

She'd seen herself in the restroom mirror. Except for her pink cheeks, she was a pasty blob.

"What I'll do," she said as decisively as possible, "is wait for the bus to Denver."

"That's a five-hour wait." Apparently he'd read the schedule, too.

"I'll sleep until it comes."

"On one of those chairs?" The man didn't forget life's little details.

"Those old scoop seats from the sixties are more comfortable than they look. One of my friends was into retro decorating."

"Boyfriend?"

There was an irrelevant question if she'd ever heard one.

"Female," she lied. She didn't want to explain about Mad Milt McDonald whose idea of a date was prowling through salvage yards.

"I don't like to leave you—sick and all, that is."

"I'm twenty-six years old. I can take care of myself."

"Really? That old?" He took her hand and started leading her toward the bus waiting room.

"How old did you think?" Should she be insulted? In the mists of her mind, she didn't really care if he thought she was thirty.

"Twenty-one, twenty-two."

"No way!"

"You told me already. I was just kidding."

He wasn't. They'd spent the night together and hadn't bothered to exchange vital statistics. Was he a morning person or a night person? Did he eat his salad first or crunch on it all through the meal? Did he like tall brunettes?

"How are old are you?" she asked.

"Thirty-two in March."

"Over the hill." She didn't mean it, but it was unusual to find a gorgeous bachelor his age still unencumbered by a wife, ex-wife or significant other.

She was leaning on his arm, wishing she didn't feel like melting gelatine. Maybe she should go with him, but what if she got sick to her stomach in the truck?

"I hate leaving you here," he said.

"It's a public place." Every step she took, she discovered a new ache. Fat lot of help she'd be to Jane if she brought the flu with her.

"I suppose I could wait for the bus." He sounded lukewarm.

"No, you have a wedding to break up. If you don't get there, they may live happily ever after."

"You don't understand the situation."

"What's not to understand? Boy loves girl, plans to marry same. Along comes the big bad wolf—I mean, brother..."

He opened the door of the bus depot and practically pushed her inside.

"Let me give you my card," he said.

He dug one out of his billfold and handed it to her. She looked at it but had no idea what it signified.

"Call me when you get to Phoenix so I know where to send your things."

"Oh, sure. And I have to settle for the car and the train and the meals. I must owe you a bundle."

"It's the least of my worries." He walked over to the lockers and retrieved his overnight bag. "Here's your duffel and the key to the other one."

She wanted to whimper like a little lost girl. She definitely didn't want him to leave, and she hated his plan to scuttle a wedding.

"The trucker won't wait," he said. "Take care of yourself."

If I don't, who will? she thought miserably.

"Thanks for everything," she said woodenly.

"Nice getting to know you."

He left.

Why didn't he ask for her sister's phone number or arrange to meet her in Phoenix?

She flopped down in one of the faded green chairs, too exhausted to worry about comfort, or the answer to her question. Jane needed her, and she couldn't get to her. Closing her eyes, she tried to sink into oblivion, but Rick's face swam behind her lids. Was this what it was like to let someone get under your skin?

A HALF HOUR LATER Rick was still worried about Kim. The trucker was a talker, glad to have a passenger, but Rick was hard-pressed to keep up his end of the conversation. He liked problems with logical solutions, not the sticky morass created by his brother's infatuations. The last time he'd talked to Brian, his sibling had been bullheaded about a prenuptial agreement. He claimed it showed a lack of trust and insulted the woman he loved.

What was so terrible about taking a simple precaution? He couldn't get through to Brian, and now he had Kim on his mind. She had looked steamrolled, drained of the vitality he'd come to enjoy. Probably she had a virus, or maybe she was only exhausted. He was pooped himself, but the driver had refused to let him pay for the ride, making him feel obligated to stay awake and make an occasional comment even though his mind was back at the dingy waiting room.

When the bus did come, she'd be on it for hours. What if she were seriously ill? Granted, she was good at getting help from strangers—he was proof of that— but what if she were feverish and incoherent? She'd been pretty spacey at the restaurant, and he wasn't at all sure she'd eaten anything. His pile of eggs had been suspiciously large.

He looked at his watch after they'd been on the road forty-five minutes. He had a hard time believing it was only Saturday. This trip seemed to be taking forever. If Brian hadn't postponed the wedding, he'd only have a few hours left to get to Phoenix.

Snow pelted the broad windshield, and the driver's conversation slacked off as he concentrated on worsening road conditions. Rick started to miss the friendly drone of his voice. He found that he missed another friendly voice, as well.

AT THE BUS STATION, Kim was only dimly aware of the ticket agent coming to work and a few passengers wandering into the waiting room. The big clock on the wall showed a half hour until the bus departed for Denver. She should buy her ticket and retrieve her wardrobe, but she couldn't muster enough energy to get out of the chair. Her head still ached, and her throat felt as if she'd been gargling with sand. She tried to think of options other than getting on the bus. Maybe if she sat there long enough, she'd turn into a statue and someone would haul her away. Or maybe another ten minutes of dozing would revive her. She closed her eyes again, depending on the low conversation of other passengers to wake her in time.

She awoke abruptly, not sure whether minutes or hours had passed.

"Kim, wake up."

She knew that soft, coaxing voice.

"The bus leaves in ten minutes. Do you want to be on it?"

She cautiously peeked out under her lashes. Why did people admire the long, spikey things? They only got in the way of seeing clearly.

"Kim, are you with me? Wake up!"

She focused reluctantly, then knew what it meant to feel a flood of joy.

"Rick, why are you here?"

"That's what I've been asking myself," he said with a self-deprecating laugh.

"How did you get here?" She was trying to focus on practical details to make sure she wasn't dreaming.

"Hay truck to Fort Powell, then I rented some kid's beat-up old pickup at a service station there. It's cheaper to fly on the Concord than travel with you."

"I thought you'd left." Chalk squeaking on a board made a prettier sound than her voice.

"I did. What about the bus? Are you up to it? I paid the kid with the truck enough to have him get it here, or there's a motel in Fort Powell if you need to rest awhile."

"You have to get to Phoenix."

She had to call her sister. There was no way she could go to her house feeling like this. It was a bitter disappointment, but it would be worse to let Peter or Jane catch what she had.

"Maybe a few hours sleep in a bed..." Rick suggested hopefully. "I saw a grocery store in Fort Powell. I'll get you some aspirin."

"Last call," a sweet-faced woman with a halo of gray curls called out.

Kim was alert enough now to realize the woman was the ticket agent, and they were on the verge of missing the bus to Denver.

"We won't be going now," Rick said, walking toward the counter. "Can we get a schedule for Denver?"

"Won't be going..." Kim stood and the room reeled.

Rick returned from the ticket window, stuffing a printed schedule into his pocket. "There's always another bus," he said matter-of-factly.

"But your brother's wedding..."

"We'll talk about it later."

She slept in the pickup, her head on Rick's shoulder, and awoke to see an unlit neon sign for the E-Z Sleep Motel.

"Stay here," he said as he got out.

Did he think she'd hop out and race over to the E-Z Roll Bar and Bowling Alley across the street? Stop it! She reminded herself to be nice to him. He had come back to rescue her. She forgot from what.

He returned with a key attached to a piece of lumber vaguely shaped like a Z. It took a minute to connect it to the E-Z Sleep Motel. She was even slower realizing he only had one key.

"Where will you be?" she asked, beginning to have visions of stretching out on a real bed.

"I'll check out the grocery store, make a few phone calls. Don't worry about me. You need rest."

"Thank you."

She was beginning to have warm, mushy feelings about him. Was it possible—no, no way. He only *seemed* like Mr. Right because she was feverish, fuzzy-brained, out of her head. Such a shame! He was sexy and adorable, and he even had a sweet side. If only he didn't think weddings were wakes for carefree bachelorhood....

6

KIM HADN'T SEEN blond furniture since Mad Milt
McDonald bought a pile of it at an estate auction, but
the motel room had one saving grace: a king-size bed.
It didn't matter that the walls were lackluster tan, the
rug threadbare gold, and the only picture was calen-
dar-art, an autumn scene with dark orange blobs the
color of the bedspread. At least she could stretch out
in comfort and sleep.

She sat on the edge of the bed to pull off her boots,
but they seemed too far away. She bent over and
groped for the left one, but the room started to spin.

"Let me do that." Rick dropped to his knees,
blocking her headlong tumble to the floor.

"Wow, I'm dizzy."

He did that nice thing with his fingers on her forehead again.

"You're burning up. Maybe I should take you to
a hospital."

"No, all I need is some sleep."

Hospitals were good. She'd met her best boyfriend
ever in the emergency room when she'd fallen rock
climbing. Of course, after a wonderful six months,
he'd decided to work for a relief agency in Guatemala. She wanted to volunteer and go with him, but
her computer skills weren't in high demand in a place

with no electricity. At least it had been a sweet parting.

"It wouldn't hurt to have an emergency room check you out," Rick insisted.

Easy for him to say. He probably had medical insurance. Hers had expired with the end of her job, and she already owed him her life savings for tickets and whatever else. Her sister would help if asked, but the whole point of the trip was for *her* to help *Jane* for a change.

"It's too much of a hassle to go there and sit around," she said, not untruthfully.

"Let me get your boots."

He pulled off first her right and then her left boot. It was a good sign she could tell which was which. Then he rolled down her kneesocks and peeled them off.

She didn't know what to say. He was making her feel like a pampered child, but in a nice way.

He took one sole in the palm of his hand and gently massaged the top of her foot with his other. How could he come in from the frigid air and still have warm hands? She tended to be ticklish, but the way he manipulated her toes was pure heaven. She embarrassed herself by moaning with pleasure.

"That feels wonderful. My neck is jealous."

"Did sleeping in a chair at the bus depot give you a few kinks?" He was working his magic on her other foot.

"I should have stayed on the train," she said wearily.

"Move toward the end of the bed," he said, standing and earning merit points for not saying, "I told you so."

"This was my big chance to do something for my sister. Without Jane, my life would have been pretty wretched as a kid. She was a mother when I needed one, and she's still my best friend."

"She sounds like a special person, but that doesn't surprise me."

She half expected him to say she was special, too, but he didn't. Instead he started kneading the back of her neck, putting subtle pressure where it ached.

"You're good at this," she murmured.

"Thanks. I like getting a professional massage myself, so I've learned a few things."

She imagined him lying on a table on his tummy with only a towel to cover his firm bottom. It would be sheer pleasure to rub lotion into his sleek shoulders and back. She loved the thought of relaxing his tense calf muscles with the palms of her hands and pummeling away the tension in his strong thighs with the edges of her hands.

"Am I hurting you?" he asked.

"No, it feels much better." Her head lolled from side to side. "How can I thank you?"

"Why don't you take your clothes off—"

"I'm not that thankful!"

"I wasn't... I meant, you should get into something more comfortable and get some sleep. I'll go get some aspirin."

"I'm too tired to bother."

She yanked aside part of the bedspread and crawled toward a plump white pillow.

"At least take off your skirt so you'll be more comfortable."

The white headrest was her life raft. Another few inches and she could clutch it and rock herself to sleep the way she had as a little girl. Her head hit the pillow, but her eyes popped wide open. A thought was nagging at her. There was something she had to know.

She looked up at Rick and remembered.

"Why are you being so mean to your brother?"

"I'm not." He took a deep breath but didn't seem annoyed by her question. "Brian has had one very bad experience with marriage, and his track record with women is abysmal. I want him to slow down, not jump into another disastrous relationship. He's hardly known the woman six weeks. What would it hurt to get to know her better before committing himself to marriage?"

"You don't believe in love at first sight?" She turned onto her back and stared up at him.

"No. It's just chemistry, pheremones, or to be blunt, sex. When you came down the escalator, I wanted to forget the luggage and carry you over my shoulder to a nice private place."

"Like a caveman..." Her shiver had nothing to do with her raging fever.

"But aside from getting me arrested it would have been a darn stupid thing to do."

She was disappointed. It was only pretend, so why didn't he tell her what else he'd wanted to do?

"I don't see why, assuming she—I—was willing."

"Were you?"

"I didn't know you."

"Exactly!"

He didn't need to sound so triumphant.

"But if you knew I was an eligible bachelor making a comfortable living," he went on, "and I dangled a diamond the size of an egg in front of you, wouldn't you be tempted whether you knew much about me or not?''

''Certainly not.'' She was angry now, but she'd bite off her tongue before she explained that love and romance meant too much to her to marry for any other reason. The fever made her lightheaded but not idiotic enough to bare her heart to an unbeliever.

''Then you're not the kind of woman my brother usually hooks up with.''

''But it's your brother's life,'' she said tiredly.

''I know.''

He ran his fingers through his hair, repeatedly brushing it back from his forehead. It was the first time she'd seen him fidget. She sensed it wasn't a good time to give him advice.

''All I want him to do is give it some time and thought,'' he said. ''Is that unreasonable?''

She recognized a rhetorical question when she heard one. Rolling over on her side, she closed her eyes and saw lights dance on the insides of her lids.

RICK WATCHED her sleep longer than he'd planned, not that Fort Powell, Nebraska, offered much in the way of diversions. He couldn't explain it, even to himself, but something was happening to him. He felt so darned responsible for Kim, even though it had never been his idea for her to tag along. In fact, thanks to her, he was in more trouble than ever, his chance of heading off Brian's wedding lessening with every passing hour.

How long would she be sick? She was an amazingly robust woman, but how long would it take what he suspected to be a virus to run its course? Who would take care of her if he didn't stick around? He'd already thought of calling her sister, but he didn't want to be responsible for upsetting a woman who was struggling with a difficult pregnancy.

He stepped closer to the bed, intending to cover her, then wondered about the skirt twisted around her thighs. It looked so uncomfortable, he persuaded himself to try straightening it around her legs. She was soundly sleeping, so he wasn't worried about waking her. Damn, even her stuffy-sounding little snore was cute!

He doubted he'd ever seen a shapelier pair of legs, long and slender with the right amount of fullness in the calves and thighs. It was almost criminal to hide them under a long skirt. He tried to rearrange the bunched-up fabric, but it wasn't working. There was no way he could make her more comfortable without doing what he'd told her to do earlier: take off the skirt. The waist was elastic, so he gripped it with his fingers and carefully worked it over her hips and down her legs.

The cheeks of her bottom were only half-covered by high-cut pink panties, and she looked cute and tempting and breathtakingly erotic with her backside provocatively revealed.

He wondered if altruism had anything at all to do with his compulsion to stay with her. Was he being as simpleminded as Brian, letting a woman get under his skin when he'd just met her?

Impatient with himself, his brother and his unwanted traveling companion, he left the motel room without bothering to zip his coat or put on gloves. He needed to cool down in a big way.

THREE HOURS LATER Rick had exhausted the resources of the town—and himself. He bought some necessities at the town's only grocery store and lunched at the E-Z Bar while bowlers thundered balls down the six lanes. The crash of pins and the excited squeals weren't enough to distract him from his troubles.

At least lunch hit the spot. His burger was juicy and hot, and the cup of chicken soup that came with it had never seen the inside of a can. He arranged for a takeout order for Kim and went to the lobby where he'd seen a pay phone.

Brian answered on the first ring. Rick wondered for an instant why he wasn't at work, then remembered it was still the weekend.

"Bro!" Brian usually called him that when he wanted something. "I've got good news and bad news. Which do you want to hear first?"

Rick hated this game.

"Give me the bad."

"Melinda's mother got stung by a bee."

"Is she allergic?"

"No, but she got nailed right on the nose. It's as red and swollen as a clown's honker. She doesn't want anyone to see her until it's back to normal, so we've had to postpone the ceremony until next Saturday. We'll have it just before the reception. Melinda is disappointed, but she's a good sport."

Rick wanted to hoot with pleasure. Brian's bad news was great for him. He'd get to Phoenix in plenty of time to try talking some sense into his brother.

"What's the good news?" he asked.

"I had a long talk with Melinda about a prenuptial. She wants me to get one. That way I'll never have any doubt she's marrying me because she's crazy about me.''

"She sounds like a sensible woman," Rick said. "I'm glad."

"Of course, I'm not going to do it."

"What? You said she thinks it's a good idea."

"Yeah, but I don't. What kind of message would it give the woman I love? I'm going into this for the long haul. We've had the talk, and I'm happy with my decision. So when do you think you'll get here?"

Rick explained his situation without telling his brother about Kim, only that he was stranded because a semi rammed the overpass. Brian's bad news was good for him, but he was mega shortsighted about the prenuptial. He still needed to get to Phoenix and drum some sense into his brother, but at least he had a little more time. He absolutely had to talk to Brian—and their attorney—before the wedding.

He made his goodbyes, picked up the chicken soup, paid the kid at the service station to use his truck another day and went back to the motel where he tried to rent a second room.

"Sorry," the clerk said, peering at Rick through owl-eyed glasses that made his face look perfectly round. "I'm all booked up for tonight. Got a bunch of railroad fellows coming in."

"Where's the nearest place I can get a room?"

"Maybe Kearney. Can't say for sure."

Great! He mumbled thanks and went to check on Kim. Like it or not, she was going to have a roommate. It would be harder on him than her.

The bed was empty when he got back, but he heard the shower running behind the closed door of the bathroom. He took off his jacket, put the container of soup by the heater with a vague idea of keeping it warm, and eyed the unused portion of the bed. He was tired enough to sleep standing up, but darned if he'd let that space go to waste.

"Oh, I didn't hear you come in!" Kim came through the door a few minutes later swaddled in a long robe covered with swirls of pink and red. It clung to her curves, making him wish she'd wear plaid flannel or thick terry cloth.

"I brought you some soup and aspirin for your fever."

"I can't thank you enough for coming back for me. I've made so much trouble for you."

He shrugged, unwilling to admit, even to himself, that he wasn't in a hurry to part company with her anymore. He could have refused to share the rental car, and he should have insisted she wait for a plane in Chicago, but somewhere along the way he'd started enjoying her company.

"How are you feeling?"

"Not great, but I had a good nap. Think I woke up because I'm hungry. Funny, though, I don't remember taking my skirt off."

She gave him the evil eye—at least, it felt that way—and challenged him to deny doing it.

"You looked uncomfortable." He tried to sound nonchalant, but inside he was squirming.

She stared him down without saying anything.

I'm not going to apologize, he told himself, not her.

"I brought you chicken soup from the bowling alley. It's pretty good. They sent a plastic spoon and some crackers with it."

The business of setting it up on the room's small

writing desk gave him something to do besides telling her they'd be roomies for the night.

She praised the soup, dutifully swallowed the pills, and thanked him profusely, all the while eyeing him warily. What did she want him to do, tell her she had the sexiest legs and the cutest butt he'd ever seen?

"I called my brother," he said instead.

"Has he rescheduled the wedding?"

"Yes. The mother of the bride got stung by a bee on the end of her nose."

"On the end of her nose?" She crushed another cracker into her soup, not the way he liked to eat it. "Can she breathe?"

"I guess, but she doesn't want to be seen until the swelling goes away. They're going to get married before the reception next Saturday, so I'm going to forget about hitching a ride and take the bus to Denver tomorrow."

"So we can spend the night here. I'm glad. I still feel semirotten. Did you get a room?"

However she felt, she looked great to him. Her curls were damp but bouncy, and the lingering blush of pink on her cheeks only made her more beautiful. Worse, she had him wondering what she was wearing under the long wrap.

"Yeah, the only one left. This one."

He held his breath, wondering whether she'd object. Considering the effect she was having on him, he probably deserved to be booted out.

"I guess it doesn't matter. I look even worse than I feel. Maybe I'll take another nap."

She slept while he tried to watch a basketball game on TV. He dozed in the wooden-armed chair but kept waking up because there was no headrest—and no way he could forget the woman curled up in bed only a few feet away. He could make a really bad mistake in this situation. Kim would take anything that happened between them very seriously, and the better he knew her, the more sure he became that she wasn't into casual sex. She wanted a permanent relationship, and he wasn't a candidate for the position.

He needed a cold shower.

When she woke again, it was nearly eight o'clock in the evening. He went back to the bowling alley bar and brought club sandwiches and huge cups of decaf coffee to the room. He wolfed all of his and half of hers.

After a shower—warm not cold because nothing was going to make him indifferent to Kim—he wrapped up in the bedspread to sleep on top of the blanket on the far side of the big bed.

"I think my fever has broken for sure," she said from her side.

"Good." He kept his back resolutely turned toward her.

"One little problem."

"What?" Her whole existence was a problem to him.

"I'm wide awake. I slept most of the day."

"Watch TV. I don't mind."

"I don't want to keep you awake."

What did she think she was doing?

"Nothing can," he lied. "I'm bushed." Nothing except the thought of her long legs wrapped around him.

"You probably want me to shut up."

He imagined how quiet she would be if he covered

her mouth with his and kissed her until she could only gasp with pleasure.

"No, that's okay. I'm glad you're feeling better."

The bedspread twisted around him was scratchy and smelled stale. As soon as she went to sleep, he was going to toss it aside and get under the blanket.

"I've never been so out of it. Of course, I can't remember the last time I had a fever. Must have been when I was a kid," she mused.

He tried not to listen, but her words were like warm honey spreading over him, entrapping him in her sweetness. Her voice was definitely on the long list of things he liked about her.

"I don't know what I would have done without you," she said.

"Someone else would have helped you. Strangers like to be kind to you, not that you're not perfectly capable of taking care of yourself."

She certainly had a gift for making a man want to look after her. Why else was he here, hugging his side of the bed even though he was sharing it with a woman he ached to take in his arms. A cold shower couldn't reach the place where she was affecting him the most: in his weary, weak-willed brain.

"Tell me a story," she said in a coaxing voice.

"What?"

He propped himself up on one elbow, seeing her dimly in the light filtering toward them from the bathroom door. She was sitting up, hugging her knees.

"You know, a bedtime story."

"I don't know any. Telling stories wasn't my parents' style even when one of them happened to be around at bedtime."

"That's too bad. Oh, before I forget, I owe you for

a phone call. I called my sister while you were getting the sandwiches.''

The way her conversation skipped around kept him off balance, or maybe just being with her did that.

"How is she?"

He tried to resign himself to a long chat, but his mind wasn't on what she was saying. What could he do to get her to sleep? Didn't she realize what she was doing to his steadily weakening willpower?

"She said fine, but she sounded tired. She made the mistake of telling Peter I was coming. He was camped out by the front door in his pajamas at six this morning."

"Sounds like a cute kid. You'll be seeing him soon now that you're feeling better. You are still feeling better, aren't you?" He didn't need to ask. He could tell just by listening to her, but he was struggling to find a safe topic.

"A lot better. I hope it's only a twenty-four-hour bug."

"Sleep helps, I've heard."

She rustled as she sank back on the pillow. He tried not to imagine what, if anything, she was wearing under the pink-and-red robe.

Hot and bothered as he was, he was relieved. He'd been scared seeing her so sick, and the fact that he'd felt compelled to come back for her was scary, too. He'd been like a fish taking bait when he picked up the first of her scanty panties at the Detroit airport. As long as she was out of it from fever, there was no way he could get the hook out.

"I'm waiting for my story," she teased.

He enjoyed her mischievous demand in spite of himself. At least it was a sign she was herself again.

"Start one for me, then I'll see what I can do," he said.

"All right. Once upon a time there were two handsome princes. One of them wanted to get married, but the bigger, stronger, older prince said, 'No, no, no. You cannot get married.'"

She giggled, and it didn't take a smack on the side of the head to alert him to her ulterior motive.

"Now it's your turn. Finish it," she urged.

"The older prince—he was also more handsome—locked his brother in the dungeon and put the would-be bride to work scrubbing clothes in the stream. End of problem. End of story."

"That's a terrible ending!" She sat up again with more noisy rustling.

"I never claimed to be a good storyteller."

"Tell me one thing. Does the mean older prince hate all weddings or just his brother's?"

"Marriage isn't the issue. The witty, brave, talented older prince was trying to save his foolish younger brother from making a terrible mistake. The kid had ravished enough peasant girls and seduced enough widows without making an idiot of himself over a silly husband-hunting girl."

"How do you know she was silly?"

"An educated guess. Now go to sleep."

"Easy for you to say. You didn't nap all day."

"Kim, please, let me get some sleep."

"Sorry." She sounded sweetly penitent. "I should be nice to you after all you've done for me."

"You're forgiven. Good night."

"Don't you think putting his brother in a dungeon was pretty harsh?"

"All right. He can be locked in a nice, warm tower with dancing girls to entertain him."

"He's still locked up."

"Kim, it's a story. Why are you obsessing over a made-up story?"

"I'm not, but I read a book about interpreting fairy tales. They always have secret meanings. Do you know why Sleeping Beauty really slept?"

He groaned loudly, glad she didn't know his secret. He had a very clear idea what he'd like to do to one chatty princess.

7

"WELL, HERE WE ARE. Denver."

Kim looked at the crowd in the busy airport concourse, then fell into step beside Rick.

"We're still nowhere until we can get on a plane to Phoenix," he grumbled.

He'd slept a lot on the eight-hour bus trip, but it hadn't put him in a good mood, Kim noticed.

"Maybe we've used up all our bad luck," she suggested hopefully.

She'd actually enjoyed the bus ride. When she wasn't dozing on his shoulder, she had the pleasure of watching him sleep. When his face was relaxed and his dark blond hair tumbled over his forehead, he looked boyish and cuddly.

They'd talked on the bus, too. He told her about playing baseball, a sport he still loved, at the University of Arizona. She had to admit she was never unhappy with a tennis racket in her hand. They liked to listen to the same jazz musicians, and he donated blood whenever there was a blood drive. He didn't seem to get tired of hearing about Jane, Peter and Luke, but he didn't say much about his own family.

"I don't like this," he said suspiciously. "Seems like there are too many people for a Sunday night."

He sidestepped a gum-chewing blonde who gave him a sizzling look. Kim wanted to play warrior

queen and send the bimbo sprawling, but her saner
self was appalled at her possessiveness. What made
her think she needed to protect Rick from predatory
females? Rick was only an accidental traveling companion. He might as well go to Guatemala for all the
hope she had of becoming more than a casual ac-
quaintance.

"Denver is a major hub. There are always lots of
people," she reminded him.

"You're right. I'm looking for trouble. What else
could possibly go wrong on this trip?"

What could? She didn't want to know.

They had to stand in a line that inched forward two
baby steps at a time, but when their turn finally came,
they hit the jackpot. In one hour and some odd
minutes they'd be winging their way to Phoenix. Rick
checked her bags but held on to his own, which could
squeak by as a carry-on. He wouldn't have to go to
baggage pickup when they reached their destination.
She would. Did he plan it that way so there wouldn't
be any long goodbyes?

"Hungry?" he asked as they made their way to
their gate.

"I don't think we have time to eat."

"We'll be lucky if we get peanuts on the plane.
I'm going to grab a quick snack."

"I'd rather wait where I can look out the window
and make sure our plane doesn't sneak off without
us."

"There's plenty of time. Come with me."

"Why?"

"I'm getting used to having you around." He
smiled, but she wasn't sure it was a compliment.

"Anyway, you need to drink something. You're probably still dehydrated from the fever."

"I'm perfectly healthy now."

"At least let me buy you a soda."

He took her arm. She thought of pulling away, but what was the point? He gave warm fuzzies just by touching the sleeve of her jacket. This was the last leg of their trip, and she really, really did want to spend every minute of it with him. If only he weren't so pigheaded about weddings!

He led the way to a restaurant near their departure area, a classy niche with subdued lights and waiters in white jackets.

"Do we have time for a fancy place?"

"They're used to people with planes to catch."

She followed him to seating for two in a dark corner, just the place for a couple who wanted to cozy up and rub knees under the table. She slung her purse out of her way toward her back without removing the strap that crossed her chest. No need to bother taking off her jacket. She liked to line up for planes before the pilot went onboard, and she hated mad dashes. Hopefully they'd get food and be on their way without a hassle. She sat on the edge of the chair to signify she was ready for a hasty departure.

"Just hot tea for me." She couldn't help glancing at her watch.

"How about splitting a turkey melt with me? I won't have time to eat a whole one myself."

"Maybe just a bite." Her stomach was hollow, but she wouldn't admit it now. "We may have to carry it onto the plane. This place is busy."

As if to prove her point, the back of her chair was jostled by a patron hunting for a table.

Rick surprised her by reaching across the small table and laying his hand on top of hers.

"I won't be in a rush to forget this trip," he said.

Even in the dim light, his electric blue eyes mesmerized her.

"It's not over yet," she murmured, confused by his words, and his intense gaze.

Much as she enjoyed being with him, she couldn't relax until the plane was in the air with them on it. Rick tried to get the attention of a waiter, and finally one ambled over.

"I'm Gerald. I'll be your server this evening, sir. Can I get you something from the bar?"

"What imported beer do you have?" Rick asked.

Next he'd want to know about the turkey farm where their sandwich got its start!

"We have to catch a plane," she interrupted. "We're in a big hurry."

"Of course, I understand." Gerald had exceptionally large teeth in a mouth that stretched from ear to ear when he smiled.

Rick ordered some German beer with twenty syllables in the name, and the waiter tried to sprint off to get it. Kim was too quick for him. She grabbed his starchy white sleeve.

"We're in a *big* hurry."

"We'll order now," Rick said, lending halfhearted support to her urgency. "Bring us one turkey melt and an order of steak fries with two plates. And a pot of hot tea."

"Herbal or—"

"Surprise me! We don't want to miss our plane," Kim interrupted.

"I'll get your order right out," he promised.

"We're not in trouble yet," Rick said, seemingly amused by her impatience.

"Easy for you to say. You have all week to wreck the wedding. My sister needs me now."

The beer came quickly, dark, nasty-looking stuff that he drank one tiny sip at a time. The waiter brought her water so hot it was boiling in the pot and a dish of foil-wrapped tea bags in a dozen or so flavors. She wasted a minute checking out the choices, then tore open a packet of Raspberry Rapture and figured the stuff would be cool enough to drink about the time the plane landed in Phoenix.

The food came after a nail-biting wait, but their server forgot—or didn't deign to bring—the extra plate.

"Don't even think of asking!" Kim warned Rick, plopping her half of the sandwich on a napkin. "They'll be boarding any second now."

She bit into crisp, buttery toast and hot melted cheese with strings that tangled on her fingers as she tried to separate them from the sandwich.

"Don't hurry," Rick said with maddening calm. "It's a lot easier to board after the rush is over."

"Would that be somewhere over Flagstaff?"

He laughed.

If this was their first fight, it wasn't a very satisfactory one.

She stopped looking at her watch and nibbled at the sandwich until Rick was ready to leave. He was right. The plane never took off the minute people boarded. Had she ever been on a plane when someone didn't dash on at the last second? Of course, as one of the dutifully prompt passengers, she thought the latecomers were arrogant and inconsiderate.

"We have plenty of time," Rick said encouragingly. "Enjoy the sandwich."

Stop reading my mind and finish that glass of German pond water, she thought.

"Look," he said, pointing to the complicated face of his watch after he finished the last swallow. "Perfect timing. Our row should be boarding as we walk up."

"Spiffy." She'd never said that word before, but these were desperate times. She needed a whole new vocabulary for a cross-country jaunt that went from crisis to crisis.

They both stood, and the server bounded over with the quickness of a bunny with its tail on fire.

"I'll take that for you, sir."

Rick handed over some bills and didn't ask for change.

"Let's go," he said.

She stepped away from the table, but something was drastically wrong. Another two steps confirmed it.

"Oh no!"

"What's wrong?"

"I've been robbed!"

"Are you sure?"

"Rick, I've been carrying this purse forever. I know when it's too light."

She began digging to the bottom, confirming the worst.

"My billfold is gone."

"I saw you put it back after you showed your I.D. at the airline ticket counter."

"Yes, I did, but look! It's gone!"

"The bag never left your shoulder. I had it in sight the whole time. Well, almost. I did read the menu."

"Someone bumped my chair. That had to be when it happened."

"We should call airport security."

"We'll miss the plane!"

He took her arm and hustled her out of the restaurant area.

"What was in your billfold?" he asked.

"My money, except for change I threw in the bottom of my purse. All my identification, even my birth certificate because I'm moving. Social Security card, all my adorable photos of Peter..."

"Credit cards?"

"No, I only have a couple. I put them in the bottom of my purse. My billfold was too stuffed with my passport and—"

"Passport?"

"I got one to go to Guatemala, but things didn't work out."

"What didn't work out? Never mind, this is bad."

"Of course it is! It will take forever to replace all those papers. I'll be a living, breathing Jane Doe."

"It's worse than that."

"That's not possible!"

"An identity thief may have it. There was enough stuff in there for someone else to become you."

"I better go to airport security."

"Before you do anything, let's see if we can find your billfold."

"It's not under the table!"

"No, but a thief will get rid of it as soon as he takes what he wants. My guess is, it's in a trash container somewhere near here."

"So we tip over cans." It wasn't much of a plan, but she didn't have a better one.

"If we're lucky, they won't be full," he said glumly.

"If I were a thief, I'd duck into a restroom for a private look at the loot."

"Good thinking. I'll check the men's. You check out the waiting areas."

"The thief could be a woman."

"I didn't see a woman come into the restaurant."

"Do you notice every female who happens to stroll into an eating place where you're partaking?" There was a lot about Rick Taylor she didn't know.

"Usually." He had the grace to look sheepish. "It's a gift. All men have it."

"The plane will be leaving."

"Let's hurry. Maybe we'll get lucky."

Rick headed for the nearest men's room. She went to a deserted waiting area near the restaurant and peered into the black interior of a trash receptacle. She couldn't—she just couldn't—plunge her arm into the damp depths of discarded cups, dirty napkins and soggy soda-soaked newspapers.

"Yuck!" She looked around, hoping for airport security to come to her rescue. No one looked even faintly official.

She yanked the top off the trash container, pulled out the black bag and squeezed the outside from the bottom up as cups and clutter spilled over the top. The only solid object in the bag was a mustard-stained pink sneaker.

No time to worry about cleanup. Their plane could leave any second. Kim ran to the next trash container, horribly embarrassed by the mess she left behind. Af-

ter twenty-six years of depositing her own refuse with
conscientious neatness, she was turning into a serial
litterer.

The next receptacle really gave her pause. How
could a sweet, adorable baby leave behind such a dis-
gusting souvenir? Kim held the top of this bag shut
and stomped on it with her boot. No billfold-size
lumps, but people were beginning to mutter at her.

Where was Rick? She caught a few words from a
speaker. Airport announcers had to be fluent in some
language that wasn't English. This one seemed to be
speaking an exotic native dialect and chewing salt-
water taffy.

She started looking under seats, in drinking foun-
tains, anywhere a clever thief might discard the legal
proof that she was herself. What if a really rotten
criminal bought her identity? She might end up
wanted by Interpol and the Canadian Mounted Police!

"I've been robbed!" she hissed at a couple of frat-
boy types who were watching her with far too much
interest. "I'm trying to find my billfold."

"Like some help?"

"Oh, I couldn't ask...." Sure she could! "But I'd
love some. I'm hoping the person who stole it took
the money out and threw the rest away."

"Just what I'd do," the tall thin one said.

"Not me. I'd keep anything that came from you as
a trophy," his round-faced friend said.

She sent them in one direction and went in another
herself. How did the thief remove the billfold from
her shoulder bag without alerting her? Okay, she
didn't have a brilliant early-warning system in her
brain, but the pickpocket was good—maybe a pro.

Would he do anything as obvious as throwing away the empty wallet out in the open?

The next trash container she found wasn't full. As scavenger hunts went, this one ranked below trying to grab fishing worms on a dark golf course. She stomped on the liner from this receptacle and smashed some plastic cups, then tossed the bag back in. What felt so gooey? She looked at her hand and saw green, sticky, icky, nauseating green slime.

"Icky, icky, icky."

She made a beeline for the nearest female pictograph and pushed the soap nozzle seven or eight times before her hands felt thoroughly de-slimed.

She didn't know where Rick was, but those boys were sweet to help. The least she could do was give them some encouragement that didn't involve touching any more alien goo herself.

She hurried to catch up with them, past the deserted area where she should have waited for their plane. Deserted! Not a single passenger was waiting to board.

A bored-looking airline employee was talking on the phone.

"Has the flight to Phoenix left?" She discovered how it felt to have her heart pounding in her throat.

"Hold a sec," he said on the phone. "Yes, ma'am. Did you have a reservation?"

"Yes, yes, yes." This wasn't happening! She'd fallen asleep, and the whole trip was part of a zany dream.

"Sorry, miss."

"But my luggage is on that plane."

Tightlipped, the clerk punched a few keys on his computer keyboard. "No, ma'am. Since you didn't get on the plane, they took your luggage off. Security regulations. You'll have to go to the ticketing area and talk to one of our representatives."

She turned away, imagining a mountain of red tape between her and her wardrobe.

"You're the computer whiz," she muttered aloud. "Run the data."

Billfold status: missing. Luggage status: missing. Rick Taylor status: also missing.

She looked in both directions and saw her two overly eager Galahads bearing down on her at a fast trot, one of them waving something in the air.

Waving something!

"You found it!"

"Maybe this is yours," round-face said. "Or maybe it's not. Is your name Kimberly—let's see— Grant?"

"Yes, that's me."

"Can you prove it?"

"Give it to her, Biff."

She liked that tall boy.

"There's a lot of stuff in this. I can't hand it over to just anyone."

"Don't be a total jerk." His friend snatched at it, but ol' Biff wanted his pound of flesh.

"Here, I can prove it." Kim dug down to the bottom of her purse, past her address book and the emergency package of peanut butter crackers and pulled out a credit card. "There's my name."

"No more fooling around," the friend said. He grabbed her billfold away from Biff and handed it to her.

"I am so thankful," she said. "What's your name?"

"Gilbert—Gil for short. Glad we could help."

"I can't thank you enough!" She reached up, took Gil's chin in her hand and kissed him as noisily as she could just south of his lips.

"You just did!" He grinned broadly.

"Oh, thanks for the help, Biff," she added off-handedly.

She walked away as round-face sputtered and whined.

Her passport was still jammed into the side opening. She found her Social Security card, her pictures, even her Michigan driver's license. It hardly mattered that the thief had cleaned out her remaining bills and even emptied out the coins. She had her identity back.

What she didn't have was Rick. Was he following a trail of waste receptacles out of the terminal? Or had he finally washed his hands of her troubles and walked out of her life forever? Suddenly she wasn't so elated about the billfold. She was stranded in Denver, many long snowy miles from Jane, and she didn't know where Rick was.

She walked dejectedly into the deserted waiting area. Even the airline official with the phone had left. For lack of anything better to do, she started scrubbing off the billfold with one of the hand wipes she always kept in her purse. She'd forgotten to ask the boys where they'd found it. Maybe she would rather not know.

"You got it!"

Rick came up behind her, startling her so much she dropped the billfold and scattered some of the contents.

"A couple of boys found it for me."

"Figures." He stooped and gathered the fallen bits and pieces.

"What do you mean, figures?"

"You're very good at getting strangers to help you."

She stared at him through narrowed eyes. If he planned to blame this whole mess on her...

"I am terribly sorry," he said softly.

She sat down with a thump on her jean-clad rear. This whole thing with Rick was getting to be too much for her.

"At least don't be sarcastic."

"I'm not! You wanted to go directly to the waiting area. I insisted on eating...."

"In a fancy place where the waiter needed a fire-cracker down his pants to get him moving."

"Guilty. I'm really sorry. It's my fault we missed our ride this time."

"It is, isn't it?" She stood and looked at his hang-dog expression. He looked as if he were scratching behind his ears.

She giggled a little, then a lot. She couldn't stop. Peals of laughter rolled out of her throat while she bobbed up and down in mirth.

Rick was laughing with her, a full-throated, sexy outburst that reverberated to the ceiling.

"We're stranded again, and they tossed my lug-gage off the plane, and we've paid for a ride we're not using, and I've never had anything like this happen to me," she gasped breathlessly.

He bent over and put his hands on his knees. He couldn't stop laughing either.

"Rick, are you okay?"

"No, of course I'm not."

He straightened, grabbed her shoulders, and locked his lips on hers.

This was no simple kiss. He hugged her so tightly her toes left the ground. He kissed her so hard, she had to wiggle her lips into the open position and kiss him back. Was the earth moving?

He lowered her feet to the floor, but the earth was still quaking.

"I thought..."

What was it she meant to say? Who knew he could do that with his tongue? The insides of her cheeks would never feel the same again.

"Need any more help, Kim-ber-ly?"

Biff, the round-faced boy, stepped so close she could feel his shoulder bump hers.

"This is one of the young men who found my billfold," she said breathlessly.

"Thanks a lot." Rick pumped his hand.

"Yeah, some job, digging through all that garbage."

"It meant a lot to my friend...." Rick was fishing out his money clip. "Thanks for your trouble."

"You should share that with Gil!" Kim yelled at the boy's retreating back.

"Yeah, like he shared with me," he called over his shoulder.

"You didn't need to do that," she told Rick.

"You handed out your own reward?"

"Not exactly. The thief took all my money. But I did thank them."

She decided not to say how.

"Here we are, stranded again." He put his arm around her shoulder.

"I guess we'd better find my bags and see when we can get another flight."

"Yes to the bags. No to the flight."

"No?"

"No."

"Then how?"

"The one sure way. I'm driving."

"It's so far!"

"Just eight hundred miles or so."

"It's dark out."

"Happens at night."

"Why did you kiss me?" No harm throwing that one in.

"Damned if I know."

"Car rental?"

"Quicker than dogsled or snowmobile."

"I'm going to owe you a year's salary."

"Lucky for me you still have an identity so I can find you if you default."

He hoisted his carry-on and started walking.

"This time I'll drive partway," she insisted, race-walking to keep up.

8

"TALK TO ME. I'm getting sleepy." Rick switched on the wipers to brush away an accumulation of snow.

"When someone asks me to talk, I can't think of anything to say." Kim sounded sleepy herself. "You could let me drive."

"There's no place to stop and switch. Tell me more about your nephew, Peter."

He decided to leave the wipers on, much as he hated the back and forth sweep of the blades. Light snow had started falling in Colorado Springs, getting heavier beyond Pueblo, and now it was a significant downfall of white blanketing the car, the highway and the rugged high ground in all directions.

"He loves anything that wiggles, squirms or drools. Once he caught a little lizard. He isn't supposed to bring livestock into the house, so he hid it in a cookie jar on top of the fridge—don't ask how he reached that high. Jane had a cleaning woman with a raging sweet tooth—you can guess the rest. She didn't even stay to clean up the pieces."

"And you're going there to keep him out of trouble?"

He yanked her chain so she'd forget about driving. The weather was getting worse, and they'd had to settle for a little subcompact with front-wheel drive from Econo-Cars. He felt safer with his hands on the wheel—nothing to do with her driving skills, but she did seem to live by Murphy's Law.

"More likely we'll get into trouble together," she admitted.

Regretfully her soft laugh was lost in the racket of the wind. It was becoming one of his favorite sounds, not a good sign. She was in his thoughts most of the time, another disturbing indication that the sooner this trip was over, the better.

"Are you still sleepy?" she asked. "We could play silly questions."

"What's that?"

"We take turns asking questions. Here's my first one. Have you ever gone skinny-dipping in the daylight? If you can say yes, you get a point. If you have to say no, I get one. First person to get twenty-one wins."

"Yes."

"You have? In the daylight? The game doesn't work unless you're absolutely honest."

"Still yes."

"Did people see you?"

"Is that question part of the game?"

"No, I'm just curious."

"Yes, a lot of other Boy Scouts. My turn. Have you ever kissed someone you've just met?"

"You saw!"

"Saw what?"

"Saw me kiss Gil—one of the boys who found my billfold. His dopey friend was being cute, not giving it to me. He's the one you rewarded."

"I take that as a yes." He laughed to himself, marveling at how easily she kept him entertained.

"Score is one to one. My turn," she said. "Have

you ever wanted a wedding of your own? Remember, you have to be honest."

"No."

"You've never met someone so special you wanted to be with her always?"

"Is that your next question?"

He couldn't say what she wanted to hear, but he did feel badly about it.

"This is a dumb game," she said. "Anyway, I just made it up to keep you awake. If you're sleepy, let me drive."

"I'm wide awake now."

He decided it was safer to entertain himself. He let his imagination kick into high gear, and he could see her long, luscious body in animal print panties and nothing else. Unfortunately his mind conjured up a white fence around her with deadly sharp pickets to ward off seducers. Only a man with a mounted diamond could get to her.

Maybe the altitude was making him hallucinate. He peered ahead into thickly falling snow, and his brother's problems receded in importance. He was still grateful to the bee who'd nailed the nose of Brian's would-be mother-in-law, but he had a much more immediate concern. And she was sitting next to him.

SITTING BESIDE RICK, Kim felt secure even in the face of the worsening storm. The last thing she wanted to do was drive, but he didn't need to know that. He was so stubborn, so shortsighted, so...

How could he kiss her the way he had at the airport and not admit they belonged together? She used to be scornful of clinging women, but she wanted to hang on to him for dear life.

"Snow's coming down harder," he said.

Sure, talk weather, she thought crossly, wishing she could throw a few snowballs at him before they drove back to desert country.

"Starting to blow a lot, too." He swerved to the left to avoid a drift encroaching on his lane of the highway.

"Look at the lights up ahead," she cried out.

"What the devil!"

He gradually slowed, coming to a stop a few yards from a metal barricade. A highway patrolman in a heavy parka was waving an oversize flashlight.

"The highway is closed, sir," he said when Rick cracked his window. "The Red Cross has a shelter set up in the Community Church. Take this exit and turn left at the light, then right at the third light."

"Any chance of getting a motel room?"

"Doubt it very much."

Rick eased the car down a recently plowed exit ramp where drifts were already reforming. The heavy snowfall dimmed the lights of the city and made the small interior of the car seem like a snug cocoon. Kim peered at her watch but couldn't see the hands.

"What time is it?" she asked.

His high-tech illuminated clock on a strap did everything but sing out the hour.

"Three-ten. Sorry about this, Kim."

"What was our option? Sacking out on the floor of the airport? At least this is something new. I've never been a refugee before."

He found the emergency shelter marked by a big sign on the door of the church.

"You'll have to help me remember where I park," he said, brushing snow away from the license plate after parking in the dimly lit church lot. "Many hours of this, and the car will be buried."

Kim's teeth were chattering more from nervousness than cold as they walked into the building. The whole situation was totally unreal, and she hugged Rick's arm, not too proud to squeeze his arm a little.

The woman who greeted them had silvery gray hair and the body of a teenager in faded jeans and a bulky red-and-white ski sweater.

"Not a fit night for man or automobile, is it?" she joked cheerfully. "We still have plenty of cots in the community room. The blankets look like aluminum foil, but they're the insulated kind our hospital uses. The facilities are down that hallway, and the coffee pot is always on. Fresh doughnuts for breakfast."

"We really appreciate this," Rick said, graciously thanking the volunteer.

They'd left their baggage in the car. Getting ready for bed was only a matter of finding an unoccupied army-style cot and taking off boots and coats. They found two together in the large, semidark room, and Rick quietly moved them closer together.

He was asleep in under thirty seconds. Kim lay wide-eyed, trying to imagine how the buzz-saw snorer to her left would look with his mouth closed. The little night sounds of dozens of people reminded her of the Phoenix zoo, every species adding its own peculiar sound to the noisy concert.

Rick shifted onto his side, no mean feat on the canvas bed, and touched her arm.

She held her breath, then whispered his name to be sure he was really asleep. She liked the heaviness of his hand on her upper arm, and she liked feeling connected to him while he slept. With a little strategic maneuvering, she covered his hand with her blanket and snuggled against his palm. When he reached over and cupped her breast, she froze, sure he was awake. But his breathing was regular, and his hand stayed on the outside of her cashmere sweater.

Even his unconscious touch was enough to send sparks to the juncture of her thighs. She covered his hand with hers to keep it there.

She was in trouble, big, big trouble. When they first met, she'd been attracted to him, but her interest had been superficial, easy to pass off as temporary. Then he'd come back for her because she was sick. Not only did he care for her, he filled an emptiness she'd always carried around, even when she was with people who meant a lot to her. Now she cared about him more than was sane or sensible. He still wasn't right for her, but it was too late to forget him without lots of pain.

He turned again and withdrew his hand. She was lying wide-eyed in a room full of strangers, and she'd never felt more alone. It seemed an awfully long time before she slept.

SHE AWOKE hearing little voices.

"We're not supposed to wake her up."

"I'm not. I'm just looking."

Kim squeezed her eyes shut tighter. If the voices were coming from little green aliens, she didn't want to see them.

"Go away," she mumbled.

"She said something."

"She said, 'Go away.'"

Kim cautiously opened one eye and saw a chocolate-covered doughnut hovering over her face. She'd been right about the little alien part, but they were pink-cheeked, not green.

"Where do you kids belong?"

They giggled but stood their ground.

"There's no VCR," one of the raven-haired cherubs complained.

"I got the last chocolate doughnut," his slightly taller female sidekick said.

"Nice for you." Kim eyeballed her wristwatch. It was nearly ten o'clock.

"Jason, Joanie, leave the lady alone!"

The children wandered away, and Kim stood, looking around a beige-tiled all-purpose room with pale green walls and tables stacked against a far wall. It seemed crowded now that people were upright and milling around. The blanket on Rick's cot was folded into a neat aluminum square and laid on top of the pillow, but he was nowhere to be seen.

Kim washed up as best she could, using dispenser soap and institutional brown paper towels, then indulged in one of the few remaining powdered-sugar doughnuts. Rick was still among the missing. She did a quick search of the building from sanctuary to Sunday school wing. By the time she thought to check the parking lot, she had a very bad feeling.

Their rented car was supposed to be the fifth vehicle to the right of a light pole. From the doorway she counted four car-shaped mounds of snow and an empty spot. The lot had been plowed recently, and the falling snow hadn't yet obscured the tire tracks Rick left when he'd driven away without her.

Was he going to leave her stranded with no luggage, no cash—thanks to the airport thief—and no goodbye?

"Rick Taylor, I could learn to hate you!"

She needed to call Jane. Her sister always knew what to do, but if Kim talked to her now, she was sure to cry and upset Jane. Kim squared her shoulders, deciding against it. It was time she stopped dumping her miseries on Jane.

She went back to the common room and joined a group clustered around a small TV watching the weather report.

"Raton Pass closed... Storm not abating... Snow accumulations up to..."

Wherever Rick was, he wasn't on his way to Phoenix. The highway was blocked and might stay that way for days. She put her woes on a back burner and volunteered to help entertain the little army of kids stranded in the shelter.

RICK WAS GONE longer than he'd expected. He checked out every hotel, motel and bed-and-breakfast on Bat Masterson Boulevard and branched out wherever he got a lead. He ignored no-vacancy signs and stooped to offering monetary incentives, but the old town on the Santa Fe trail was packed full of stranded motorists.

Traveling by himself, he would have slept at the shelter until the pass was open, but he wanted to be alone with Kim. He felt as if he'd known her forever, but they were barely acquainted. He needed time to work out what was going on between them. Getting to know each other better in a room with a hundred other people would be next to impossible.

He stopped for coffee at the Red Dog Cafe where

the only thing colorful was the name, and sat at the counter beside a couple of telephone linemen. One was lean, weatherbeaten and quiet, but the big guy with him started a conversation right away. After a few moments of weather and sports, Rick asked the big question: "Any idea where I can get a room? Town seems to be booked solid."

"My aunt has a B&B on the east side. She's particular who she rents to. Even has a travel agent screen her bookings, but she probably got some cancellations because of the storm."

"If you got deep pockets," his partner said morosely.

"Tell her Art sent you—Art Gries. I do jobs around the place for her when I have time."

"I really appreciate it," Rick said, introducing himself and picking up the linemen's tabs.

He followed directions to a blue-and-gray Victorian place with Christmas-card gingerbread. It was the last house on a street that ended in a huge expanse of snow-swept scrub land at the foot of a massive flat-topped peak. He supposed it was romantic at the right time of year, but with the wind whipping through thin cotton trousers and his ears turning to outcrops of ice, he'd prefer a desert rat's vintage trailer.

Unfortunately, it was this or share Kim with legions of bored travelers. People gravitated to her like bears to honey. He was proof of that.

Mrs. de la Farge answered the metallic tinkle of a hand-turned doorbell wearing a lavender taffeta dressing gown that strained over massive breasts and fell to the floor in rows of ruffles. Every auburn hair was lacquered in place, and Rick could only assume there was human skin under a colorful mask of makeup.

She was almost six feet tall and so dignified in her theatrical way, he let her intimidate him for a few moments.

Mrs. de la Farge didn't admit to the possibility of having a vacancy until he mentioned her nephew's name. Then she fleeced him with the expertise of a carnival barker. He could stay at a five-star hotel in New York City for what she charged for a suite of two bedrooms—all she claimed to have. He had to sign a credit card chit for three nights in advance.

Their lodging squared away, he drove back to the church shelter with a satisfied grin on his face. He'd checked out their rooms, and he didn't feel overcharged.

At first he couldn't find Kim, when he'd arrived back at the shelter. She wasn't helping set up the sandwich lunch or socializing in the common room. He wandered into the Sunday school wing and found her sitting on the carpet in one of the rooms surrounded by pint-size people.

Her hair was a rumpled mass of sable curls, and the tiny dimple in her right cheek was so kissable he felt weak-kneed. She was intent on telling a story, acting it out with squeaky dialogue and gruff roars. She didn't see him, and he enjoyed the tale more than the kids. At the end she started crawling on hands and knees, leading her enthralled audience around the room and nearly colliding with his legs.

"You're back!" she shouted upon seeing him. She finished circling the room, her pert jean-covered bottom up in the air like one of the kid's, and they all tumbled around her when she stopped. Rick was enchanted by her performance. He might be confused about his feelings for her, but he ached to gather her in his arms.

A couple of women came into the room to usher the children out for lunch. Kim stared up at him with a pout that made him wish for a white flag.

"Of course, it's none of my business where you go," she said.

She ignored the hand he offered and rose gracefully to her feet.

"Did you think I deserted you?" he asked.

"I didn't give it much thought one way or another."

"Liar."

"All right, I was worried about my luggage."

He pushed the door shut, glad it was solid with no windows.

"Not your ride?"

"That too, I suppose. But I can take care of myself."

"I'm sure you can." He grinned.

She was wandering around the little tables, keeping furniture between them. He was enjoying her evasiveness, but he'd like even more to capture her between his arms.

"I guess you came back because the pass is still closed," she said.

"Is it?"

"You know darn well it is."

She got careless and didn't move fast enough when he jumped over a cluster of chairs. He caught her shoulders and found the softness of her sweater familiar. Maybe he hadn't just dreamed about cupping her breast in the night.

"I should go help with the children's lunch."

"You don't have time."

"According to the weather report, I have several days."

She squirmed loose, leaving him with warm hands for the first time that day.

"I've found a place for us to stay."

"I'm perfectly happy here."

He saw she wasn't going to give an inch.

"Too bad. Don't know what I'll do with two rooms and the biggest clawfoot tub west of the Mississippi."

"For real?" The green in her eyes flashed her skepticism.

"That's where I've been—combing the town for a vacancy."

"A couple of people tried and came back here. Why were you so lucky?"

"I had coffee with a telephone lineman who has an aunt—but you're not interested. You're having too much fun here."

"I am."

"Tell me, are you mad because I left without waking you, or because I came back?"

"You could have left a note."

"I expected to be back sooner."

"You really do have two rooms?"

"Would I lie to you?"

"I suppose I have to go with you—you have my best underwear. But I'll put one of the rooms on my credit card."

"It's a done deal. We'll settle later."

"Let's go eat lunch with the kids before we leave."

"You go. I'll shovel the steps and sidewalk."

He needed to cool off.

IT WAS AFTER four o'clock when Mrs. de la Farge ushered them to the General Dodge suite with the formality of a head-of-state receiving lesser dignitaries.

"These horsehair sofas were brought west by my ancestor, Pierre de la Farge, when he came to invest in silver mining in the 1860s."

She was heavily corseted under a floor-length black taffeta gown and rustled like an army on the move.

"Breakfast is served from seven until nine in the morning room," she said. "All my suites have private parlors with liquid refreshments available on the honor system."

Kim had to clamp her hand over her mouth not to giggle as Mrs. de la Farge's heavy footsteps receded down the curving grand staircase.

Once they were situated in their rooms, Rick gave her the first turn in a deep, spacious tub surrounded by black wall tiles decorated with golden swans. She'd never used a black towel, and she'd certainly never sat in lavender scented water behind an unlocked door wishing someone would scrub her back.

While Rick took his bath, she lay on the canopied bed in a pink-and-white room with long narrow windows draped in ruffled chintz. The pink plush carpeting was deep enough to conceal her little toe, and the wallpaper was a garden of floating pink roses on an ivory background. It was a ten-year-old girl's dream room, but the fantasies it inspired in her were R-rated. She'd be all alone with Rick for another day, maybe two. Anything could happen and probably would, but then where would she be?

He was making her face a shameful little truth about herself: Much as she loved Jane, sometimes she envied her. Her sister had fallen into the kind of relationship Kim had longed for since her first kiss when she and Stanley Green stayed after school on the last day before vacation to help their sixth grade teacher clean the classroom. Stan the Man, playground bully and chaser of girls, had dirty fingernails and smelled like bologna sandwiches, but she'd adored him.

She didn't see her first love all summer. In the fall she was still smitten, but he'd preferred tormenting Erika, the first girl in the class to need a B-cup bra.

She heard Rick walking through the parlor to his room and raced over to crack her door, but she was too late to see how he looked wearing a towel.

"Bad girl," she scolded herself.

Nothing good could come of her latest crush. Rick hated weddings and would walk out of her life as soon as the forces of nature stopped conspiring against them.

She wasn't going to sit around this love nest like a decoy, waiting for him to score. The town was full of stranded travelers, and there had to be action somewhere. She plumbed the depths of her wardrobe case and came up with a short emerald-green jersey dress that hugged her curves like a second skin and playfully swirled around her thighs. Not forgetting the weather, she pulled on black tights and shoes with platform soles thick enough to keep her toes out of the snow. She was going to have some fun.

She flounced out to the parlor and found Rick.

He was so darn sure of himself, he was wearing a short navy velour robe and nothing else—that she could see. She wavered about going out when she saw his long, sexy legs and the sprinkling of dark hairs at the deep V of his neckline. Would it be so terrible to curl up on one of the sofas, even at the risk of Mrs. de la Farge's censure?

"You're dressed," he said bleakly.

"You did plan on having dinner?" she asked coyly, hoping he didn't guess the effect he had on her.

"I thought maybe pizza...."

"There's a phone book."

She walked over to a small writing desk that probably came west on the back of a pregnant mule—no, mules weren't into that. Flipping to the restaurant section of the Yellow Pages, she started making suggestions.

"There's a Family Buffet—no fun there. We could do Chinese—no, here's something better. Foxy Fred's Roadhouse. Live music every night, line dancing, two-inch steaks, sixty-one brands of beer."

"I don't know..."

"My treat—get dressed." Please, get dressed! "They take every credit card in existence, so I can handle it."

"It's cold out there. I thought we could—"

"I bet you did!" And get some clothes on before my resolve weakens, she silently added.

WHEN THEY got to the roadhouse, Kim could see it was *the place* to party in Tobago. They had to wait to be seated at one of the small, black laminated tables crowded around a shiny wooden dance floor. The live music was vintage country with a huge bare-bellied guitar player singing in a small, soft voice that belied his size.

"Hey, tourist! Did you get a room?"

The man barreling down on them was another kind of big: tall, wonderfully tall, with lumberjack shoulders under his plaid flannel shirt and jeans so tight it was obvious he was huge everywhere.

"Your name was the magic word," Rick said cordially.

"Hey, you're not gonna get a table before midnight. Come join us."

"I don't want to butt in," Rick said.

"I'm here with my cousin—no problem."

He was talking to Rick but looking at her. Kim knew when she was being mentally stripped, and this good ol' boy was down to her panties already. She opened her mouth to protest joining him, then changed her mind. What could happen in a crowded roadhouse with Rick as chaperone? It wouldn't hurt him to know she didn't need him for a good time.

"Sounds like fun," she chirped in, ignoring Rick's glare.

They followed the big guy to a table in a dark corner and waited while he cadged chairs from other tables for the two of them.

"I'm Art Gries," he said. "Fanny is my aunt."

"Mrs. de la Farge," Rick explained.

"Old Fargie was her second husband. She's had three more since he took off for California with a blond exotic dancer, but Fanny likes to use his name. Gives her place class."

"Kim Grant." She offered her hand, and he clasped it with pleasing gentleness.

"My cousin, Mac Gries. He drove a semi up from Kansas City. He's stuck here like you folks, so he's staying with me."

Art insisted they dig into a platter of Buffalo wings

already on the table as he signaled a waitress in cut-off jean shorts, cowboy boots and a fringed vest for another pitcher of beer. She couldn't have come quicker if Art had had her on a string.

Kim had been in bigger roadhouses, but none livelier or louder. When the band took a break, it was like sudden deafness.

"Where you folks going?" Cousin Mac asked.

"Phoenix." Rick talked road conditions with the trucker while Art turned on his considerable store of charm for Kim's benefit.

She didn't exactly discourage him, but she didn't want him following her back to the B&B. If he thought she and Rick were a couple, she wasn't going to set him straight.

Art couldn't care less whether they were, she soon realized. He was one of those big, gorgeous men who were so darn nice women thought of them as pals—until they were hooked.

"Ever line dance?" he asked.

"A few times. I have two left feet," Kim admitted.

"I have two right." He flashed a foxy grin. "How about giving it a try?"

She didn't look at Rick, and he didn't say anything. When the line started forming, she followed Art to the dance floor with at least a good show of enthusiasm.

RICK HAD had more fun dancing with his mother's age-defying, overdressed friends when she roped him into duty as an extra man at her interminably long country club parties. His new good buddy was dancing with Kim—again. Cousin Mac had been up for thirty hours or so and looked about to nod off in a plate of nachos. The shelter was starting to look inviting to Rick.

"Oh, I'm out of breath!" Kim plopped down on a chair across from him and took deep breaths that unnecessarily called attention to two of her spectacular assets.

Good ol' Art was chatting up a table of women on the far side of the smoky room, but he'd be back. He would certainly be back.

"Is he sleeping?" She nodded at the trucker who'd finally succumbed, sleeping with his chin on his chest.

"He's beat. His cousin should take him back to his place."

"He's okay, I guess. The place will close in another hour or so. Sure you wouldn't like to try a line dance?"

"No, thanks."

Darned if he'd go out and stomp around like a clod after she'd spent the evening fancy-stepping with the king of the line dancers. He felt petty and didn't much like himself, but his idea had been to spend the evening alone with Kim.

"I thought you'd be more fun," she said.

"I'm having fun," he lied.

"Is your brother having a dance at his reception?"

She had a one-track mind: wedding, wedding, wedding.

"I have no idea."

"You're not going to stop it, you know."

"No?"

"When people are really in love, outsiders don't matter."

"Are you speaking from experience?"

His plan to learn more about her had bombed, and

his unsatisfied curiosity was eating at him. He wanted to talk about her, not his brother.

"I've had some close friends."

"I'm not asking about friends."

"Nothing worked out, so what does it matter?"

Was that sadness in her voice? His intuition told him she was multi-layered, but he had yet to get more than a glimpse of the inner woman.

Damn! He hated pop psychology—his mother's hobby when she wasn't playing golf or getting married. Now he was hanging on every word Kim said, analyzing her every statement. She was a scatterbrain who lost her underwear on an escalator and her billfold in a restaurant. Why was he taking her so seriously?

"Hey, babe, last chance to dance." Art approached the table like a big jungle cat stalking its prey. Rick wished the guy wasn't so damn likable.

"Oh, I'm pooped," Kim protested halfheartedly.

"You'll like the grand finale. Have you ever done the can-can western-style?"

"Sounds like you're a regular here," Rick said.

"Usually just on the weekend, but I wanted to show Mac a good time as long as he's stranded here."

"Looks like he's had all the fun he can handle," Rick said, but they were on their way to the dance floor and didn't hear.

He liked watching Kim dance almost more than he hated seeing her dance with Art. The men and women were across from each other—that part he did like— and legs were flying. Kim kicked her skirt waist-high above her tights. She wasn't a great dancer—she was out of step as often as not—but she stole the show with her long gorgeous legs and infectious enthusiasm.

He should be out there with her. Why didn't he compete with Art for her attention? He was sulking and wasn't proud of it. Worse, he was jealous of a woman he'd only known a few days and a man she'd probably never see again.

The noise and smoke had given him a headache, or maybe it was passively watching Kim cavort with a stranger. He wanted her to prefer being with him, to choose him over any other man, but he couldn't bring himself to make the commitment that would do that.

He was being a jerk, but he didn't know how—or if—he could change.

9

RICK PUT HIS ARM around her shoulder as they shuffled through drifting snow in the parking lot of the roadhouse. Kim shivered as icy wind buffeted her face and she regretted not wearing pants, but not nearly as much as she regretted wasting the chance to spend an evening alone with Rick. She couldn't even remember what she'd been trying to prove.

"You look like a snowman," he said, brushing off her coat and hood before opening the car door.

"Snow*man?*"

"Snow queen?"

"Good save." When they reached the car, she slid onto the seat and hugged herself to get warm.

They drove to the main business section without passing another car, but snowplows were keeping the roads passable in town. She sat on her side, wishing divided front car seats had never been invented. This was a night made for snuggling, and body heat was only one of the reasons she wanted to wrap herself around Rick. She put her hand on the bend of his elbow, but he moved it to rest on the muscular swell of his thigh.

"I need some razor blades," he said in a husky voice. "There's an all-night convenience store at the service station up ahead."

"I can hardly see the neon sign."

She peered through the flurry of fast-moving crystals wondering if each flake really had a unique design. No two people were exactly alike, so maybe it was true of snow. Certainly there was no other man like Rick, and she wanted him more each moment they spent together.

He ran into the store while she waited in the car with the heater running.

When they were once again en route to the B&B, she had to admire how quickly he'd acquired a knack for winter driving. He parked on the street near their temporary lodging and made a path for her to follow to the front door, but snow still clung to her tights and caked on her shoes. They both stomped and brushed at their clothes on the front porch, then Rick used the key he'd been given to open the door.

The madame, as they'd jokingly started calling Mrs. de la Farge, kept a square plastic mat inside the front door, but there was half a mile of highly polished hardwood floor and stairs between them and their rooms.

"She'll banish us if we leave tracks," Kim whispered.

She stepped out of her shoes and looked down at tights already beaded with melting snow that threatened to drip on the floor.

Rick bent and took off his boots, then tried to empty the snow trapped in his cuffs.

"Only one solution," he whispered. "We'd better take off everything that's wet."

They made bundles of their coats so melting snow wouldn't leak, but Kim knew her tights were soaked to midcalf.

"Don't look." She turned her back and peeled them down her legs and off her feet.

He was watching, his face softened by a look that turned her insides mushy.

"Your turn," she said softly.

His zipper slid down so slowly she could hear the separation of each tiny tooth. He wiggled his pants over lean hips, and a startling bulge strained against the black knit of his briefs.

She embarrassed herself by staring. Even in the dim light from a leaded glass lamp on the hall table, she could tell his thighs were sun-bronzed up to the pale crease where his torso began. He lifted one foot in slow motion, then the other, stepping free of his trousers and bending to wad them into a bundle with his coat.

The plastic mat was cold on her bare soles, but she couldn't will herself to move.

"Let's go to bed," Rick said.

He said it as if they were a couple who always shared sleeping space, but his simple words were more seductive than any elaborate sexual charade.

"Yes, it's been a long day."

Was she agreeing to more than the trek up the stairs? She didn't know.

She gathered her wet things and followed him, suppressing a nervous giggle but not the trembling sensations radiating downward from her shoulders to her thighs.

"This feels like sneaking in after curfew on a high-school date," she said in a stage whisper.

"I wouldn't put it past Fargie to ground us."

He waited for her to come up beside him on one of the wide steps, then put his arm around her.

"Or put us in detention." She was giggling now.

"Detention in a room with you. I could handle that." He dropped his hand lower, locking it onto her waist and pulling her hip against his.

"I wonder if there are other guests," she said.

"I don't." His voice was low and throaty. She liked that in a man she wanted to seduce.

He unlocked the single door to their suite, let her step in ahead of him, and dropped his clothing on another plastic floor protector.

Kim looked around the suite as though seeing it for the first time: a small Victorian parlor with a burgundy-and-blue Oriental rug. A Gone-with-the-Wind lamp in a window alcove illuminated when Rick flicked the switch by the door. To the left she saw the familiar bedroom and the bathroom behind two doors, but the room on the right was mysterious territory.

"This room is cozy at night," she said.

She put her clothing on the floor beside his as he closed the door to the corridor.

"Yes."

"I'm glad Mrs. de la Farge is a phony. It makes her so much more fun."

"Do you really want to talk about her?" he asked.

"Not really."

"Or her nephew?"

She enjoyed the undertone of annoyance in his voice.

"I guess not."

"Are you cold?" He took her hand and led her away from the cold, grainy mat.

"Freezing."

He took her in his arms, sliding one warm leg between her chilled limbs. She pressed her thighs against his knee, enjoying the heat of his skin.

"How did you stay so warm?" she asked.

"Internal combustion."

He lowered his head and finally, at long last, after waiting all evening, kissed her.

She closed her eyes and decided this was the sweetest moment of her life. His lips moved from one corner of her mouth to the other in a kiss as potent as it was chaste.

"You are so beautiful," he murmured. "I've never met anyone like you."

He held her in the circle of his arms. His lips brushed her closed lids, then pressed against her forehead.

"Are you getting warmer?" he asked softly.

"Somewhere between a boiling cauldron and a blast furnace."

Without thinking, she burrowed her hands under his camel hair sports coat and cocoa-brown turtleneck and rubbed the smooth skin on his back.

He shivered but didn't pull away.

"Your fingers are like icicles."

"Sorry." She started to take her hands away.

"No. What kind of man would I be if I didn't help you warm up?"

"A snowman with an ice ball for a heart."

"Is that what you think I am?"

"I don't know what kind of man you are," she said seriously.

"You need to get under a nice thick comforter," he said, stepping back when she took her hands away.

"All my bed has is a thin spread and one of those

insulated things motels use. They only work if you don't move away from the one spot you've warmed.''

''Would you like to trade rooms?''

''I couldn't ask you to sleep in a little girl's pink paradise.''

''You haven't seen my room.'' He laughed and took her hand, leading her to door number two.

''If Mrs. de la Farge has a split personality, her evil half conjured up this room,'' Rick said. ''Or maybe she dreamed it up bingeing on boiler makers.''

He turned on the only light, an ornate brass floor lamp with purple swans circling a gold fringed shade. The walls had patterned red brocade wallpaper above ebony-stained wainscotting, and the Oriental rug was a garden of deep reds, purples and blues. The bed had a heavily carved antique headboard and footboard with high posts at every corner, but new metal side supports held a modern double-bed size mattress. The velveteen comforter was deep mulberry, and looking at it was enough to make Kim feel hot.

''And here are the sheets.'' He flipped back the comforter to reveal shiny black linens with a pearly white pattern of exotic jungle vines and flowers.

''Crawl in. You need to get your body temperature up,'' he urged.

She sat on the edge, nervous about where this was going but falling so much in love his soft urgency had the weight of command. He stood over her, and she knew this was a turning point. She could go to the other room or stay the night with Rick. She glanced at her right shoulder first, then her left, as if she expected a cartoon devil and angel to whisper conflicting advice into her ears. Her conscience remained silent, but her heart was thundering the only possible answer.

"I guess I should take my dress off," she said in a tiny voice so unlike her normal one she felt possessed.

"Let me help you with the zipper."

He sounded hesitant, a little unsure of himself.

She felt odd, as if she should reassure him, but she was the one risking her heart.

Rick stepped behind her and found the tab of the long back zipper. She felt cool air steal down the length of her spine as he pulled it open.

He maneuvered the dress over her head with just enough awkwardness to be endearing, then stood back shaking his head.

"Are you disappointed?"

Her instinct was to wrap her arms across her scantily clad breasts, but they'd traveled a long way together. She wasn't going to be a coward after everything they'd been through together.

"Oh, yeah, I'm really disappointed." The way he said it belied his words. "I'm looking at the most beautiful breasts in creation...."

She'd made her choice, and it had nothing to do with words. She reached out and took his hand, guiding it to her breast.

Still standing in front of her, incongruously dressed in a sports coat and briefs, he took the weight of her breast in one hand and explored it with the other, his thumb and forefinger slowly circling the satiny surface, around and around, getting closer and closer to her nipple without touching it. She closed her eyes and surrendered to pure ecstasy.

He breached the cloth barrier of her bra so suddenly

she gasped. His thumb and forefinger rolled the pebble-hard nub of her nipple until the pleasure was intense enough to be painful.

"Your sleeve is scratchy," she said to give herself a moment of respite, afraid she'd embarrass herself by being too eager.

He grinned sheepishly and stripped off his jacket and shirt, tossing them aside on the floor.

"Hey, you didn't hang up your clothes."

She said the first thing that came into her head rather than let him realize she was over the top already. Men liked to be the aggressors. Didn't it say so in all the women's magazines? Come to think of it, she hadn't read one in ages. Maybe the rules had changed.

"This from a girl who left a trail of panties in a public place? I like the ones you're wearing." He nodded at the skimpy peach bikinis that matched her bra.

"Do you?"

She stood and cavorted, twirling around in the small space between them. He stopped her by pulling her against him, back against his front, the hardness of his arousal prodding her bottom while he slid his hand down the satin triangle of her panties. He hooked his thumbs on the edges and peeled them down below her cheeks, then kissed her shoulders and the back of her neck while he caressed her bare bottom.

"You're still cold," he murmured near her ear.

"Not inside." She wiggled out of her panties and kicked them aside.

He released the back snap of her bra and sent it flying across the room.

She wanted to look at him, all of him, but he stayed behind her, holding her in the circle of his arms while he caressed both her breasts with lazy, mesmerizing strokes. He nuzzled the back of her neck and pressed his cheek against the mat of curls flattened by the hood of her jacket.

Her pleasure deepened, and she was content to have his caresses go on forever, but he surprised her by taking both nipples between his strong fingers and stretching them gently forward. Currents of sensation were hot-wired to her groin, intensifying when he lowered her to the bed and began caressing the flesh of each breast.

Was she visibly shaking? She didn't know, but her nipples were swollen and hard when he took the first into his mouth and suckled with devastating effect.

"You taste fantastic," he whispered, teasing the other pinkish-brown knob with his teeth as he lay beside her.

She wanted him to say the magic words, but they were both moving beyond talk. She reached out to him and found the barrier of his briefs gone. A little shy about his nudity, she quickly drew her hand away.

They'd never talked about other lovers, but, oh, he did know exactly how to please her. He warmed her from the tips of her fingers to the tops of her feet with deep, passionate kisses and soft seductive caresses.

"Do you like this?" he asked softly, tentatively touching the downy softness above her thighs.

Her moans were the only answer she could muster. He tickled her torso with sweet little kisses until the delicious sensation of his lips and the rhythmic movement of his hand clouded her mind. His face was bristly and felt just as she'd dreamed it would, delightfully erotic on her tender skin. He ran his prickly chin from the hollow between her breasts to the softest part of her thigh.

Just when she thought she'd blank out from sensual overload, his tongue speared her intimately. Her eyes teared with happiness, and she clutched his head.

"I love your five o'clock shadow," she murmured, a half-truth that didn't begin to tell him what he was doing to her. "Never use those razor blades."

"I forgot!" He startled her by rolling off the bed and leaving her bereft.

"What's wrong?"

"You didn't really think I stopped for blades, did you?"

She was appalled by her own carelessness. She'd never failed to protect herself. Her only explanation was that Rick already seemed like part of her, a man she could trust wholly and completely.

"Sweetheart, I am sorry." He picked up her hand and kissed her fingers one by one. "They're in my coat pocket."

She watched him walk to the doorway, his bottom round and firm and terribly cute in the muted light of the period lamp. He was a beautiful man, and oh, how she wanted him.

When he returned to the room, he dropped a large box on the bedside table.

"Come here," he said, and pulled her against him on the bed, skin caressing skin for the whole of their length. He kissed her hard on the lips and filled her mouth with his tongue.

She forgot she'd ever been reticent and circled his arousal with her fingers, gently stroking the velvety soft skin. She was a little awed by the size of him, the hardness of him, and by her own eroticism, so unlike anything she'd experienced before. She loved the scent of him and wondered if the perfume of her body pleased him as much.

She watched spellbound as he parted her with his finger, gently probing for her magic spot. She grabbed his hand, not to pull it away but because the intensity of his touch was electrifying.

He reached for a foil-wrapped packet with his free hand and she stopped him. "I'd like to do that, but I don't know if I'll do it right."

"You will."

She was encouraged by his grin and soft directions when she wiggled into a position sitting in front of him with her legs over his thighs, her toes buried under the pillows. Giddy with anticipation, but still shamelessly greedy when it came to feeling his skin against hers, she leaned toward him and held him in her arms.

With his arms around her, she cuddled against his chest and stroked his satiny, slightly salty skin with her tongue. She nibbled one of his milk-chocolate nipples, wondering at how tiny they were compared to his broad masculine chest.

Rick was breathing hard, and she was having trouble catching her breath. She looked into his eyes, locking her hands behind his neck and inhaling deeply, absolutely sure she'd never been so totally aroused.

"Come here." He supported her back with one hand and did thrilling things with the other.

"Is this possible?"

His arousal was touching her, but she'd never tried—never thought...

He scooted closer and proved it was.

"If it doesn't feel right, stop me," he said. "All right?"

"All right," she echoed, bracing herself for tremendous pressure, afraid she'd be inadequate for this huge man she realized she loved to distraction.

"Relax," he murmured, sliding his free hand under her bottom and half lifting, half encouraging her to receive him.

She rose up to meet him, stunned by the overwhelming wealth of sensations. He moved slowly inside of her while he steadied her with gentle kisses. Only by clinging to his arms did she stay upright and consciously abandon her resistance, delighted when he closed his eyes and pushed into her with unhurried passion.

She watched his face, jaw rigid and lids tightly clenched, and realized he was giving her the gift of empowerment. In this sitting position, he couldn't thrust hard enough to bring himself to climax unless she helped.

She clenched and unclenched her bottom, writhing in a superhuman effort to draw him deeper and deeper into her. Her breath was as ragged as his, but something was happening. The heavy old bed vibrated, and the intensity built. They were moving in sync, their bodies slick from the exertion.

She heard little shrieks but didn't connect them to her. Both of them were on overdrive, straining for completion.

She exploded, and he exploded, then he fell backward on the generous pile of pillows and carried her, still connected, with him. Covering her mouth with his, he held her so close he had to feel the aftershocks rocketing through her body.

"Oh, Kim.... You are terrific." He separated from her and hugged her in the crook of his arm, playfully tweaking her breast.

"I guess you did okay, too."

"You guess?"

He threw one leg over hers to imprison her in the nicest possible way.

"I'm pretty certain." She sighed contentedly, torn between the need to sleep and not wanting their first time to end.

"For a girl with no sense of rhythm, you really can move," he mused.

"No sense of rhythm!" She wiggled under his heavy leg but didn't want him to move it. "How can you say that?"

"I watched you dance."

"Oh." She reached down and did some tweaking of her own. "Why didn't you dance with me?"

He didn't answer.

"Because I can't stay in step?"

He rolled her onto the pillows beside him and leaned over her.

"No."

"Then why?" She didn't try to hide her hurt feelings.

"I preferred watching you."

"Not good enough." She teased his lips with her little finger until he took it into his mouth and gently suckled. She pulled it away.

"I wanted to stay here," he grumbled.

"You're that fond of pizza?"

"It's a meal."

"There's no TV." She'd just realized it.

"I'm not addicted to it."

"Well, it didn't matter whether you danced with me or not," she lied. "I had a good partner."

"Yeah, he's a nice guy."

Kim noticed he didn't use the big dude's name.

"Guess I should go back to my bed." She gave him a quick peck on the end of his lovely, strong nose.

"Give me one reason why."

"I'm not sleepy. I'll keep you awake," she teased.

"Is that a promise?"

She squirmed toward the edge of the bed, but he put out his arm to block her.

"What a nice arm you have, Brother Wolf." She patted his bicep, liking the bulge of muscle, the sleekness of his shoulder. Was there anything about this man she didn't adore?

Yes, there was, but they were snowbound for at least another day or two. She didn't want to think of him as a wedding-buster.

He kissed her long and hard, then raised his head and smiled sweetly. "Are you sure you're warm now?"

He pulled the heavy comforter over them and burrowed down under it. "Turn over," he said in a muffled voice.

It would take a bulldozer with a backhoe to get her out of his bed. She slowly rolled over, wiggling a whole lot more than necessary.

He made a tent of the comforter, letting it rest across his arched back as he trailed his lips down her spine.

"Don't go to sleep on me," he said from the depths of the velveteen cocoon.

"As if I could," she murmured contentedly, loving the way he massaged her shoulders and rained little kisses on her back. "Did you learn this from your masseuse?"

He shoved aside the heavy comforter and turned his attention to first one leg, then the other. She giggled when he brushed his lips over the backs of her heels and squirmed with pleasure when he kissed the backs of her knees.

He caressed the backs of her thighs, and she was definitely wide awake. She tried anticipating what he'd do next, and ripples of desire flowed through her. When he did wonderful things at the end of her spine, she wasn't sure she could endure another moment of such electrifying pleasure.

"Rick..."

"Ummm..."

How could she ask whether he could make love again? Weren't men sensitive about performance levels?

"Are you ready yet?" she blurted out.

He gave her a noisy little love tap on the fullness of her bottom and an order: "Roll over."

He was enormous. He swayed over her and parted her thighs with his hands.

"No more Mr. Nice Guy?" she quipped, then regretted it. This wasn't a good time to get cute.

He didn't wait for her fumbling hands to take care of protection. This time the rhythm of his lovemaking carried both of them. His thrusts were harder and deeper, tapping into something so elemental and satisfying she gave herself up completely to sensation.

She dug her nails into his back without meaning to and lifted her hips to intensify a pleasure that throbbed on and on and on until he shuddered and held her tight.

"Do you have any idea how special you are?" he whispered, pulling up the cover and cuddling beside her.

There were other words she'd rather hear, but she fell asleep before she could dwell on them.

10

RICK WOKE UP wanting to make love to Kim again. She was curled up by his side, her bare bottom snuggled against his hip, and he couldn't imagine a nicer way to begin the day.

The window shade was murky gray, but with so much reflected light from the snow, it was hard to guess what time it was. He reached over to the nightstand and checked his watch.

Would it be mean to wake her before seven when they couldn't leave town anyway? It was tempting. He wanted to know whether she was grouchy or sweet first thing in the morning. Did she like wake-up sex? Would it be as good between them as last night?

He wasn't used to sleeping on a big mound of pillows, and the back of his head ached.

Maybe it was just dehydration, he thought, realizing his throat was dry and scratchy. Careful not to wake her, he reluctantly crawled out of bed, shivering when cold air assailed him. The bizarre lamp was still a dimly illuminated smudge against the garish wall, and he pulled the chain on the way out to make the room darker for Kim to sleep.

By the time he returned from getting a drink of water, he was shaking from the cold. For what he'd paid for the room, Mrs. de la Farge should at least give them some heat.

Kim had turned onto her stomach and slipped off the pillows, but she was still asleep. He crawled into bed, careful not to wake her, and burrowed under the comforter. He wanted to hold her against him, but his cold skin would give her a rude awakening.

Last night he'd had the best sex of his life, so why did he feel so rotten? He edged closer to Kim's warm body but was still too chilly to hug her.

When he woke again, he saw his own robe gaping open over Kim's lovely breasts.

"You're wearing my robe," he mused.

"I took a bath. I'd like to get some of my underwear from your bag."

"On one condition." He deserved the headache that had crept over his eyes, but he had to ask. "Model my favorites."

"You mean, do a lingerie show?" She sounded unsure, then unexpectedly giggled. "Why not? You've seen all of it anyway—and all of me."

She was gorgeous when color flooded her cheeks. Her damp hair was a mass of ringlets, and her full pink lips were even sexier without lipstick.

"The black thing first." Inwardly he was groaning, wondering how much titillation he could take.

She tossed his robe on the end of the bed and went over to turn on the lamp. Even naked, she walked like a model, the provocative wiggle of her bottom only adding to her stunning presence.

She unzipped his bag and rummaged in the corners, pulling out a handful of her silky undies.

"The rules are you stay there and watch, no getting out of bed and no comments," she said sternly.

"Not even a wolf whistle or two?"

"Absolutely not, or the show is over."

"You're a cruel woman."

She grinned and slipped into the lacy one-piece black thing. Just thinking about it after brief glimpses had helped him to stay awake driving in bad weather. Watching her put it on was beyond anything he could have imagined. It involved her leaning over and sort of shaking her breasts into the top.

"Wait a minute." She scampered from the room on bare feet and was gone at least half an eternity.

He propped himself up on the pillows, pulled the comforter up to his chin because he still couldn't get warm, and ached with impatience.

"Ta dum!"

Her entrance was worth waiting for. She was wearing black spike heels and every man's dream-lingerie. From the tiny spaghetti straps to the hem that barely touched the tops of her thighs, it left little to his imagination. The peep-hole lace showed the sexy dark triangle below her navel and the rosy buds of her breasts.

"Come here." He was begging and didn't care.

"Oh, no. You wanted a fashion show."

She grabbed a handful of undies and ducked out the door, much to his disappointment. But he was more then compensated when she pranced in wearing the jungle print panties and a wisp of matching cloth across her breasts. She twirled, arms above her head, and undulated her hips provocatively.

"Where did you learn that?"

"It's something women just know. Are you going to pick a winner when I'm done?"

"Do you want me to?"

"Sure, why not?"

"Change in here. Please."

"It's sort of embarrassing."

He laughed so hard he doubled over.

"Well, it is." She pouted. "I've never done anything like this before. I buy nice lingerie because I like it myself."

"Don't be embarrassed," he cajoled. "I'm grateful you're sharing something special with me."

She looked skeptical but stepped out of the jungle panties and took off the bra. For some reason he thought women always undid the bra first, but if he added up all his field experience on the subject, it hardly made him an expert.

She turned her back to change panties.

Was she totally unaware how exciting it was to watch her spine curve down to the cleft in her buttocks and her shapely bottom give way to sleekly perfect thighs and legs?

She modeled reds, blues and lacy white seethroughs. Her Valentine set had big pink hearts strategically placed.

"I'm only doing one more," she said firmly, "and I'm changing in the parlor."

He nodded weakly, not sure he could survive one more.

"I never wear this," she said, sticking her head around the doorjamb. "It's not comfortable."

"Okay." He had no idea what constituted feminine comfort.

"Also," she said, poking her head into the room again, "I don't have a bra to match."

She didn't dance her way into the room this time. Arms folded across her chest, she crept in wearing a purple triangle of cloth precariously held in place by a couple of strings.

"It's a G-string," he said, trying not to laugh.

"It certainly is not! I ordered it from a lingerie catalogue."

"Sweetheart, it's still a G-string."

"How would you know? Have you ever shopped for women's panties?"

She stood with hands on her waist and elbows jutting out. Even her nipples bristled with indignation, or at least they were standing at attention.

"Never," he had to admit. "If it's not comfortable, maybe you want to take it off."

"I will." She grabbed his robe and flounced out, not what he had in mind.

He thought of following her. He'd love to sweep her up in his arms and carry her giggling and squirming to the bed, but he didn't have his usual energy. In fact, he felt hungover without having gotten drunk.

Kim returned to the bedroom, back swaddled in folds of velour that came to her knees.

"I threw it away."

"Why?"

"I told you. It's not comfortable."

"You took the trouble to pack it. Why toss it here?"

"I don't know." She was even beautiful when she sulked.

"Thank you for modeling." He said it softly, wanting her to come closer.

"I feel like an idiot."

"You shouldn't. That was the nicest thing anyone has ever done for me." He meant it.

"Really?" She stepped closer.

"You did something out of character because you knew it would please me."

"I guess."

"Come back to bed."

She was rooted to the spot, holding his robe shut with both hands.

"Does it seem cold in here to you?" He clutched the top of the comforter.

"No, not that I've noticed. Did you pick a winner?" She stayed where she was.

He liked the G-string because it revealed the most, but it seemed politic to make another choice. The white lace was breathtaking, but it reminded him of bridal wear. The animal print made him want to grab her, and the peek-hole black lace was an instant turn-on. It was almost impossible to say which he liked best when the body underneath was the real winner.

"The Valentine," he said, picking the style least likely to lead to risky explanations.

"That's my favorite!" She bounded over to him and jumped knee first on the bed. "I love Valentine's Day. It's so romantic."

Why wasn't he surprised?

"I'm cold," he said, hoping for a warm response. Not even the hot lingerie show had fully warmed him.

"Oh, poor baby." She touched his forehead with the backs of her fingers. "You feel feverish. I hope you're not getting what I had."

"I never catch anything." Being sick was too inconvenient to consider. "My last choice is that robe."

She wasn't coy. With a shrug and a wiggle, she undid it and sent the garment flying toward a small chair on the other side of the room. She missed, but he admired her good try.

"Scoot over. I'll warm you up," she promised.

He made room for her even though it meant shifting his backside to a cold spot on the sheet.

"Your feet are blocks of ice." She wasn't telling him anything he didn't know.

She ran her toes over the tops of his feet then burrowed between his legs with her knee.

"Friction creates heat," she said with the seriousness of a learned professor.

She ran her palms over his shoulders and down his arms, all the while energetically rubbing his legs with hers. All he could see was the top of her head sticking out of the mulberry comforter, but she had busy little fingers and toes that did far more than combat his shivers.

Did she have a clue what she was doing to him? His chest wasn't a block of stone, and she was working her magic dangerously close to the point of no return.

"I'm warm now," he said. Blazing hot was more like it.

She was still into friction, this time doing a tummy rub that somehow ended with her fingers surrounding a body part best left untouched unless—

He wanted her so desperately he couldn't quite believe she was taking the initiative. She hovered over him, a knee on either side of his hips, and cradled him in her hand.

"You're so big." She said it with a wholly satisfying tone of wonder. "I don't know if..."

If happened.

Now he knew she liked wake-up sex.

And she did have a sense of rhythm.

He wanted to tell her it felt like his first time, but

a corny compliment like that didn't come close to what he was feeling.

Happiness.

She made him so happy the convulsing shudder of their mutual release was only a small part of it.

"You're fantastic," he whispered, wrapping his arms around her, not sure he could ever let go.

RICK DOZED OFF almost instantly, but Kim couldn't sleep. She wanted to savor every minute with him. She adored the tickle of his silky leg hair on her calves and the way he curled his hand under his chin when he turned to sleep on his side.

Wind howled around the peaks and dormers of the stately old house, no doubt piling drifts on the highway faster than man-made equipment could hope to push them aside. She counted on her fingers the days since she'd started this odyssey to Phoenix. How could it only be Tuesday? Her whole life had changed in less than a week.

She snuggled closer, trying not to worry about anything outside their little haven. Jane knew the weather situation and, good big sister that she was, she'd deliberately made herself sound chipper on the phone yesterday.

Rick hadn't said anything about the wedding recently, but she was sure he hadn't changed his mind. He was hell-bent on saving his brother from a fate worse than a lifetime of picnics in Death Valley.

Little wisps of hair were growing below the trim styling at the back of his neck, the sign of a busy man who hadn't had time to get a haircut. What did she know about his ordinary life? He had a house in a posh part of Phoenix, but he hadn't given her a description so she could visualize it. What did he do with his friends? Did he like parties or quiet evenings with one special person?

She couldn't even be sure he wasn't involved with someone. He wasn't the kind of person who shared his private life with a stranger, and now that they weren't strangers there were so many questions she'd like to ask if she weren't afraid of the answers.

He stirred, stretched lazily, and rolled over on his back.

"Are you all right?" She propped herself up on one elbow and showed admirable restraint by not throwing herself on top of him.

"Shouldn't I be asking you that question?"

He grinned boyishly, and she decided to worry about his personal life later.

"I was asking about your health."

"I'm fine."

He sat up, shook his head, and sank back onto the pillows.

"I'm just a little dizzy," he admitted. "Do you suppose we can get some breakfast?"

"Let me check the time."

She reached over to the inlaid mother-of-pearl top of the nightstand and picked up his heavy watch.

"It's nearly eleven."

"Bummer. Breakfast was seven to nine."

"We'll see about that!"

She hopped out of bed and snatched her jungle panties from a nearby chair. Her white lacy bra was the first one she saw on top of Rick's things in his overnight bag, so she slipped into it.

"You're not color-coordinated," he teased.

"What do you want, breakfast or another style show?"

"Ta dum!"

"You paid for breakfast. You're going to get it."

She dressed quickly in her room in jeans and an Arizona State sweatshirt, trying to pretend he wasn't hovering in the doorway to the pink bedroom looking rakishly irresistible in his little short robe.

When she tried to leave, he blocked her way.

"Seriously, are you all right with what happened?" He put his hands on her shoulders and focused his devastating blue eyes on her.

"Right as rain—make that snow." She tried to be flip but it fell flat.

"You're a special person. I'd never want to do anything to hurt you."

"Then be quiet because you're making me feel like a one-night stand!"

To his credit, he looked like a man who'd just been slapped—hard.

"You're not!"

"Well, one night, one morning," she grumbled, not at all proud of her outburst. "I'm going to scare up some breakfast."

She scored a small triumph with the madame. For a woman who lived to intimidate, she wasn't all that tough, especially when Kim got her started talking about the chimney repairs she wanted their friend, her nephew, to do in the spring.

Kim returned to their room with a heavy tray of breakfast offerings: cold sliced ham, warm English muffins with a honey pot on the side, lemon-filled Danish, individual servings of cereal, a pitcher of milk, another of orange juice, and a thermos of steaming hot coffee.

Rick was back in bed.

"Breakfast is served in the parlor," she announced with exaggerated cheerfulness.

"Thanks, sweetheart, but maybe I'll just have some juice in here if you brought any."

"You're sick," she accused sympathetically. "You have the same thing I did."

"I just need a nap. Did you get a road report?"

"Mrs. de la Farge had the radio on. Our odds of getting through the pass today are almost as good as the Donner party's were."

"Cheer me up some more," he teased.

"Terrible for you, being stuck here when you need to head off a wedding."

"Terrible," he repeated, grinning broadly. "But I could be consoled by breakfast in bed."

"So you have your appetite back?"

"I'll force myself."

She carried the tray to the bedside table, slipped out of her jeans and shoes, and propped herself beside him on the pillows.

"I can't remember ever having breakfast in bed," she mused, carefully pouring a little milk on a serving of cereal.

"Me neither. I don't suppose you'd..." He opened his mouth like a baby bird waiting for a worm.

"Sure, why not?"

She held a spoonful of cereal to his lips and giggled when a drop of milk ran down his chin.

"There must be a knack to this," she said, blotting his chin with a pink linen napkin.

"Keep practicing," he urged.

She did, but when the honey on the muffin dribbled down his chest, she did the only thing a good hostess could. She caught it with her tongue.

And when he humbly implored her to let him have the same dessert, she laughingly stripped off her sweatshirt and bra and let him dab her nipples with the sticky nectar.

"I thought you weren't hungry," she said, wiggling, giggling and running her fingers though the back of his hair as his tongue busily savored her.

He insisted on counting the spots on her jungle-print panties, and they played a new version of her Truth game: all the questions involved body parts. He won, twenty-one to twelve. No way would she let him think he was the hottest hunk in the universe!

Later in the afternoon they napped. When he woke her, the wind had calmed down, and the shade they'd never bothered to raise showed the dusky gray beginnings of another winter night.

"I don't think I can cadge dinner out of the madame," she said lazily.

"We'll go out." He stretched languidly and nuzzled her hand. "What are you in the mood for?"

She let her fingers spider-walk on his torso and teased his belly button with her little finger.

"Food, I meant," he said.

"Are you sure you feel well enough to go out? I could go and bring something back. Or there's always pizza delivery."

"I'm more in the chicken-soup mood."

"Darn, I know you've caught my bug."

"Don't blame yourself. If you had it, I want it."

"At least it's a short-lived virus. What are your symptoms?"

"Lecherous thoughts and perpetual desire."

"You're terrible!"

She tweaked his nose and slid out of bed.

When they finally made it outdoors, they had to wade through hip-deep drifts to get to the car, but they lucked out on the wind pattern. Rick was able to drive the car free without arduous shoveling, although for a few minutes Kim was sure the engine wasn't going to start.

Apparently quite a few stranded motorists and snowbound residents had cabin fever. The family-style restaurant they found on Bat Masterson Boulevard had a twenty-minute wait. They spent the time standing in companionable silence, watching the flow of diners in and out of the eatery.

Rick's face was ruddy from the cold wind, but his darkly shadowed eyes gave him away—he still wasn't feeling at all well.

The owners had wildly embraced the junk-decor of the eighties, and their server seated them in a battered wooden booth with a boat paddle and a ratty-looking hobby horse suspended overhead. The wall was colorful if not particularly appetizing with tin signs, framed old-time photos, a mouse trap, a rusty clamp-on ice skate and assorted snatches of barbed wire. Kim looked for a unifying theme and decided it was early yard sale.

"This sounds good," she said, taking a laminated menu from their server who introduced herself with the perkiness of a candidate for asparagus queen.

"What does?" He'd already scanned the somewhat sticky menu and laid it aside.

"Western-style barbecued ribs with seasoned home

fries and the chef's famous horseradish cabbage slaw.''

Now that he was thawing out, he looked even more peaked.

''Or maybe I'll just have a big salad,'' she said out of kindness to him, remembering how she'd felt when she was sick.

She ordered the taco shell salad with chicken, cheddar cheese and a dozen or so other ingredients. It came swimming in ranch dressing.

Rick opted for the turkey club on dry toast. She ate half of that, too.

''Good thing I fed you,'' he teased on the way home. ''Making love gives you one gigantic appetite.''

''We did miss lunch, you know.''

''I didn't even notice. Guess my mind was somewhere else.''

Dare she hope his mind was on her—them—possibly even a future together after their whirlwind trip together? She just didn't know what to think, instead she watched as the traffic thinned to nothing as they headed to the far side of town.

11

HAD SHE HONESTLY THOUGHT this day wouldn't come? After being snowbound for a few days, they were leaving together, but Kim still felt as though she had to say goodbye to Rick.

Sure, they'd be in the car for another seven hundred and fifty miles, but would they ever again share a bath in a tub big enough to float a cabin cruiser? Would they sit through a matinee in the balcony of an ornate old movie theater? Already she couldn't remember the name of the film, but she'd never forget holding hands with Rick in the flickering darkness, sharing a bag of buttery popcorn, rubbing knees, and necking like the oversexed teenagers who no doubt enjoyed the local passion pit.

"This will be a first," he said, coming up behind her and cupping her breasts over her crewneck yellow sweater. "The two of us in time for one of Fargie's breakfasts."

She turned in the circle of his arms and wrapped her arms around his neck, her lips parted for his deep kiss.

"Umm…when is checkout time?" she asked.

"Don't tempt me, woman. Another eye-opener like this morning's, and I'll walk out of here like a bow-legged cowboy—if I can walk at all."

"You have such a way with words." She nipped at his lower lip.

"If you're ready, let's eat. The highway's open, but I don't expect to make good time."

They went down the curving oak staircase, Kim leading the way to the breakfast room because she'd been there to badger Mrs. de la Farge for a tray the last two mornings.

The room had wallpaper with green vines and little yellow flowers on a white background, and the lace curtains framed a cluster of long narrow windows looking out at the snowy peak in the distance. There was only one table, large and round with a bright green tablecloth and four place settings of china that nearly matched the wallpaper. Two of the chairs were occupied by a big iron-jawed man with thinning gray hair and a woman with reddish-pink curls and a round beaming face. Her skin was deeply scored with wrinkles, emphasized rather than concealed by a liberal dusting of powder.

"Well, here are the honeymooners," the woman gushed. "We were so hoping we'd get to meet you. Harold and I spent our honeymoon in this very house fifty-two years ago. Of course, then it was Mrs. Flannagan's boarding house, and we were lucky she agreed to rent to a married couple."

"Are you going to eat your bacon, Josie?" Harold asked.

"Now you know it's not good for you."

He took several pieces with his fingers and chomped them down with mechanical efficiency.

"Sit down, sit down," Josie urged after Kim did the polite thing and introduced themselves, first names only to avoid explanations. "On Thursday

Fanny always makes Belgian waffles, not that you lovebirds care what's on the menu."

"We're not...." Kim started to say.

"You're in the General Dodge Suite, you know. Harold and I stayed in your suite two years ago."

"Three," he corrected her.

"No, Harold, I'm sure it was two. We come to visit Harold's aunt, but she's in a senior living facility, so we always take a room here."

"Nursing home." Harold stabbed a section of thick waffle from Josie's plate.

"Anyway, it is so romantic to have honeymooners here. I was hoping you'd come to breakfast at least once before we leave."

"We're not honeymooners," Kim said, prompted by the less-than-pleased look on Rick's face.

"Oh, don't be shy with an old married couple like us. We know how newlyweds are."

Mrs. de la Farge's plump, sweet-faced cook-server came out with fresh-squeezed orange juice and took their orders for scrambled eggs and sausages to go with their waffles.

Rick tried a few conversation-starters with Harold, but basketball, weather and road conditions didn't drown out Josie's monologue on the joys of young love. He gave up and sat, grim-faced and silent.

Kim ate so fast she was done before her stomach knew she'd started.

When they were packed and in the car, Rick still hadn't commented on the honeymoon thing.

"I guess when you're old, everyone younger looks like a newlywed," she said.

"I hope this thing starts." Rick tried the ignition for the fifth or sixth time.

The car started, but Kim decided he wasn't going to comment on being mistaken for honeymooners. He didn't believe in marriage, so Josie's overblown enthusiasm was probably only an irritant to him.

Kim settled down on the seat beside him. She was Cinderella leaving the ball, but no one would chase after her with a glass slipper. Her prince had turned into the pumpkin.

"Are you sure you're feeling well enough to go all the way to Phoenix?" she asked.

"I'm fine now. It was just a twenty-four-hour bug like yours."

"Our germs were at least first cousins," she admitted. "But if you get tired, I'll drive."

"Maybe when we get beyond Albuquerque."

The sun was shining, and the snow sparkled like diamonds, a good excuse to hide her glistening eyes behind sunglasses. They had a lot to talk about, but Rick had made livelier conversation with Harold.

"Road's a little icy in spots," he said. "We won't make good time."

"We've had our good time," she grumbled, but he didn't rise to the bait.

Now was the time when she needed to hear that she was wonderful, beautiful, special, etcetera, etcetera, etcetera. Pillow talk didn't count unless she heard the same thing after the fact. All she was getting from Rick was a lot of quiet time and scenery she was in no mood to appreciate.

They reached Albuquerque in the early afternoon. It was one of Kim's favorite cities with the rugged Sandia Mountains towering on the skyline, and she hated having to rush through it.

"I've always wanted to be here for the balloon festival," she said when Rick made a brief stop for gas and a drive-through burger. "Old Town is so much fun."

"Pretty touristy, isn't it?"

"Pretty touristy, isn't it," she muttered under her breath when he went inside to pay for the gas.

When he came back, she was behind the wheel.

"I'll spell you," she said.

"Okay." There was no enthusiasm, but he didn't object.

She drove, he slept.

He drove, she slept.

The turnabout naps made sense since Rick was gung-ho to travel all the way to Phoenix that night. He wanted to be there on Friday to sabotage the wedding, dash his brother's hopes for the future and ruin the poor bride's happiness. This was assuming he could succeed. She couldn't believe two people truly in love would let an outsider change their plans.

She had to bite her tongue more than once that day to keep from telling him he had no right to interfere. He knew how she felt, of course. His wedding crusade was a black pall hanging between them as they drove toward home and their separate lives.

When it was his turn to drive again, she feigned sleep more than she actually dozed. Their days in Tobago had been incredibly sweet, but they'd dulled her enthusiasm for living with Jane until the babies came. Much as she loved her sister's family, her heart ached to have a home and family of her own—with Rick.

RICK WAS GLAD when he got the wheel back after a rest stop. He checked the map and decided they were making fairly good time, but Tobago to Phoenix was a hell of a long drive. They'd started later than he would have liked, and the patches of ice in the mountains had slowed them down.

"I'm not so sure about making Phoenix tonight," he admitted when Kim slid into the passenger seat beside him.

"It's easy to fall asleep driving after dark," she said.

He wouldn't worry much if he were alone. Crack the window and turn up the radio, and he trusted himself to stay alert. But he'd be gambling with Kim's safety, and he didn't want to risk another driver's late-night carelessness.

"What if we find a motel in Flagstaff and leave early tomorrow morning?" he suggested. "We can drive down to Phoenix from there in less than two hours."

He didn't add that this would still give him time to keep an appointment with their family attorney. If he lost the argument on the wedding, he could still press for the prenuptial agreement.

Kim was a romantic. She hated his hardheaded attitude, but she didn't understand Brian's abysmal record with women. Her opinion mattered more than he could have dreamed possible, but he wasn't sure what to do about her. First he had to deal with another gold-digger in his brother's life.

"Flagstaff is fine," she agreed.

It was dark when they exited at Flagstaff. Rick loved this part of his home state, especially the stately Ponderosa pines that thrived in the high altitudes. Tonight he was too tired to do anything but head for the first motel with a vacancy sign. Maybe the virus had hit him harder than he thought, but he had a vision of a soft pillow, a firm bed and Kim sound asleep in his arms.

They found a generic room in a motel utterly devoid of character or cuteness. It was relaxing after three nights with bordello decor, but Rick was tired enough to pitch a tent in the freeway median and get a good night's sleep.

"Order in pizza?" he suggested hopefully as Kim turned up the heating unit under the window.

"Good idea. I like everything but bacon and Canadian bacon."

"You don't like Canadian bacon?"

She was continually saying and doing things that convinced him she wasn't like anyone he'd ever known. He was even eager to hear her rationale on pizza toppings.

"I love it, but not on Italian pizza. It's like putting spaghetti sauce on chow mein noodles."

"Point taken." He laughed. "So you want anything else? Bread sticks, maybe?"

"No thanks. We do have to go over our expenses so I can pay you back for my share."

He wouldn't dream of sticking her with any part of the exorbitant bill for the bed-and-breakfast, but the last thing he wanted tonight was a financial reckoning.

"Don't worry. I'm still holding your lingerie hostage."

Sitting cross-legged on the bed, they shared a deliciously greasy pizza loaded with stringy cheese, Italian sausage, mushrooms, green peppers and sauce so good it smelled almost as good as it tasted.

"This is the best pizza I've ever had," she said,

pulling off another piece and catching the cheese dripping from the tip with her tongue.

"Want to use the shower first?" he offered, almost too tired and full to take his pants off before he fell into bed.

"Doesn't matter."

It did matter. If he went first and she joined him, his urgent need for a good night's sleep would take second place to the chemistry between them. Whenever she touched him, she short-circuited his brain.

"You go first," he urged.

The minute the bathroom door closed behind her, he stripped down to his briefs, dimmed the light and crawled onto the far side of the king-size bed. He didn't doubt he'd be sound asleep before the shower turned off.

Sleep he did, a solid eight hours according to the watch he'd been too beat to take off. He woke up and stretched, but something wasn't right. His arm reached out and found nothing but empty bed.

Kim! He sat up and was greatly relieved to see her sleeping on the far edge of the king-size bed. His first instinct was to scoot over and hold her in his arms, but he knew what would happen. They hadn't mastered the quick wake-up kiss—maybe never would.

The bitter truth was he had to get to Phoenix as soon as possible. He got up, grabbed his shaving kit and headed toward the shower.

She was dressed when he came out with one of the skimpy motel towels wrapped around his waist.

"Do you mind if we grab coffee in a drive-through on our way out of town?" he asked.

"Good morning to you, too."

"Good morning, sweetheart." He brushed a quick kiss on her lips.

She stepped back and pursed her lips thoughtfully. He supposed women were used to being eyeballed from head to toe, but it was a new sensation for him. She scrutinized him so intently he was too embarrassed to drop the towel and pull on his underwear.

"The bathroom is all yours," he said, oddly relieved when she grabbed her toothbrush bag and disappeared behind a closed door.

Ten minutes later he had their bags in the car. He expected her to offer to drive, so he headed her off by holding the passenger door open. Not that he had any complaints. She was a darn good driver. But he was too anxious about his brother's situation to ride without anything to do.

He tried the ignition and, as usual, the little subcompact didn't want to start. Five or six tries was the morning average. He lost count after a dozen futile tries, wondering if he'd have to scare up a new battery before they could be on their way.

"It's flooded," Kim said.

She was right, and he had to wait impatiently until he could try again. Finally the starter caught. The motor whined, wheezed and clanked with jarring vibrations.

"What's wrong?" she asked.

"I'm not a mechanic," he snapped, knowing he should apologize for biting her head off but too irritated to do it.

He stepped out and did what men always did in the face of mechanical breakdown: Reached in to pull the hood lever, then propped it open.

By the time he looked at it, the motor had died.

"Try to start it," he told Kim.

She shimmied over to the driver's seat, a feat he would have admired if he hadn't been mad enough to kick the car all the way to Phoenix.

The motor sputtered to life, rattled, clanged and died again. Then nothing. Kim couldn't restart the dead motor, and neither could he.

He appreciated all the things she didn't say.

"What now?" It was a rhetorical question, and he asked it. They were a hundred and fifty miles from Phoenix, and they were worse off than they had been in Detroit.

"Here's the rental agreement. There's an emergency number," she said, handing it to him.

"I guess this qualifies as an emergency."

"I'm sure they'll bring up a replacement," she said hopefully.

On the seventh or eighth round of pressing numbers for services he didn't need, he got through to a human being.

"I need a replacement right away," he said after a long recitation of the car's woes.

"There is a small problem, sir."

Of course.

"The corporation has gone into Chapter Eleven. Royal Rentals has contracted to handle client accounts until the final settlement. Here's what you need to do."

He made notes on skimpy pages of motel notepaper.

"We have to have it towed. This is the code number to give the tow truck driver," he told Kim.

"Want me to call? Damsel in distress and all?"

"No, I have to be doing something."

An hour and seventeen minutes later the big rig came and hooked up the compact. They crowded into the cab with the driver.

"It's a truck rental place," Kim said when they pulled onto a lot on the outskirts of town.

"We do Royal Rental's repair work," the driver assured her. "Just a few forms for you folks to fill out."

Rick was pretty sure it would take less paperwork to apply for a small business loan. When he finally handed in the sheath of forms, the manager was sympathetic—a very bad sign.

"We'll start processing these right away," he assured them. "You should get your refund within ninety days."

"I want a car, not a refund." He also wanted to punch something, but he tried to be reasonable. "I have to get to Phoenix."

"Sorry, we don't have rental cars here. We're only a servicing agent."

"My lease promised a replacement if the car I rented breaks down."

"Royal Rentals doesn't offer that service. Your agreement is with—"

"Yes, I know. Just tell me how I can get a car."

"Sorry. The nearest rental depot is at the Phoenix airport."

"If I could get to the Phoenix airport, I wouldn't need a car."

"Can we rent a truck?" Kim asked.

"All we have are moving trucks."

"Fine, I'll take one," he said.

"Sorry, sir. I won't have one available until noon tomorrow."

"So where does that leave us?"

"You'll have to call the emergency number on your rental agreement. They'll make arrangements for a replacement vehicle."

"That's how I got here!"

"Can we get the luggage?" Kim asked.

They hauled their bags out of the derelict little compact.

"She was nice while she lasted," Kim said dejectedly. "There's a truck stop half a mile or so down the road."

"You're willing to hitch a ride?"

"You have a lot better chance of getting a ride without all my luggage. Anyway, Jane will go into early labor if she finds out I hitchhiked with a trucker. Have you seen all the runaway-truck ramps on the way down the mountains?"

"Yeah. The steep inclines are hard on brakes. What will you do if I go?"

"Take a cab back to the motel. Get the room for another night and make that company bring me a car."

"I don't know…"

"If you wait for the rental, you might miss the wedding."

"Will you be all right?"

"People always help me."

"You're super." He kissed her full on the mouth, hesitated, then said, "I'll never forget this…or you."

12

RICK PRESSED a kiss on her mouth and some bills into her hand. His lips were cold.

She hated having to take his money and swore to herself she'd pay every cent she owed him even if it meant borrowing from Jane, which was a major no-no in her life. The thief who stole her money deserved a million tickle-tortures.

"Take a cab back to the motel...."

He started giving her detailed instructions about cutting through the red tape and getting another car. She didn't take in any of it. Foolishly she'd let herself nourish a flicker of hope for a future with Rick—maybe not marriage, but at least a chance to be with him.

All he really cared about was ruining his brother's wedding. He was leaving her on a truck lot in a strange town with a wreck of a rental car and some patronizing advice. Granted she'd told him to go, but that was so he could refuse and tell her being with her was the most important thing in his life.

"I can handle it," she interrupted.

"Sure you can."

He smiled but she wasn't buying it.

Then he was gone, race-walking down the road, a crusader off to save his brother from the horrors of matrimony.

If he felt the way she did, he wouldn't have left, never mind that she'd told him to. His brother's wedding was important, but it was tomorrow, not today. He was obsessed with preventing, not celebrating, the happy event.

The trouble with tests was the possibility of flunking them. She'd scored a big F with Rick, and it hurt, hurt, hurt.

She wanted to weep and wail, but she still had the problem of getting home. Car, bus, pack mule—the mode of transport didn't much matter. She started by calling a taxi, waiting long enough for it to have come from Denver, and checking into the motel where they'd stayed together.

By coincidence she got the same room. She used her credit card. It was bad enough she had to pay the cabbie with Rick's money.

Before she tackled the rental agency's handy toll-free customer service number again, she had to call Jane.

"Janie," she said with forced cheerfulness when her sister answered the phone. "I'm getting closer. Flagstaff."

"Great! You'll be here in what, two hours?"

"Maybe tomorrow. The rental car broke down. I have to try to get a replacement. It isn't looking good for today."

"Oh, Kim, I'm sorry you've had so much trouble because of me. But guess what? Luke is home! He came back early because he was worried about me."

Jane was bubbling with happiness, and Kim was glad for her sake. Still, she couldn't help feeling deflated. After everything she'd done to get to Phoenix, Jane didn't need her. She had her wonderful husband, but what did Kim have? She wasn't eager to intrude on their reunion, and her traveling companion—she didn't know what else to call Rick—didn't think twice about abandoning her to wage his campaign against marital bliss.

"Peter wants to say hello."

She listened to her nephew's excited babble: Daddy was going to build a tree house for him. Daddy had brought him a lion....

"Not a live one." Luke took the phone and told Kim how much he appreciated all she'd done to try to get home. He offered to drive to Flagstaff to get her, but she adamantly refused. She needed a little time before she plunged into the cozy world of their happiness.

"Don't you dare leave your wife," she warned.

"No chance of that!"

She hung up and forced herself to tackle the car-rental fiasco again. They finally agreed to rush a car up to Flagstaff as soon as they had one available. Of course, they wouldn't have a driver before noon tomorrow. Meanwhile, they were faxing some forms to the motel office for her to fill out and return immediately.

Jane didn't need her, and Rick was gone. If a man really loved a woman, wouldn't he forsake all others to fill out forms with her?

Maybe Rick's concern for his brother was admirable, but his desertion was a bitter awakening for her. She believed in true love with all her heart and soul, but maybe they were too different to bridge the gulf between them.

She got through what was left of the day by watching soap operas and eating potato chips from the motel's vending machine. The melodramas on the screen had easy solutions: just write the bad guys out of the scripts. Life should be so simple.

For dinner she ordered pizza but ended up throwing most of it into the motel's Dumpster. It didn't taste the same without Rick to share it.

She fell asleep that night with a grainy black-and-white werewolf film flickering on the TV screen.

It was bad enough to wake up with a talk show host grinning vacuously at the foot of the bed, but the knocking had to go. Someone was pounding on the door, and it was only—she checked the clock on the nightstand—a little after eight.

She had to answer in case it was the replacement car, but she had a whole lot to say about being woken up this early with no warning.

For one joyful instant she imagined Rick on the other side of the door, but a quick peek through the spy hole dashed that hope. She cracked the door, leaving the chain on.

The man was short and slight with a pencil-line mustache, but his clothes made him look impressive: a navy blazer with silver buttons and a uniform cap, hard-billed and official-looking.

"Miss Grant," he read from a clipboard.

"Yes."

"Your limo is ready at your convenience."

"My limo?"

"I'll be waiting over there."

He pointed at a stretch limo taking up three or four parking spaces across from her door.

She'd read the riot act to the rental company, but she hadn't expected *this* kind of compensation.

"The car rental people sent you?" she asked.

"No, ma'am. I drive for Executive Limousine Service. Here are my credentials." He flashed a license and a fancy ID. "If you'd like to verify them, I can give you our 1-800 number."

She peered out at the gorgeous dove-gray vehicle.

"No, I guess the limo gives you pretty good confirmation, but who ordered it?"

"I'm sorry, I don't have that information. Is there anything I can do to facilitate your departure?"

"I'll put my bags out when I'm ready."

Leave it to Luke and Jane to surprise her like this! She'd arrive in style even if it had taken a week.

She showered and dressed quickly. They might be paying by the hour, so there was no point dawdling in this dismal motel room.

The only thing missing in the luxurious interior of the stretch limo was Rick. They should be making the last leg of the trip together.

The driver, William, stowed her luggage, opened the rear door and showed her the refrigerator where a perfect cold breakfast was waiting for her: a fruit bowl with strawberries and melon balls, cream cheese in three flavors and a platter of bagels, sweet rolls and fancy rolled ham. She had her choice of juices in small bottles, or she could go all out and drink champagne.

She opted for champagne and strawberries as a starter. If she weren't missing Rick so much, this would be a blast: legroom to stretch her whole length, a deep wine-colored interior that reeked of elegance and an intercom should she wish to communicate with William behind the glass partition that separated them.

By the time she sampled everything in the miniature fridge and polished off the slender single serving of champagne, she was sleepy. If she'd known about the limo, she wouldn't have watched the late, late horror movie.

SHE AWOKE with a start. This wasn't I-17 to Phoenix. She knew an expressway from a switchback, and this definitely wasn't the divided highway.

"Where are we?" she asked.

William didn't respond. Of course not! She had to use the intercom.

Apparently she'd overused it. In her panic she boomed out the question again. "Where are you taking me?"

He was too well trained to wince at the volume of her voice.

"To Sedona, Miss Grant. The intercom is quite sensitive."

"I want to go to Phoenix." She moderated her voice level, trying to remember if she'd ever read a book where the heroine was kidnapped in a limo.

What a perfect way to allay a victim's suspicions! She'd been so gullible she was embarrassed as well as scared silly.

"My work sheet is very specific, Miss Grant. It gives a Sedona destination. You're welcome to call the home office to confirm it."

There was a plan. Anyone could answer a number he gave her and say whatever a kidnapper's accomplice would say. Or he could be telling the truth, and she'd sound like an idiot.

She was bigger than William, and she was on to him. Was there any way she could barricade herself in the back until help came?

She tested the cell phone. It was working. Was she overreacting? After all, how many kidnap victims got a champagne breakfast?

Suddenly she felt ridiculous. Luke's grandfather lived in Sedona. Maybe they'd decided to meet her at his palatial home. The posh town nestled among the red rocks was a mecca for tourists and a haven for the wealthy. She giggled at the thought of a white slavery ring operating there.

The driver negotiated the sharp curves on the mountain switchback as if born to drive, but Kim wasn't sure he could find the house without her help. Roads were twisty-turny, and residences were hard to locate.

She switched on the intercom, but was speechless when the limo turned down a private road with an arched gate and a sign reading Los Paradiso. She was sure she'd never gone this way before.

The limo came to a stop in a circular drive in front of a Spanish-style resort hotel. She briefly noted tennis courts, stables and a fenced pool, then all she could see was the man standing beside the curb.

Rick must have stopped the wedding, then rushed up here, but why?

He opened the door of the limo himself.

"You had me brought here!" She was too agitated to know whether she was angry or elated.

He smiled. His face had a soft, adoring look that further confused her.

"Did you get your brother to call off the wedding?"

She'd never once thought he could succeed, but it was the only explanation. Otherwise he'd be in Phoenix suiting up for the ceremony.

"Let's talk about it in our room."

"Our room?"

She looked at the hand he was offering but didn't move.

"Please come out."

"My sister is expecting me in Phoenix."

"Not anymore. I talked to her."

"She doesn't even know you."

"Actually I went to their house, but she promised not to tell you. She's doing well. Those two are really in sync. Luke cut short his trip because he had a hunch Jane needed him."

"Peter is expecting me," she said.

"He's pretty busy playing construction man with his dad. He bangs nails in a board with a real hammer. I have scars from holding nails for him."

"Really?" One more thing she didn't quite believe.

"Just kidding, but I did check my pockets for lizards when I left."

"When did you do all this?"

"Let's talk upstairs."

Rick walked over to the driver and complimented him on a job well done. He handed William a bill that made the man grin like a lottery winner and begin energetically unloading her luggage.

"I haven't said I'd stay."

She scurried out and watched a hotel employee in a dark suit, white shirt and sky blue tie take possession of her bags.

Rick took her hand, and she had no choice, short of throwing a tantrum on the clay tiled entryway, but to go with him.

"You're mad because I left you in Flagstaff," he said for her ears only.

"I'm not mad. I managed fine. A car is coming at noon—a car is coming!"

"I canceled it."

"How did you know I'd fall for your limo trick? And when did you have time to visit my sister and hire a limo and wade through the Chapter Eleven mess to cancel my ride and find a room here and—"

"I have a staff."

"I thought you were a computer consultant."

"I am, but I can't run a corporation alone."

"How many employees?"

"Thirty or so."

"Oh." She decided to shut up.

They walked through a lobby with a statue of a nymph presiding over a swiftly flowing pond with giant goldfish. The gleaming white stucco walls made a wonderful background for the best collection of Native American weaving she'd ever seen, and the management was so discreet she didn't even spot the registration desk.

An elevator was waiting open for them, and they rode to the top floor. Rick put his hand on her waist to guide her to their door, and she was almost afraid of how wonderful it felt.

Her bags were already in the room.

Rick must have stopped the wedding, or he wouldn't be here. But how could she stay here with him if he'd ruthlessly destroyed two people's happiness?

The room was spacious and beautiful with the Southwestern decor and muted desert colors she loved. The king-size bed matched the light carved oak dresser and wardrobe but in no way crowded the space.

Rick closed the door and pulled her into his arms, kissing her so sweetly she almost convinced herself nothing else mattered.

But it did.

"Did you ruin the wedding?"

She squirmed in his embrace, but he showed no intention of releasing her.

"No."

"They wouldn't listen to your objections?"

"I didn't make any."

"You didn't?"

"I want to talk about us, not them."

She wanted that, too, but she didn't understand about the wedding. Did he have a major falling out with his brother? She hated that possibility.

"Why aren't you in Phoenix for the wedding?"

"It's a meaningless, archaic ceremony, and they certainly don't need me."

"A wedding isn't meaningless!"

"Sit down, and I'll tell you the whole story."

He pulled her down beside him on the bed and sandwiched her right hand between both of his.

"Tell me," she urged.

"I got a ride right away with a trucker hauling appliances. Washing machines and clothes dryers made in Iowa."

"Never mind that!" She knew he was teasing her with an excess of details, and her impatience was at the bursting point.

"I went home and cleaned up."

"Rick! Next you'll tell me you checked your answering machine and opened your mail."

He grinned and squeezed her hand.

"No, I went straight to my brother's place. His

fiancée was there. They've already set up housekeeping, so to speak.''

"You probably hated that. They didn't ask your permission."

"Let me tell my story." He lifted her hand to his lips and nibbled her fingertips until she yanked her hand away.

"Tell me about the wedding."

"I met Melinda," he went on, "and I learned a lesson."

"Did you like her?" she asked hopefully.

"I adored her on sight. She's delightful. Cute and petite and blond and—"

"You've made your point!"

She pulled her long jean-clad legs closer to the edge of the bed to make their length less obvious and wished she'd thought to dress up for her limousine adventure. No one ever called her petite.

"The best part is she's madly in love with Brian, although what she sees in my brother is a mystery to me."

"You really like her." She had to confirm the important part.

"Yeah, I like her, and there's not a gold-digging bone in her body. In fact, she's probably better off financially than my brother, a fact he neglected to mention. He said he wanted me to like her for herself, which sort of leaves me feeling like a jackass."

"You should have met her before you had a hissy fit about the wedding."

"Thank you for trying to make me feel better," he said, grinning sheepishly. "I shouldn't have assumed Brian was making another colossal mistake, but his track record is my defense. How could I know both Taylor brothers would get lucky?''

"I want to hear more about that part."

"You wanted the whole story. You're going to get it," he said firmly.

"Then tell me why you're missing your brother's wedding to this wonderful petite woman."

"He doesn't want me there."

"No! I can't believe that."

"I talked his ear off until three in the morning, telling him how wonderful you are. He told me I was an idiot to leave you, and for once my brother is smarter than I am. He insisted nothing was more important than finishing our trip together."

"I told you to go," she reminded him weakly.

"You had the courage to send me on my way even though you hated the idea of interfering in a wedding."

She shrugged, and he put his arm around her shoulders.

"It wasn't just the wedding," he admitted with obvious effort. "I was running away from you."

"From me?"

She stiffened, suddenly fearful this was his idea of dumping her gently.

"I know you're looking for permanence, a lasting commitment. I've never had the courage to take that step. I always blamed my reluctance on my parents, on their marital failures, but the truth is I was scared to take the risk."

"I want to be with you for as long as you'll have me, no strings attached," she admitted to both herself and him.

This was his cue for the big kiss. She was going

to fall apart if he didn't take her in his arms and tell her exactly how he felt about her.

He stood instead and went down on his knees, taking both of her hands in his.

"I love you, Kim. I want to marry you if you'll have me."

"Oh!"

She blinked. He was still there.

"I know we haven't known each other very long," he continued. "If you feel you need more time…"

"Time." Her brain had turned to cheesecake.

"I'll wait as long as you like, but I don't want to," he said.

"Neither do I." She finally managed an intelligent response.

"Does that mean…"

"Do you really want to get married?"

"I want to marry you. I love you, Kim. You're the yin to my yang, or is it the other way around? Walking away from you in Flagstaff turned my whole world upside down. I stopped caring about anything but you."

"You feel that way now—"

"I'll love you always. If you want a picket fence—"

"A what?"

"Picket fence. You know, white pointed boards around a little clapboard house."

"Wouldn't that look silly in Phoenix? Fenced-in cactus and sand."

"This proposal isn't going at all the way I planned. Nothing with you does."

He stood and pulled her into his arms.

"Are you taking it back?" She loved him so much

she was afraid to believe he really wanted to marry her.

"No, no, no."

He punctuated his denial with hard, emphatic kisses she could feel all the way to her toes.

"How long are you going to make me suffer?" he asked, coming up for air.

"At least the rest of your life."

She hugged him tight and wiggled against the soft cotton of the baby-blue knit he was wearing under a charcoal sports coat.

"You're going to make me wait that long to tell me you love me?"

He sounded stricken, and she wanted more than anything in the world to make him happy.

"Of course I love you! I adore you. I love you to pieces. I never dreamed I could love anyone as much as I love you."

She put her hands on the sides of his head and pulled his mouth to hers, covering it with noisy, enthusiastic kisses.

He lifted her, all of her, as if she were petite, and laid her on the gloriously large bed.

"Wait!" She rolled to the far side, stood, and ripped off the lovely cactus flower bedspread and a boring beige chunk of insulated cloth that served as a blanket. The sheets were desert pink with sand-colored stripes, and she loved them. She loved the room, she loved the hotel, and she loved the surprise of coming there in a limo.

But mostly she loved Rick.

He was grinning across the bed at her, already tossing his jacket aside and pulling off his shirt. She studied every inch of that magnificent chest.

"Stop!" she cried out.

"Why?" He looked puzzled but left the shirt bunched around his pecs.

"If we're going to celebrate, this has to be special."

"Everything about you is special." The way he said it gave her goose bumps.

"Freeze. Don't even think of moving," she said.

She circled the bed on quaking legs, wondering if she knew how to show him how much she loved him.

She was going to give it a darn good try.

Married! She was engaged to marry Rick Taylor, and she was high on happiness.

She worked the shirt over his head and leaned forward to press her lips against the silky skin of his chest. All the fears she'd had of losing him were forgotten, and her tongue moved down to his sexy flat stomach.

He pulled his belt free of the loops on his trousers, but she loosened the top and slid the zipper down over the bulge of his arousal. She started to slide them over his hips, but something hard in his pocket made her hesitate.

"Ah, you've found it."

He reached into his pants pocket and took out a dark velvety ring box.

"You even had time to get me a ring?"

"I made time. A friend opened up his store at six this morning."

"When were you going to give it to me?"

"You'll find out."

He tossed the box on the bed without opening it and completed what she'd started, shedding the rest of his clothes. Then he looked at her with hooded eyes, the strong planes and angles of his face softened by passion.

She'd seen that look before. She shivered in expectation.

He pulled down her jeans first, then her drab faded everyday pink cotton panties.

"I haven't seen these before."

"I didn't expect today to be a special day."

She felt a little silly standing bare-bottomed in shoes, kneesocks and a sweater while he looked at the worst underwear she owned.

"Skin the rabbit," he said, beaming from ear to ear.

"What?"

"I had a nanny."

"You had a nanny? For real?"

"Imported from jolly old England. She'd always say, 'skin the rabbit' before she yanked my shirt off."

"There's so much about you I don't know."

"I suspect I'll never know everything about you."

"I hope not." She giggled because he was working her sweater over her upraised arms.

"You did wear a pretty bra."

He unhooked her second-best white lace and tumbled her onto the bed.

"I still have my shoes and socks on."

"Kick them off."

He was obviously more interested in her undressed parts.

"You've never kissed me there before." She managed to slip out of one shoe.

"Give me time. I'll get to all your parts if you're patient."

She wasn't patient. She loved him. She loved him

to touch her. She loved him to kiss her. She loved what he was doing.

She circled his bottom with her legs and hugged him against her with all her strength.

"That shoe does have to go."

He took care of it.

"I've been going crazy without you. I love you so much I'm certifiable."

"I was afraid I'd never see you again."

"There was never a chance of that."

"You didn't say—"

"I was afraid to believe someone as special as you are had come into my life."

"Believe!"

"I love you," he murmured into her ear.

He said it, and this pillow talk counted. It really counted. So did his kisses, long, slow, hard kisses, his tongue deep at the back of her throat and his hands stroking her to the edge of delirium.

He entered her slowly and gently. She watched his face, loving the flush of color on his cheeks and the fragile paleness of his lowered lids. His lashes were long and spiky, and his hair fell forward over his forehead as he rose above her.

"Your eyes are open." He met her gaze with a look of liquid intensity.

"I want to keep my eyes on you always," she whispered.

"You don't need to. I won't disappear."

"Promise?"

"Swear."

It wasn't possible, but she loved him even more. He electrified her, made her spirit soar and her flesh convulse with pleasure.

"Nice for a wake-up," she teased when he collapsed beside her, imprisoning her with an arm and a leg.

"Can't be a wake-up. I haven't been to bed yet."

"Since Flagstaff?"

"Yes. Five minutes away from you, I knew I wanted you back if I had to crawl all the way from Phoenix to get you."

"I thought..." No, she didn't want to spoil this deliciously happy moment.

"Thought what?"

"In Flagstaff I thought... No, I was silly."

"Do we have to play the question game?"

He burrowed his fingers between her thighs, and she floated on wave after wave of unremitting pleasure.

"No question game," she begged, her mind too clouded by sheer ecstasy to concentrate.

"Let me guess. You thought because I didn't make love to you, I didn't care about you?"

"No...not exactly."

"We're playing the truth game." His finger slid deep into her moist heat, and she felt dizzy with renewed desire.

"I was afraid you didn't want—"

"Sweetheart, you plain pooped me out. I needed time to recharge my batteries."

"I understand... I don't expect... I mean, no one does it every night."

"Don't count on that."

He kissed her lids and the tip of her nose, then teased her lips with his.

"Umm. How long do we have this room?" she asked dreamily.

"They don't rent it by the hour." He laughed.

"I meant, maybe you need a nap?"

"Not yet." He reached across her and retrieved the ring box. "You haven't seen this yet. If you don't like it…"

"No chance."

He snapped open the posh little box and took out a giant sparkling diamond set in gleaming gold.

"I don't like gaudy settings with lots of little chips. This is flawless, just like you."

He held it up for her to admire, and it nearly took her breath away.

"It's so beautiful."

"So are you."

He reached down and lightly squeezed her breast, then laid the ring on her nipple.

She squealed at the cold metal, but the sensation was so different it was erotic.

"Doesn't it go on my finger?"

It was a shocking turn-on, and so was the way his tongue teased the hard little knob inside the ring.

"Of course, I want the world to see it on your finger and know you're mine. But I imagined it lying on your breast when I picked it out. Just for me to see."

She shivered. She wasn't cold.

"I love it," she whispered.

"I love you."

"Me too."

"How do you feel about a Las Vegas wedding?"

"How would we get there?"

"Plane, train, camel caravan."

"With our luck in traveling, the plane would break

down, the train would catch on fire, and the camels would bog down in a sand storm.''

''Point taken. Phoenix?''

''In Jane's living room, but we'll have to race the stork.''

''Luke said it wouldn't be long,'' he said.

''Peter will love being our ring bearer.''

''No way unless you handcuff the ring to his wrist.''

''You did get to know him.''

He picked up the ring and slid it onto her finger.

''Not as well as I want to know you, darling.''

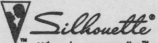

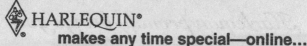

If you enjoyed what you just read,
then we've got an offer you can't resist!

Take 2 bestselling
love stories FREE!

Plus get a FREE surprise gift!

Clip this page and mail it to Harlequin Reader Service®

IN U.S.A.
3010 Walden Ave.
P.O. Box 1867
Buffalo, N.Y. 14240-1867

IN CANADA
P.O. Box 609
Fort Erie, Ontario
L2A 5X3

YES! Please send me 2 free Harlequin Duets™ novels and my free surprise gift. Then send me 2 brand-new novels every month, which I will receive months before they're available in stores. In the U.S.A., bill me at the bargain price of $5.14 plus 50¢ delivery per book and applicable sales tax, if any*. In Canada, bill me at the bargain price of $6.14 plus 50¢ delivery per book and applicable taxes**. That's the complete price—what a great deal! I understand that accepting the 2 free books and gift places me under no obligation ever to buy any books. I can always return a shipment and cancel at any time. Even if I never buy another book from Harlequin, the 2 free books and gift are mine to keep forever.

So why not take us up on our invitation. You'll be glad you did!

111 HEN C24W
311 HEN C24X

Name	(PLEASE PRINT)	
Address	Apt.#	
City	State/Prov.	Zip/Postal Code

* Terms and prices subject to change without notice. Sales tax applicable in N.Y.
** Canadian residents will be charged applicable provincial taxes and GST.
  All orders subject to approval. Offer limited to one per household.
  ® and ™ are registered trademarks of Harlequin Enterprises Limited.

DUETS00

MAITLAND MATERNITY

Where the luckiest babies are born!

In March 2001, look for

BILLION DOLLAR BRIDE
by Muriel Jensen

**Billionaire Austin Cahill doesn't believe
in love or marriage—**

he only wants to marry in order to produce an heir. Single
mom and wedding planner Anna Maitland is horrified by his
old-fashioned attitude. So when Austin proposes a marriage
of convenience, will Anna be able to refuse him...
now that she's fallen in love with him?

*Each book tells a different story about the
world-renowned Maitland Maternity Clinic—
where romances are born, secrets are revealed...
and bundles of joy are delivered.*

HAR~~~~~~ ~~~~~~uette®

Make~~~~~~ *~~~~~~mes alive*™

Visit us at www.eHarlequin.com   MMCNM-7